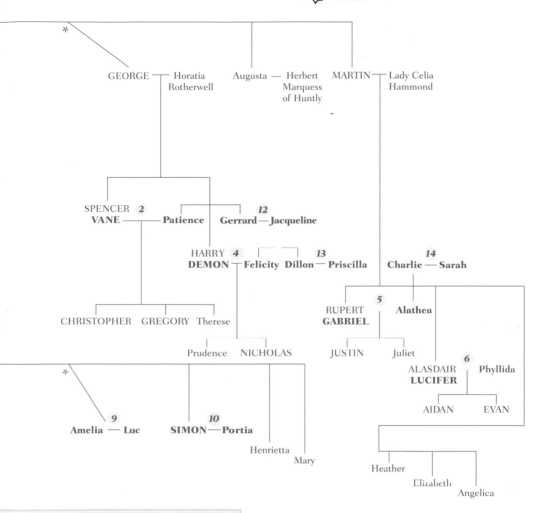

* GEORGE — Horatia Rotherwell

Augusta — Herbert Marquess of Huntly

MARTIN — Lady Celia Hammond

SPENCER **2 VANE** — **Patience**

12 **Gerrard** — **Jacqueline**

HARRY **4 DEMON** — **Felicity** Dillon — **13 Priscilla**

14 **Charlie** — **Sarah**

CHRISTOPHER GREGORY Therese

Prudence NICHOLAS

RUPERT **5 GABRIEL** **Alathea**

JUSTIN Juliet

ALASDAIR **6 LUCIFER** Phyllida

AIDAN EVAN

*

9 Amelia — **Luc**

10 **SIMON** — **Portia**

Henrietta Mary

Heather Elizabeth Angelica

MALE Cynsters in capitals
❋ denotes twins
Children born after 1825 not shown

Where the Heart Leads

ALSO BY STEPHANIE LAURENS

Cynster Novels

The Taste of Innocence
What Price Love?
The Truth About Love
The Ideal Bride
The Perfect Lover
On a Wicked Dawn
On a Wild Night
The Promise in a Kiss
All About Passion
All About Love
A Secret Love
A Rogue's Proposal
Scandal's Bride
A Rake's Vow
Devil's Bride

Bastion Club Novels

Beyond Seduction
To Distraction
A Lady of His Own
A Gentleman's Honor
The Lady Chosen
Captain Jack's Woman

Where the Heart Leads

STEPHANIE LAURENS

WM

WILLIAM MORROW

An Imprint of HarperCollins*Publishers*

WHERE THE HEART LEADS. Copyright © 2008 by Savdek Management Proprietory Ltd. All rights reserved. Printed in the United States of America. No part of this book may be used or reproduced in any manner whatsoever without written permission except in the case of brief quotations embodied in critical articles and reviews. For information address HarperCollins Publishers, 10 East 53rd Street, New York, NY 10022.

HarperCollins books may be purchased for educational, business, or sales promotional use. For information please write: Special Markets Department, HarperCollins Publishers, 10 East 53rd Street, New York, NY 10022.

FIRST EDITION

Library of Congress Cataloging-in-Publication Data
Laurens, Stephanie.
    Where the heart leads / Stephanie Laurens. — Ist ed.
        p.   cm.
    ISBN 978-0-06-124339-4
    I. Title.
    PR9619.3.L376W49 2008
    823'.92—dc22   2007028899

08 09 10 11 12 WBC/RRD 10 9 8 7 6 5 4 3 2 1

The Honorable Barnaby Adair's Investigations Involving Cynster Connections

Cornwall, June 1831
Assisting Gerrard Debbington, brother of Patience Cynster, brother-in-law of Vane Cynster, and Miss Jacqueline Tregonning
In: The Truth About Love

Newmarket, August 1831
Assisting Dillon Caxton, cousin of Felicity Cynster, brother-in-law of Demon Cynster, and Lady Priscilla Dalloway
In: What Price Love?

Somerset, February 1833
Assisting Lord Charles Morwellan, Earl of Meredith, brother of Alathea Cynster, brother-in-law of Gabriel Cynster, and Miss Sarah Conningham
In: The Taste of Innocence

London, November 1835
Assisting Miss Penelope Ashford, sister of Luc, Viscount Calverton, sister-in-law of Amelia Cynster
In: Where the Heart Leads

The Fulbridge-Ashford Family Tree

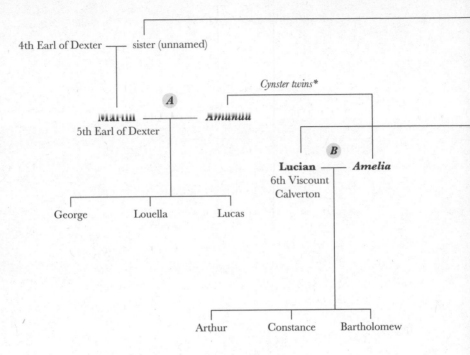

4th Earl of Dexter —— sister (unnamed)

Cynster twins*

Martin —— **A** —— **Amanda**
5th Earl of Dexter

Lucian —— **B** —— *Amelia*
6th Viscount
Calverton

George   Louella   Lucas

Arthur   Constance   Bartholomew

Connections to Cynsters noted*

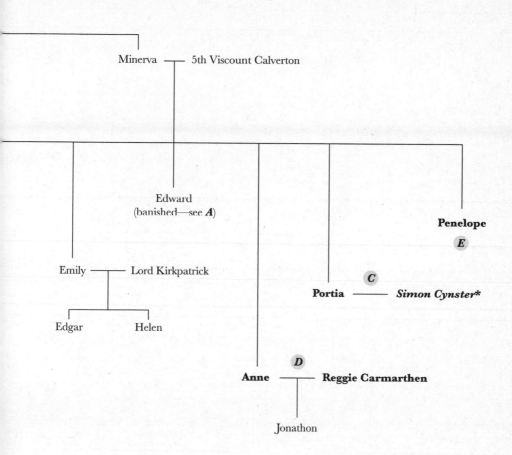

Minerva —— 5th Viscount Calverton

Edward
(banished—see *A*)

Penelope

E

Emily —— Lord Kirkpatrick

C

Portia —— *Simon Cynster**

Edgar   Helen

D

Anne —— **Reggie Carmarthen**

Jonathon

*See Cynster Family Tree

1

November 1835
London

"Thank you, Mostyn." Slumped at ease in an armchair before the fire in the parlor of his fashionable lodgings in Jermyn Street, Barnaby Adair, third son of the Earl of Cothelstone, lifted the crystal tumbler from the salver his man offered. "I won't need anything further."

"Very good, sir. I'll wish you a good night." The epitome of his calling, Mostyn bowed and silently withdrew.

Straining his ears, Barnaby heard the door shut. He smiled, sipped. Mostyn had been foisted on him by his mother when he'd first come up to town in the fond hope that the man would instill some degree of tractability into a son who, as she frequently declared, was ungovernable. Yet despite Mostyn's rigid adherence to the mores of class distinction and his belief in the deference due to the son of an earl, master and man had quickly reached an accommodation. Barnaby could no longer imagine being in London without the succor Mostyn provided, largely, as with the glass of fine brandy in his hand, without prompting.

Over the years, Mostyn had mellowed. Or perhaps both of them had. Regardless, theirs was now a very comfortable household.

Stretching his long legs toward the hearth, crossing his ankles, sinking his chin on his cravat, Barnaby studied the polished toes of his boots, bathed in the light of the crackling flames. All *should* have been well in his world, but . . .

He was comfortable yet . . . restless.

At peace—no, *wrapped* in blessed peace—yet dissatisfied.

It wasn't as if the last months hadn't been successful. After more than nine months of careful sleuthing he'd exposed a cadre of young gentlemen, all from ton families, who not content with using dens of inquity had thought it a lark to run them. He'd delivered enough proof to charge and convict them despite their station. It had been a difficult, long-drawn, and arduous case; its successful conclusion had earned him grateful accolades from the peers who oversaw London's Metropolitan Police Force.

On hearing the news, his mother would no doubt have primmed her lips, perhaps evinced an acid wish that he would develop as much interest in foxhunting as in villain-hunting, but she wouldn't—couldn't—say more, not with his father being one of the aforementioned peers.

In any modern society, justice needed to be seen to be served even-handedly, without fear or favor, despite those among the ton who refused to believe that Parliament's laws applied to them. The Prime Minister himself had been moved to compliment him over this latest triumph.

Raising his glass, Barnaby sipped. The success had been sweet, yet had left him strangely hollow. Unfulfilled in some unexpected way. Certainly he'd anticipated feeling happier, rather than empty and peculiarly rudderless, aimlessly drifting now he no longer had a case to absorb him, to challenge his ingenuity and fill his time.

Perhaps his mood was simply a reflection of the season—the closing phases of another year, the time when cold fogs descended and polite society fled to the warmth of ancestral hearths, there to prepare for the coming festive season and the attendant revels. For him this time of year had always been difficult—difficult to find any viable excuse to avoid his mother's artfully engineered social gatherings.

She'd married off both his elder brothers and his sister, Melissa, far too easily; in him, she'd met her Waterloo, yet she continued more doggedly and indefatigably than Napoléon. She was determined to see him, the last of her brood, suitably wed, and was fully prepared to bring to bear whatever weapons were necessary to achieve that goal.

Despite being at loose ends, he didn't want to deliver himself up at the Cothelstone Castle gates, a candidate for his mother's matrimonial machinations. What if it snowed and he couldn't escape?

Unfortunately, even villains tended to hibernate over winter.

A sharp *rat-a-tat-tat* shattered the comfortable silence.

Glancing at the parlor door, Barnaby realized he'd heard a carriage on the cobbles. The rattle of wheels had ceased outside his residence. He listened as Mostyn's measured tread passed the parlor on the way to the front door. Who could be calling at such an hour—a quick glance at the mantelpiece clock confirmed it was after eleven—and on such a night? Beyond the heavily curtained windows the night was bleak, a dense chill fog wreathing the streets, swallowing houses and converting familiar streetscapes into ghostly gothic realms.

No one would venture out on such a night without good reason.

Voices, muted, reached him. It appeared Mostyn was engaged in dissuading whoever was attempting to disrupt his master's peace.

Abruptly the voices fell silent.

A moment later the door opened and Mostyn entered, carefully closing the door behind him. One glance at Mostyn's tight lips and studiously blank expression informed Barnaby that Mostyn did not approve of whoever had called. Even more interesting was the transparent implication that Mostyn had been routed—efficiently and comprehensively—in his attempt to deny the visitor.

"A . . . lady to see you, sir. A Miss—"

"Penelope Ashford."

The crisp, determined tones had both Barnaby and Mostyn looking to the door—which now stood open, swung wide to admit a lady in a dark, severe yet fashionable pelisse. A sable-lined muff dangled from one wrist, and her hands were encased in fur-edged leather gloves.

Lustrous mahogany hair, pulled into a knot at the back of her head, gleamed as she crossed the room with a grace and self-confidence that screamed her station even more than her delicate, quintessentially aristocratic features. Features that were animated by so much determination, so much sheer will, that the force of her personality seemed to roll like a wave before her.

Mostyn stepped back as she neared.

His eyes never leaving her, Barnaby unhurriedly uncrossed his legs and rose. "Miss Ashford."

An exceptional pair of dark brown eyes framed by finely wrought gold-rimmed spectacles fixed on his face. "Mr. Adair. We met nearly two years ago, at Morwellan Park in the ballroom at Charlie and Sarah's wedding." Halting two paces away, she studied him, as if estimating the quality of his memory. "We spoke briefly if you recall."

She didn't offer her hand. Barnaby looked down into her uptilted face—her head barely cleared his shoulder—and found he remembered her surprisingly well. "You asked if I was the one who investigates crimes."

She smiled—brilliantly. "Yes. That's right."

Barnaby blinked; he felt a trifle winded. He could, he realized, recall how, all those months ago, her small fingers had felt in his. They'd merely shaken hands, yet he could remember it perfectly; even now, his fingers tingled with tactile memory.

She'd obviously made an impression on him even if he hadn't been so aware of it at the time. At the time he'd been focused on another case, and had been more intent on deflecting her interest than on her.

Since he'd last seen her, she'd grown. Not taller. Indeed, he wasn't sure she'd gained inches anywhere; she was as neatly rounded as his memory painted her. Yet she'd gained in stature, in self-assurance and confidence; although he doubted she'd ever been lacking in the latter, she was now the sort of lady any fool would recognize as a force of nature, to be crossed at one's peril.

Little wonder she'd rolled up Mostyn.

Her smile had faded. She'd been examining him openly; in most others he would have termed it brazen, but she seemed to be evaluating him intellectually rather than physically.

Rosy lips, distractingly lush, firmed, as if she'd made some decision.

Curious, he tilted his head. "To what do I owe this visit?"

This highly irregular, not to say potentially scandalous, visit. She was a gently bred lady of marriageable age, calling on a single gentleman who was in no way related very late at night. Alone. Entirely unchaperoned.

He should protest and send her away. Mostyn certainly thought so.

Her fine dark eyes met his. Squarely, without the slightest hint of guile or trepidation. "I want you to help me solve a crime."

He held her gaze.

She returned the favor.

A pregnant moment passed, then he gestured elegantly to the other armchair. "Please sit. Perhaps you'd like some refreshment?"

Her smile—it transformed her face from vividly attractive to stunning—flashed as she moved to the chair facing his. "Thank you, but no. I require nothing but your time." She waved Mostyn away. "You may go."

Mostyn stiffened. He cast an outraged glance at Barnaby.

Battling a grin, Barnaby endorsed the order with a nod. Mostyn didn't like it, but departed, bowing himself out, but leaving the door ajar. Barnaby noted it, but said nothing. Mostyn knew Barnaby was hunted, often quite inventively, by young ladies; he clearly believed Miss Ashford might be such a schemer. Barnaby knew better. Penelope Ashford might scheme with the best of them, but marriage would not be her goal.

While she arranged her muff on her lap, he sank back into his armchair and studied her anew.

She was the most unusual young lady he'd ever encountered.

He'd decided that even before she said, "Mr. Adair, I need your help to find four missing boys, and stop any more being kidnapped."

Penelope raised her eyes and locked them on Barnaby Adair's face. And tried her damnedest not to see. When she'd determined to call on him, she hadn't imagined he—his appearance—would have the slightest effect on her. Why would she? No man had ever made her feel breathless, so why should he? It was distinctly annoying.

Golden hair clustering in wavy curls about a well-shaped head, strong, aquiline features, and cerulean blue eyes that held a piercing intelligence were doubtless interesting enough, yet quite aside from his features there was something about him, about his presence, that was playing on her nerves in a disconcerting way.

Why he should affect her at all was a mystery. He was tall, with a long-limbed, rangy build, yet he was no taller than her brother, Luc, and while his shoulders were broad, they were no broader than her brother-in-law Simon's. And he was certainly not prettier than either Luc or Simon, although he could easily hold his own in the handsome stakes; she'd heard Barnaby Adair described as an Adonis and had to concede the point.

All of which was entirely by the by and she had no clue why she was even noticing.

She focused instead on the numerous questions she could see forming behind his blue eyes. "The reason I am here, and not a host of outraged parents, is because the boys in question are paupers and foundlings."

He frowned.

Stripping off her gloves, she grimaced lightly. "I'd better start at the beginning."

He nodded. "That would probably facilitate matters—namely my understanding—significantly."

She laid her gloves on top of her muff. She wasn't sure she appreciated his tone, but decided to ignore it. "I don't know if you're aware of it, but my sister Portia—she's now married to Simon Cynster—three other ladies of the ton, and I established the Foundling House opposite the Foundling Hospital in Bloomsbury. That was back in '30. The house has been in operation ever since, taking in foundlings, mostly from the East End, and training them as maids, footmen, and more recently in various trades."

"You were asking Sarah about her orphanage's training programs when we last met."

"Indeed." She hadn't known he'd overheard that. "My older sister Anne, now Anne Carmarthen, is also involved, but since their marriages, with their own households to run, both Anne and lately Portia have had to curtail the time they spend at the Foundling House. The other three ladies likewise have many calls on their time. Consequently, at present I am in charge of overseeing the day-to-day administration of the place. It's in that capacity that I'm here tonight."

Folding her hands over her gloves, she met his eyes, held his steady gaze. "The normal procedure is for children to be formally placed in the care of the Foundling House by the authorities, or by their last surviving guardian.

"The latter is quite common. What usually occurs is that a dying relative, recognizing that their ward will soon be alone in the world, contacts us and we visit and make arrangements. The child usually stays with their guardian until the last, then, on the guardian's death, we're informed, usually by helpful neighbors, and we return and fetch the orphan and take him or her to the Foundling House."

He nodded, signifying all to that point was clear.

Drawing breath, she went on, feeling her lungs tighten, her diction growing crisp as anger resurged, "Over the last month, on four separate occasions, we've arrived to fetch away a boy, only to discover some man has been there before us. He told the neighbors he was a local official, but there is no central authority that collects orphans. If there were, we'd know."

Adair's blue gaze had grown razor-sharp. "Is it always the same man?"

"From all I've heard, it could be. But equally, it might not be."

She waited while he mulled over that. She bit her tongue, forced herself to sit still and not fidget, and instead watch the concentration in his face.

Her inclination was to forge ahead, to demand he act and tell him how. She was used to directing, to taking charge and ordering all as she deemed fit. She was usually right in her thinking, and generally people were a great deal better off if they simply did as she said. But . . . she needed Barnaby Adair's help, and instinct was warning her, stridently, to tread carefully. To guide rather than push.

To persuade rather than dictate.

His gaze had grown distant, but now abruptly refocused on her face. "You take boys and girls. Is it only boys who've gone missing?"

"Yes." She nodded for emphasis. "We've accepted more girls than boys in recent months, but it's only boys this man has taken."

A moment passed. "He's taken four—tell me about each. Start from the first—everything you know, every detail, no matter how apparently inconsequential."

Barnaby watched as she delved into her memory; her dark gaze turned inward, her features smoothed, losing some of their characteristic vitality.

She drew breath; her gaze fixed on the fire as if she were reading from the flames. "The first was from Chicksand Street in Spitalfields, off Brick Lane north of the Whitechapel Road. He was eight years old, or so his uncle told us. He, the uncle, was dying, and . . ."

Barnaby listened as she, not entirely to his surprise, did precisely as he'd requested and recited the details of each occurrence, chapter and verse. Other than an occasional minor query, he didn't have to prod her or her memory.

He was accustomed to dealing with ladies of the ton, to interrogating young ladies whose minds skittered and wandered around subjects, and flitted and danced around facts, so that it took the wisdom of Solomon and the patience of Jove to gain any understanding of what they actually knew.

Penelope Ashford was a different breed. He'd heard that she was something of a firebrand, one who paid scant attention to social restraints if said restraints stood in her way. He'd heard her described as too intelligent for her own good, and direct and forthright to a fault, that combination of traits being popularly held to account for her unmarried state.

As she was remarkably attractive in an unusual way—not pretty or beautiful but so vividly alive she effortlessly drew men's eyes—as well as being extremely well connected, the daughter of a viscount, and with her brother, Luc, the current titleholder, eminently wealthy and able to dower her more than appropriately, that popular judgment might well be correct. Yet her sister Portia had recently married Simon Cynster, and while Portia might perhaps be more subtle in her dealings, Barnaby recalled that the Cynster ladies, judges he trusted in such matters, saw little difference between Portia and Penelope beyond Penelope's directness.

And, if he was remembering aright, her utterly implacable will.

From what little he'd seen of the sisters, he, too, would have said that Portia would bend, or at least agree to negotiate, far earlier than Penelope.

"And just as with the others, when we went to Herb Lane to fetch Dick this morning, he was gone. He'd been collected by this mystery man at seven o'clock, barely after dawn."

Her story concluded, she shifted her dark, compelling eyes from the flames to his face.

Barnaby held her gaze for a moment, then slowly nodded. "So somehow these people—let's assume it's one group collecting these boys—"

"I can't see it being more than one group. We've never had this happen before, and now four instances in less than a month, and all with the same modus operandi." Brows raised, she met his eyes.

Somewhat tersely, he said, "Precisely. As I was saying, these people, whoever they are, seem to know of your potential charges—"

"Before you suggest that they might be learning of the boys through someone at the Foundling House, let me assure you that's highly unlikely. If you knew the people involved, you'd understand why I'm so sure of that. And indeed, although I've come to you with our four cases, there's nothing to say other newly orphaned boys in the East End aren't also disappearing. Most orphans aren't brought to our attention. There may be many more vanishing, but who is there who would sound any alarm?"

Barnaby stared at her while the scenario she was describing took shape in his mind.

"I had hoped," she said, the light glinting off her spectacles as she glanced down and smoothed her gloves, "that you might agree to look into this latest disappearance, seeing as Dick was whisked away only this morning. I do realize that you generally investigate crimes involving the ton, but I wondered, as it is November and most of us have upped stakes for the country, whether you might have time to consider our problem." Looking up, she met his gaze; there was nothing remotely diffident in her eyes. "I could, of course, pursue the matter myself—"

Barnaby only just stopped himself from reacting.

"But I thought enlisting someone with more experience in such matters might lead to a more rapid resolution."

Penelope held his gaze and hoped he was as quick-witted as he was purported to be. Then again, in her experience, it rarely hurt to be blunt. "To be perfectly clear, Mr. Adair, I am here seeking aid in pursuing our lost charges, rather than merely wishing to inform someone of their disappearance and thereafter wash my hands of them. I fully intend to search for Dick and the other three boys until I find them. Not being a simpleton, I would prefer to have beside me someone with experience of crime and the necessary investigative methods. Moreover, while through our work we naturally have contacts in the East End, few if any of those move among the criminal elements, so my ability to gain information in that arena is limited."

Halting, she searched his face. His expression gave little away; his broad brow, straight brown eyebrows, strong, well-delineated cheek-bones, the rather austere lines of cheek and jaw, remained set and un-revealing.

She spread her hands. "I've described our situation—will you help us?"

To her irritation, he didn't immediately reply. Didn't leap in, goaded to action by the notion of her tramping through the East End by herself.

He didn't, however, refuse. For a long moment, he studied her, his expression unreadable—long enough for her to wonder if he'd seen through her ploy—then he shifted, resettling his shoulders against the chair, and gestured to her in invitation. "How do you imagine our investigation would proceed?"

She hid her smile. "I thought, if you were free, you might visit the Foundling House tomorrow, to get some idea of the way we work and the type of children we take in. Then . . ."

Barnaby listened while she outlined an eminently rational strategy that would expose him to the basic facts, enough to ascertain where an investigation might lead, and consequently how best to proceed.

Watching the sensible, logical words fall from her ruby lips—still lush and ripe, still distracting—only confirmed that Penelope Ashford was dangerous. Every bit as dangerous as her reputation suggested, possibly more.

In his case undoubtedly more, given his fascination with her lips.

In addition, she was offering him something no other young lady had ever thought to wave before his nose.

A case. Just when he was in dire need of one.

"Once we've talked to the neighbors who saw Dick taken away, I'm hoping you'll be able to suggest some way forward from there."

Her lips stopped moving. He raised his gaze to her eyes. "Indeed." He hesitated; it was patently obvious that she had every intention of playing an active role in the ensuing investigation. Given he knew her family, he was unquestionably honor-bound to dissuade her from such a reckless endeavor, yet equally unquestionably, any suggestion she retreat to the hearth and leave him to chase the villains would meet with stiff opposition. He inclined his head. "As it happens I'm free tomorrow. Perhaps I could meet you at the Foundling House in the morning?"

He'd steer her out of the investigation after he had all the facts, after he'd learned everything she knew about this strange business.

She smiled brilliantly, once again disrupting his thoughts.

"Excellent!" Penelope gathered her gloves and muff, and stood. She'd gained what she wanted; it was time to leave. Before he could say anything she didn't want to hear. Best not to get into any argument now. Not yet.

He rose and waved her to the door. She led the way, pulling on her gloves. He had the loveliest hands she'd ever seen on a man, long-fingered, elegant, and utterly distracting. She'd remembered them from before, which was why she hadn't offered to shake his hand.

He walked beside her across his front hall. "Is your carriage outside?"

"Yes." Halting before the front door, she glanced up at him. "It's waiting outside the house next door."

His lips twitched. "I see." His man was hovering; he waved him back and reached for the doorknob. "I'll walk you to it."

She inclined her head. When he opened the door, she walked out onto the narrow front porch. Her nerves flickered as he joined her; large and rather overpoweringly male, he escorted her down the three steps to the pavement, then along to where her brother's town carriage stood, the coachman patient and resigned on the box.

Adair reached for the carriage door, opened it, and offered his hand. Holding her breath, she gave him her fingers—and tried hard not to register the sensation of her slender digits being engulfed by his much larger ones, tried not to notice the warmth of his firm clasp as he helped her up into the carriage.

And failed.

She didn't—couldn't—breathe until he released her hand. She sank onto the leather seat, managed a smile and a nod. "Thank you, Mr. Adair. I'll see you tomorrow morning."

Through the enveloping gloom he studied her, then he raised his hand in salute, stepped back, and closed the door.

The coachman jigged his reins and the carriage jerked forward, then settled to a steady roll. With a sigh, Penelope sat back and smiled into the darkness. Satisfied, and a trifle smug. She'd recruited Barnaby Adair to her cause, and despite her unprecedented attack of sensibility had managed the encounter without revealing her affliction.

All in all, her night had been a success.

Barnaby stood in the street, in the wreathing fog, and watched the carriage roll away. Once the rattle of its wheels had faded, he grinned and turned back to his door.

Climbing his front steps, he realized his mood had lifted. His earlier despondency had vanished, replaced with a keen anticipation for what the morrow would bring.

And for that he had Penelope Ashford to thank.

Not only had she brought him a case, one outside his normal arena and therefore likely to challenge him and expand his knowledge, but even more importantly that case was one not even his mother would disapprove of his pursuing.

Mentally composing the letter he would pen to his parent first thing the next morning, he entered his house whistling beneath his breath and let Mostyn bolt the door behind him.

2

Good morning, Mr. Adair. Miss Ashford told us to expect you. She's in the office. If you'll come this way?"

Barnaby stepped over the threshold of the Foundling House and waited while the neatly dressed middle-aged woman who'd opened the heavy front door in response to his knock closed it and secured a high latch.

Turning away, she beckoned; he followed in her wake as she led him across a wide foyer and down a long corridor with rooms opening to left and right. Their footsteps on the black-and-white tiles echoed faintly; the unadorned walls were a pale creamy yellow. Structurally the house seemed in excellent order, but there was no hint of even modest ornamentation—no paintings on the walls or rugs upon the tiles.

Nothing to soften or disguise the reality that this was an institution.

A brief survey of the building from across the street had revealed a large, older-style mansion, painted white, three stories with attics above, a central block flanked by two wings, with large graveled yards in front of each wing separated from the pavement by a wrought-iron fence. A straight, narrow path led from the heavy front gate to the front porch.

Everything Barnaby had seen of the structure screamed solid practicality.

He refocused on the woman ahead of him. Although she wasn't wearing a uniform, she reminded him of the matron at Eton with her quick, purposeful stride, and the way her head turned to scan each room as they passed, checking those inside.

He looked into the rooms, too, and saw groups of children of various ages either seated at desks or in groups on the floor, listening with rapt attention to women, and in one case a man, reading or teaching.

Long before the woman he was following slowed, then halted before a doorway, he'd started making additions to his mental notes on Penelope Ashford. It was the sight of the children—their faces ruddy and round, features undistinguished, their hair neat but unstyled, their clothes decent but of the lowest station—all so very different from the children he or she would normally have any dealings with that opened his eyes.

In championing such powerless, vulnerable innocents from a social stratum so very far removed from her own, Penelope wasn't indulging in some simple, altruistic gesture; in stepping so far beyond the bounds of what society deemed appropriate in charitable works for ladies of her rank, she was—he felt certain knowingly—risking society's disapprobation.

Sarah's orphanage and her association with it wasn't the same as what Penelope was doing here. Sarah's children were country-bred, children of farmworkers and local families who lived, worked, or interacted with the gentry's estates; in caring for them, an element of noblesse oblige was involved. But the children here were from the slums and teeming tenements of London; in no way connected with the aristocracy, their families eked out a living however they could, in whatever way they could.

And some of those ways wouldn't bear polite scrutiny.

The woman he'd followed gestured through the doorway. "Miss Ashford is in the inner office, sir. If you'll go through?"

Barnaby paused on the threshold of the anteroom. Inside, a prim young woman was sitting, head down, at a small desk in front of a phalanx of closed cabinets, busily sorting through a stack of papers. Smiling slightly, Barnaby thanked his escort, then walked across the room to the inner sanctum.

Its door, too, stood open.

On silent feet, he approached and paused, looking in. Penelope's office—the brass plaque on the door read HOUSE ADMINISTRATOR—was a severe, undecorated, white-walled square. It contained two tall cabinets against one wall, and a large desk set before a window with two straight-backed chairs facing it.

Penelope sat in the chair behind the desk, her concentration fixed on a sheaf of papers. A slight frown had drawn her dark brows into an almost horizontal line above the bridge of her straight little nose.

Her lips, he noted, were compressed into a firm, rather forbidding line.

She was wearing a dark blue walking dress; the deep hue emphasized her porcelain complexion and the lustrous bounty of her richly brown hair. He took due note of the glints of red in the heavy mass.

Raising a hand, he rapped one knuckle on the door. "Miss Ashford?"

She looked up. For one instant, both her gaze and expression remained blank, then she blinked, refocused, and waved him in. "Mr. Adair. Welcome to the Foundling House."

No smile, Barnaby noted; she was all business. He told himself that was refreshing.

His own expression easy, he walked forward to stand beside one chair. "Perhaps you could show me around the place, and you could answer my questions as we walk."

She considered him, then glanced at the papers before her. He could almost hear her mentally debating whether to send him on a tour with her assistant, but then her lips—those ruby lips that had eased back to their natural fascinating fullness—firmed again. Laying aside her pen, she stood. "Indeed. The sooner we can find our missing boys, the better."

Coming around the desk, she walked briskly out of the room; brows rising faintly, he turned and followed—once again in a woman's wake, although this time his guide did not figure in his mind as the least bit matronly.

She nevertheless managed a commendable bustle as she crossed the outer office. "This is my assistant, Miss Marsh. She was once a foundling herself, and now works here ensuring all our files and paperwork are in order."

Barnaby smiled at the mousy young woman; she colored and bobbed her head, then refixed her attention on her papers. Following Penelope into the corridor, Barnaby reflected that the denizens of the

Foundling House were unlikely to encounter many tonnish gentlemen within their walls.

Lengthening his stride, he caught up with Penelope; she was leading him deeper into the house, striding along almost mannishly,
clearly dismissive of the currently fashionable glide. He glanced at her
face. "Do you have many ladies of the ton involved in your work
here?"

"Not many." After a moment, she elaborated. "Quite a few come—
they hear of it from me, Portia, or the others, or our mothers and
aunts, and call intending to offer their services."

Halting at the intersection with another corridor leading into one
wing, she faced him. "They come, they look—and then they go away.
Most have a vision of playing Lady Bountiful to suitably grateful urchins." A wicked light gleamed in her eyes; turning, she gestured
down the wing. "That's not what they find here."

Even before they reached the open door three doors down the corridor, the cacophany was evident.

Penelope pushed the door wide. "Boys!"

The noise ended so abruptly the silence rang.

Ten boys ranging in age from eight or so to twelvish stood frozen,
caught in the throes of a general wrestling match. Eyes wide, mouths
acock, they took in who had entered, then quickly disengaged, jostling
to line up and summoning innocent smiles that regardless appeared
quite genuine. "Good morning, Miss Ashford," they chorused.

Penelope bent a stern look on them. "Where is Mr. Englehart?"

The boys exchanged glances, then one, the biggest, volunteered,
"He just stepped out for a minute, miss."

"And I'm sure he left you with work to do, didn't he?"

The boys nodded. Without another word, they turned to their
desks, righting the two that had been upended. Picking up chalks and
slates, they sat on the benches and resumed their work; glancing over
a few shoulders, Barnaby saw they were learning to add and sub-
tract.

The sound of swift footsteps echoed down the corridor; an instant
later, a neatly dressed man of about thirty appeared in the doorway.

He took in the boys and Penelope, then grinned. "For a minute I
thought they must have killed each other."

A few smothered chuckles escaped from the class. With a nod for

Penelope, and a curious look for Barnaby, Englehart moved to the front of the room. "Come along, lads—three more sets of sums and you can take your turn outside."

Muffled groans sounded, but the boys buckled down; more than one had his tongue clenched between his teeth.

One raised a hand and Englehart went to him, bending over to read what was on the boy's slate.

Penelope surveyed the group, then rejoined Barnaby just inside the door. "Englehart takes the boys of this age through their reading, writing, and arithmetic. Most gain at least enough to be employed as more than just basic footmen, while others become apprentices in various trades."

Noting the earnestness in the boys' interaction with Englehart, and the way he responded to them, Barnaby nodded.

He followed Penelope outside. Once she'd closed the door, he said, "Englehart seems a good choice for that job."

"He is. He's an orphan, too, but his uncle took him in and had him educated. He works in a solicitor's firm in a senior position. The solicitor knows of our work, so allows Englehart to give us six hours a week. We've other tutors for other subjects. Most volunteer their services, which means they truly care about their students and are willing to work to extract the best from what most would regard as less than ideal clay."

"It appears you've attracted considerable—and useful—support."

She shrugged. "We've been lucky."

Barnaby suspected that once she had a goal in mind, luck was incidental. "The relatives who give over their wards to this place—do they visit first?"

"Those who can usually do. But regardless we always visit the child and guardian in their home." She glanced up and met his eyes. "It's important we know what background they come from, and what they're used to. When they first come to stay, many are frightened—it's a new and often strange environment for them, with rules they don't know and customs that seem peculiar. Knowing what they're used to means we can help them settle in."

"You do the visiting." He didn't make it a question.

She raised her chin. "I'm in charge, so I need to know."

He couldn't think of any other young lady who would willingly go where she must; it was becoming obvious that making assumptions about her, or her likely behavior or reactions, based on the norm for young ladies of the ton was an excellent way to find himself wrong-footed.

She led him on, stopping in this classroom or that, showing him the dormitories, presently empty, and the infirmary and dining hall, lecturing him on their practices, introducing him to staff they met along the way. He drank it all in; he enjoyed studying people—he considered himself something of a connoisseur of character—and the more he saw, the more he found himself fascinated, most of all by Penelope Ashford.

Strong-willed, dominant as opposed to domineering, intelligent, quick-witted and mentally astute, dedicated and loyal; by the end of their tour he'd seen enough to be certain of those qualities. He could also add prickly when pushed, high-handed when challenged, and compassionate to her toes. The latter shone through every time she interacted with any of the children; he was prepared to take an oath that she knew every name and every history of the more than eighty children under the house's roof.

Eventually they returned to the main foyer. Penelope couldn't think of anything further she needed to show him to make her point; he was refreshingly observant and apparently able to deduce without having matters explained in minute detail. Halting, she faced him. "Is there anything further you need to know about our procedures here?"

He looked at her for a moment, then shook his head. "Not at present. All appears straightforward, well thought out, and established." He glanced back into the house. "And on the basis of what I've seen of your staff, I agree that it seems unlikely any of them are involved, even in passing information to the . . . for want of a better word, kidnappers."

His blue gaze refixed on her face; she fought to appear unconscious as he studied her eyes, her features.

"So my next step will be to visit the scene of the latest disappearance, and to question the locals and learn what they know." His lips curved, beguilingly charming. "If you'll give me the address, I won't need to take up any more of your time."

She narrowed her eyes, let her jaw firm. "You needn't worry about my time—until we have our four boys back, this matter takes precedence over all else. Naturally I'll accompany you to Dick's father's lodgings—aside from anything else, the neighbors don't know you and are unlikely to readily speak to you."

He held her gaze. She wondered if they were going to have the argument she knew would eventually come then and there . . . but then he inclined his head. "If you wish."

His last word was drowned by the clatter of footsteps. Penelope swung around to see Mrs. Keggs, the matron, come hurrying up the corridor.

"If you please, Miss Ashford, I need a few minutes of your time before you go." Coming to a halt, Mrs. Keggs added, "About the supplies for the dormitories and the infirmary. I really should get the order out today."

Penelope hid her vexation—not for Mrs. Keggs, for the need was acute, but over the unfortunate timing. Would Adair try to use the delay as an excuse to cut her out of the investigation? She turned back to him. "This will take no more than ten . . . perhaps fifteen minutes." She didn't ask if he would wait, but forged on, "After that, we'll be able to set out."

He held her gaze steadily; she could read nothing in his blue eyes other than that he was evaluating, weighing. Then the line of his lips eased, not in a smile but as if he were inwardly amused.

"Very well." From beyond the now open front door the sound of boys' voices reached them; he tipped his head in that direction. "I'll wait outside, observing your charges."

She was too relieved to ask what he expected to observe. She nodded briskly. "I'll join you shortly."

Giving him no chance to change his mind, she turned and, with Mrs. Keggs, set off down the corridor to her office.

Barnaby watched her go, appreciatively noting the brisk sway of her hips as she strode so purposefully along, then he turned and, smiling more definitely, went out into the gloomy day.

Standing on the porch, he scanned the yard to the right; a bevy of children, boys and girls about five and six years old, were laughing and shrieking as they chased one another and threw soft balls. Looking to the left, he discovered a similar number of boys, all in the seven- to twelve-years-old age group into which the missing boys would have merged.

Stepping down, he let his feet take him in that direction. He wasn't looking for anything specific, yet experience had taught him that snippets of what at the time seemed extraneous information often turned out to be crucial in solving a case.

Leaning against the side of the house, he let his gaze range over the group. They came in all sizes and shapes, some pudgy, heavyset, and thuggish looking, others scrawny and thin. Most moved freely in their games, but a few limped, and one dragged one foot.

Any similar group of tonnish children would have been more physically homogenous, with similar features, similar long limbs.

The one element these children shared, with one another and with children from his sphere, was a certain carefreeness not normally found in pauper children. It was a reflection of confidence in their security—that they would have a roof over their heads and reasonable sustenance, not just today but tomorrow as well, and into the foreseeable future.

These children were happy, far more than many of their peers would ever be.

A tutor was seated on a bench on the opposite side of the playground, reading a book but glancing up every now and then at his charges.

Eventually one of the boys—a wiry, ferret-faced lad of about ten—sidled up to Barnaby. He waited until Barnaby glanced down at him before asking, "Are you a new tutor, then?"

"No." When more was clearly expected, he added, "I'm helping Miss Ashford with something. I'm waiting for her."

Other boys edged closer as the first mouthed an "Oh." He glanced at his friends, then felt emboldened enough to ask, "What are you, then?"

The third son of an earl. Barnaby grinned, imagining how his interrogators would react to that. "I help people find things."

"What things?"

Villains, generally. "Possessions or people they want to find."

One of the older boys frowned. "I thought bobbies did that. But you're not one of them."

"Nah," another boy cut in. "Bobbies are about stopping things getting nicked in the first place. Finding nicked stuff is another game."

Wisdom from the mouths of babes.

"So . . ." His first questioner eyed him measuringly. "Tell us a story about something you've helped find." His tone made the words a hopeful plea rather than a demand.

Glancing at the circle of faces now surrounding him, perfectly aware that every boy had taken note of his clothes and their quality, Barnaby considered. A movement across the yard caught his eye. The tutor had noticed his charges' interest; he raised a brow, wordlessly asking if Barnaby wished to be rescued.

Sending the tutor a reassuring smile, Barnaby looked down at his audience. "The first object I helped restore to its owner was the Duchess of Derwent's emerald collar. It went missing during a house party at the Derwents' estate . . ."

They peppered him with questions; he wasn't surprised that it was the house party itself, the estate, and how "the nobs" entertained themselves that was the focus of their interest. Emeralds were something beyond their ken, but people fascinated them, just as people fascinated him. Listening to their reactions to his answers made him inwardly chuckle.

Inside her office, Penelope noticed that Mrs. Keggs's attention had drifted from her and fixed on some point beyond her left shoulder. "I think that should hold us for the next few weeks."

She laid down her pen and shut the inkpot lid with a clap; the noise jerked Mrs. Keggs's attention back.

"Ah . . . thank you, miss." Mrs. Keggs took the signed order Penelope handed her. "I'll take this around to Connelly's and get it filled this afternoon."

Penelope smiled and nodded a dismissal. She watched as Mrs. Keggs rose, bobbed a curtsy, then, with one last glance out of the window at Penelope's back, hurried out.

Swiveling her chair, Penelope looked out of the window—and saw Adair held captive by a group of boys.

She tensed to rise, but then realized she had it wrong; *he* was holding the boys captive—no mean feat—with some tale.

Relaxing, she studied the scene, examining her surprise; despite all she'd heard of him she hadn't expected Adair to have either the necessary facility, or the inclination, to interact freely with the lower orders—certainly not to the extent of stooping to entertain a group of near-urchins.

Yet his smile appeared quite genuine.

A little more of the wariness she'd felt over consulting him eased. Her fellow members of the governing committee were all out of London; although she'd informed them of the first three disappearances, she hadn't yet sent word of the most recent—nor of her plan to enlist the aid of Mr. Barnaby Adair. In that, she'd acted on her own initiative. While she was certain Portia and Anne would support her action, she wasn't so sure the other three would. Adair had made a name for himself assisting the police specifically in bringing members of the ton to justice—endeavors that hadn't been met by universal approval within the ton.

Lips firming, she slapped her palms on the arms of her chair and pushed to her feet. "I don't care," she informed her empty office. "To get those boys back, I'd enlist the aid of the archfiend himself."

Social threats had no power to sway her.

Other sorts of threats . . .

Eyes narrowing, she studied the tall, elegant figure surrounded by the ragtag group. And reluctantly conceded that at some level he did, indeed, represent a threat to her.

To her senses, her suddenly twitching nerves—to her unprecedentedly wayward brain. No man had ever made her think distracting thoughts.

No man had ever made her wonder what it would be like if he . . .

Turning back to her desk, she closed the order ledger.

After leaving his house last night she'd told herself that the worst was over, that when next she saw him his impact on her senses would have faded. Waned. Instead, when she'd looked up and seen him filling her doorway, his blue gaze fixed so *consideringly* on her, all rational thought had flown.

It had taken real effort to keep her expression blank and pretend she'd been mentally elsewhere, somewhere he hadn't reached.

Clearly, if she wished to investigate by his side she was going to need the equivalent of armor. Or else . . .

The notion of him realizing how much he affected her, and smiling in that slow, arrogant *male* way of his, didn't bear thinking about.

She pressed her lips together, then firmly reiterated, "Regardless, I don't care."

Collecting her reticule and gloves from beneath the desk, chin rising, she headed for the door.

And the man she'd recruited as the Foundling House's champion.

3

At the behest of Dick's father, Mrs. Keggs and I visited two weeks ago." Penelope gazed out of the hackney at the passing streetscape. They'd hailed the carriage from the rank outside the Foundling Hospital; the driver had happily taken them up, and rattled away to the east at a good pace.

Their progress had slowed once they'd turned into the narrow, crowded byways of what Londoners termed "the East End." A conglomeration of ramshackle, cheek-by-jowl houses, tenements, shops, and warehouses originally built around long-ago villages outside the old city wall, over the centuries the rough buildings had merged into a mean, dark, often dank sprawl of hodgepodge, rickety habitation.

Clerkenwell, the area into which they were heading, wasn't quite as bad—as overcrowded and potentially dangerous—as other parts of the East End.

"He—Dick's father, Mr. Monger—had consumption." She swayed as the hackney turned into Farringdon Road. "It was clear he wouldn't recover. The local doctor, a Mr. Snipe, was there, too—it was he who sent us word when Mr. Monger passed away."

On the seat opposite, Adair had been frowning—increasingly—ever since they'd ventured into the meaner streets. "You received Snipe's message yesterday morning?"

"No. The previous night. Monger died about seven o'clock."

"But you weren't at the Foundling House."

"No."

He turned his head and looked at her. "But if you had been . . ."

She shrugged and looked away. "In the evenings, I never am."

Of course, given the four missing boys, she'd now instructed that news of a guardian's death be conveyed to her immediately wherever she might be. Next time there was an orphan to retrieve, she would take her brother's carriage, and his coachman and a groom, and plunge into the East End regardless of the hour . . . but she saw no point in stating that in the present company.

She'd known Adair was at the very least acquainted with her brother—and guardian—Luc; she could guess what he was thinking— that Luc couldn't possibly approve of her going into such areas, more or less by herself. And certainly not at night.

In that he was perfectly correct; Luc had little idea what her position as "house administrator" entailed. And she would very much prefer to keep him in ignorance.

Glancing out of the window, she was relieved to see that they'd almost reached their goal; distraction lay to hand. "In this instance, three of the neighbors saw and spoke with the man who took Dick away the morning after Monger died. Their description of the man matches that given by the neighbors in the previous three cases."

The carriage slowed almost to a stop, then ponderously turned into a street so narrow the carriage could barely pass down it.

"Here we are." She shifted forward the instant the carriage halted, but Adair was before her, grasping the carriage's door handle, forcing her to ease back to allow him to open the door and step down.

He did, then blocked the exit while he looked around.

She bit her tongue and battled the urge to jab him—sharply— between the shoulder blades. Very nice shoulders, encased in a fashionable overcoat, but they were in her way . . . she had to content herself with glaring.

Eventually, unhurriedly—oblivious—he moved. Stepping aside, he offered her his hand. Clinging to her manners, she steeled herself and surrendered her fingers; no, the effect of his touch—of feeling his long, strong fingers curl possessively around hers—still hadn't waned. Waspishly reminding herself that it was at her request that he was there—taking up far too much space in her life and distracting her—she let him hand her down, then quickly slid her fingers free.

Without glancing at him, she started forward, waving at the hovel before them. "This is where Mr. Monger lived."

Their arrival had naturally drawn attention; faces peered out through grimy windows; hands edged aside flaps where no glass had ever been.

She glanced at the building next door; a wooden table was set along its front. "His neighbor is a cobbler. He and his son both saw the man."

Barnaby saw a shabby individual peering at them from beneath the overhang under which the cobbler's table was set. Penelope started toward him; he followed at her heels. If she noticed the squalor and dirt that surrounded her, let alone the smells, she gave no sign.

"Mr. Trug." Penelope nodded to the cobbler, who warily bobbed his head. "This is Mr. Adair, who is an expert in investigating strange occurrences, like Dick's disappearance. I wonder if I can trouble you to tell him about the man who came and took Dick away."

Trug eyed Barnaby, and Barnaby knew what he was thinking. What would a toff know of disappearing urchins?

"Mr. Trug? If you please? We want to find Dick as soon as we can."

Trug glanced at Penelope, then cleared his throat. "Aye, well—it were early yesterday morning, barely light. Fellow came knocking on old Monger's door. Me son, Harry, was about to head out to work. He stuck his head out and told the bloke Monger was dead and gone." Trug looked at Barnaby. "The bloke was polite enough. He came over and explained he was there to fetch young Dick away. That's when Harry yelled fer me."

"This bloke—what did he look like?"

Trug looked up at Barnaby's blond curls. "Taller'n me, but not as tall as you. Nor as broad of shoulder. Bit heavier round the middle. Stocky like."

"Did you notice his hands, by any chance?"

Trug looked surprised, then his expression turned thoughtful. "Didn't look to be a bruiser, now I think on it. And not a navvy or anything like—his hands weren't callused. Shopworker or . . . well, like he said. Worked for the authorities."

Barnaby nodded. "Clothing?"

"Heavy coat—nothing special. Cloth cap, the usual. Work boots like we all wear round here."

Barnaby didn't follow Trug's gaze as it lowered to his polished Hessians. "What about his speech—his accent?"

Looking up again, Trug blinked. "Accent? Well . . ." Trug blinked again, then looked at Penelope. "Stap me, but I hadn't thought of that. He came from round here. East End. No question."

Penelope looked at Barnaby.

He met her gaze, then turned to Trug. "Is your son in?"

"Aye." Trug lumbered around to head inside. "He's back here—I'll fetch him."

The son verified all his father had said. When asked for a guess as to the man's age, he pursed his lips, then opined, "Not old. Maybe about me own age—twenty-seven that'd be."

He grinned at Penelope. From the corner of his eye, Barnaby saw her eyes narrow, her dark gaze turn flinty.

"Thank you." He nodded to both Trugs and stepped back.

"Aye, well." Trug senior settled back behind his bench. "I know Monger wanted young Dick to go with the lady, so don't seem right this other bloke should steal him. Who knows what he's got in mind for him—he'll be forcing the poor little beggar up a chimney, like as not."

Penelope paled, but her expression only grew more determined. She, too, nodded to the Trugs. "Thank you for your help."

Turning, she joined Barnaby. She waved at the tiny house on the other side of Dick's father's abode. "We should talk to Mrs. Waters. Dick spent the night with her, so she saw and spoke to the man, too."

Summoned by a bell hanging beside her door, Mrs. Waters emerged from the depths of her cramped home. A large, motherly woman with a florid complexion and limp gray hair, she confirmed the Trugs' description. "Aye, twenty-five years old, I'd say, and he was from round here somewheres, but not close. I know most on the nearby streets, and he's not a local, so to say, but yes, he'd be an East Ender born and bred, the way he spoke."

"So he was too young to be a bailiff or anything like that." Penelope glanced at Barnaby.

Mrs. Waters snorted. "Not him—he wasn't a leader of anything, nor in charge of anything, I'll take my oath."

Barnaby was struck by her certainty. "Why do you say that?"

Mrs. Waters's brow furrowed in thought, then she said, "Because he wasn't even in charge of what he was doing. He was careful spoken. *Really* careful—like someone had taught him what to say, and how to say it."

"So you think he'd been sent here to do a job—he was an errand boy, as it were."

"That's it." Mrs. Waters nodded. "Someone had sent him to fetch Dick, and that's what he did." Her face clouded; she looked up at Barnaby. "You find that beggar and get Dick back. A good boy he was, never any trouble, no malice in him at all. He don't deserve whatever those bastards"—she glanced at Penelope—"begging your pardon, miss, are planning for him."

Barnaby inclined his head. "I'll do my best. Thank you for your help." He held out his hand to Penelope. "Miss Ashford?"

She didn't take his hand, but after thanking Mrs. Waters, she walked by his side back to the hackney. She had to take his hand to climb into the carriage. After instructing the driver to return to the Foundling House, Barnaby joined her and shut the door.

Slumping on the seat, he ran through what they'd learned, trying to see what it suggested.

She broke into his thoughts. "So it's possible Dick is not all that far away." Eyes narrowed, she stared apparently unseeing across the carriage. "Does that suggest anything—any specific activity?"

He considered her, then said, "The East End is a large and densely populated area." *Moreover, one teeming with vice.*

She grimaced, then refocused on him. "So—what next?"

"I think . . . if you're agreeable, I'd like to lay what we know before a friend—Inspector Basil Stokes of Scotland Yard."

Her brows rose. "The police?" After a moment of returning his regard, she said, "To be perfectly honest I can't imagine Peel's Police Force evincing much interest in missing pauper boys."

His smile was as cynical as her tone. "In the normal way of things, you would unfortunately be correct. However, Stokes and I go back a long way. And at this stage all I'll do is alert him to the situation and ask for his opinion." He paused, then went on, "Once he's heard what we know . . ."

If Stokes, like Barnaby, felt his instincts pricking . . .

But he didn't need to share such thoughts with Penelope Ashford. He shrugged. "We'll see."

He returned Penelope to the Foundling House, then took the hackney on to Scotland Yard. Entering the bland and unremarkable building that now housed the Metropolitan Police Force, he made his way to Stokes's office unchallenged; most in the building knew him by sight, and by reputation.

Stokes's office was on the first floor. When Barnaby reached it, the door stood open. He paused just outside, looking in, a slow grin lifting his lips at the sight of his friend, coat off, sleeves rolled up, laboriously writing reports.

If there was one thing Stokes did not appreciate about his increasing success and status, it was the inevitable report writing.

Sensing a presence, Stokes glanced up, saw him, and smiled. Delightedly. He laid down his pen, pushed aside the stack of papers, and sat back. "Well, well—what brings you here?"

Anticipation rang in his tone.

With a laugh, Barnaby walked into the office—not tiny, thankfully, but of a size just large enough to accommodate four people at a pinch. Set before the window, the desk with its chair faced the door. A cupboard stood against one wall, packed with files. Stokes's greatcoat hung from the coat hook on the wall. Slipping the buttons of his own elegant overcoat free, Barnaby let it fall open as he sank into one of the two chairs before the desk.

He met Stokes's slate-gray eyes. Of similar height and build to Barnaby, dark-haired, with rather saturnine features, Stokes was peculiarly classless. His father had been a merchant, not a gentleman, but courtesy of his maternal grandfather, Stokes had been well educated. Because of that, Stokes had a better grasp of the ways of the ton, and therefore a better chance of dealing with the denizens of that elite world, than any other inspector presently on Peel's force.

In Barnaby's opinion, the force was lucky to have Stokes. Aside from all else, he was intelligent and used his brain. Which in part was why they'd become close friends.

Which in turn was why Stokes was eyeing him with such undisguised eagerness; he hoped Barnaby was about to save him from his reports.

Barnaby grinned. "I have a case that, while not in our usual way of things, might just pique your interest."

"At present that wouldn't be hard." Stokes's voice was deep, rather gravelly, a contrast to Barnaby's well-modulated tones. "All our villains have gone on holiday early this year, or else they've retired to the country because we've made it too warm for them here. Either way, I'm all ears."

"In that case . . . I've been asked by the administrator of the Foundling House in Bloomsbury to look into the disappearance of four boys."

Succinctly, Barnaby outlined all he'd learned from Penelope, from his observations at the house, and during their trip to Clerkenwell. As he did, a gravity he hadn't allowed Penelope to see infused his voice and his expression.

By the time he concluded with, "The most pertinent fact is that it was the same man who whisked each of the four boys away," he looked and felt distinctly grim.

Stokes's face had hardened. His eyes had narrowed, darkening. "You want my opinion?" Barnaby nodded. "I don't like the sound of it any more than you do."

Sitting back in his chair, Stokes tapped one spatulate fingertip on his desk. "Let's consider—what use could someone make of four— at least four—seven- to ten-year-old boys, all from the East End?" Without pause, Stokes answered the question. "Brothels. Cabin boys. Chimney sweeps. Burglars' boys. Just to cite the more obvious."

Barnaby grimaced; folding his hands over his waistcoat, he looked up at the ceiling. "I'm not so sure of the brothels, thank heaven. Surely they wouldn't restrict themselves to the East End for such prey."

"We don't know how widespread this is. We might have heard about the East End cases simply because it's the administrator at the Foundling House who called you in—and they deal mostly with the East End."

"True." Lowering his gaze, Barnaby fixed it on Stokes. "So what do you think?"

Stokes's gaze grew distant. Barnaby let the silence stretch, having a fairly good idea of the issues with which Stokes was wrestling.

Eventually, a slow, predatory smile curved Stokes's thin lips. He refocused on Barnaby. "As you know, normally we'd have no chance of getting permission to put any real effort into this—into finding four pauper boys. However, those possible uses we mentioned—none of them are good. All are, in themselves, crimes worthy of attention. It occurs to me, what with the way your recent success in dealing with tonnish villains has played out politically, and given the governors are so constantly exhorting us to be seen to be evenhanded in our efforts, that perhaps I might present this case as an opportunity to demonstrate that the force is not solely interested in crimes affecting the nobs, but equally prepared to act to protect innocents from the lower walks of life."

"You might point out that at present, crime among the nobs is at a seasonal low." Tilting his head, Barnaby met Stokes's gaze. "So, do you think you can get permission to work on this?"

A moment passed, then Stokes's lips firmed. "I believe I can make this play into their prejudices. And their politics."

"Anything I can do to help?"

"You might drop a line to your father, just to shore up support in case of need, but other than that . . . I believe I'll manage."

"Good." Barnaby sat up. "Does that mean you, specifically, will be joining in?"

Stokes looked at the stack of papers by his elbow. "Oh, yes. I'm definitely dealing myself into this game."

Grinning, Barnaby rose.

Stokes looked up. "I should be able to catch the commissioner later today. I'll send word as soon as I get clearance." Rising, Stokes offered his hand.

Barnaby clasped it, then released it and saluted. "I'll leave you to your persuasions."

He headed for the door.

"One thing."

Stokes's voice halted Barnaby in the doorway; he looked back.

Stokes was already clearing away his papers. "You might like to ask the Foundling House's administrator if there was anything those boys had in common. Any common feature—were they all small, all tall, all large, all thin. From good homes or the dregs. That might give us some clue as to what whoever has snatched them wants them for."

"Good idea. I'll ask." With another salute, Barnaby left.

• • •

He'd said he'd ask, but he didn't need to ask that day.

He didn't need to seek out Penelope Ashford that very afternoon to pick her brains. She'd mentioned she was usually only at the Foundling House in the mornings. Even if he found her, wherever she might be, she wouldn't have her files to consult.

Of course, all he'd learned of her suggested that she would be able to answer Stokes's question without the need for any files.

Barnaby halted on the steps of Stokes's building. Hands sunk in the pockets of his greatcoat, now done up against the chilly breeze, he contemplated the buildings across the street while debating pursuing Penelope Ashford, albeit in search of answers.

Being the sort of woman she was, if he hunted her up, she would assume he'd done so to question her.

Reassured, he smiled, strode down the steps, and set out for Mount Street.

By dint of asking a streetsweeper, he located Calverton House, and plied the knocker. A moment passed, then the door opened and an imposing butler met his gaze, brows rising in magisterial inquiry.

Barnaby smiled with easy charm. "Is Miss Ashford in?"

"I regret Miss Ashford is presently from home, sir. May I tell her who called?"

Smile evaporating, he looked down, wondering if he should leave any message. Predicting how Penelope might react—

"Mr. Adair, is it not?"

He looked up at the butler, whose expression remained entirely uninformative. "Yes."

"Miss Ashford left word that should you call, sir, I was to inform you she'd had to accompany Lady Calverton on her afternoon rounds, as part of which she anticipated being in the park at the customary hour."

Barnaby hid a grimace. The park. At the fashionable hour. A combination of place and time he habitually avoided. "Thank you." He turned and went down the front steps. On the pavement he hesitated, then turned west.

And walked toward Hyde Park.

It was November. The skies were overcast, the breeze chill. Most of the glittering horde that populated the ton's ballrooms had already decamped for the country. Only those associated with the corridors of power remained, as Parliament had not yet risen. It soon would, and then London would be all but devoid of tonnish society. Even now, the rows of carriages to be found lining the Avenue should have thinned significantly.

There wouldn't be that many dowagers and matrons, let alone sweet young things, to see and wonder why he was intent on speaking with Penelope Ashford.

Crossing Park Lane, he strode through the gates and on, cutting across the lawns to where the carriages of the ladies of the haut ton always gathered.

His estimation of the park's inhabitants proved both right and wrong. The gossipy matrons and giggling girls were thankfully absent, but the gimlet-eyed dowagers and the sharp-eyed political hostesses were very much in evidence. And courtesy of his father's prominence and his mother's connections, he was instantly identifiable—and of interest—to all of those.

The Calverton carriage was drawn up on the verge in the center of the line of carriages, ensuring he passed under the eyes of at least half the assembled ladies as he skirted the fringes of those passing back and forth. Lady Calverton was engaged in earnest conversation with two contemporaries; beside her, Penelope looked distinctly bored.

Lady Calverton saw him first. She smiled as he approached the carriage. Penelope glanced his way, then straightened, her characteristic animation infusing her features, making them glow.

"Mr. Adair." Lady Calverton held out her hand, recalling him.

He took her gloved fingers and bowed over them. "Lady Calverton."

Behind their gold-rimmed spectacles, Penelope's eyes gleamed. He met them, and politely inclined his head. "Miss Ashford."

She smiled easily; social assurance was something neither she nor Portia lacked. Turning to her mother, she said, "Mr. Adair is assisting me with inquiries into the backgrounds of certain of our charges." She looked at Barnaby. "I daresay you have more questions, sir."

"Indeed." He, too, could play the social game. He glanced at the lawns nearby. "I wonder, Miss Ashford, if perhaps we might stroll while we talk?"

She smiled approvingly. "An excellent idea." To her mother she said, "I doubt we'll be long."

Swinging open the carriage door, he offered her his hand. She grasped it and climbed down. Releasing him, she shook out her skirts, then seemed mildly surprised when he offered his arm.

She took it, hesitantly laying her hand on his sleeve; to him her touch seemed almost wary.

Interesting. He doubted there was much in the ton, or out of it, that could make her . . . cautious. Yet he sensed it was that—and perhaps a need to seize control—that had her saying as they moved away from the carriage and the other strollers nearby, "I take it you spoke with your friend, Inspector Stokes. Have you learned anything?"

"Other than that Stokes is inclined to amuse himself by investigating these disappearances?"

The look she turned on him was gratifyingly wide-eyed. "You persuaded him to take up the case?"

Temptation bloomed, but chances were that she would meet Stokes at some point. "Not so much persuaded as assisted him to find reasons he should. Personally he was quite willing, but the force has its priorities. In this instance, Stokes felt he could make a case for action that would appeal to the commissioner." He met her eyes. "He hasn't yet received permission to put this case on his list, but he seemed confident of gaining approval."

Penelope nodded and looked ahead. Police support was far more than she'd expected. Consulting Barnaby Adair had clearly been the right thing to do—even if her witless senses hadn't yet learned how to be calm when near him. "You called Stokes a friend. Have you known him long?"

"Several years."

"How did you meet?" She looked up. "Well—an earl's son and a policeman. There had to be some event that brought him into your orbit. Or was it through your own investigating?"

He hesitated, as if remembering. "A bit of both," he eventually conceded. "I was present at the scene of a crime—a series of thefts at a country house party—and he was sent to investigate. I was a close friend of the gentleman most wished to blame. Both Stokes and I were, in different ways, a little out of our depth. But we found we dealt well together, and our combined knowledge—mine of the ton, Stokes's of the ways of criminals—proved successful in addressing the crime."

"Simon and Portia were much struck by Stokes. They spoke highly of him after the events at Glossup Hall."

Adair's smile turned subtly affectionate. Penelope sensed he was pleased and proud on his friend's behalf even before he said, "That was Stokes's first major murder case in the ton alone. He did well."

"How was it you didn't accompany him into Devon? Or don't you always work together on cases within the ton?"

"Usually we work together—it's quicker and more cerain that way. But when the report came in from Glossup Hall, we were in the middle of a long-standing case involving members of the ton here in London. The commissioner and the governors elected to send Stokes to Devon, leaving me to continue the investigation here."

She'd heard of the scandal that had ensued; naturally, she had questions, which she promptly posed. Said questions were so insightful and so succinctly phrased, he found himself answering readily, seduced by a mind that saw and understood. Until one of the park gates loomed before them. He blinked, then glanced around. They'd walked, more or less in a straight line, away from the Avenue. She'd distracted him with her interrogation—he hadn't even asked her what he'd come there to learn. Lips setting, he checked and turned her about. "We should return to your mother."

Penelope shrugged. "She won't mind. She knows we're discussing serious matters."

But none of the other grande dames do. Biting back the words, he quickened his stride.

"So what questions did Stokes raise?" Penelope asked. "I assume there were some."

"Indeed. He asked if there were any traits or characteristics the four missing boys share." He forbore giving her any example, not wanting to color her response.

She frowned, her straight dark brows forming a line above her nose. They continued to walk, rather briskly, while she thought. Eventually she volunteered, "They are, all four of them, rather thin and slight, but they're healthy and strong enough—wiry, if you like.

And all struck me as nimble and quick. But they aren't all the same height. In fact, I can't think of any other characteristic they have in common. They weren't even the same age."

It was his turn to frown. After a moment, he asked, "How tall was the tallest?"

She held up her hand level with her ear. "Dick was about this tall. But Ben—the second one who disappeared—was more than a head shorter."

"What about their general appearance—were they attractive children, or . . . ?"

She shook her head decisively. "Plain and totally unremarkable. Even if you dressed them well, they would never rate a second glance."

"Blond hair or brown?"

"Both—varying shades."

"You said they were nimble and quick—did you mean quick as in movement, or quick-witted?"

Her brows rose. "Both, actually. I was looking forward to teaching all four boys—they were bright, all of them."

"What about backgrounds? They were all from poor homes, but were these four from more stable families, likely to be better behaved, perhaps easier to train, more tractable?"

She pursed her lips, but again shook her head. "Their families weren't of any one sort, as such, although all four had gone through difficult times, even for the East End. That's why the boys were destined for us. All I could say is that there was no hint of any criminal associations in any of the four families."

He nodded, looking ahead—to where her mother waited in her carriage, staring rather pointedly their way.

Penelope hadn't noticed; she was busy studying his face. "What does that—what they look like and so on—tell you? How does it help?"

His gaze raking the line of carriages, Barnaby inwardly swore. How long had they been away? He should never have allowed her to distract him with her questions. Countless dowagers were peering at them, some even wielding lorgnettes. "I don't know." *But I can guess.* "I'll take your answers back to Stokes, and see what he says. He's better acquainted with that world than I."

"Yes, please do." Penelope halted beside the carriage door and fixed her gaze on his face. "You will inform me of what he thinks, won't you?"

Adair looked down and met her gaze. "Of course."

She narrowed her eyes, ignoring all the curious glances focused so avidly on them. "As soon as practicable."

His lips thinned.

Uncaring of propriety, she tightened her grip on his arm, perfectly prepared to cling if he dared try to leave without promising . . .

Blue eyes like flint, he tersely conceded, "As you wish."

She smiled and let him go. "Thank you. Until next we meet."

He held her gaze for a moment longer, then nodded. "Indeed. Until then."

Steely warning rang in his tone, but she didn't care; she'd won her point.

He handed her into the carriage, took his leave of her mother, then, with another curt nod, strode off. She noted his direction—toward Scotland Yard, where Peel's police had their headquarters; leaning back against the seat, she smiled a satisfied smile. Despite her senses' preoccupation with him, she'd managed that encounter rather well.

4

Stokes was on his feet behind his desk, tidying it before leaving for the day, when Barnaby strode in. Stokes looked up, took in his friend's features. "What?"

Penelope Ashford is going to be a problem. Barnaby drew in a controlled breath. "I asked Miss Ashford about the four boys."

Stokes frowned. "Miss Ashford?"

"Penelope Ashford, Portia's sister, currently the Foundling House's administrator. She said all four boys were thin, wiry, nimble, and quick—both in movement and wits. She considered them brighter than the norm. Other than that, they range in age from seven to ten years old, are of widely differing heights, totally unprepossessing, and have no other indicative characteristics in common."

"I see." Eyes narrowing, Stokes dropped back into his chair. He waited while Barnaby walked in and sat in one of the chairs facing the desk, then said, "It sounds like we can cross all arms of the flesh trade off our list."

Barnaby nodded. "And one at least is far too tall to be useful as a chimney boy, so that's off the list, too."

"I ran into Rowland of the Water Police an hour ago—he was here for a meeting. I asked if there was any shortage of cabin boys. Apparently the opposite is the case, so there's no reason to imagine these boys are being pressed into service on the waves."

Barnaby met Stokes's gaze. "So where does that leave us?"

Stokes considered, then his brows rose. "Burglars' boys. That's the most likely use for them by far—thin, wiry, nimble, and quick as they are. The fact they're unremarkable is an added bonus—they wouldn't be looking for any boy too pretty or noteworthy in any way. And in that part of the city . . ."

After a moment, Stokes continued, "There have, on and off over the years, been tales—true enough by all accounts—of, for want of a better description, 'burglary schools' run in the depths of the East End. The area is crowded. In some parts, it's a warren of tenements and warehouses that not even the local bobbies are happy going into. These schools come and go. Each doesn't last long, but often it's the same people behind them."

"They move before the police can close them down?"

Stokes nodded. "And as it's usually impossible to prove they—the proprietors—are involved in any citable crime, one we could take before a magistrate, then . . ." He shrugged. "By and large they're ignored."

Barnaby frowned. "What do these schools teach? What do burglars' boys need to be taught?"

"We used to think they were used as lookouts, and perhaps they are when the burglar operates in less affluent neighborhoods. But the real use of burglars' boys is in thieving from the houses of the more affluent, especially the ton. Getting into houses in Mayfair isn't that easy—most have bars on the ground-floor windows, or those windows are too small, at least for a man. Thin young boys, however, can often wriggle through. It's the boys who do the actual lifting of the objects, then pass them out to the burglar. The boys, therefore, need to be trained in creeping about silently in the dark, on polished wood and tiled floors, over rugs, and around furniture. They're taught the basic layout of ton houses, where to go, where to avoid—where to hide if they rouse the household. They learn how to tell good-quality ornaments from dross, how to remove pictures from their frames, how to pick locks—some are even taught to open safes."

Barnaby grimaced. "And if something goes wrong . . . ?"

"Precisely. It's the boy who gets caught, not the burglar."

Barnaby stared at the window behind Stokes. "So we have a situation that suggests a burglary school is operating, training boys most likely for use in burgling the houses of the ton . . ." He broke off and met Stokes's eyes. "Of course! They're getting ready to commit burglaries over the festive season, while the ton is largely not in residence."

Stokes frowned. "But most ladies take their jewelery with them to the country—"

"Indeed." Barnaby's burgeoning enthusiasm remained undimmed. "But this lot—whoever they are—aren't after jewelery. The ton packs up house only in terms of clothing and jewelery, and staff—they leave their ornaments, many of which are treasures, behind. Those things remain with the houses, usually with a skeleton staff. Some houses are left with only a caretaker."

Barnaby's excitement had infected Stokes. His gaze drifted as he thought, then pinned Barnaby. "We're getting ahead of ourselves, but let's assume we're right. Why four? Why in the space of a few weeks snatch four boys for training?"

Barnaby grinned wolfishly. "Because this group is planning a succession of robberies—or has more than one burglar who's planning to be active over the coming months."

"While the ton is away from London." His features hardening, Stokes murmured, "It could be worth it. Worth the effort they've already invested to identify four likely lads—and there might be more—and organize to whisk them away."

A moment passed, with both men following their thoughts, then Barnaby met Stokes's eyes. "This could be big—a lot bigger than it appears at present."

Stokes nodded. "I spoke to the commissioner earlier. He gave me leave to investigate appropriately—the emphasis being on appropriately." Stokes's dark smile curved his lips. "I'll speak with him again tomorrow, and tell him what we now think. I believe I can guarantee having a free hand after that."

Barnaby smiled cynically. "So what's our next step? Finding this school?"

"It's most likely in the East End, somewhere not far from where the boys lived. You said it's unlikely the boys were identified as potential scholars by any of the Foundling House's staff. If so, then the most likely explanation for how our 'schoolmaster' heard of the four, and more, knew exactly when and how to send a man to fetch them, is that the schoolmaster and his team are locals themselves."

"The neighbors were certain the man who fetched the boys was from the East End, and that he was merely an errand boy—someone trained in what to say to convince them to surrender the orphans to him."

"Exactly. These villains know the local ropes well because they're locals."

Barnaby grimaced. "I have no idea how to go about searching for a burglary school in the East End. Or anywhere else, for that matter."

"Looking for anything in the East End isn't easy, and I'm no more familiar with the area than you."

"The local force?" Barnaby suggested.

"I'll notify them, but I don't expect to get much direct help. The force is in its infancy and predictably not well established in that area." A minute passed, Stokes tapping one finger on the desktop, then he seemed to come to a decision. He pushed back from the desk. "Leave it with me. There's someone I know who knows the East End. If I can get them interested in the case, they might consent to help us." He rose.

Barnaby rose, too. He turned to the door. Stokes came around the desk, snagged his greatcoat from its hook, and followed.

Barnaby paused in the corridor; Stokes halted beside him. "I'll go off and rack my brains to see if there's some other way to advance our cause."

Stokes nodded. "Tomorrow I'll see the commissioner and tell him our news. And I'll see my contact. I'll send word if they're willing to help."

They parted. Barnaby went outside into the gathering dusk. Again he paused on the building's steps to take stock.

Stokes had something to do—an avenue to pursue. He, on the other hand . . .

The compulsion to act—to not simply sit waiting for Stokes to send word—rode like a goblin on his shoulders. Whispering in his ear.

If he spoke with Penelope Ashford again, now he had some idea of their direction, he might winkle more useful information from her. He had little doubt her brain was crammed with potentially pertinent facts. And he had more or less promised to let her know what Stokes thought.

Pushy female.

Difficult female . . . with lush, ripe lips.

Distracting lips.

Thrusting his hands into his pockets, he continued down the steps. The one problem with speaking with Penelope Ashford that night was that to do so he would have to meet her somewhere in the ton.

Evening had come, and with it Penelope had been forced to don what she considered a disguise. She had to convert from being herself to being Miss Penelope Ashford, youngest sister of Viscount Calverton, youngest daughter of Minerva, the Dowager Lady Calverton, and the only unmarried female in the clan.

That last designation grated, not because she had any desire to change her marital status but because it somehow set her apart. Set her on a pedestal that she cynically viewed as akin to an auction block. And while she never had the slightest difficulty dismissing the mistaken assumptions too many young gentlemen inevitably made, the need to do so irked. It was irritating to have to suspend her thoughts and find patience and polite words to send importuning gentlemen to the rightabout.

Especially as, while she might be standing by the side of a ballroom, she was usually mentally elsewhere. Thermopylae, for example. To her the ancient Greeks held a far greater allure than any of the youthful swains who tried to catch her eye.

Tonight's venue was Lady Hemmingford's drawing room. Fashionably gowned in green satin of such a dark hue it was almost black—having been forbidden by her family from wearing black, her color of choice—Penelope stood by the wall, a political soiree in full voice before her.

Regardless of her boredom with—indeed, antipathy to—such social events, she couldn't cry off. Her unfailing attendance with her mother at whatever evening functions the Dowager chose to grace was part of the bargain she had struck with Luc and her mother in return for Lady Calverton remaining in town when the rest of the family had departed for the country, thus allowing her to continue her work at the Foundling House.

Luc and her mother had flatly refused to countenance her remaining in London on her own, or even with Helen, a widowed cousin, as chaperone. Unfortunately, no one could see Helen, sweet tempered and mild, as being able to check her in any way, not even Penelope. Despite her brother's unhelpful stance, she could see his point.

She also knew that an unvoiced part of their bargain was that she would consent to being paraded before those members of the ton still in the capital, thereby keeping alive her chances of making a suitable match.

Within the family, she did her best to openly quash such thoughts; she saw no benefit in marriage at all—not in her case. When out in society, she, if not openly, then subtly and unrelentingly, discouraged gentlemen from imagining she might change her mind.

She was always taken aback when some young sprig proved too dense to read her message. *I'm wearing spectacles, you dolt!* was always her first thought. What young lady wishful of contracting a suitable match came to a ton event with gold-rimmed spectacles perched on her nose?

In reality, she could see enough to get by without her spectacles, but things were fuzzy. She could manage within a restricted area like a room, even a ballroom, but she couldn't make out the expressions on people's faces. In her teens, she'd decided knowing what was going on around her—every little detail—was far more important than projecting the right appearance. Other young ladies might blink myopically and bumble about in an attempt to deny their shortcoming, but not her.

She was as she was, and the ton could simply make do with that.

Chin elevated, gaze fixed on the cornice across the room, she continued to stand by the side of the Hemmingfords' drawing room, debating whether among the more recently arrived guests there were any with whom she—or the Foundling House—might benefit from conversation.

She was distantly aware of music issuing from the adjoining salon, but resolutely ignored the tug on her senses. Dancing with gentlemen invariably encouraged them to imagine she was interested in further acquaintance. A sad circumstance given she loved dancing, but she'd learned not to let the music tempt her.

Suddenly, with no warning whatsoever, her senses . . . ruffled. She blinked. That most curious sensation slid over her, as if the nerve endings beneath her skin had been stroked. Warmly. She was about to look around to identify the cause when a disturbingly deep voice murmured, "Good evening, Miss Ashford."

Blond curls; blue, blue eyes. Resplendent in evening black-and-white, Barnaby Adair appeared by her side.

Turning to face him, she smiled delightedly and, without thinking, gave him her hand.

Barnaby grasped her delicate fingers and bowed over them, seizing the moment to reassemble his customary suave composure, something she'd shattered with that fabulous smile.

What was it about her and her smiles? Perhaps it was because she didn't smile as freely as other young ladies; although her lips curved readily and she bestowed polite accolades as required, those gestures were dim cousins of her true smile—the one she'd just gifted him with. That was so much more—brighter, more intense, more open-hearted. Unguarded and genuine, it evoked in him an impluse to warn her not to flash those smiles at others—evoked an underlying covetous desire to ensure she kept those smiles just for him.

Ridiculous. What was she doing to him?

He straightened, and found her still beaming, although her smile itself had faded.

"I'm so glad to see you. I take it you have news?"

He blinked again. There was something in her face, in her expression, that touched him. Shook him in a most peculiar way. "If you recall," he said, with a valiant attempt at a dry, arrogant drawl, "you insisted I inform you of Stokes's thoughts as soon as practicable."

Her cheeriness didn't abate. "Well, yes, but I had no hope you would brave this"—she flicked a hand at the fashionable gathering— "to do so."

She had, however, had the foresight to once again instruct her butler to tell him her direction. Barnaby hesitated, then glanced briefly at the groups conversing nearby. "I take it you would rather talk of our investigation than of the latest play at the Theatre Royal."

This time her smile was both smug and confiding. "Indubitably." She looked around. "But if we're to talk of kidnappers and crime, I suspect we should move to a quieter spot." With her fan, she indicated the corner by the archway into the salon. "That area tends to remain clear." She glanced at him. "Shall we?"

He offered his arm and she took it; only because he was watching her closely did he see the momentary girding of her senses. He affected them. He'd known that from the first moment he'd laid eyes on her—in that instant she'd walked into his parlor, and seen him—not in a crowd of others but alone.

Steering her across the drawing room, necessarily stopping here and there to exchange greetings with others, gave him time to consider his unusual reaction to her. It was understandable enough; his reaction was a direct consequence of her reaction to him. When she smiled so unguardedly, it wasn't because she was responding to him as a handsome gentleman—the glamour most young ladies never saw beyond—but because she saw and was responding to the man behind the façade, the investigator with whom, at least in her mind, she was interacting.

It was his investigative self she smiled at, the intellectual side of him. That was what had made him feel so strangely touched. It was refreshing to have his manly attributes overlooked—dismissed as inconsequential—and instead be appreciated for his mind and his accomplishments. Penelope might wear spectacles, but her vision was a great deal more incisive than her peers'.

They finally reached the corner. There they were somewhat isolated from the main body of guests, cut off by the traffic into and out of the salon. They could talk freely, yet were in full view of the company.

"Perfect." Drawing her hand from his sleeve, she faced him. "So! What did Inspector Stokes deduce?"

He suppressed the urge to inform her that Stokes hadn't been the only one deducing. "After considering all the possible activities in which boys of that age might be employed, it seemed that by far the most likely in this case would be burglary."

She frowned. "What do burglars want with young boys?"

He explained. She exclaimed.

Eyes sparkling behind her lenses, she categorically stated, "We must rescue our boys without delay."

Taking note of the determination ringing in her tone, Barnaby kept his expression impassive. "Indeed. While Stokes is assessing his contacts in order to search for this school, there's another route I believe we should consider."

She met his gaze. "What?"

"Are there any other similar boys who might be orphaned soon?"

She stared at him for an instant, her dark eyes wide. He'd expected her to ask why; instead, in a bare instant, she'd fathomed his direction and, from her arrested expression, was only too ready to follow it.

"Are there?" he prompted.

"I don't know, not off the top of my head. I go on all the visits, but sometimes a year can pass between a child being entered into our files and the guardian actually dying."

"So there's a list of sorts, of potential upcoming orphans?"

"Not a list, unfortunately, but a stack of files."

"But the files have an address, and a basic description of the boy?"

"Yes to the address. But the description we take is just age and eye and hair color—not enough for your purpose." She met his gaze. "However, I can often remember the children, certainly those I've seen recently."

He drew breath. "Do you think—"

"Miss Ashford."

They both turned to see a young gentleman bowing extravagantly.

He straightened and beamed at Penelope. "Mr. Cavendish, Miss Ashford. Your mama and mine are great friends. I wondered if you'd care to dance? I believe they're preparing for a cotillion."

Penelope frowned. "No, thank you." She seemed to hear the frost in her tone; she thawed enough to add, "I'm not especially fond of cotillions."

Mr. Cavendish blinked. "Ah. I see." He was clearly unaccustomed to being refused.

Although Penelope's discouraging mien didn't ease, he shifted as if to join their conversational group.

She reached out and seized his arm, and forcibly turned him about. "That's Miss Akers over there." She directed his attention down the room. "The girl in the pink dress with the rosebuds rioting over it. I'm sure she'd love to dance the cotillion." She paused, then added, "She's certainly dressed for it."

Barnaby bit his lip. Cavendish, however, meekly bobbed his head. "If you'll excuse me?"

He glanced hopefully at Penelope, who nodded, brisk and encouraging. "Of course." She released his arm.

With a nod to Barnaby, Cavendish took himself off.

"Now." Penelope turned back to Barnaby. "You were saying?"

He had to cast his mind back. "I was wondering—"

"My dear Miss Ashford. What a pleasure it is to find you gracing this event."

Barnaby watched with interest as Penelope stiffened, and turned, slowly, her expression hardening, to face the interloper.

Tristram Hellicar was a gazetted rake. He was also undeniably handsome. He bowed elegantly; straightening, he nodded to Barnaby, then turned his devastatingly charming smile on Penelope.

Who was demonstrably unimpressed. "Tristram, Mr. Adair and I—"

"Whatever you were, dear girl, I'm here now. Surely you wouldn't throw me to the wolves?" A leisurely wave indicated the other guests.

Behind her lenses, Penelope's rich brown eyes narrowed to slits. "In a heartbeat."

"But consider, sweet Penelope, my being here with you is making all those other bright young sprigs keep their distance, relieving you of the need to exert yourself to diplomatically dismiss them. Rigby has just arrived, and you know how exhaustingly devoted he can be. And Adair here is no real protection—he's far too polite."

Barnaby caught the glinting glance Hellicar threw him, well aware the man was assessing him and his possible connection to Penelope. There was a latent warning in that look, but Hellicar wasn't sure if he was a rival for Penelope's affections, and without proof would only go so far.

He could have given Hellicar some sign easily enough, but he was enjoying the exchange and what it was revealing too much to cut it short. Aside from all else he was absolutely certain Penelope had no idea that Hellicar, reputation aside, was seriously pursuing her.

What was equally fascinating was that Hellicar, while having the nous to recognize that she wasn't the usual sort of female, and therefore wouldn't respond to the usual sort of blandishments, had no real clue how to charm her.

And if half the tales told of Hellicar were true, he was a past master at charming ladies of the ton.

He'd failed dismally with Penelope.

Hellicar continued his lighthearted banter, seeming not to realize she only grew progressively more rigid. Eventually she cut through his prattle without compunction.

"Go away, Tristram." Her voice was even, and cold as steel. He'd clearly fallen entirely from grace. "Or I'll tell Lord Rotherdale what I saw in Lady Mendicat's parlor."

Hellicar blinked, then paled. "You saw . . . you wouldn't."

"Believe me, I saw, and I would. And I'd relish every moment of the telling."

Lips compressing, eyes narrowing, Hellicar studied her face—and her set expression—and decided she wasn't bluffing. Accepting defeat, he bowed, rather less fluidly than before. "Very well, fair Penelope. I'll retire from the lists. For now." He glanced at Barnaby, then looked at Penelope. "However, if your aim is to lead an unfettered existence, then chatting so animatedly to Adair here isn't a clever way to convince all those yearning puppies that you're uninterested in a stroll to the altar. Where one goes, others might venture."

Turning away, he said, "Be warned, Adair—she's dangerous."

With a salute, Hellicar departed.

Penelope frowned. Increasingly direfully. "Rubbish!"

Barnaby fought to suppress a smile. She was dangerous—dangerously unpredictable. He hadn't needed Hellicar's warning, yet for him her threat stemmed from his fascination; he'd never before encountered a gently bred lady who, intentionally and with perfect understanding, stepped entirely beyond society's bounds whenever she felt like it and knew she could get away with it.

For the first time in longer than he could remember, he was enjoying himself at a ton function. He was being entertained in a novel, entirely unexpected way.

"At least he's gone." Penelope turned back to him. "So"—she frowned—"where were we?"

"I was about to ask—"

"Miss Ashford."

She actually hissed in disapproval as she swung to face their latest interruption. Young Lord Morecombe. She dismissed him summarily, ruthlessly disabusing him of the notion that she had the least interest in hearing about the latest play, let alone his curricle race to Brighton.

Morecombe was followed by Mr. Julian Nutley.

Then came Viscount Sethbridge.

While she dealt with him, and then Rigby, who true to Hellicar's prediction proved the most difficult to dismiss, Barnaby had ample time to study her.

It wasn't hard to see why those hapless gentlemen were drawn to brave her sharp tongue. She was highly attractive, but not in any common way. The dark hue of her gown made her porcelain skin glow. Even her spectacles, which she no doubt assumed detracted from her appearance, actually enhanced it; the gold rims outlined her eyes, while the lenses faintly magnified them, making them appear even larger, emphasizing her long, curling dark lashes, the rich, dark brown irises, and the clear intelligence that shone from their depths.

With the vibrancy that infused her features, indeed, her whole being, she was a striking package, even more so when viewed against the pale, meek, pastel uniformity of the other young ladies on the marriage mart.

He seriously doubted she understood that, far from being a deterrent, her waspish nature and high-handed attitude to her would-be suitors was, in her case, having the opposite effect. Her behavior had established her as a prize to be won, and the gentlemen who circled her were perfectly cognizant of the intangible cachet attached to winning her hand.

Listening to her deal with—and in Rigby's case, drive off—all those who had dared to get in the way of her learning what he, Barnaby, had to say, it was perfectly obvious that she considered gentlemen, as a species, to be significantly less intelligent than she.

He had to admit that in the majority of cases she was correct, but not all gentlemen were dolts. A compulsion to point that out, to score at least one point for his sex, and perhaps along the way nudge her into some comprehension of her attractiveness to males and what underpinned that—thus rendering a service to her hapless would-be suitors—burgeoned, teased, and tempted.

"Finally!" With one last glare at Rigby's departing back, Penelope once again turned to him.

Before she could speak, he held up a staying hand. "I fear Hellicar was correct. If we stand here chatting, too many will see it as a continuing invitation to join us. Might I suggest, in pursuit of our common goal, that we take advantage of the waltz the musicians are apparently about to play?"

He half bowed, and offered his hand.

Penelope stared at it, then at him. The introductory bars of a waltz floated over the surrounding conversations. "You want to waltz?"

One brown brow quirked. "We'll be able to talk sufficiently privately without risk of interruption." He studied her eyes. "Don't you waltz?"

She frowned. "Of course I do. Not even I could avoid being taught to waltz." Girding her loins, steeling her senses, she put her fingers in his. She had to learn what he'd been trying to tell her, and in light of her annoying suitors, the dance floor held the most hope of success.

He turned her toward the salon. "From which comment I take it you tried."

Drawing in a slow breath past the constriction in her lungs, she looked up, puzzled . . .

"To avoid being taught to waltz."

She blinked. Prayed he wouldn't guess his touch had so scrambled her wits she'd lost track of his words. She looked ahead. "I didn't at first see any point in my mastering such a skill, but then . . ." Lightly, she shrugged, and let him steer her onto the floor, then turn her into his arms.

They closed around her—gently, correctly—yet still her senses quaked. She inwardly swore at them to behave. Despite her irritating reaction to him, this was, she told herself, an excellent idea.

She'd dropped her opposition to being taught to waltz when she'd discovered that waltzing could be exhilarating and exciting. She rarely indulged these days because so many partners had disappointed her.

She fully expected Adair to disappoint her, too—which would be a very good thing. Once she discovered he was a less-than-adequate dance partner, her swooning senses would immediately lose interest. There was no better way to cure them of their ridiculous obsession with him.

Head high, chin tilted to just the right angle, a confident smile curving her lips, she stepped out—and immediately found herself following, rather than leading.

It took a moment for her to adjust, but that was one point in his favor.

Then she recalled she didn't want him to impress her, not in this arena.

Unfortunately . . .

Her cause withered and died as, her gaze locked on his face, she felt herself being whirled effortlessly down the room, checking and swirling along with the other couples precessing around the floor. It wasn't simply the ease with which he moved her—she was slight enough that most gentlemen managed that—but the sense of power, of control, of harnessed energy he brought to the simple revolutions of the waltz.

Far from being freed, she was caught, trapped.

And despite it being precisely *not* what she'd wanted, she found her lips curving more genuinely, found herself relaxing into his loose embrace as she accepted that yes, he could waltz. That yes, she could give herself over to his mastery and simply enjoy.

It had been so long since she'd taken pleasure in a waltz.

His blue eyes searched her face, then his lips quirked. "You obviously changed your mind and paid attention to your dance master."

"Luc, my brother. He was a dictatorial taskmaster." She gave herself one more moment to enjoy the sensation of floating around the floor, of his strong thighs brushing her skirts as they whirled, before asking, "Now, at last, we can complete our conversation. So what was it you wanted to know?"

Barnaby looked down into her wide brown eyes, and wondered why she hadn't wanted to waltz. "I was going to suggest that if you could identify any other boys who might be orphaned in the near future and who met the kidnappers' criteria, we might put a watch on them, both to identify the kidnappers if they come calling and, ultimately, to protect the boys from being snatched."

She blinked. Her eyes widened. "Yes, of course. What an excellent idea!" She breathed the words as if being visited by revelation. Then she snapped free and briskly took charge. "I'll go through the files tomorrow. If I find any possible candidate—"

"I'll meet you at the Foundling House tomorrow morning." He smiled. Intently. If she thought he was going to let her loose on the hunt, she would need to think again. "We can go through the files together."

She eyed him as if evaluating her chances of dismissing his offer, yet he was quite sure she understood it was no offer, but a statement of fact. Eventually, her lips—forever distracting—eased. "Very well. Shall we say eleven o'clock?"

He inclined his head. "And we'll see what we can find."

Looking up, he whirled her through a turn, then started back up the room. Another glance at her face confirmed she was enjoying the dance as much as he.

She was, even in this, the antithesis of the norm. Most young ladies were tentative; even when they were excellent dancers they were passive, not just allowing but relying on a gentleman to steer them around the floor. Penelope had no truck with passivity—not even during a waltz. Even though, after those first few steps, she'd consented to him leading, the fluid tension that invested her slender limbs, the energy with which she matched his stride, made the dance a shared endeavor, an activity to which they both contributed, making the experience a mutual, shared pleasure.

He would happily dance half the night with her . . .

Abruptly, he hauled his mind off the track of considering what different dances they might indulge in. That wasn't why he was waltzing with her. She was Luc Ashford's sister, and his association with her was purely driven by his investigation.

Wasn't it?

He looked down at her face as he swirled her to a halt—at those ruby lips slightly parted, at her lovely eyes and the madonnalike face that no amount of severe grooming would ever disguise—and wondered just how truthful he was being.

How willfully blind.

She stepped out of his arms. He let them fall and smiled—charmingly. "Thank you."

Smiling in return, she inclined her head. "You waltz very well—much better than I'd expected."

He noted the dimple in her left cheek. "I'm delighted to have been of service."

She chuckled at the dry reply.

Taking her hand, he set it on his sleeve and turned her toward the drawing room. "Come—I'll return you to your mother. And then I must leave."

He did. As he walked from the drawing room, he felt a certain contentment from his evening's entertainment—something he very definitely hadn't expected, either.

Penelope watched his broad shoulders until he passed out of sight. Only then did she even bother to try to marshal her wits and assess the situation.

When she did . . . *"Damn!"* She muttered the word beneath her breath. She could find no fault with Barnaby Adair—not in his investigative capabilities, nor yet, and most surprisingly, in his gentlemanly attributes. That was not a good sign. Normally, certainly after she'd conversed with a gentleman twice, she'd already dismissed him from her mind.

Barnaby Adair she couldn't dismiss. Not least because he wouldn't be dismissed.

Quite what she was going to do about him she didn't know, but it was patently clear she would have to do something. It was either take some action to nullify his effect, or continue to suffer her wayward wits and wretchedly preoccupied senses.

The latter wasn't an option. And until she accomplished the former, she wasn't—clearly wasn't—going to be able to manage him as she wished.

5

The next morning at nine o'clock, Inspector Basil Stokes stood on the pavement in St. John's Wood High Street, staring at the door of a small shop. After a moment, he squared his shoulders, walked up the two steps, opened the door, and went inside.

A bell above the door jangled; two girls working at a bench at the rear of the narrow rectangular space looked up. They blinked, then exchanged quick glances. One—Stokes took her for the elder—laid aside the bonnet she was trimming and came forward to the small counter.

Hesitantly she asked, "Can I help you, sir?"

He could understand her confusion; he wasn't the usual run of customer for a milliner's establishment. Glancing around, he almost winced at the feathers, lace, ribbons, and fripperies draped over pegs and adorning hats of various shapes. He felt comprehensively out of place, as if he'd stepped uninvited into a lady's boudoir.

Returning his gaze to the girl's round face, he stated, "I'm here to see Miss Martin. Is she in?"

The girl eyed him nervously. "Who shall I say wants her, sir?"

He was about to give his title, then realized Griselda—Miss Martin—would likely not appreciate her staff knowing she was being visited by the police. "Mr. Stokes. I daresay she'll remember me. I'd like a moment of her time, if she can spare it."

Like many others, the girl couldn't decide his social status; she bobbed a curtsy just to play safe. "I'll ask."

She disappeared through a heavy curtain that cut off the back of the shop. Stokes looked around. Two mirrors hung along one wall.

He caught sight of himself in one, framed by confections of feathers and lace, fake flowers and spangles displayed on the wall behind him. He quickly looked away.

A mumble of voices came from beyond the curtain, drawing nearer. He locked his gaze on the curtain as it parted—and a vision every bit as lovely as he recalled walked through.

Griselda Martin was neither tall nor short, neither plump nor slender. She had a round face with pleasant features—large cornflower-blue eyes framed by lush black lashes, a wide brow, an upturned nose across which a band of freckles marched, rosy cheeks, and rosebud lips. Her thick, sable hair, secured in a knot at the back of her neck, framed her face. Although her style was a far cry from tonnish beauty, she was, to Stokes, perfect in every way.

Her eyes were the sort that should have been twinkling, but when she looked at him they were serious, careful—a trifle wary. "Mr. Stokes?"

She, too, avoided using his title. He inclined his head. "Miss Martin, I wonder if you could spare me a moment—I'd like to discuss a business matter."

She appreciated his sensitivity in not mentioning the police before her staff. She thawed slightly; after a second's consideration, she turned to her assistants. "Imogen, Jane—you can take the deliveries around now."

Both girls, who'd been listening and watching avidly, looked deflated. But, "Yes, Miss Martin," they chorused, and set aside their work.

"If you'll wait just a moment," Griselda murmured to Stokes.

He nodded and moved to one side, trying to make himself as unobtrusive as possible, not easy given he was over six feet tall and broad shouldered to boot. He watched as the girls assembled various parcels and hatboxes, then donned cloaks and hats. Sharing their bundles, they headed for the door, glancing at him curiously as they passed.

The instant the door shut behind them, Griselda asked, "Is this about that business in Petticoat Lane?"

Anxiety threaded through her voice; Stokes hurried to reassure her. "No, not at all. The villain was transported, so you have nothing to fear from him."

She exhaled. "Good." Banked curiosity appeared in her eyes.

She tilted her head slightly. "To what, then, do I owe this visit, Inspector?"

To the fact that I can't get you out of my head. Stokes cleared his throat. "As I mentioned before, the force, and I, were very grateful for your assistance in the matter of the Petticoat Lane attack." She—along with a host of others—had seen a man beat a woman nearly to death. Of all the onlookers, only she and an old, almost blind crone had been willing to stand witness to the crime; without Griselda's testimony, the case would have been impossible to prosecute. "That, however, isn't the matter that brought me here."

Putting his hands behind his back, he crossed his fingers. "When I saw your statement about Petticoat Lane, I learned that, although you live and work in this area now, you grew up in the East End. Your father still lives there, and you yourself are widely known, at least within a certain pocket."

She frowned. "I might have improved my speech to better deal with my customers, but I've never hidden my origins."

"No—which in part is what has brought me here." He glanced at the front of the shop, confirming they were not about to be disturbed by any customers, then turned back to her. "I have a case involving boys disappearing from the East End. Young boys, seven to ten years old, born and bred in that area. These boys are newly made orphans. On the morning after their parent or guardian dies, some man has been appearing, saying he's been sent by the authorities to fetch the boy. In the cases we know of, the parent or guardian had made arrangements for the orphan to be admitted to the Foundling House, so the neighbors have been handing the boys over, only to discover mere hours later, when the Foundling House people arrive, that the man has no connection with them."

Frown deepening, she nodded, encouraging him to continue.

He drew breath, battling an odd constriction banding his chest. "I don't have any contacts in the East End. The police force there is not well established. I wondered . . . I know it's asking a lot of you—I do understand how the authorities are viewed—but . . . I wondered if you would be willing to lend your aid, in whatever way you felt able to. We believe these boys are being snatched to be trained for use as burglars' boys."

Her eyes widened. "A burglary school?" From her tone she knew precisely what that was.

He nodded. "I need to find someone who can tell me whether there's been any talk of some particular villain setting up a school recently."

Folding her arms, she softly snorted. "Well, there's no point asking your rozzers. They'd be the last to know."

"Indeed. And please believe that I don't intend to imply that you would know, either, but I hoped that you might know someone who might know a name, or an address."

She studied him, her blue gaze steady and candid. He fell silent, feeling that if he pushed she would refuse.

Griselda felt torn. She did know the East End; that was why she'd been so determined—and worked so long and hard—to leave it. She'd completed an arduous apprenticeship, then slaved, scrimped, and saved to be able to rent her own premises, and then she'd worked all but around the clock to establish herself.

She'd been successful, and had largely left the East End behind. Now here was this handsome police inspector asking if she was willing to go back into the stews. For him and his case.

No, she corrected herself—he wasn't asking for himself. He was trying to help four young boys who hailed from the same slums she'd left. She knew of the Foundling House by reputation; those boys would have had a chance to better themselves if they'd gone there, as their dying relatives had arranged.

Four young boys' futures. That was what was at stake here.

She no longer had brothers; she'd lost all three in the wars years ago. The oldest had been twenty when he'd died; they'd never truly had a chance to live their lives.

Eyes narrowing, she asked, "These four lads. How long ago were they taken?"

"It's been happening over the past few weeks, but the last was only two days ago."

So there was a chance they might be saved. "You're sure it's a burglary school?"

"That seems the most likely." Without prompting, Stokes described the boys, thus eliminating the other likely scenarios. He didn't elaborate on those alternatives; he didn't need to—she knew the realities of the world she'd left.

He fell silent again. He didn't press her; he waited . . . a predator nonetheless, but he was taking great care not to let that side of himself show.

She considered not helping, and inwardly sighed. "I can't tell you what I don't know, but I can ask around. I visit my father every week. He doesn't get about much these days, but he hears everything, and he's lived in the area all his life. He might not know who's set up a school recently, but he'll know who's run schools in the past, and who might still be in that line of business."

The tension that had held him eased. "Thank you. I'll be grateful for anything we can learn."

"We?"

He shifted. "Given I've asked you to revisit the area, I must insist that I go with you. As protection."

"Protection?" She gave him a bemused, intentionally faintly patronizing look. "Inspector—"

She broke off, rethinking what she been about to say: that in the East End, it would not be she but he who would need protection. She swallowed the words because she'd finally allowed herself a proper look at him as he stood there taking up too much space in her little shop.

She'd seen him—briefly met him—before, but that had been in a watch house in a milling throng of big men; they'd camouflaged him. Today he was by himself, and she couldn't miss his lean hardness, nor the way he moved, both sending a clear message that he could handle himself—easily—in a brawl.

Some gentlemen of the ton had that same dangerous edge—one that glinted through their polished exteriors, reminding the wise that underneath the sophistication beat a heart not civilized at all.

She'd been staring. Clearing her throat, she said, "I really don't need any guard, Inspector. I visit my father regularly."

"Perhaps, but the incident in Petticoat Lane could still have repercussions, and as in this instance you would be venturing into the area at my behest, I hope you can see that I couldn't in all conscience allow you to proceed unescorted."

"But—"

"I really must insist, Miss Martin."

She frowned. His tone might imply he was requesting, but the expression on his dark-featured face, the flat gray of his eyes, stated unequivocally that, for whatever convoluted male reason, he wasn't going to shift his stance. She knew that look; she'd seen it on her brothers' and father's faces often enough.

Which meant arguing would be futile. And Imogen and Jane would return soon, and she'd rather he was gone before they did.

Inwardly she sighed—again. In reality it would be no skin off her nose to walk into the East End with a man of his ilk at her heels. More than one woman would give a great deal for the privilege, and here he was offering, for free. She nodded. "Very well. I'll accept your escort."

He smiled.

She suddenly felt unsteady. Was this what it felt like to go weak-kneed?

Just because he'd smiled at her?

Second thoughts about the wisdom of allowing him any closer crowded into her brain.

"So . . ." He was still smiling. "I assume your girls will be back soon?"

She blinked. Then she met his eyes—gray, changeable, stormy. "I can't go now—I've only just opened."

"Ah." He sobered; his smile faded. "I'd hoped—"

"This afternoon," she heard herself say. "I'll close early—at three o'clock. We can go and see my father then."

He held her gaze, then nodded. "Thank you. I'll return here at three o'clock."

He didn't smile again; she told herself she was grateful. But his lips did ease as he inclined his head politely. "Until then, Miss Martin." He turned and walked to the door. Opening it, he glanced back, then went out.

The instant the door shut, her feet moved of their own accord, taking her down the shop to the door. She reached up to still the tinkling bell.

Watching Stokes's greatcoat-swathed shoulders retreat along the street, she wondered what she was doing.

And why. It wasn't like her to react to a handsome face, although his held a darkly rugged appeal that was difficult to ignore.

When he'd disappeared from her sight, she frowned, then turned and headed back to the bonnet she'd been feathering. If, thanks to him, she was going to be closing early, she needed to get back to work.

At ten o'clock that morning, Barnaby walked unheralded into Penelope's office in the Foundling House—surprising her in the act of searching through a stack of files.

Glancing up and seeing him, she blinked.

He smiled, all teeth. She was standing beside her desk. He strolled to her side. "Any luck?"

After a fraught second of simply staring at him, her distracting lips compressed and she returned her attention to the papers she was leafing through. Rather tightly, she said, "There's one boy I remember, but I can't recall his name. He lives with his mother somewhere in the East End, and she's dying."

He nodded at the files. "Are all these of about-to-be-orphaned children?"

"Yes."

There had to be dozens, a sobering thought.

After a moment, she paused, then reached out and pushed the stack across the desk toward him. "You could weed out the girls, and those under six years of age, or not in the East End. The details, unfortunately, are scattered throughout the pages."

He dutifully opened the next file, and scanned. They settled into a rhythm, he discarding the files of girls, younger children, and those outside the East End, while she studied the details of the remaining files, searching presumably for some feature that would tell her she'd found the likely lad she recalled.

Ten minutes passed in silence; her stiffness gradually eased. Eventually, without looking up, she stated, her tone almost accusing, "You got here an hour early."

Scanning the contents of the next file, he murmured, "You didn't seriously think I'd let you hie off on your own?"

From the corner of his eye, he saw her lips tighten. "I was under the impression gentlemen of your ilk lay abed until noon."

"I do." *When I have female company in said bed, and—* "When not chasing villains."

He thought he heard her humph, but she said nothing more. He continued to eliminate files; she continued to read.

"This is it—him." Holding up the file, she read, "Jemmie Carter. His mother lives in a tenement between Arnold Circus and Bethnal Green Road."

She glanced through the file again, then laid it on the pile.

He watched while she rounded her desk, picking up her reticule, and wondered if any purpose would be served by attempting to dissuade her.

Chin high, she swept past him on her way to the door. "We can get a hackney across the street."

She didn't even glance back to see if he was following. He turned and stalked in her wake.

Fifteen minutes later, they were rocking side to side in an ancient hackney as it rolled deeper and deeper into the stews. Barnaby eyed the decaying and decrepit façades. The Clerkenwell Road had been bad enough; he wouldn't have brought any lady into this area, not by choice.

Leaning back against the seat, he studied Penelope. Holding tight to a strap, she was gazing steadily out at the dismal streets.

He couldn't put his finger on what, but something had changed. He'd expected some resistance, yet on walking into her office he'd encountered an amorphous yet steely barrier, effectively shielding her from him. When he'd taken her hand to help her into the hackney, she'd tensed as usual, but as if his effect on her was now muted to the point of triviality.

As if she'd dismissed it, and him, as inconsequential.

It was one thing to have his mental acuity rated more highly than his personal attributes; it was quite another to have said attributes entirely ignored.

He'd never considered himself vain—he was quite sure he wasn't—and he certainly wasn't the sort of gentleman who expected ladies to fall swooning at his feet, yet her refusal to acknowledge him as a man, her refusal to acknowledge the effect he had on her, was definitely starting to grate.

The carriage entered Arnold Circus, then drew in to the side of the narrow street.

"Far as I can go," the jarvey called down.

Meeting Penelope's gaze with a narrow-eyed look, Barnaby opened the door and stepped down. He glanced around, then moved to the side, giving her his hand as she descended and joined him. He looked up at the jarvey. "Wait here."

The man met his eye, read the message therein, and tapped the bill of his cap. "Right, sir."

Releasing Penelope's hand only to grip her elbow, he faced south. "Which street?"

"Which miserable alley" would have been more accurate.

She pointed to the second opening yawning on their right. "That one."

He guided her to it, then escorted her along, ignoring her narrow eyes and the thin-lipped looks she cast him. He wasn't letting go of her, not in this area; if he did she'd sweep ahead, expecting him to follow in her wake—from where he wouldn't be able to see trouble looming until after she walked into it.

He felt positively medieval.

She couldn't complain; the cause lay at her door.

It had been gloomy in Bloomsbury, but as they entered the narrow passage a depressing darkness closed in. The air hung oppressively close; no sun could reach between the overhanging eaves to warm the dank stones and rotting timbers. No breeze stirred the heavy miasma of smells.

The street had once been cobbled, but few stones remained. He steadied Penelope as she picked her way along.

Teeth gritted against the sensation of his fingers—long, strong, and warm—wrapped about her elbow, his grip, firm and uncompromisingly male, distracting her in ways she hadn't imagined possible, Penelope uttered a small prayer of relief when she recognized Mrs. Carter's door.

"This is it." Halting before it, she raised her free hand and rapped smartly.

While they waited for a response, she swore she would—without further delay—find some way to overcome Barnaby Adair's effect on her. It was that or succumb, and that she'd never do.

The door cracked open with a protesting creak. At first she thought it had come unlatched of its own accord, but then she glanced down and spotted the narrow, pinched face of a child peering out from the darkness within.

"Jemmie." She smiled, pleased her memories had been accurate.

When he didn't respond—didn't open the door wider—but remained staring warily up at her—and at Barnaby beyond—she realized that with the lack of light, he couldn't see her well enough to recognize her.

Smile brightening, she explained, "I'm the lady from the Foundling House." Waving at Barnaby, she added, "And this is Mr. Adair, a friend. We wondered if we might speak with your mother."

Jemmie studied her and Barnaby with large unblinking eyes. "Mum's not well."

"I know." Her voice softened. "We know she's not very well at all, but it's important that we speak with her."

Jemmie's lips quivered; he pressed them tight to still them. His small face tightened, holding worry and fear close. "If'n you're here to tell her you can't take me after all, you can just go. She don't need to hear anything more to worry her."

Moving slowly, Penelope crouched down so her face was level with Jemmie's. She spoke even more gently. "It's not that at all—just the opposite. We're here to reassure her—to tell her that we're definitely going to be looking after you, and that she's not to worry."

Jemmie stared into her eyes, then blinked rapidly. He studied her face, then glanced up at Barnaby. "Is that right?"

"Yes." Barnaby left it at that, the simple truth.

The boy heard it, accepted it. After examining him for a moment more, Jemmie edged back from the door. "She's in here."

Penelope rose, eased the door wider, and followed Jemmie into the short hall. Barnaby followed, ducking beneath the lintel. Even inside, if he stood straight the top of his curls came uncomfortably close to the peeling ceiling.

"This way." Jemmie led them into a room that was cramped, but infinitely cleaner than Barnaby had expected. Someone—he glanced at Jemmie—was making a huge effort to keep the place tidy and passably clean. More, there was a tattered bunch of violets perched in a pot on the windowsill, the splash of intense color incongruously cheery in the drab room.

A woman lay on a makeshift bed in one corner. Penelope moved past Jemmie and went to her side. "Mrs. Carter." Without hesitation, Penelope lifted the woman's hand from the rough blanket, cradling it between her own, even though, blinking in surprise, Mrs. Carter hadn't offered it. Penelope smiled warmly. "I'm Miss Ashford from the Foundling House."

The woman's face cleared. "Of course. I remember." A soft smile flitted over a face made gaunt by constant pain. Mrs. Carter had once been a pretty woman with fair hair and rosy cheeks, but the body in the bed was wasted, skin hanging on bone; her hand lay limp between Penelope's.

"We're here just to check on you and Jemmie, to make sure all's as well as might be at present, and to reassure you that when the time comes, we'll make sure Jemmie is taken care of. You've no need to worry."

"Why, thank you, dear." Mrs. Carter was too far gone for social awe to have much hold on her. Turning her head on the pillow, she looked toward her son and smiled. "He's a good boy. He's been taking such good care of me."

Regardless of her body's state, the brightness in Mrs. Carter's blue eyes suggested that she was yet some way from departing this earth. She still had some time left with her son.

"Let me tell you what Jemmie will be doing once he joins us." Penelope skimmed through the procedures Jemmie would go through in becoming a foundling, and moved briskly to the activities and facilities the house provided for its charges.

Barnaby glanced down at Jemmie, by his side. The boy wasn't listening to Penelope's words; his eyes were glued on his mother. As it became obvious Penelope's choice of subject was indeed soothing the sick woman, the tension in Jemmie's slight body eased.

Glancing back at the bed, Barnaby felt an unaccustomed tightness grip his chest. He couldn't imagine watching his mother die, even worse watching her waste slowly away before his eyes. Even less could he imagine doing so all alone.

An entirely unexpected gratefulness for his family—even for his mother, annoyingly determined female that she was—was joined by a certain respect for Jemmie. The boy was coping, and coping well with a situation Barnaby wouldn't want to face. Couldn't imagine facing.

He looked again at Jemmie. Even in the poor light, it was clear he was unnaturally thin and scrawny.

"So that's what will happen." Smiling easily, brightly, Penelope scanned Mrs. Carter's features. "We'll leave you now, but rest assured we'll fetch Jemmie when the time comes."

"Thank you, dear." Mrs. Carter looked up at Penelope as she straightened. "I'm glad my Jemmie's to go with you. I know you'll take good care of him."

Penelope's smile wobbled a trifle. "We will."

She turned for the door.

The room was so cramped, Barnaby had to edge around to let her past. Before turning to follow, he looked at Mrs. Carter, met her gaze, and inclined his head. "Ma'am. We'll make sure Jemmie's safe."

Turning to the door, he noticed Jemmie's attention had remained on his mother. He touched the boy's shoulder. When Jemmie looked up, he pointed to the hall.

A slight frown on his face, Jemmie followed him. With Penelope waiting just inside the front door, the tiny hall was crowded, but at least they could speak without disturbing Mrs. Carter. Jemmie paused just past the doorway, from where he could keep his mother in view.

Halting, Barnaby reached into his waistcoat pocket and drew out all the small change he was carrying. He couldn't give Jemmie any sovereigns; possession of such wealth would put the boy at risk. "Here." Reaching out, he caught one of Jemmie's bony hands, turned it up, and poured the coins into his narrow palm.

Before Jemmie could react beyond a tightening of his jaw, he continued, "This isn't charity. It's a present for your mother. A surprise present. I don't want you to tell her about it, but you have to promise faithfully that you'll use the money in the one way that will mean most to her."

Jemmie's gaze had locked on the pile of copper and silver in his hand. His lips had pressed tight. A long moment passed before he looked up at Barnaby. His expression wasn't suspicious but wary. "What's the way that will mean most to her?"

"You have to eat." Barnaby held Jemmie's gaze. "I know her appetite is poor, but there's nothing you or anyone can do about that. Don't waste the money on delicacies to tempt her—they won't work. She's past that. But the one thing that will make her happy, make her last weeks and months happier, is to see you well. I know it'll feel wrong when she's not eating, but for her, you have to force yourself to eat—more than you have been."

Jemmie dropped his gaze.

Barnaby paused, felt the tightness in his chest as he drew in another breath. "*You* are the most important thing in her life—the most important thing she's leaving behind. You are the one thing that matters most to her now, and you need to respect that, and take care of that—take care of you—for her."

He hesitated, then dropped a hand on Jemmie's skinny shoulder, lightly gripped, then released him. "I know it's not easy, but that's what you have to do." He paused, then asked, "Will you promise?"

Jemmie didn't look up. He kept his gaze fixed on the pile of shiny coins. A glistening droplet fell to slide over and into the pile. Then he nodded. "Yes." His voice was the barest whisper. "I promise."

Barnaby nodded, even though Jemmie couldn't see. "Good. Hide the coins."

Turning away, he joined Penelope by the door. She'd been watching silently. Her gaze remained on his face for an instant longer, then she turned, opened the door, and stepped outside. Ducking again, Barnaby followed her into the murky lane.

Jemmie, rubbing his sleeve across his face, came to the door. "Thank you." He looked up at Barnaby, then at Penelope. "Both of you."

Barnaby nodded. "Just remember your promise." He trapped Jemmie's gaze. "We'll be back to fetch you when the time comes."

Turning away, he took Penelope's arm. They made their way back toward Arnold Circus.

Looking ahead, Penelope said, "Thank you. That was very well done."

Barnaby shrugged. He glanced back at Mrs. Carter's door; it was shut. "So how do we keep Jemmie out of the hands of our villains?"

Penelope grimaced. "I had assumed we'd warn Mrs. Carter, and Jemmie, too, but as he said, she doesn't need any more worries."

Barnaby nodded. "And neither does he." After a moment, he went on, "And warning him won't do any good anyway. If our villains want him, they'll snatch him, and scrawny as he is he won't be able to fight them. Better for him if he doesn't try."

The bustle and brighter, less-shadowed gloom of Arnold Circus drew nearer. "I'll speak with Stokes." Barnaby glanced around as they emerged into the circular space. "He'll get the local bobbies to keep an eye on the house. What about neighbors? Are there any we could approach?"

"Unfortunately, neighbors aren't much use in this case. Mrs. Carter has only recently moved here—they used to live in a better street, but once she could no longer work, and Jemmie had to spend more time looking after her, they couldn't meet the rent. Her landlord here is an old friend of the family—he's not charging them anything for the rooms. It was he who convinced Mrs. Carter to send for us. But there's no one nearby she's comfortable with—no one she'd be happy watching over the place, or her and Jemmie. The landlord lives some streets away."

Reaching the hackney, Penelope halted, jaw firming. "I'll send to the landlord and alert him. I'm sure he'll keep as close an eye on the Carters as he can. I'll ask him to send word if he or anyone he knows sees anything suspicious."

Opening the door, Barnaby grasped her hand and helped her climb up, then followed her into the carriage. The instant the door clicked shut, the jarvey called to his horse and they set off on the long journey back to more fashionable streets.

"That seems all we can do." Barnaby looked out at the drab streetscape. His tone suggested he wished it weren't so, that there was something more definite they could reasonably do to protect Jemmie while not worrying his mother, possibly unnecessarily.

Penelope grimaced again; she, too, looked out of the window. And inwardly wrestled with not her conscience but something closely aligned—her sense of rightness, of truth, of giving praise where it was due.

Of acknowledging the totality—the humanity—of Barnaby Adair.

She would much rather consider him a typical ton gentleman, far distanced from the world through which the hackney was rolling—a man uninterested in and untouched by the wider issues she confronted every day.

Unfortunately, his vocation—the very aspect of him that had compelled her to seek his help—was proof positive that he was otherwise.

Seeing him deal with Jemmie, hearing the commitment in his voice when he'd told Mrs. Carter, a poor woman with no claim on his notice other than her need, that he would keep Jemmie safe, had made closing her eyes and her mind to his virtues—so much more attractive to her than any amount of rakish charm—impossible.

When he'd arrived at the Foundling House that morning, she'd been determined to keep him rigidly at a distance. To keep all their dealings purely business, to suppress each and every little leap her unruly nerves might make, giving him no reason whatever to imagine he had any inherent effect on her.

Her resolve had wavered—illogically—when he'd arrived early, demonstrating a far better grasp of her determination and will than any man of her acquaintance. But she'd quickly bolstered her resolve with said will and determination, and stuck to her plan of how to deal with him.

And then . . . he'd behaved in ways few other gentlemen would have, and earned her respect in a way and to a degree that no other man ever had.

In less than an hour, he'd made her plan untenable. She wasn't going to be able to ignore him—even pretend to ignore him—not when he'd made her admire him. Appreciate him. As a person, not just as a man.

Her gaze on the rundown houses slipping past, she inwardly acknowledged that in dealing with him, she would need to think again.

She needed a better plan.

Silence reigned until the hackney drew up outside the Foundling House. Barnaby shook himself free of his thoughts—of the disturbingly persistent need to stop Penelope from making visits such as the one just concluded. Opening the carriage door, he got out, handed her down, then paid off the jarvey, adding a hefty tip.

As the grateful jarvey rattled away, he turned, remembered not to grip her arm as he had in the stews—a protective action only their surroundings had excused—and instead took her hand and wound her arm in his.

She cast him a swift glance, but allowed it. He swung open the gate and they walked up the path to the house's front door.

He rang the bell.

She drew her hand from his arm and faced him. "I'll write a letter to Mrs. Carter's landlord immediately."

He nodded. "I'll contact Stokes and explain the situation." He met her eyes. "Where will you be this evening?"

Her large dark brown eyes blinked at him. "Why?"

Irritation swamped him, heightened by her transparently genuine blank look. "In case I think of anything more I need to know." He made it sound as if he was stating the obvious.

"Oh." She considered, as if mentally reviewing her diary. "Mama and I will be at Lady Moffat's party."

"I'll look you up if I need any further information." To his relief, the door opened. He nodded to Mrs. Keggs, bowed briefly to Penelope, then turned and walked away.

Before he said something even more inane.

6

At three o'clock that afternoon Stokes presented himself at Griselda Martin's front door. She was waiting to let him in. The blinds screening the front window and the glass panel in the door were already drawn. Her apprentices were nowhere in sight.

She noted the hackney he had waiting in the street. "I'll just get my bonnet and bag."

He waited in the doorway while she bustled back behind the curtain, then reappeared a moment later, tying a straw bonnet over her dark hair. Even to Stokes's eyes, the bonnet looked stylish.

She came forward, briskly waving him down the steps ahead of her. She followed, closing and locking the door behind her. Dropping the heavy key into her cloth bag, she joined him on the pavement.

He walked beside her the few paces to the hackney, opened the carriage door, and offered her his hand.

She stared at it for a moment, then put her hand in his. Very aware of the fragility of the fingers he grasped, he helped her into the carriage. "What direction should I give?"

"The corner of Whitechapel and New Road."

He conveyed the information to their driver, then joined her inside. The instant the door shut, the carriage jerked and started rolling.

She was seated opposite him; he couldn't stop his gaze from resting on her. She didn't fidget, as most did under his eye, but he noticed she was clutching the bag she'd placed in her lap rather tightly.

He forced himself to look away, but the façades slipping past couldn't hold his attention. Or his gaze; it kept returning to her, until he knew if he didn't say something, his steady regard would unnerve her.

All he could think of was, "I want to thank you for agreeing to help me."

She looked at him, met his gaze squarely. "You're trying to rescue four young boys, and possibly more besides. Of course I'll help you—what sort of woman wouldn't?"

What sort of woman had he expected her to be?

He hastened to reassure her. "I only meant that I was grateful." He hesitated, then went on, "And if truth be told, not all women would be keen to get involved with the police."

She studied him for a moment, then gave a soft sniff and looked away.

He felt fairly certain the dismissive sniff had been directed at women who wouldn't get involved, not at him.

After further cogitation, he decided silence was the better part of valor. At least after their exchange, however brief, she was no longer clutching her bag quite so nervously.

As directed, the hackney halted at the corner of Whitechapel Road and New Road. Stokes descended first. Griselda found herself being handed down with the same care he'd used to help her into the carriage. It wasn't a courtesy to which she was accustomed, but she rather thought she could get used to it.

Unlikely as that was to be; Stokes and she were here on business, nothing else.

He ordered the driver to wait for them. Dragging a breath into lungs that seemed suddenly tight—she must have laced her walking gown too tightly—she lifted her chin and waved down the street. "This way."

During the drive she'd surreptitiously watched him, studying his dark-featured face for any sign of him turning up his nose as they'd penetrated deeper into the old neighborhoods. She wasn't ashamed of her origins, but she knew well enough how the East End was viewed. But she'd detected no hint of contempt, no turning up of his arrogant, bladelike nose.

Then, as now, he looked about him with a certain detached interest.

He strode easily, effortlessly, by her side, scanning the ramshackle houses pressed tight together, holding one another up. He saw all there was to see, but evinced no sign of passing judgment.

She felt just a little easier—less tense—as she led the way down Fieldgate Street, then took the second turning on the left, into familiar territory. She'd been born and raised in Myrdle Street. They drew level with her father's house; she paused beside the single front step and met Stokes's eyes. "I was born here. In this house." Just so he'd know.

He nodded. She looked, closely, but saw nothing in his face or his changeable gray eyes but curiosity.

Feeling rather more confident as to how the next half hour would go, she raised a hand and tapped on the door—three sharp raps—then opened the door and went in.

"Grizzy-girl! That you?" Her father's voice was scratchy with age.

"Yes, Da, it's me. I've brought a visitor." Setting down her bag in the tiny front room, she led the way into the room beyond.

Her father was propped up in his bed-cum-chair, an old ginger cat curled up in his lap, purring under his hand. He looked up as she entered, eyes brightening as they met hers, then widening as they moved on to fix on the presence at her back.

She was relieved to see that her father was wide awake, and also reasonably pain-free. "Did the doctor call this morning?"

"Aye." Her father's reply was absentminded. "Left another bottle of tonic."

She saw the bottle on the scarred dresser.

"Who's this?" Narrow-eyed, her father was studying Stokes.

Griselda sent Stokes a brief, warning look. "This is Mr. Stokes." She drew a deep breath, then said, "Inspector Stokes—he's an inspector from Scotland Yard."

"A rozzer?" Her father's tone made it clear that wasn't an occupation he held in high regard.

"Yes, that's right." She pulled up a chair and sat, taking one of her father's hands in hers. "But if you'll let me explain why he's here—"

"Actually," Stokes cut in. "It might be better, sir, if I explain why I've prevailed on your daughter to arrange this meeting."

She glanced at Stokes, but he was looking at her father.

Who grumped, but nodded. "Aye—all right. What's this about then?"

Stokes told him, simply, directly, without any embellishment.

At one point her father cut him off to wave him to a stool. "Sit down—you're so damned tall you're giving me a crick."

She caught the flash of Stokes's smile as he complied, then continued his tale. By the time he'd completed it, her father had lost all suspicions of this rozzer at least. He and Stokes were soon engrossed in evaluating the likely local villains.

Feeling unexpectedly redundant, Griselda rose. Stokes glanced up, but her father reclaimed his attention. Nevertheless, as she left the room, she felt the weight of Stokes's attention. In the cramped lean-to kitchen, she raddled the stove, then boiled the kettle and made tea. Returning to the front room, she extracted the biscuits she'd remembered to stuff in her bag, then laid them out on a clean plate.

Arranging the teapot, three mugs, and the plate on a wooden tray, she carried it into the small bedroom. Her father brightened at the sight of the biscuits; she felt her heart constrict when Stokes noticed, reached over, lifted the plate, and offered it to him. Delighted, her father helped himself, then returned to their discussion.

After handing out the mugs, Griselda sat. She didn't listen, but instead let the cadence of her father's voice wash over her, watched his face, more animated than she'd seen it in years—and silently gave thanks that she'd agreed to bring Stokes to see him.

Having an interest in life kept old people living; she wasn't yet ready to let her father go.

They finished their tea, and the biscuits. She rose, tidied the tray, and carried it back to the kitchen. She returned in time to see Stokes get to his feet, tucking his black notebook into his pocket while he thanked her father for his time.

"And your help." Stokes smiled easily; he had, she'd noticed, a smile that, although he didn't flash it often, inspired confidences. "Your information is exactly what I needed." His gaze locked with her father's, his smile grew wry. "I know assisting the rozzers with their inquiries isn't something that's encouraged around here, so I doubly value your help."

Her father, she could tell, was inwardly preening, but he hid it behind a manly nod and a gruff, "You just find those boys and get them back."

"If there's any justice in this world, with your help, we will." Stokes glanced at her.

She went to her father and fussed, straightening the blanket over his legs, reminding him that Mrs. Pickles next door would bring his dinner in an hour, then she kissed him on the cheek and bade him good-bye. He was settling down for a nap, an unusually contented smile on his face, when she joined Stokes in the tiny front room. Picking up her bag, she led the way to the door.

Stokes held it for her, then followed her out, making sure the latch caught behind them.

They were walking up the street when he asked, "Is he your only family?"

She nodded. Hesitated, then added, "My three brothers were killed in the wars. My mother died when we were young."

Stokes nodded.

He said nothing more, merely strode along by her side, yet within a few paces she felt compelled to add, "I wanted him to move to St. John's Wood with me." She gestured about them. "There's no call for a milliner around here. But he was born in this street, too, and this place is his home, with all his friends around, so here he'll stay."

She felt Stokes's glance, sharper, more assessing, but even now not judgmental. "So you come and visit him often."

Not a question, but she nodded. "I come as often as I can, but that's usually only once a week. Still, he has others—like Mrs. Pickles and the doctor—to keep an eye on him, and they all know how to reach me if there's any need."

He nodded again, but said nothing more. The obvious question leapt to her tongue; she bit it, then decided there was no reason she should. "Do you have any family living?"

For a long moment, he didn't answer. She was wondering if she'd stepped over some invisible line when he replied, "Yes. My father's a merchant in Colchester. I haven't seen him . . . not for a while. Like you, my mother died some time ago, but I was an only child."

He said no more, but she got the impression that he hadn't just been an only, but also a lonely child.

The jarvey was where they'd left him. When they were in the

hackney heading back to St. John's Wood, she asked, "So what now with your investigation?"

Stokes glanced at her; his hesitation suggested he was considering whether he should tell her or not, but then he said, "Your father gave me eight names of possible schoolmasters. He had directions for some, but not all. I'll need to check each one to see if they might be the villain behind our lads' disappearances, but any inquiries will have to be made very carefully. The last thing we want is for the schoolmaster, whoever he is, to realize we're taking an interest. Once he does, he'll up stakes and disappear into the slums, taking the boys with him— we'll never catch him and we'll have scuppered our chance to rescue the boys."

She nodded. After a moment she said, "You can't just wander in and ask, you know." Catching his eye, she wondered why she was doing this—why she was about to get further involved in a police investigation. "The locals will know who—and what—you are. No matter what disguise you put on, you'll still not be 'one of us.'"

He grimaced. "There's little option beyond using the local rozzers, and they—"

"Won't be spoken to, either." She paused, then said, "I, however, can still move among the locals. They know who I am—they trust me. I'm still one of them."

He'd tensed. A dark turbulence came into his eyes. "I can't let you do that. It's too dangerous."

She shrugged. "I'll dress down, let my accent come through. And there'll be far less danger for me than for you."

He held her gaze, and she knew he was torn.

"You need my help—those boys need my help."

Lips compressed, he stared at her, then he leaned forward, forearms on his knees. "I'll agree to you asking questions on one condition, and one condition only. I go with you."

She opened her mouth to point out the obvious.

He silenced her with an upraised hand. "I can pass well enough in disguise, as long as I don't have to talk. You can do the talking. I'll be there purely for your protection—but I must be there, or you don't go."

She longed to ask him how he intended to stop her, but if her father heard she was asking questions about schoolmasters he would worry, and there was no question but that having Stokes at her shoulder would, even in the roughest sections of the East End, count as very good protection.

Relaxing back against the seat, she nodded. "Very well. We'll go together."

Some of the tension holding him eased.

She glanced out, and realized they were back in St. John's Wood High Street. The carriage rocked to a halt before her door. Stokes descended, and handed her out. She could, she decided, get used to being treated like a lady.

Shaking out her skirts, she glanced at her door, then turned and met his gaze. "So when should we go back?"

He frowned. "Not tomorrow. I should share the information we've uncovered with a colleague—the one who brought the case to my attention. He might have news that will help us to fix on which of our possible villains is the most likely."

"Very well." She inclined her head. "I'll wait to hear from you."

He fell in beside her as she walked the few feet to her front steps. As she climbed them, then hunted for her key and unlocked the door, she was aware of him looking at the shop, as if with new eyes.

The door open, she turned and regarded him, brows lifting faintly in query.

His elusive smile flashed. He looked down for a moment, then lifted his head. "I was just thinking you must have worked very hard to get from the East End to here." His eyes trapped hers. "That in itself is a significant accomplishment. That you've retained the ability to move in your original circles—while I'm grateful for the benefits that brings my investigation"—he paused, then continued, his voice lower, softer—"I also find that admirable."

He held her gaze for a breathless instant, then inclined his head. "Good evening, Miss Martin. I'll be in touch in a day or so, once I have news."

He turned and made his way unhurriedly down the steps.

It took a moment and more to shake free of her surprise, to register that yes, he had indeed paid her a compliment, and no little one at that. Feeling suddenly exposed, she stepped inside and shut the door, then hesitated. With one fingertip she eased aside the blind—and watched his departing back, savoring the elegant lines, the muscular grace of his stride, until he climbed into the hackney and shut the door.

With a mental sigh, she let the blind fall and listened to the clop of hooves slowly fade.

That evening, Barnaby did something he'd never done. He propped one shoulder against a fashionable matron's wall and over the heads of the assembled throng studied a young lady across the room.

For once he was grateful that the matron in question, Lady Moffat, had a drawing room whose small size was at odds with her extensive acquaintance. Despite the continuing exodus of ton families from the capital, enough remained to ensure that the crowd packed into the limited space gave him adequate cover.

Within the ton, such cover was thinning by the day. Just when, for the first time in his life, he had need of it. His mother, he felt sure, would laugh herself into stitches if she learned of his predicament.

She'd laugh even more if she could see him.

He didn't have any question to ask Penelope yet here he was, watching her. He'd decided he may as well obsess over her in person, rather than sit at home staring into the fire and seeing her face in the flames. Alone, by himself, he would think of nothing but her; no other subject, not even the puzzling case she'd brought him, served to break her spell.

The saner, more rational part of him felt he should be stubbornly resisting her lure. The rest of him, led by a more primitive side he hadn't previously thought he possessed, had already surrendered.

As if the notion flitting about the corners of his mind were inevitable.

As if it were a truth he couldn't—wouldn't be able to no matter how hard he tried—deny.

His sophisticated self scoffed, and assured him he was merely intrigued by a lady so very different from all others he'd met.

His more primitive self wasn't listening.

His more primitive self was observing the men gathering about

her through ever-narrowing eyes. When Hellicar swanned into contention, he inwardly swore, pushed away from the wall, and headed in
her direction.

Penelope was holding her own against an annoying clutch of
would-be suitors when she glimpsed Barnaby through the crowd. The
whirl of emotions that afflicted her when she realized he was heading
her way was a warning; excitement, trepidation, and a seductive thrill
were a novel and unsettling mix.

Sternly ordering her stupid senses to bear up, she refocused on
Harlan Rigby's aristocratic countenance. He was presently holding
forth on the pleasures of the chase, something she was well acquainted
with having grown up in Leicestershire with hunting-mad brothers.
Unfortunately it was beyond Rigby's comprehension that a mere
female might know anything about anything. Even more unfortunately, as he was possessed of a sizable fortune along with passable
looks, not even Hellicar at his most pointed had succeeded in punc-
turing Rigby's self-assurance, let alone opened his eyes to the simple
fact that the route to her favors did not lie in belittling her intelligence.

Rigby was an afflicting ailment she had yet to learn how to treat.

Barnaby appeared, by some magic convincing the younger gentlemen to make space for him beside her. That left her flanked by him
and Hellicar, but still facing Rigby.

Smiling welcomingly, she gave Barnaby her hand. Rigby paused in
his ponderous discourse while Barnaby bowed and he and she exchanged greetings, but then Rigby drew breath, opened his large
mouth—

"It seems rather stuffy in here." Apparently oblivious of Rigby,
Barnaby trapped her gaze. He'd kept hold of her hand; he lightly
squeezed her fingers. "It's too cold to stroll the terrace, but perhaps
you'd care to take a turn in the salon." He raised his brows. "I believe
that's a waltz commencing, if you'd care to indulge?"

She beamed delightedly. Anyone who saved her from Rigby and
his views on the best way to husband hounds was worthy of her un-
dying gratitude. "Thank you. It is rather oppressive. A waltz will be
just the thing."

Inclining his head, Barnaby set her hand on his sleeve, covering
her fingers with his.

Nerves clenching at the subtle touch, she turned to her circle of unwanted admirers. "If you'll excuse us, gentlemen?"

Most had watched the byplay between her and Barnaby with interest, much along the lines of where he went, they might soon follow.

All except Rigby. Frowning, he fixed her with a puzzled look. "But, Miss Ashford, I've yet to tell you of my success with the latest round of crossbreeding with whippets." His tone made it clear he couldn't believe she didn't want to hear every last detail.

She wasn't sure how to answer; the very thought she might want to know such a thing made her brain seize.

Her white knight stepped in. "I find it hard to believe, Rigby, that you're unaware that Calverton, Miss Ashford's brother, is a renowned breeder of prize hounds." Barnaby's lips curved. "Are you smothering her with your procedures in the hope of winkling family secrets from her?"

Rigby blinked. "What?"

A snort sounded on Penelope's right—Hellicar smothering a bark of laughter. The other gentlemen fought to hide smiles.

Barnaby's smile turned apologetic. He glanced at Penelope, then nodded to Rigby. "I'm desolated to cut short your time for interrogating Miss Ashford, old man, but the lady desires to waltz." With a general nod, he drew her out of the circle. "If you'll excuse us?"

All the others bowed, amused. Rigby simply stared as if he couldn't believe she was deserting him.

But she was, for a much more challenging proposition. Barnaby led her to the archway separating the drawing room from the salon beyond, in which couples were dancing. A string quartet was crowded into an alcove at one end, laboring to be heard over a hundred conversations. They'd just played the opening bars of a waltz.

"I didn't think my ears had played me false." Barnaby glanced down and met her eyes. "Were you serious about dancing, or were you merely seizing the opportunity to escape Rigby?"

He was giving her a chance to avoid the effects that waltzing with him was sure to provoke. If she was wise, she'd take it . . . but she wasn't such a coward.

"I would like to waltz." *With you.* She didn't say the words, but the sudden intentness in his eyes made her wonder if he'd heard them—guessed them. Without another word, he drew her forward, onto the floor, into his arms, then whirled her into the swirling throng.

As previously with him, the revolutions of the dance swept her away. Left her senses giddy. Left her wits reeling.

Pleasurably.

They didn't speak again, exchanged not one word, not aloud. But their gazes locked and held, and communication seemed to flow without speech, on another plane, in a different dimension. In a different language.

A language of the senses.

One large hand, warm and strong at her back, the other clasping her fingers firmly, he held her with a confidence that left her free to relax, to dispense with her customary distrust of her partners and revel in the swirling motion, the quick, tight turns, the reverses and checks, in the masterful way he steered her around the floor.

Masterful men, she concluded, had their place—even with her.

The music flowed over and around them. The magical moment stretched; the subtle pleasure sank to her bones, taking hold and soothing her in some inexplicable way. Like a large warm hand stroking her senses.

She felt like a contented cat. If she could have, she would have purred. Instead, she didn't—couldn't—stop smiling, softly, gently, as they whirled and she floated on a cloud of delight.

After a time, he smiled, too, in that same, quietly satisfied way. They didn't need words to communicate their shared pleasure.

Too soon the musicans reached the end of the measure. Barnaby halted with a flourish. He bowed; she bobbed the regulation curtsy, and with an inward sigh returned to the world.

He settled her hand on his sleeve and turned her toward the drawing room.

Her senses were still waltzing, but her wits had reconnected—enough to recall her to the pertinent point that as he was there, he must have questions.

She glanced at his face, waited a heartbeat, but he seemed in no rush to pursue his inquiries. She looked ahead, smiling politely at those they passed. She was content to let the moment stretch, to just be together, him and her, with no investigation intruding—content to imagine, just for that moment, that investigating wasn't the reason he was there.

But it was, and now she'd thought of it . . . inwardly sighing, she asked, "What was it you wanted to know?"

He looked down at her, puzzlement clear in his blue eyes.

"The investigation," she prompted. "What did you come here to ask?"

The expression in his eyes blanked, then his lips tightened and he looked ahead; locating her mother, he tacked in her direction.

"Well?" she prodded, hoping he realized her mother had no knowledge of the situation at the Foundling House. That they even had a situation, let alone that she'd recruited him to investigate and she was investigating, too.

"Just give me a minute to think," he muttered, still looking ahead. Not looking at her.

She blinked. Perhaps he'd forgotten what he'd come to ask, and couldn't remember. Perhaps the waltz had distracted him, too.

Or perhaps . . .

He led her to a spot beside the chaise on which her mother sat, chatting to Lady Horatia Cynster. Both ladies smiled benevolently at their approach, but immediately returned to their discussion.

Suddenly very certain she needed to know what had brought him to Lady Moffat's, she drew her hand from his sleeve, faced him, and fixed him with an interrogatory stare.

Barnaby met it. Lips firming, he extemporized, "Stokes wasn't in when I called this afternoon. I left a note explaining the situation with Jemmie Carter—Stokes will no doubt order a guard, but I'll go and see him tomorrow morning regardless. Wherever he was, he was working on this case—he and I need to consolidate what we know and plan our next step."

Penelope's eyes lit up. "I'll come, too."

Barnaby inwardly swore; he'd only told her what he had to excuse his presence, not to tantalize her. "There's no need—"

"Of course there is. I'm the one who knows most about these boys—the four who've been taken and Jemmie." Her dark eyes darkened further; he got the impression she was expending effort not to frown. "Besides," she continued, her diction crisp, "I'm the one who initiated the investigation—I have a right to know what's being done."

He argued. In forceful terms, albeit keeping his voice low.

She regarded him mulishly, and gave not one inch. When he ran out of arguments, she tartly commented, "I don't know why you bother. You know perfectly well I won't change my mind—and if I choose to call on Inspector Stokes, there's nothing you can do to stop me."

He could think of a few things, but all involved rope. Exasperated, he exhaled through his teeth. "All right."

She gifted him with a smile—a tight one. "See? That didn't hurt a bit."

"Much you know."

She heard the mumbled grumble, but forbore to comment. She looked out at the guests. "What time do you imagine calling on Stokes?"

Lips tight, he considered, then surrendered. "I'll call for you at ten."

She didn't react for a moment, then inclined her head. "I'll be waiting."

A warning, but he'd expected no less. Once she set her mind on a path she was . . . as ungovernable as he.

In his mind he could hear his mother laughing riotously.

He had half a mind to retreat, to excuse himself and depart. From the way she held herself, slightly stiff by his side, and the quick side-long glances she darted his way, that was what she expected him to do. To cut his losses and run.

But he'd already lost all he could that night; there was nothing more he could concede.

And the night was yet young; there would probably be another waltz or two, and in this style of gathering there were no sharp-eyed dowagers keeping track of who danced how many times with whom.

He glanced at Lady Calverton, still absorbed with Lady Cynster. Perhaps there was more he could salvage from the night; he might as well remain, and reap what benefits he could.

In that vein, the first order of business was to thaw the ice maiden by his side. Glancing at her clear profile, he asked, "Is Rigby always so pompous?"

She glanced at him, suspicious, but after a moment, she answered. After that, courtesy of him paying close attention, enough to keep the reins firmly in his grasp, the remainder of the evening went his way.

"Good evening, Smythe." The gentleman who called himself Mr. Alert—he prided himself on being forever alert to the possibilities fate sent his way—watched as his henchman, silhouetted against the moonlit night as he stood in the open French door, glanced around the unlit parlor.

The town house in St. John's Wood Terrace had proved very useful to Alert. As usual when he met with his rougher associates, the only source of light in the room was the glowing embers of a dying fire.

"Do come in and sit down." Alert clung to his fashionable drawl, knowing that it emphasized the distinction between himself and Smythe. Master and servant. "I don't believe we need any great deal of light to conclude our business—do you?"

Smythe fixed him with a hard, direct, but carefully unchallenging glance. "As you wish." A large, hulking brute of a man, surprisingly quick and agile for his size, he stepped over the threshold, closed the door carefully, then picked his way around the shadowy furniture to the armchair set opposite the one Alert occupied by the hearth.

Relaxed in his chair, legs crossed, the picture of a gentleman at his ease, Alert smiled encouragingly as Smythe sat. "Excellent." He drew a sheet of paper from his coat pocket. "I have here the list of houses to which we'll need to gain access. Eight addresses in all, all in Mayfair. As I made clear at our last meeting, it's imperative—absolutely essential—that we burgle all these houses in a single night." He locked his eyes on Smythe's. "I take it you and Grimsby have made suitable arrangements?"

Smythe nodded. "Grimsby is still a few boys short, but he says he'll have all eight soon."

"And you're confident not only that he can supply the right number and style of boy, but that the training he provides will be up to scratch?"

"Aye. He knows the ropes, and I've used boys from him before."

"Indeed. But this time you're working for me. As I believe I've stressed, this is a game with high stakes, far higher than any you've played for previously." Alert held Smythe's gaze. "You need to be sure—indeed, you need to be able to assure me—that your tools will be up to the task."

Smythe didn't blink, didn't shift. "They will be." When Alert's expression made it clear he expected more, he grudgingly added, "I'll make sure of it."

"And how do you propose to do that?"

"I know where he's getting the boys. With the date you've given me, we've time to make sure we have the right number, and have them properly trained." Smythe hesitated, as if—finally—considering the eventualities, then went on, "I'll stop by Grimsby's and make sure he understands how . . . serious we are about this."

Alert permitted himself a small smile. "Do. I see no reason for us to find ourselves in difficulties because Grimsby didn't adequately comprehend, as you put it, the seriousness of our endeavor."

Smythe's gaze dropped to the list in Alert's hand. "I'll need those addresses."

The addresses were Alert's primary contribution to their game, together with the list of items to be stolen—he prefered the term "liberated"—from each house. "Not just yet." Lifting his gaze, he met Smythe's frown. "I'll hand it over in good time for you to do the necessary reconnoitering, but as you said, we've plenty of time."

No fool, Smythe understood that Alert didn't trust him. A moment passed, then he stood. "I'll get moving, then."

Remaining seated, Alert nodded a dismissal. "I'll arrange our next meeting as I did this one. Unless I leave word otherwise, we'll meet here."

With a curt nod, Smythe retraced his steps to the French door, and let himself out.

Wreathed in shadows, Alert smiled. All was going according to plan. His need for money had in no way eased—indeed, courtesy of the visit he'd endured yesterday from the fiend into whose clutches he'd unwittingly fallen, and the latest arrangement for repayment to which he'd been forced to agree, that need would only escalate with every passing day—yet his salvation was at hand. There was, he'd discovered, a certain satisfaction—a thrill, in fact—in cheating fate, and society, through the simple application of his admittedly devious brain.

He had no doubt that with his knowledge and Smythe's talents— and Grimsby's tools—he would come about, and that handsomely. As

well as freeing him from the shackles of London's most notorious
cent-per-cent, his scheme would significantly bolster his nonexistent
fortune.

Fate, as he well knew, favored the bold.

Glancing down at the list of houses he still held, he considered
it—and saw superimposed the other, even more important list that
was its mate, the list of the items to be liberated from each house.

He'd chosen carefully. Only one item from each address. Chances
were they wouldn't even be missed, not until the families returned in
March, and possibly not even then. And once they were . . . the staff
of the houses would be the obvious suspects.

By all accounts, Smythe was a master of his trade. He—or rather
the boys he used—would be in and out without leaving any trace.

And there wouldn't be any fences involved to later assist the authorities. He'd eliminated the need. Knowing the world of the ton as
he did—and the Lord knew he'd studied it avidly—he'd appreciated
that a judicious choice of items would ensure immediate resale, and
on his terms.

He already had collectors keen to acquire the items, no questions
asked. Selling to such people would ensure they never even contemplated exposing him. And the prices they were willing to pay would
easily free him of the debt currently weighing him down, even with
the constantly increasing load.

Slipping the list of houses back in his pocket, he smiled even more
broadly. Of course, the items were much more valuable than he'd intimated to Smythe, but he couldn't imagine that a burglar from the
East End would ever guess their true worth.

He would need to be careful, but he could handle Smythe, and
Smythe would handle Grimsby.

All was going precisely as he wished. And soon he would be as
wealthy as everyone in his life thought him to be.

7

The following morning, on Barnaby Adair's arm, Penelope climbed the steps of a nondescript building on Great Scotland Yard.

Her curiosity was running high. She'd heard all the commonly told tales of Peel's Police Force, the tonnish rumblings that had accompanied its establishment and consequent development over the last years, but this was the first time she'd come into contact with members of said force. More, other than Adair, she knew of no one who had visited its headquarters; she was agog to see what the place was like.

As he ushered her into the front foyer—a depressingly ordinary area in uninspiring shades of gray—she looked around, keen to see whatever there was to be seen. Quite aside from appeasing her natural inquisitiveness, concentrating on absorbing all she could about the police force helped avoid absorbing more about Adair—his nearness, his strength, his unfailing handsomeness—items from which her misbehaving senses steadfastly refused to be distracted.

Inwardly lecturing herself, she studied the only distraction the foyer offered—a little man in a dark blue uniform seated on a high stool behind a raised counter along one side. He glanced up, saw her—but then saw Adair. Raising a hand in an acknowledging salute, the man returned to his ledgers.

She frowned and looked about. Other than some clerk disappearing into the nether regions there was no one else around. "Is this where they deal with criminals? It seems awfully quiet."

"No. This building houses the senior investigating officers. There are bobbies in the building next door and a watch house down the street." She felt Adair's gaze touch her face. "We won't be running into any villains today."

Inwardly she grimaced, and prayed Stokes proved better fodder for distraction. After last night and the two reckless waltzes she'd shared with Adair, she needed something to focus on—something other than him. The increasing intensity of her reaction to him was disturbing in a way that tantalized as much as bothered her.

He steered her to the stairs at the end of the foyer. As they climbed, she reminded herself that thinking of him as Adair, rather than Barnaby, would help in keeping him at a sensible distance. Despite her earlier resolution, she'd yet to define a way forward—a way of dealing with him that would nullify the effect he had on her nerves, her senses, and, to her supreme irritation, sometimes her wits.

Unfortunately, her failure to devise an effective plan had left her wayward senses free to seize the day and slip their leash, and wallow as they would. As they had during those waltzes last night. As they had this morning when he'd arrived as promised to escort her there.

As they still were.

Mentally gritting her teeth, she vowed that the instant she had a moment to spare, she was going to find some way to make them stop.

At the head of the stairs Adair guided her to the right, down a long corridor. "Stokes's office is down here."

He led her to an open door; his hand brushed the back of her waist as he ushered her through, sending unwelcome awareness streaking through her.

Luckily, the man—gentleman?—seated behind the desk gave her something else to think about. He glanced up as she entered, then laid aside his pen and rose.

To his full, imposing six-foot height.

After returning from Glossup Hall, Portia had described Stokes to her, but as Portia had, by then, been engaged to Simon Cynster, her description had, Penelope now realized, lacked a certain depth.

Stokes was, to her eyes, quite fascinating. Not in the same way Adair, close by on her right, was, thank heaven; Stokes engaged her curiosity and piqued her interest on quite a different plane. She immediately sensed he was something of an enigma; while her mind instantly latched on to that promising fact, her senses and her nerves remained entirely unaffected.

Walking forward, she smiled and held out her hand. "Inspector Stokes."

He studied her for a heartbeat, then reached across the desk and shook her hand. He shot a quick glance at Adair. "Miss Ashford, I presume?"

"Indeed. Mr. Adair and I are here to consult with you on the matter of our missing boys."

Stokes hesitated, then looked at Barnaby, who had no difficulty reading the questions in his friend's eyes.

"This Miss Ashford is even less conventional than her sister." He let Stokes read his resignation—that he hadn't brought her there willingly—then moved to position one of the chairs before the desk for her.

She sat, smiling amiably. Stokes resumed his seat. Setting another chair beside Penelope's, Barnaby sat and crossed his legs. He harbored not a single doubt that Penelope was set on immersing herself in all aspects of the investigation. He and Stokes would have to, at some point, draw a line and curtail her involvement, although he'd yet to fathom exactly how.

Regardless, until she reached the point beyond which it was unsafe for her to go, he saw no real benefit in attempting to rein her in.

Stokes focused on him. "I got your note about the Carters. I had cause to visit Aldgate watch house this morning, and discussed the situation with the sergeant there." He glanced at Penelope. "We have to exercise caution so that we don't alert those involved to our interest in them—if we do, we'll lose all chance of rescuing the boys already taken. If Mrs. Carter's death is imminent, then mounting an around-the-clock watch would possibly be worth the risk—possibly." He locked eyes with Penelope. "Do you know if she's expected to die soon?"

She held his gaze, then grimaced and glanced at Barnaby. "After meeting her, I would have to say no."

"So it could be weeks, even months, before this boy, Jemmie, becomes a target?" Stokes pressed.

Penelope sighed. "I checked with Mrs. Keggs—the Foundling House's matron—after seeing the Carters yesterday. Mrs. Keggs has trained as a nurse. She's visited the Carters recently, and her opinion, confirmed by the local doctor, is that Mrs. Carter has at least three months more."

Stokes nodded. "So Jemmie Carter is not at immediate risk, and setting a watch on him might well work against us. However, if our more direct avenues of investigation fail, we may need to pursue him and others like him to pick up a trail."

Remembering Jemmie, seeing the boy in his mind's eye, Barnaby reluctantly nodded. "You're right—a watch for any length of time might well put the boys already taken at greater risk." Meeting Stokes's gaze, he asked, "So if you 'had cause to visit' an East End watch house this morning, can I infer that you've found some other way forward?"

Stokes hesitated. To Barnaby it was clear he was feeling his way over Penelope; he wasn't at all sure how much he should say before her.

Penelope spoke before he could. "Rest assured, Inspector, nothing you say will shock me. I'm here to assist in whatever way I can, and am determined to see our four missing boys rescued and the villains exposed."

Stokes's brows rose a fraction, but he inclined his head. "A laudable stance, Miss Ashford."

Barnaby hid a smile; Stokes had clearly been polishing his tact.

"Very well." Stokes settled his forearms on his desk and clasped his hands. He glanced from Penelope to Barnaby. "As I mentioned yesterday, I knew of a contact who I hoped would help me gain better insight into the identities and whereabouts of burglary schoolmasters who might be currently active in the East End. Through my contact, I was introduced to a man who's lived all his life in the area. He gave me eight names, together with some addresses, although by the nature of their business these villains move constantly so the latter are likely not to be of much help."

Stokes drew a sheet from a pile beside his blotter. "This morning I visited Aldgate watch house. The police there verified my list, and added one more name." He glanced at Barnaby. "So we have nine individuals to pursue." He transferred his gaze to Penelope. "But we have no guarantee at this point that any of these men are involved in this particular case."

Following Stokes's gaze, Barnaby saw Penelope nod—saw the gleam of engaged alertness in her eyes.

"That's excellent progress, Inspector—you've moved a great deal faster than I'd dared hope. I do understand that nothing is yet certain, but we now have a place to start—a route through which to learn more of active burglary schools. Your contact has certainly advanced our cause materially—can I ask you for their name? I'd like to send a note from the Foundling House expressing our gratitude. It never hurts to encourage people when they've been helpful."

Barnaby inwardly winced. He straightened in his chair. He was about to explain to Penelope that revealing contacts was something an investigator never did, when he saw something that froze the words in his throat.

Color was rising in Stokes's lean cheeks.

Observing the phenomenon, registering Penelope tilting her head as she did the same, Barnaby eased back in his chair again, and left Stokes to her.

Raising her brows, she prompted, "Inspector?"

Stokes shot Barnaby a glance—only to see that he'd get no help from him. He was now as intrigued as Penelope. Lips thinning, Stokes cleared his throat and met Penelope's gaze. "Miss Martin, a milliner in St. John's Wood High Street, hails originally from the East End. I met her while investigating another crime to which she was a witness. When I approached her with our present case, Miss Martin suggested introducing me to her father—he's lived in the area all his life, and now he's bedridden he spends most of his days listening and talking about what's going on around about."

"He gave you the names?" Penelope asked.

Stokes nodded. "However, as I said, we've no guarantee our list will lead to your four boys."

"But those individuals, even if they're not connected in any way with this latest incident, are surely the most likely to have heard if someone else is actively involved in their trade. They might well be able to help us locate our villain and thus rescue the boys."

Stokes shook his head. "No—it won't be that easy. Consider."

As Stokes leaned forward, Barnaby noticed that his friend was rapidly losing his reticence over interacting with Penelope; like Barnaby, he was starting to treat her as a coinvestigator.

"If we go into the East End," Stokes continued, "and openly inquire whether any of these men are currently running a burglary school, no one will say they are, *even* if they are. Instead, the instant we go away, whoever we ask will most likely send word to the men we've inquired about, and tell them questions are being asked. That's how the East End operates. It's an area that has its own rules, and by and large those rules don't encourage interference from ouside, especially from the rozzers, as they term us. The certain upshot of us making open inquiries will be that the villains—be they the ones on our list or someone else—will hear of our interest in short order, and they'll close up shop and move, taking the boys with them, and taking even greater care to hide their tracks."

Sitting back, Stokes shook his head. "We'll never catch them by asking questions."

Frowning, Penelope replied, "I see." She paused for only an instant before continuing, "From that I gather that you intend to go into the area in disguise, locate these men, and observe their activities from a distance—thus establishing whether they are currently running a burglary school, and if our boys are with them."

Stokes blinked; he glanced at Barnaby, as if seeking guidance. Unsure of Penelope's direction, Barnaby had none to give.

When Stokes looked back at her, she trapped his gaze. "Is Miss Martin assisting you in that endeavor?"

Stokes's eyes widened fractionally; he hesitated, then reluctantly admitted, "Miss Martin has agreed to assist us in furthering our investigations along the lines you've indicated."

"Excellent!" Penelope beamed.

Stokes, seeing her smile, wasn't the only one suddenly uneasy. Eyeing her delight, Barnaby felt his instincts go on full alert.

"So"—Penelope glanced from Stokes to Barnaby, then back again—"when are we to meet with Miss Martin to make our plans?"

Shocked into immobility by the implication of her words, Barnaby didn't shake free fast enough to stop Stokes from admitting, "I intend to meet with her tomorrow afternoon." Stokes regarded Penelope with a disbelief even greater than Barnaby's. "But—"

"You aren't going." Barnaby infused the statement—a statement that plainly had to be made—with absolute, unshakable conviction.

Turning her head, Penelope blinked at him. "Of course I am. We have to sort out the details of our disguises, and how best to work to uncover what we need to learn."

Stokes dragged in a breath. "Miss Ashford—you cannot venture into the East End."

She turned her gaze—growing darker by the second—on Stokes. "If a milliner from St. John's Wood can transform herself back into a woman who would pass without comment in the East End, then she'll know how to disguise me to a similar degree."

Barnaby found himself literally lost for words. He knew she would scoff if he described her as a beauty, but she was the type of lady who turned men's heads. Effortlessly. And that was a feature that couldn't be disguised.

"If Mr. Adair"—Penelope cast him a hard look—"who I'm sure is expecting to join in your hunt, but will need to be equally disguised to do so, and I, join you and Miss Martin in pursuing our inquiries, those inquiries will proceed significantly faster."

"Miss Ashford." Clasping his hands on the desk, Stokes made a valiant effort to retreat to a formal, authoritarian position. "It would be unconscionable of me to allow a lady like you—"

"Inspector Stokes." Penelope's voice acquired a precise diction that brooked no interruption whatever. "You will notice that Mr. Adair is remaining silent. That's because he knows that argument on this issue is futile. I do not require permission from you, nor him, to pursue this matter. I'm bound and determined to see our four boys rescued and the villains prosecuted. Moreover, as administrator of the Foundling House, I am arguably morally obliged to do all I can in that endeavor." She paused, then added, "I'm sure, if I request Miss Martin's help in this matter, she will assist me regardless of your views."

Barnaby glimpsed salvation, the way out of this argument for him and Stokes. He caught Stokes's gaze. "Perhaps, in light of Miss Ashford's strongly held notions, we should leave the question of her involvement until after we've met with Miss Martin?"

Thus leaving it to Miss Martin to pour the cold water of reality over Penelope's enthusiasm. He had little doubt that a sensible, worldly milliner—someone used to dealing with fashionable, headstrong ladies—would know just how to convince Penelope that she needed to leave the investigating to others. Miss Martin would unquestionably do a better job of dissuading Penelope than either he or Stokes.

Doubtless having reached the same conclusion, Stokes slowly nodded. "That's a reasonable suggestion."

"Good. That's settled." Penelope looked at Stokes. "What time tomorrow, and where shall we meet?"

They agreed to meet outside Miss Martin's shop in St. John's Wood High Street at two o'clock the following afternoon.

"Excellent." Penelope rose and shook hands with Stokes.

Turning to the door, she caught Barnaby's eye. "Are you remaining, or leaving, too, Mr. Adair?"

"I'll see you home." Barnaby waited for her to start for the door before exchanging a long-suffering glance with Stokes. "I'll see you tomorrow."

Stokes nodded. "Indeed."

Turning, Barnaby fell in at Penelope's heels—following in her wake. He no longer minded; the view from that position was sufficient compensation.

"Grimsby? You there, old man?" Smythe ducked beneath the low beams of Grimsby's ground-floor room. Word had it that Grimsby owned the whole house—all three floors of rickety tenement on Weavers Street.

Hearing a grumbled response from above, Smythe waited by the dusty counter. Around him all manner of old wares clogged the floor, piled here and there with no apparent order. Grimsby claimed to sell bric-a-brac, but Smythe knew most of the goods traded through the shop were stolen. He'd sold stuff he'd lifted through Grimsby himself on occasion.

A heavy, shuffling step on the stairs at the back of the shop heralded the descent of the store's owner from his rooms on the first floor. The floor above that was where the boys Grimsby tutored learned their lessons. The attic above, concealed unless you knew where to look, was where the boys slept.

Smythe straightened as Grimsby appeared out of the dusty murk. The man was aging, and now carried a considerable paunch, but there was intelligence still alive in the beady eyes that narrowly studied Smythe.

"Smythe." Grimsby nodded. "What're you after?"

"I'm after bearing a message from our mutual friend."

Grimsby's expression—of canny malicious avarice—didn't change. "What's he want?"

"He wants to be assured that you'll provide the tools for his lark as agreed."

Grimsby's features eased. He shrugged. "You can tell him we've encountered no difficulties."

Smythe narrowed his eyes. "I thought you were two boys short?"

"Aye, we are. But unless he's changed his timetable, we've plenty of time to get the last two in and trained up fer you."

Smythe hesitated, then glanced back at the shop door, confirming there was no one lurking. He lowered his voice. "You still picking off the orphans?"

"Aye—best source of what we need with no one to raise a ruckus. Used to be we had to pick 'em off the streets, and there's always the risk of a hue and cry that road. But taking the orphans from round here—no one's fussed."

"So what's your prospects for these last two boys? When will you have them?"

Grimsby hesitated, then, beady eyes narrowing, said, "I don't tell you how to run your business, now do I?"

Smythe straightened. "Give over, Grimsby—I'm the one who has to deal with Alert. And what he's got on is big."

"Aye—and just who put your name up for that, heh?"

"You, you old reprobate, but that's all the more reason I'll hold you to your promise to get me all eight boys. Eight, all properly trained and trialed. And that takes time—time you're running out of."

"What in thunder do you need eight fer, anyway? Never heard of a caper that needs eight all at once."

"Never you mind why. The way Alert's playing this, it's possible I might need all eight boys to do what he wants."

Grimsby looked suspicious. "You aiming to leave the nippers behind?"

"Not aiming to, no. But I don't want to have to tell Alert I can't finish his runs because some boy got stuck in a window, or tripped over a footman on his way out. Trained or not, they make mistakes, and Alert—as you know—isn't a forgiving man."

"Aye, well, that's the only reason I've come out of retirement—to appease Mr. Bloody Alert."

Smythe studied Grimsby. "What's he got on you, old man?"

"Never *you* mind. Getting you to see him, and then getting you these boys, that's my end of things."

"Exactly what Alert sent me to remind you." Smythe's gaze hardened. "So what of these last two boys? I need them—I want to be able to tell Alert that we have all eight as planned."

Grimsby eyed him for a long moment, then said, "Plenty of orphans littering the streets, but not the sort we need. Suddenly they're all lumbering oxes, or simpletons, or worse. No use, is what they are." He paused, then leaned nearer, lowering his voice, "When I told you I'd have the eight, I had eight in mind. We've got six of 'em. But with these last two, their sick relatives ain't turned out to be as sick as I'd heard."

Smythe read Grimsby's expression, read his beady little eyes—read between his words. Thought of Alert and his high-stakes game. "So . . . how sick are they—these ailing relatives? More to the point, what's their names and where do they live?"

Throughout the next day, Sunday, Penelope was forced to possess her soul with what patience she could—until at last she and Barnaby—Adair—reached St. John's Wood High Street. Instructed to stop outside the milliner's shop, the hackney slowed, rolling along as the driver studied the façades.

The carriage halted before a single-fronted, white-painted shop. Drawn blinds screeened the interior, but the sign swinging above the door read GRISELDA MARTIN, MILLINER.

Barnaby—Adair—got out and handed her down. While he paid the jarvey, Penelope considered the three steps leading up to the front door, then turned and saw Stokes walking down the street toward them.

He nodded politely as he joined her. "Miss Ashford." Over her head, he nodded to Barnaby. "Miss Martin should be expecting us."

Penelope promptly walked up the steps and tugged the bellpull beside the door. She heard the bell peal inside.

A minute later, light footsteps came hurrying toward the door. A click sounded, and the door swung inward. Penelope looked up into lovely blue eyes set in a sweet, round, rosy-cheeked face. She smiled. "Hello. You must be Miss Martin."

The woman blinked, then noticed Barnaby and Stokes on the pavement. Stokes quickly stepped forward. "Miss Martin, this is—"

"Penelope Ashford." Stepping forward, Penelope held out her hand. "I'm very pleased to meet you."

Miss Martin glanced at Penelope's hand, then hesitantly took it, shook it, then added a bob for good measure.

"No, no." Penelope moved farther into the shop, drawing Miss Martin with her. "There's no need for any ceremony. You've been very kind in agreeing to help us find our missing boys. I truly am very grateful."

Following Penelope inside, Barnaby could see the "Us?" forming in Griselda Martin's eyes. When her gaze shifted to him, he smiled reassuringly. "Barnaby Adair, Miss Martin. I'm a friend of Stokes's and like Miss Ashford—who is the administrator of the Foundling House where the missing boys should have gone—am most sincerely grateful for your assistance."

Stokes stepped over the threshold and closed the door behind him. He caught Miss Martin's eye. "I hope you'll excuse this invasion, Miss Martin, but—"

"The truth, Miss Martin," Penelope cut in, "is that I jockeyed Stokes into allowing me to come to meet you, together with himself and Mr. Adair. I'm absolutely determined to rescue the four boys who've been taken, and I gather you have a plan to go into the East End and search for clues to the burglary school in which they've likely been enrolled."

Barnaby had a sudden sinking premonition that allowing Penelope to talk freely with Miss Martin would lead to disaster. But then Miss Martin frowned, and he hoped he was wrong.

Penelope hadn't taken her eyes from Miss Martin's face. In response to the frown she nodded. "Indeed. I daresay you're wondering why a lady of my station is so interested in the welfare of four East End boys. The answer is quite simple. While they may not have been handed over to the Foundling House, as was intended, they were, nevertheless, made into our care. Those boys are our charges, and as the administrator of the house, I will not simply turn my back and let them be taken, denied the life that their parents arranged for them, to be instead inducted into a life of crime. That wasn't their intended destinies, and I will move heaven and earth if necessary to return them to their proper course."

Watching her face, Barnaby understood that when she said "heaven and earth," she meant it literally. The fierceness that lit her dark brown eyes and tightened her animated features bore testimony to her resolution, her unwavering determination.

Then she smiled, banishing the image of a warrior-goddess. "I hope you understand, Miss Martin, that I can't simply sit at home and wait for news. If there's any way at all I can help in locating these boys and rescuing them, as I believe there is, then I must be here, doing."

Behind him, Barnaby heard Stokes shift restlessly. He clearly hadn't anticipated Penelope's appeal to Miss Martin, much less its fervor. Despite being able to see quite clearly just where Penelope's persuasion was going to land them—with her going into the East End in disguise—Barnaby had to, albeit grudgingly, admire her honesty, as well as her strategy.

Miss Martin had remained silent throughout Penelope's declaration. She was studying Penelope's face; the frown on her own had faded, but remained in her eyes.

Barnaby was tempted to say something, to try to mute Penelope's appeal, but sensed if he spoke, he might well achieve the opposite. He was sure Stokes felt the same; with her characteristic directness, Penelope had shifted the discussion onto a plane on which they, mere men, held much less clout.

Everything hinged on how Miss Martin reacted to Penelope's words.

Penelope tilted her head, her gaze still fixed on Miss Martin's face. "I hope you can set aside any reservations you might have over my social status, Miss Martin. No matter the relative quality of our gowns, we are women before all else."

A smile slowly broke over Miss Martin's face. "Indeed, Miss Ashford. So I've always thought. And please, call me Griselda."

Penelope beamed. "If you will call me Penelope. Now!" She turned to survey Barnaby and Stokes, then glanced at Griselda. "To our plans."

Barnaby exchanged a thin-lipped look with Stokes; Penelope had won that skirmish before they'd fired a shot. But the battle wasn't yet over.

Miss Martin—Griselda—waved to the rear of the shop. "If you'll come up to my parlor, we can sit and discuss how best to manage things."

She led the way past the counter and through the heavy curtain. Beyond lay a small kitchen, the space all but filled with a large deal table on which feathers, ribbons, lace, and beads lay spread.

Penelope surveyed the feminine clutter. "Do you decorate all your bonnets yourself?"

"Yes." Griselda turned to a narrow flight of stairs. "I have two apprentices, but they're not working today."

She climbed the stairs, Penelope followed close behind. Barnaby went next; the stairs were so narrow he and Stokes had to angle their shoulders.

At the top of the stairs, Barnaby stepped into a cozy room that extended in a bow window over the front of the shop. At the other end, opposite the bow window, a wall cut across the space. Through an open door he glimpsed a bedroom, with a narrow window looking over the rear yard.

He followed the ladies to where a sofa and two mismatched armchairs were arranged before the small fireplace. A mound of coals was still glowing, throwing off a little heat, just enough to ease the chill. Barnaby eyed Penelope's pelisse; it was still done up—she was warm enough. He and Stokes had opened their heavy greatcoats, but kept them on as they sat.

Griselda Martin, a woolen shawl about her shoulders, sank into one armchair as Penelope claimed that end of the sofa. Barnaby sat next to her; Stokes took the other armchair. Barnaby caught Griselda's eye. "Stokes has explained the situation, and that we need to gain information about the individuals he's identified, but that we must do so without raising any suspicions, not those of the individuals nor indeed of anyone else, or we risk losing the boys forever."

Griselda nodded. "What I was going to suggest . . ." She glanced at Stokes; he nodded for her to go on. She drew breath, then said, "There's markets in Petticoat Lane and Brick Lane. Most of the men my father named work in and around those areas. Both markets will be in full swing tomorrow—if I go and pretend to look over the various wares, it won't be hard to slip in a question about this man or that here and there. People ask after others they know all the time at the market stalls. Because I have the right accent, no one will think twice about me asking—they'll answer freely, and I know how to jolly them along to get anyone who knows something to tell me all."

She glanced at Stokes. "The inspector has insisted that, as it's a police matter I'm assisting with, he will accompany me." She looked back at Penelope and Barnaby, and her expression was concerned. "But I honestly don't think it would be wise for either of you to come with us. You'll never pass. The instant people see you, they'll know something's afoot, and they'll watch and say nothing."

Barnaby glanced at Penelope. He intended to accompany Stokes and Griselda—Stokes had seen him in disguise and knew he could pull the transformation off. But if there was any chance Penelope would accept Griselda's warning and agree not to go into the East End . . . there was no reason to mention his plans.

Penelope met Griselda's eyes, held them. "You're a milliner, so you know how different bonnets can change a woman's appearance. You know what makes women look drab just as much as you know how to make them appear stunning." She smiled, a swift, engaging gesture. "Think of me as a challenge to your skills—I need you to fashion a disguise that will allow me to move through the East End markets without anyone thinking I don't belong."

Griselda met her gaze, then openly studied her. Her eyes narrowed, considering.

Barnaby held his breath. Once again he was tempted to speak and state the obvious—that there was no disguise that would adequately dim Penelope's startling vitality, let alone her innate aristocratic grace. Once again instinct cautioned him to keep his lips tightly shut. He exchanged a glance with Stokes; his friend was similarly on tenterhooks, wanting to influence the outcome and knowing they would be damned if they tried.

Penelope bore Griselda's scrutiny with unimpaired confidence.

Eventually, Griselda pronounced, "You'll never pass as an East Ender."

Barnaby wanted to cheer.

"*But*," Griselda continued, "I could, in the right clothes, with the right hat and shawl, see you as a Covent Garden flowerseller. They come to the markets quite often, plying their wares there during the hours the nobs aren't around their normal haunts, and most importantly, many of them are . . . well, they're by-blows, so your features won't mark you as a fraud."

Barnaby shot a horrified look at Stokes.

Stokes returned it with interest.

Then Griselda grimaced. "Be that as it may, while we might be able to disguise your appearance, the instant you open your mouth you'll give yourself away."

Barnaby glanced at Penelope, expecting to see her deflating with disappointment. Instead, she glowed.

"You needn't worry about me, love." Her voice sounded quite different—still her, but a different her. "I can speak any number of languages—Latin, Greek, Italian, Spanish, French, German, and Russian among them—so East End to me is just another language, one easier to master, and one I hear every day."

Barnaby hated to admit it, but he was impressed. Crossing his arms, he sank back against the sofa; glancing at Stokes—seeing his own inner consternation mirrored in his eyes—he shrugged.

They'd lost the battle, too.

Griselda was openly amazed. "That was . . . perfect. If I wasn't looking at you, I would have thought you were from . . . oh, somewhere around Spitalfields."

"Indeed. So once adequately disguised, I'll be able to help gather the information we need." She glanced at Barnaby, and sweetly asked, "I assume you'll be accompanying us, too?"

He narrowed his eyes at her. "Count on it." He looked at Griselda. "Don't worry about me—Stokes can confirm my disguise will work."

Stokes nodded. "As will mine." To Griselda he said, "We've done this before."

She studied his face, then nodded. "Very well." She looked back at Penelope. "So we have to put together your disguise."

They eventually decided that Griselda would borrow a suitable skirt, blouse, and jacket from the maids from a nearby house. "I do their Easter bonnets for them—they'll be happy to help. And they're your size."

That settled, Stokes brought out his list of names. Together, he and Griselda worked out a sensible order in which to tackle the list.

They agreed to meet at the shop at nine o'clock the next morning.

"That'll give me time to set my apprentices to their work. Then we'll have to disguise you"—she nodded at Penelope—"and then get to Petticoat Lane. We should arrive there by half past ten, which will be the perfect time to start moving through the stalls. The crowds will be big enough by then for us to merge in."

With all decided, they shook hands, Penelope and Griselda both patently pleased with their new acquaintance, then trooped down into the shop.

Griselda showed them to the door. Following Penelope and Barnaby, Stokes paused on the doorstep to exchange a few words.

Barnaby left him to it. The hackney was waiting to return him and Penelope to Mayfair; he handed her up, then followed, shutting the door.

Dropping onto the seat beside her, he stared straight ahead, considering—not happily—what tomorrow would bring.

Beside him Penelope continued to beam, radiating eager enthusiasm. "Our disguises will work perfectly—there's no need to worry."

He crossed his arms. "I'm not worrying." His tone suggested he was far beyond that.

"You don't have to come if you don't want to. I'll be perfectly safe with Griselda and Stokes. He is a policeman, after all."

He managed not to growl. "I'll be there." A moment ticked past, then he flatly stated, "In fact, I'll be glued to your side." His temper rose as the possibilities continued to reel through his mind. "Can you imagine what your brother would say if he knew you were trooping about the East End passing yourself off as a Covent Garden *flowerseller*?" Usually more accurately termed a Covent Garden whore.

"I can, actually." She remained entirely unperturbed. "He'd go pale, as he always does when he's reining in his temper, then he'd argue, in that tight, clipped, frightfully controlled voice of his, and then, when he lost the argument, he'd lose his temper and throw his hands in the air and storm out."

She glanced sideways at him; even though he refused to meet her gaze, he could tell it was faintly amused. "Is that what you're going to do?"

Lips tight, jaw set, he debated, then evenly replied, "No. Arguing with you is a waste of time." And he now understood it was point-less.

Dealing with Penelope in his preferred manner—on a rational, logical basis—was never going to swing advantage his way. With other ladies, the rational, logical approach left him with the whip hand—but not with her. She was a past master at using the rational and logical to her own ends, as she'd just demonstrated.

Arms crossed, he kept his narrow-eyed gaze fixed ahead, stead-fastly ignoring the effervescent triumph bubbling beside him.

Both he and Stokes had fallen in with Penelope's wish to meet Griselda in the firm expectation that there would be—at best—a cer-tain stiffness between the two women. Instead, Penelope had effort-lessly reached out and bridged the social gap—and it had been she who'd done that, not Griselda. Griselda had watched and waited, but Penelope had made the effort and known just how to do it, so now there was a budding friendship there, one no one could have pre-dicted.

So . . . where he and Stokes had been a team of two, there was now a team of four.

He'd imagined going into the East End with Stokes—the two of them had worked together in disguise before. With four of them . . . the hunt would indeed go faster. Penelope's version of an East End accent had been startlingly good. She could indeed pass as a local even better than he. The four of them could split up, and get through Stokes's list faster.

Having Penelope on their team as well as Griselda would help lo-cate the four missing boys that much sooner.

And all debate aside, that was their common goal.

He glanced up as the carriage swung around a corner; they'd al-ready reached Mount Street. His gaze on the façades as the hackney slowed, he said, "Tomorrow morning get your footman to summon a hackney at half-past eight. When it arrives, give the driver Griselda's direction and get in."

The hackney halted. Reaching across to open the door, he met Penelope's eyes. "I'll join you in the hackney."

Brows rising, she studied him. He moved past her and stepped down, assisted her out, then paid off the hackney and escorted her to her brother's door.

He waited for her to ask—to demand to be told what he was planning. Instead, she turned to him with a confident smile and gave him her hand. "Until tomorrow morning then. Good day, Mr. Adair."

Feeling somehow cheated, he bowed over her hand. The butler opened the door; with a nod for that worthy, he turned, descended the steps, and strode away.

8

Penelope had learned long ago that it was never wise to encourage any gentleman to believe she needed protection. Especially not when said gentleman was of the ilk of her brother Luc, or her cousin Martin, or her brother-in-law Simon Cynster. Some men simply could not be trusted to know where to draw the line—or to even recognize that a line existed—between smothering a lady in cotton wool and being a reasonable white knight. The inevitable result of any lady accepting their protection was an ongoing battle, one the lady was forced to wage to retain some workable degree of independence.

That had certainly been her observation in the case of the aforementioned males. As she rushed to be ready at half past eight the next morning, she was increasingly certain Barnaby Adair, regardless of his eccentric pastime, belonged to the same group.

Masterful men, experience warned, were masterful all the way through.

They didn't—couldn't—change their stripes, although they might at times disguise them.

With such wisdom resonating in her mind, she bolstered her enthusiasm with a quick but substantial breakfast, then hurried into her pelisse. She reached the front door just as the hackney she'd ordered to be summoned rolled up.

Farewelling Leighton, the butler, she glanced right and left as she went down the steps, but saw no one who might be Barnaby—Adair. A footman was holding the carriage door, waiting to help her up.

She called up to the driver, "St. John's Wood High Street—the milliner's shop," then climbed in.

Settling on the seat, she nodded a dismissal to the footman. He closed the door and retreated.

The door on the other side of the carriage opened; the carriage dipped as a man climbed in.

Even though she'd been expecting an appearance, Penelope's mouth fell open. The only thing she recognized about the man who shut the door and slumped on the seat opposite was his blue, blue eyes.

The carriage started forward—then abruptly stopped, the jarvey having realized some man had joined his lady passenger.

"Miss? Is everything all right?"

Her eyes—round with amazement—still fixed on Barnaby's face, Penelope simply stared. Barnaby scowled and roughly jerked his head toward the box seat, and she recalled herself and stammered, "Y-yes—perfectly all right. Drive on."

The jarvey muttered something, then the carriage rattled into motion again. As they rounded the corner out of Mount Street, Penelope let her gaze descend, taking in all of this rather startling version of Barnaby Adair.

Disguises generally concealed, but sometimes, they revealed. She was somewhat stunned—and just a little wary—of what, courtesy of his present guise, she could see.

He frowned at her, the gesture little removed from his earlier scowl—an expression that somehow fitted his new face, the clean, austere lines smudged with soot, the lean squareness of his jaw somehow more dominant beneath the prickly growth of a day-old beard. The beard roughened his cheeks. His hair was an uncombed tumble of golden curls; he never normally looked windblown and rumpled, but now he did.

As if he'd just rolled out of some doxy's bed.

The thought flashed across Penelope's mind; she instantly banished it. Closing her mouth, she found she had to swallow; her throat had grown unaccountably dry. Her gaze continued traveling over him, across his shoulders and chest, clad in a threadbare jacket with a thin, limp, cotton shirt beneath. No cravat or collar hid the lean length of his throat.

His long thighs were encased in workman's breeches; worn, scuffed boots were on his feet. He was the very picture of a rough-and-ready lout, a navvy who worked about the docks and warehouses doing this and that—whatever paid best at the time.

A certain dangerous quality emanated from him. The aura of a male not to be crossed.

Too dangerous to cross.

"What?" Through narrowed eyes, he challenged her.

She held his gaze—the only thing instantly recognizable about him—and knew that under the rough clothes and equally rough behavior he was still the same man. Reassured, she smiled mildly and shook her head. "You're perfect for the part." *Of escorting me in my flowerseller's disguise.*

She didn't voice the latter words, but if the sharpness in his gaze was any guide, he'd understood her meaning.

He humphed, then folded his arms across his chest, put his head back, and lapsed into uncommunicative silence.

Her smile spontaneously deepening, Penelope looked out the window so he wouldn't see.

As the carriage rattled on, she pondered that dangerous quality she sensed in him; it wasn't a characteristic he'd assumed for the role but something intrinsic, inherent in him.

Her earlier thoughts returned to her, now colored by a deeper insight. In view of her strengthening suspicion that Barnaby Adair was as one with her brother, cousin, brother-in-law, and their ilk, it seemed obvious—as demonstrated by the present situation—that with such men, the sophistication they displayed when going about their tonnish lives was the disguise. It was when they stripped off the outer trappings of polished civility—as Barnaby now had—that one glimpsed the reality concealed.

Given that reality . . . she wasn't entirely sure what to do with her revelation. How she should react.

Whether she should react at all, or instead pretend she hadn't noticed.

They passed the journey in silence, she busy with her thoughts, fueled by burgeoning curiosity.

The carriage eventually halted outside Griselda's shop. Barnaby uncrossed his long legs, opened the door, and stepped down. He hunted in his pocket and tossed some coins to the driver—leaving Penelope to descend from the carriage on her own.

She did, then closed the carriage door. Barnaby cast her a sharp glance, checking, then, thrusting his hands in his pockets, he slouched up Griselda's steps, flung open the door, waited for Penelope to join him, then—stepping entirely out of character—he extravagantly bowed her through.

"*Strewth!* He's a toff!"

The muttered words came from the jarvey on the box.

Pausing in the doorway, Penelope glanced at Barnaby's face as he straightened and looked at the driver; the lean planes appeared harder, more edged, than she'd ever seen them. As she watched, his blue eyes narrowed to flinty shards. A muffled curse from the driver was immediately followed by the sound of hooves as he whipped up his horse and rattled away.

Without waiting to catch Barnaby's eye, she swept on into the sanctuary of the shop. She wasn't at all sure she didn't share the jarvey's reservations about the man who followed at her heels.

Griselda had heard the tinkling bell. She came through the curtain behind the counter, set eyes on Barnaby—and very nearly stepped back. Her eyes widened, unconsciously matching those of her two apprentices who'd been working on the table between the counter and the curtain. They were now frozen, needles in midair.

After a fraught moment, Griselda's gaze shifted to Penelope.

Who smiled. "Good morning, Miss Martin. I believe you're expecting us?"

Griselda blinked. "Oh—yes, of course." Coloring faintly, she held back the curtain. "Please come through."

They went forward, Barnaby at Penelope's shoulder. She noticed he even moved differently—more aggressively. They passed the two girls, who dropped their gazes.

In frank amazement, Griselda shook her head at Barnaby when he halted before her. She waved them on. "Go on upstairs. I'll join you in a moment."

Penelope started up the stairs. Behind them she heard Griselda, voice muffled by the curtain, instructing her apprentices on their day's work.

Stepping into the parlor, Penelope paused. Barnaby moved past her;

he went to the bow window and stood looking out over the street. She seized the moment to study him, to examine again the fundamental hardness his unaccustomed guise allowed to show through.

A moment later, Griselda joined her.

"Well." Like her, Griselda surveyed the figure before the windows. "You'll certainly pass muster."

Barnaby turned his head and looked at them, then, with his chin, indicated Penelope. "Let's see what your magic can make of her."

Griselda caught Penelope's eye. She tipped her head toward her bedroom. "Come in here—I've got the clothes laid out."

Turning away from the presence by the window, Penelope meekly followed Griselda into the other room.

It took some time, and not a little hilarity, to transform Penelope into a Covent Garden flowerseller. Griselda firmly shut the bedroom door, giving them some privacy in which to work.

Once she was satisfied with the picture Penelope presented, Griselda had to change her own clothes. "I decided appearing down on my luck will make those who recognize me more likely to talk. Parading around as a successful milliner might get respect, but it isn't going to garner any sympathy in the East End."

Seated before Griselda's dressing table, Penelope used the mirror to adjust the angle of her hat. It was an ancient, dark blue velvet cap that had seen much better days, but with a spray of silk flowers attached to the band it looked exactly like something a flowerseller from the streets around Covent Garden would wear.

Her clothes consisted of a full skirt in cheap, bright blue satin, a once white blouse now a soft shade of gray, and a waisted jacket in black twill with large buttons.

They'd wound ribbon around the earpieces of her spectacles, and rubbed wax on the gold frames to make them look tarnished. A trug, the mark of her trade, had been discussed, but abandoned; she wasn't interested in selling any wares today.

Eyeing the overall result with satisfaction, Penelope said, "This disguise is wonderful—thank you for your help."

Tying the cords of an old petticoat at her waist, Griselda glanced at her. She hesitated, then said, "If you want to return the favor, you can relieve my curiosity."

Penelope swung around on the stool. She spread her hands. "Ask what you will."

Griselda reached for the skirt she'd chosen. "I've heard of the Foundling House, and the children who go there—the education they receive there. By all accounts, you and a handful of other ladies, some your sisters, have arranged all that. You still actively run the place." She paused, then said, "My question is this: Why do you do it? A lady like you doesn't need to sully her hands with the likes of that."

Penelope raised her brows. She didn't immediately answer; the question was sincere, and deserved a considered—equally sincere—response. Griselda glanced at her face, saw she was thinking, and gave her time.

Eventually, she said, "I'm the daughter of a viscount, now the sister of a very wealthy one. I've lived, and still live, a sheltered life of luxury in which all my needs are met without me having to lift a finger. And while I wouldn't be honest if I claimed that all that was anything other than extremely comfortable, what it's not is challenging."

Looking up, she met Griselda's gaze. "If I just sat back and let my life as a viscount's daughter unfold in the way that it would were I to surrender the reins, then what satisfaction would I gain from it?" She spread her hands wide. "What would I achieve in my life?"

Letting her hands fall to her lap, she went on, "Being wealthy is nice, but being idle and achieving nothing is not. Not satisfying, not . . . fulfilling."

Drawing in a breath, she felt that truth resonate within her. Holding Griselda's gaze, she concluded, "*That's* why I do what I do. Why ladies like me do what we do. People call it charity, and for the recipients I suppose it is, but it serves an important role for us, too. It gives us what we wouldn't otherwise have—satisfaction, fulfillment, and a purpose in life."

After a moment, Griselda nodded. "Thank you. That makes sense." She smiled. "*You* now make sense in a way you didn't before. I'm very glad Stokes remembered me and asked me to help."

"Speaking of Stokes . . ." Penelope held up a finger. They both listened and heard, muffled but distinguishable, the jingling of the bell on the door.

"His timing is excellent." Griselda shrugged into a loose jacket with a torn pocket, then picked up a shabby bonnet and placed it over her hair. They heard Barnaby's heavy bootsteps cross to the stairs and go down. Glancing in the mirror past Penelope, Griselda settled the bonnet, then nodded. "I'm done. Let's join them."

Griselda descended the stairs first. When she reached for the curtain, Penelope caught her hand and tugged her back. "What about your apprentices? Won't they think this is all rather odd?"

"Undoubtedly. Odd and more." Griselda grinned reassuringly. "But they're good girls and I've told them to keep their eyes open but their mouths firmly shut. They've got good positions here and they know it—they won't risk them by talking out of turn."

Penelope nodded. Releasing Griselda, she drew in a steadying breath; butterflies fluttered as if she were about to step out on a stage.

Griselda led the way. Looking past her, Penelope saw Barnaby and Stokes standing, talking, in the middle of the shop, two dark and dangerous characters incongruously surrounded by feathers and frippery.

The sight tugged her lips into a smile. Griselda stopped by the counter to speak with her apprentices. Stokes and Barnaby were discussing something. Stokes, facing the counter, saw her first—and stopped speaking.

Alerted by the sudden blankness in Stokes's face, Barnaby swung around.

And saw her—Penelope Ashford, youngest sister of Viscount Calverton, connected by birth and marriage to any number of the senior families in the ton—in a guise that effectively transformed her, spectacles and all, into the most refreshingly fetching, utterly engaging trollop who had ever strolled the Covent Garden walks.

He very nearly closed his eyes and groaned.

Stokes muttered something unintelligible beneath his breath; Barnaby didn't need to hear it to know that he'd be spending every minute of that day glued to Penelope's side.

She came up to them, smiling delightedly, clearly taken with her new persona.

Even as he looked down into her dark eyes, a niggling warning took shape in his brain. When stepping into the shoes of someone from a much lower station, as now, he'd always found it easy to shrug off the social restraints that applied to a gentleman of his class.

In far too many aspects, Penelope was proving to be much like him.

His jaw tightened until he thought it might crack.

She blinked up at him. "Well? Will I pass?"

It took a second to master his growl. "Well enough." Glancing over her head, he saw Griselda come forward. "Come on." He reached for Penelope's arm, then remembered and grasped her hand instead.

She started fractionally at the unexpected contact, but then smiled—still transparently delighted—up at him, and curled her fingers around his.

Swallowing a curse, he turned and towed her to the door.

They piled into a hackney for the journey to Petticoat Lane. They whiled away the minutes discussing the order in which they would approach the names on Stokes's list, and making plans should they decide to split into two groups—a decision they deferred until they were on the ground and had assessed the possibilities.

Leaving the hackney at the north end of the long street, they plunged into the teeming mass of humanity filling the space between the twin rows of stalls lining the pavements, spilling over the gutters and into the road. No driver would dream of taking his carriage down that street with the market in full cry.

Sounds and smells of all kinds assailed them. Barnaby glanced at Penelope, wondering if she might quail. Instead her expression suggested that she was eager to get on. She appeared to have no difficulty ignoring all she did not wish to notice, and drinking in all that was new, all that had been until now unknown to her.

He seriously doubted that any other viscount's daughter had ever rubbed shoulders with the denizens of Petticoat Lane.

For their part, said denizens cast her shrewd looks, but all seemed to take her at face value. With the hem of her full skirt, rather shorter than would have been acceptable in any ton venue, flirting about the tops of her well-worn half-boots, with her trim figure set off by the tight-waisted jacket, the lapels of which gaped provocatively at her breasts, all combined with her native confidence and perfectly sincere delight in all she saw, with her local accent setting the final seal on acceptance, it was hardly surprising that the locals swallowed her disguise whole.

Luckily, they also swallowed his. His face set, his expression an open warning, he hovered at Penelope's shoulder like a prepared-to-be-vengeful demon. No angel had ever looked as black and menacing as he did, not even Lucifer. It wasn't difficult to project such menace—because that was precisely what he felt.

When a grimy pickpocket edged too close to her, he met Barnaby's shoulder and a blue glare. Eyes wide, the man righted himself and scrabbled away into the crowd.

Stokes halted beside Barnaby. Directly before them, Penelope and Griselda were exclaiming over a collection of tawdry bows displayed on a rickety stand.

Glancing around, over the sea of heads, Stokes said, "Why don't you and Penelope take this side, while Griselda and I take the other?"

His gaze on Penelope, Barnaby nodded. "Figgs, Jessup, Sid Lewis, and Joe Gannon—they're the ones we're after today."

Stokes nodded. "Either along here, or in Brick Lane, we should be able to get a bead on those four. This is their turf—people here will know them. But don't push too hard—and don't let Miss Ashford, either."

Barnaby answered with a grunt. Quite how Stokes imagined he might accomplish the latter he'd love to hear. Penelope was entirely beyond his control . . .

The notion, or rather the notion of controlling a female in his present guise—and hers—sparked an idea. A glimmer of a possible means of survival. When Stokes moved forward to draw Griselda away, Barnaby swooped in, seized Penelope's hand, and tugged her along to the next stall.

She stared at him. "What's the matter?"

He explained Stokes's plan, then waved down the line of stalls. "This is our side, and we have to get on. However, now we've split up, we'll need to remain close, so I'm going to play the role of jealous lover disgruntled over the time you're spending on furbelows."

She stared even more at him. "Why?"

"Because it's a role the locals will recognize—one they'll accept."
And it would require no effort whatever for him to play the part.

She humphed; the glance she threw him suggested she didn't know
whether to believe him or not.

He answered it by looping an arm around her waist and pulling her
into his side. She stiffened; she started to glare, but he grinned evilly
and tapped her nose—thoroughly distracting her.

"No Covent Garden flowerseller would react like that," he murmured. "You claimed the role, now you have to play it."

She had to force herself to relax, but gradually, she managed it.
They moved down the line of stalls, stopping to chat here and there,
dropping the names of their targets whenever they encountered anyone who looked like they might know something.

He let Penelope choose which stallholders to approach; she seemed
to have a knack for knowing who she could strike up a useful conversation with. He left most of the talking to her—her accent was
faultless—and confined himself largely to grunts, snorts, or single-
syllable replies.

Penelope had to admit that his ploy worked, further encouraging
all who saw them to recognize them as something familiar, thus allowing them to insinuate questions about their targets into more general conversations.

Unfortunately, there was a cost. His nearness—the solidity of his
body whenever he pulled her close, the wall of male muscle against
which she was pressed every time the crowd surged and forced her
against him, the rampant possessiveness in his touch, in the large hand
that wrapped about her waist, or, in the few instances where he allowed her greater freedom, clamped about her hand—sparked a debili-
tating surge of emotions, an unsettling mix of excitement and wariness,
the skittering thrill of trepidation laced with disconcerting pleasure.

As the minutes ticked by, she felt increasingly distracted. Increasingly seduced into her assumed role.

But courtesy of their combined histrionic talents, they learned the
likely whereabouts of two of the men they sought.

Against that, she had to count the damage to her nerves and temper as fair exchange.

They reached the corner of a narrow lane down which Sid Lewis was said to live. By mutual accord, they halted. While Barnaby looked back up the street, trying to locate Stokes and Griselda, Penelope peered down the lane. "Fifth door down on the north side. I can see it." She grabbed Barnaby's coat—he had his arm around her waist, anchoring her beside him—and tugged, trying to gain his attention. "The door's open. There are people inside."

Barnaby covered her hand with his. "I can't see Stokes." He surveyed the lane. "All right. Let's look. But you stay in your role and play the part—which means you do what I tell you."

"Are you sure all males in the East End are this dictatorial?"

"Count yourself lucky. As far as I've seen, they're worse."

She humphed, but kept pace beside him as he strolled down the lane in the shadow of the southern walls.

Drawing level with the fifth hovel from the corner, she could see, through the open door, movement within. But there were few passersby in the tiny lane; loitering would draw attention—and someone was coming out of the house.

Barnaby stepped back into a doorway, hauling her with him—into his embrace. "Play along," he hissed. His head dipped; his lips cruised her cheek.

It took her a moment to steady her reeling head, to drag enough breath into her lungs—only to find her senses filled with him. His warmth surrounded her, wrapped about her—and somehow softened her bones. Somehow made her want to lean into him, to sink against the pure masculine temptation of his muscled chest.

Her reaction made no sense, but there was no denying it.

More than her wits were reeling; her senses were having a field day. She quivered inside, waiting—senses hovering, yearning—for the next elusive brush of his lips. It was lucky he was holding her, for she felt strangely weak.

Then she realized he was watching the activity across the lane around the edge of her cap.

He was using her as a shield.

She narrowed her eyes, not that he could see. Temper was an emotion she recognized and understood; she grabbed hold of it and used it to ground her.

Barnaby knew the instant she snapped free; he had to fight the urge to shift his lips to the left—so they could meet hers, those lush, ripe lips that haunted him. Instead, with his lips he brushed the rim of her ear—and felt a sensual shiver sweep through her, sensed her momentary pause, that instant when he succeeded in resuborning her wits.

The feel of her in his arms, soft, feminine, yet vibrantly alive, curvaceous yet supple, was distracting, a revelation he hadn't expected. The way she fitted so snugly against him as if she were made just for him fed that notion hovering at the edge of his consciousness, giving it more substance, more life.

Given their disguises, the relative roles they'd claimed, and that notion, he had to fight the compulsive urge to take what his alter ego would have—her lips, her mouth. Her.

While a part of his brain watched the activity across the lane, most was engaged in battling his instincts, in holding them down, keeping them back. Leashed. Controlled.

Predictably, she didn't stay distracted for long. "Don't," he hissed, sensing she was about to struggle.

She dragged in a breath, then hissed back through clenched teeth, "You're only doing this to pay me back for insisting on coming today."

As if he needed the internal turmoil. "Think what you will," he growled. "All that matters is that they believe our performance."

He tightened his arm around her waist, pulling her more fully against him; bending his head farther, he pressed his lips to the sensitive skin beneath her ear—and heard her gasp. Felt the resistance in her hands, pressed against his chest, ease, fade.

He inhaled, and the fragrance that was her wreathed through his brain. Sank to his bones. Her hair, sleek, dark, and silken, smelled of sunshine. He gritted his teeth against the inevitable effect, and whispered, "Someone's coming out."

He spread his hands on her back, shifted his head so that it appeared as if he were devouring her. At the very least kissing her witless, into submission—as the more primitive side of him wished he was.

She didn't struggle. After a moment, he murmured, his tone dry, "It appears we can cross Sid Lewis off our list."

"Why?"

Lifting his head, he eased his hold on her, setting her back on her feet but keeping her facing him. He studied the three men who'd come out of the hovel. "Unless I miss my guess, Sid Lewis is looking to shore up his position with God. Unlikely he'd be running a burglary school while entertaining the local vicar."

She glanced swiftly over her shoulder, then faced him again. "Sid Lewis is the short bald one." She'd extracted a description from one of the stallholders. "He looks ill."

"Which explains his sudden interest in religion." The man was leaning heavily on a cane. They could hear his wheezing from where they stood.

"Come on." Slinging an arm around her shoulders, he nudged her out of the doorway and started back up the lane. "Let's find Stokes. We've still got three others to investigate today."

They came up with Stokes and Griselda close to the southern end of the market. On hearing their report on Sid Lewis, Stokes grimaced. "Figgs is out of contention, too. He's in Newgate. That leaves us with Jessup and Joe Gannon in this area. Jessup, by all accounts, is a dangerous customer."

He met Barnaby's eyes.

"In that case, we'll just have to exercise greater caution." Penelope was glancing around. "Where should we try next?"

Stokes looked at Griselda. "How about stopping at a tavern for some lunch?"

The suggestion met with approval all around. Griselda suggested a public house she knew of on the corner of Old Montague Street and Brick Lane. "It's supposed to have more reliable food, and we have to head up Brick Lane anyway—the market stalls there are the most likely place for us to learn about Jessup and confirm Gannon's address."

They trooped back to Wentworth Street and cut across to Brick Lane, to the Delford Arms. The door to the taproom was set wide; after one glance inside, Stokes and Barnaby drew Griselda and Penelope on a few paces past the door. There were rough-hewn trestles with benches set on the pavement on either side of the entrance; most were occupied, but people were coming and going constantly.

"You two wait here," Stokes said. "We'll get the food and come back." He looked at the tables. "With luck, one will be free by then."

Griselda and Penelope nodded and dutifully waited, watching as their two cavaliers turned and entered the pub. Having seen the jostling throng in the tap, neither had been keen to brave it. Nevertheless . . . "They seem to share a penchant for giving orders," Penelope observed.

"Indeed," Griselda replied, distinctly dry. "I've noticed."

They both smiled, and continued to wait.

Having spent the last hours immersed in a constant babel of East End accents, Penelope's ear had improved significantly. She was indulging her skill, idly listening to the conversation of the four old but still hulking men hunched over the nearest trestle, empty plates spread before them, pint pots in their gnarled hands, when she heard the name "Jessup." She blinked, and listened harder.

After a moment, she nudged Griselda. When Griselda glanced at her, she indicated the table with her eyes. Griselda looked, then looked back at her, brows rising; the men were still talking, but no longer about anything relevant.

Penelope was about to turn and whisper when Barnaby reappeared, two plates piled with steaming shells in his hands. Just behind him, Stokes balanced a jug and four glasses on a tray.

At that moment, two men who'd been seated at the table next to the men who'd mentioned Jessup rose and shuffled away. Two others, in the dark, dusty coats of clerks, were still seated close by the wall.

Penelope grabbed Barnaby and steered him to that table. He glanced at her, but did as she wished. While he set down the plates and then slid along the bench, leaving the open end for her, she turned to Stokes and Griselda and whispered, "Those men"—surreptitiously she pointed at the next table—"mentioned Jessup. They were talking about something illegal, but I couldn't make out what."

Griselda glanced at the men again, then looked at Stokes. "I know one of them. I think he'll talk to me. Don't interrupt, or even look across. He's a leery sort, but he's known me and my family all my life."

Stokes hesitated, then, features hardening, nodded. He went to the bench and slid along it, opposite Barnaby, leaving the position at the end, closest to the men in question, for Griselda.

Both she and Penelope sat.

Griselda glanced around as she settled her skirts, as if checking who was at her back. She started to turn back, but then stopped.

Leaning to the side, she openly peered around the man directly behind her at the older man sitting opposite. "Uncle Charlie?"

The man she'd addressed stared at her for a moment, then his face creased in a smile. "Young Grizzy, ain't it? Haven't seen you in a good long while. Heard tell you'd moved up town and taken up making hats for the nobs." Shrewd eyes took in her less-than-prosperous attire. "Not doing so well these days?"

Griselda grimaced. "Fashions come and go. Turned out it wasn't such a good lark as I'd thought."

"So you're back home, then. How's yer da? Heard he's not so well these days."

"He's so-so. Doing well enough." Smiling easily, she asked after his family—the perfect way to ease into the world of local crime. The other men joined in, throwing information her way when she explained she'd only recently returned to the area; talking about crime was a local sport.

She bided her time; if at all possible, she didn't want to ask about Jessup directly. Remembering the man's reputation, his status among local criminals, and the fact they'd mentioned him at all, she eventually ventured, "So have there been any changes among the bigger villains recently?"

Charlie scrunched up his face as if thinking. "Only recent change would be Jessup. You'll remember him. Used to be big in burglary and such like. Taken himself off to Tothill Fields, he has, and set himself up in the usual trade." The "usual trade" in Tothill Fields meant prostitution.

It required no effort to look suitably interested. Especially as the information allowed her to say, "That must leave a bit of a hole hereabouts. Any word on who's filling it?"

Charlie laughed. "You're right about the hole, but there's no word of anyone rushing in to take advantage. Then again, it's the off-season. No doubt there'll be more activity come next year."

Stokes, beside her, roughly nudged her. Without looking around, he growled, "You'd best get to this, if you want any."

She shot him a glance, realized he was telling her to stop her questioning. Turning back to Uncle Charlie and the other three men, she smiled. "I'd best eat, or I'll miss out."

They all chuckled and bobbed their heads in farewell.

Still smiling, Griselda swiveled back to face the others. "Well," she said, "that was interesting."

"Eat." Stokes pushed the plate of steaming mussels and whelks toward her.

She glanced at him, aware of the dark tension still gripping his large frame, curious over what had caused it. But there was nothing—no clue—to be found in his face. With a mental shrug, she reached for a mussel. Lifting her spoon, she deftly opened the shell and scooped the mollusk in its warm juices into her mouth.

From across the table, Penelope watched, through narrowed eyes, admiring Griselda's confident wielding of the spoon. If anyone had told her, survivor of countless ton dinner parties that she was, accustomed to dealing with courses and cutlery of every conceivable type, that one day she'd be defeated by a simple spoon and a shell, she'd have scoffed.

But so it had proved.

Her fingers just didn't seem large enough, or strong enough, to hold the shell and insert and twist the spoon, at least not simultaneously.

She'd been reduced to accepting food from Barnaby's hand—a fact he, and Stokes, found amusing. They hadn't actually grinned, but she'd detected the expressions in their eyes, and she knew. Men!

Holding out her hand palm up, she waited until Barnaby set another opened mussel into it. Gripping the shell, she had to concentrate to scoop the flesh up and into her mouth without disaster, but that, at least, she could manage; if she'd had to let Barnaby feed her with a spoon, she would have lost her appetite.

Which would have been a pity. She'd never eaten such fare in her life—never sat outside in a crowded street to dine—but the little morsels of seafood were delicious, and she'd discovered she was seriously hungry.

She'd only taken a tiny sip of the ale; to her it tasted very bitter. Barnaby and Stokes, however, between them drained the jug.

Griselda quickly accounted for her share of the mussels and whelks. There were no napkins; Penelope noted the others wiped their mouths with their cuffs. Tugging the cuff of her shirt down so she could grip it, she did the same.

"You missed a drop."

She glanced around, and found Barnaby studying her face. Before she could ask where, he raised a hand and brushed his thumb over the corner of her mouth.

The frisson that raced through her shocked her. Had she been standing, it would have brought her to her knees.

"There." His eyes slowly rose and met hers. There was heat in the blue orbs, more than enough to steal her breath.

He held her gaze for a moment, and there was nothing remotely soft or gentle in his eyes.

Then his lids lowered; he smiled and eased back. With a wave, he encouraged her off the bench and to her feet.

She found herself upright, blinking, trying to get her bearings in what suddenly seemed a shifting landscape.

Stokes and Griselda—who glanced back and waved at her uncle Charlie and his mates—led the way up the street; his hand burning her back, then sliding around to rest possessively at her hip, Barnaby steered her in their wake.

She reminded herself that he was only doing it—all those unnerving, disconcerting touches—to make her regret insisting on participating in the day's events.

Unfortunately, knowing that didn't diminish the effect of said actions on her nerves, her senses.

They wended their way through Brick Lane market in much the same manner as in Petticoat Lane, but while the cheery stallholders in Petticoat Lane had offered a wide variety of wares for sale, fabrics and leather goods predominating, the Brick Lane stalls were peopled by sly-eyed characters, and fully half their goods remained concealed beneath the counter. Said goods were mostly ornaments or jewelry, or tatty furniture and bric-a-brac. Many of the trestles set out on the pavement were intended to lure customers into the gloomy sheds behind. Curious, Penelope ventured into one, and found it piled to the rafters with what appeared to be generations of musty old furniture, none of which would fare well in the light of day.

The owner, spotting her, came hurrying toward her, unctuously smiling. Looming at her shoulder, Barnaby scowled, grabbed her arm, and hauled her away.

It was Griselda who learned more of Joe Gannon, confirming that his present business premises were located in a building on Spital

Street. He apparently specialized in "selling old stuff." He was the last of the four sure to be known by those in the markets; although they kept their ears peeled, and Griselda did ask, they learned nothing of the other five men on Stokes's list.

The afternoon was waning when they regrouped at the north end of Brick Lane.

Stokes looked at Barnaby. "We've learned all we can from around here." He tipped his head to the east. "Spital Street's not far. I'm going to go and check that address we have for Gannon. He might be there. He might have moved." Stokes shrugged. "I'll go and see."

"I'll come with you." Griselda waited for Stokes to meet her eyes. "We can see what the place is like—if it's a shop it'll be easy enough to walk in and look around."

"I'll come, too," Penelope stated. "If there's any chance the missing boys are there, I should be present."

She looked not at Stokes but at Barnaby. His expression hard, lips compressed, he met her gaze. He wanted to argue, but recognized the futility. Curtly, he nodded, then looked at Stokes. "We'll all go."

They turned off Brick Lane into narrower streets that were more like passages with the upper stories of the buildings frequently meeting overhead. Reaching Spital Street, they walked along, Stokes with Griselda, her arm linked with his, in front, Penelope and Barnaby, his arm around her shoulders, following a few yards behind.

The directions they'd been given led them to an old wooden house. Narrow, its timbers faded, the windows shuttered, it fronted directly onto the street. There were two rickety stories and an attic above, no basement; an alley, just wide enough to allow a man to pass, ran down one side. There was no sign declaring it a shop of any kind, but the door was wedged ajar.

They strolled past, but saw no signs of life.

Stokes halted farther on. He and Griselda spoke, then he waited for Barnaby and Penelope to reach them. "We'll go inside. Why don't you two wait out here, just in case our inquiries lead to any action."

Barnaby nodded. He moved to lounge against a nearby wall, taking Penelope with him, his hand gripping her waist, anchoring her beside him. She rolled her eyes, but forbore to comment.

Stokes and Griselda crossed the street and disappeared into the house.

A minute ticked past. Penelope shifted her weight from one foot to the other—and immediately decided not to do so again. The movement had rubbed her hip against Barnaby's thigh. She studiously ignored the resultant wash of heat beneath her skin, and sternly lectured her witless senses to stop swooning.

They stood directly opposite the alleyway alongside the building. Staring down the length of the side wall, she noticed an irregularity.

She stepped forward. "There's a side door."

Whether she'd surprised Barnaby, or had simply broken his grip, his hand slipped from her waist. Taking advantage, she hurried across the lane and plunged into the alley. She heard him swear as he followed her. But the alley was clearly empty; she was patently not rushing into danger, so while he quickly closed the gap between them, he didn't try to catch her and pull her back.

Nearing the side door, she slowed, wondering if it led into the shop, or was another premises entirely. Caution had already laid its hand on her spine when the door cracked open, then quietly swung wide enough to allow a man to slip out. His back was to them. Peering into the building, he started to shut the door, easing it closed.

"Mr. Gannon?"

The man jumped and swore. He whirled around, flattening himself against the side of the house.

Penelope frowned at him. "I take it you are Mr. Joe Gannon, and that being so, we have some questions for you."

Gannon blinked. He looked at Penelope, and regained some of his color. But then he looked past her at Barnaby, looming at her shoulder, and transparently didn't know what to think. Warily, he asked, "Oo might be asking?"

Penelope replied without hesitation, "I'm asking with the full weight of the Metropolitan Police."

Gannon's eyes went wide. "The perlice?" He tried to see past them, then glanced the other way, to the other end of the alley. "'Ere—I ain't done nuthin'."

"That would be physically impossible." Penelope planted her hands on her hips; she'd dropped her disguise, and was now very much the haughty, demanding, commanding lady, which was what was confusing Gannon so much. "Don't lie to me, sir." Leaning forward, she all but wagged her finger in his face. "What do you know of Dick Monger?"

Gannon blinked, thoroughly rattled. "Oo?"

"He's about this tall"—Penelope held a hand at shoulder height—"a towheaded lad. Do you have him in your employ?"

She rapped the question out; Gannon all but recoiled.

"No! Only lad I got is me sister's—me nevvy. Right layabout he is, too. What would I want wif another? 'Specially if he's wanted by the rozzers." Clearly out of his depth, Gannon looked to Barnaby as if he were a lifeline. " 'Ere—if you're one of them rozzers in disguise, you shouldn't let a female like this loose. She's dangerous."

Barnaby had been thinking much the same; the sheer fear that had spiked through him in the instant before he'd realized Gannon was no threat—that instant when Penelope had been between him and the man—was something he never wanted to experience again. However . . . "Just answer her questions, and we—and the police—will leave you alone. Do you know, or have you heard, anything at all about a lad like she described?"

Eager to cooperate with the voice of reason, Gannon frowned and gave the matter due thought, but eventually he shook his head. "Ain't seen any tyke like that about 'ere. And I ain't 'eard nothing, either—not about 'im, or any other." A certain craftiness lit his eyes. "If you and the lady are after a lad that's been snitched, and yer imagining I might be using his services as a burglar's boy, I'll 'ave you know I 'aven't been on that gamble fer over two years now, not since my last stretch in the nick."

Truth rang in his voice. Barnaby glanced at Penelope, and saw she'd heard it, too. She nodded, and the stiffness of battle went out of her slight frame. "Very well," she said to Gannon, and there was still a latent warning in her tone. "I believe you. Take care you stay on the right side of the law from now on."

With that, she swung around. Coming face-to-face with Barnaby's chest. He stepped aside and let her through.

She marched off, back up the alley.

He glanced at Gannon; the man's expression stated very clearly he'd be happy never to meet such a disconcerting and disturbing female again.

With a last warning look, Barnaby swung around. In a few paces he was at Penelope's heels. A tension unlike any he'd previously experienced was riding him; bending his head so he could speak in her ear, he quietly stated, "Don't ever race into an alley ahead of me again."

His tone was flat, his diction precise.

She glanced up and back at him, puzzled. "It was empty. I wasn't in any danger." She faced forward. "And at least we now know we can cross Gannon off our list."

Emerging from the alley, she paused on the pavement. Taking note of the gathering dusk, she sighed. "I suppose we'll have to leave the other five names until tomorrow."

Seeing Stokes and Griselda on the opposite side of the street, Barnaby set his jaw, grasped her arm, and steered her in their direction, surprised to discover that, contrary to his expectations, he had something quite definite in common with Joe Gannon.

They found a hackney and piled in for the journey back to Griselda's shop. Unfortunately the hackney was one of the smaller affairs, ensuring that Barnaby had to endure Penelope's too-close proximity for the entire time.

Griselda and Stokes, seated opposite, spent the journey discussing how to tackle the five names remaining on Stokes's list. The East End was large, and as yet they had no clue as to which area each man might be operating in. In the end it was decided that Griselda would visit her father again, to see if he'd gleaned any further details. Meanwhile Stokes would inquire more closely of his colleagues at the East End watch houses. They would gather again in two days' time to assess what they'd learned, and make plans.

Penelope clearly chafed at the delay, but had little option but to acquiesce.

Eventually they reached St. John's Wood High Street. Gaining the pavement, Barnaby left Stokes to hand the ladies down and went to deal with the driver.

When the carriage rattled off, he turned, and discovered Stokes taking his leave, first of Penelope, then of Griselda. Watching Stokes half bow over Griselda's hand, watching her expression as she smiled into his eyes and bade him farewell, noting how Stokes held on to her fingers for rather longer than necessary . . . for the first time Barnaby thought to ask himself whether Stokes might have had an ulterior motive in fixing on Griselda Martin as his guide into the East End.

Well, well.

Rejoining the group, he nodded a farewell to Stokes. "I'll call by tomorrow."

Stokes nodded in reply. "I'll ask around at headquarters, too, in case anyone has any idea where these five might be lurking." With a last salute to the group, he turned and walked away.

For a moment, Griselda watched him go, then she recalled herself, threw a quick smile at Penelope and Barnaby, and led the way into her shop.

Her apprentices were ready to leave.

"Go on upstairs," Griselda urged Penelope. "I'll close up, then join you."

With a nod, Penelope headed up the stairs. Barnaby would have preferred to wait by the door until she'd changed into her own clothes and joined him—but he felt stifled by the weight of frills and bows. And he was clearly distracting Griselda's apprentices.

"I'll wait in the parlor." Girding his loins, he climbed the stairs.

Reaching the upper room, he found that Penelope had already retreated behind the bedroom door. Slouching over to the bow window, he stood, hands sunk in his pockets, looking out.

He felt . . . not at all like himself. No, not true. He felt *entirely* like himself, but with his patina of sophisticated control abraded to a thin—too thin—veneer. He had no idea why Penelope Ashford so easily and consistently got within his shields, but there was no denying that she did—that he reacted to her, that she made him react, as no other female ever had.

It was disconcerting, disturbing, and beyond distracting.

She was driving him quietly insane.

The door to the bedroom opened. He glanced around to see her emerge, once again in her own clothes, restored to her customary severely stylish state.

She'd washed her face, removing the powder Griselda had applied to dim the glow of her porcelain skin. In the light of the fading day, it shone like the costliest pearl.

Eyeing him, clearly sensing his tension yet, he was perfectly aware, unconscious of its cause, she tilted her head. "I take it Griselda is still downstairs. Shall we go?"

Turning, he waved her to the stairs. She preceded him down them; as he followed he sensed—how he didn't know, but he knew—that she had determined not to comment on what she regarded as his continuing churlish behavior.

Stepping off the last stair, she swept forward, head high, to where Griselda was checking through her cashbox.

"Thank you so much for all your help today." Warmth filled Penelope's face and colored her words. "We would never have got as far as we did without you." She held out her hands.

Griselda's answering smile as she placed her hands in Penelope's was equally warm. She assured Penelope she was pleased to have been asked.

Penelope squeezed her hands, then stretched up and touched her cheek to Griselda's. It was a common form of affection between tonnish ladies; from the surprise Barnaby glimpsed in Griselda's eyes, she recognized the gesture—and was utterly stunned that Penelope would bestow it on her.

If Penelope realized what she'd done, she gave no sign; still smiling warmly, she stepped back, drawing her hands from Griselda's and turning to the door. "We'll leave you then. Doubtless we'll meet again once Stokes or you have more news."

Griselda followed Penelope to the door. She opened it; with a last smile, Penelope went through. Barnaby summoned a smile for Griselda and saluted her as he stepped past. "Until next we meet."

She smiled. "Indeed. Good night."

Following Penelope down the steps, Barnaby halted beside her. As she had already done, he looked up and down the street. There was no hackney in sight.

He glanced around the roofline, getting his bearings. "We should be able to find a hackney on the next corner past the church."

She nodded and fell into step beside him.

Whether it was the habit of the day, or more likely ingrained gallantry surfacing instinctively, he put his palm to the small of her back as they angled across the street.

She sucked in a breath and almost jumped away from him. "Oh, do stop that. The day is over. I'm not in disguise any longer."

Caught entirely off guard, he frowned at her. "What the devil's your disguise got to do with it?"

"My disguise." With a dismissive flick of her hand, she started marching for the corner. "Your reason for behaving as you have been all day—all those little touches expressly designed to overset me."

He blinked. Lengthening his stride, he quickly overhauled her. "My reason for deliberately oversetting you." His temper started to slip its leash. "If I might ask, just how did you deduce that?"

They'd reached the church on the corner. She halted and swung to face him, the high stone wall at her back. Eyes narrowed, lit by sparks, she glared at him. "*Don't* think to play the innocent with me. Pretending to be my disgruntled lover. Holding my hand—and me—as if you owned me. Pretending to kiss me in that doorway! As I told you at the time, I was perfectly aware you were only doing such things because you didn't approve of me being there!"

She'd been serious? He could only stare blankly in the face of her tirade, shocked, not by her anger, but by the response she sparked in him.

She continued, ire unabated, "No doubt you imagine such behavior will put me off going out in disguise again. Permit me to inform you that you're sadly mistaken."

"That wasn't my intention at all." Anyone who knew him would have taken warning from his far too even, impossibly mild tone.

Penelope didn't know him that well. Eyes alight, locked on his, she drew in a huge breath. "Well, what *was* your intention then? What possessed you to behave as you have been all the damned day?"

For one tense moment, he held her gaze, then he raised his hands, captured her face, stepped close as he tipped it up and brought his lips down on hers.

And gave her her answer.

It wasn't a gentle kiss.

He was furious that she would imagine him the sort of man who would play on her senses to punish her.

When in reality he'd spent the entire day fighting the urge to ravish her.

That she'd so misjudged his motives seemed utterly incomprehensible.

And equally unforgivable.

So he took her lips, then her mouth, then he stole her breath.

Then gave the same back to her, along with the raging need he'd kept pent up all the long day.

That and only that was what had possessed him, what had driven him in a way he'd never before been.

That ragged, desperate, hungry need welled and poured through him, and into the kiss. As kisses went, this one was . . . ungovernable. One step beyond control, edged with a wildness he'd never before felt. Her lips were as ripe and luscious as he'd imagined, the soft cavern of her yielded mouth a delectable delight.

One he plundered.

Without restraint.

And she let him.

Penelope's wits weren't reeling—they'd flown. Entirely. For the first time in her life she discovered herself hostage to her senses, wholly at their mercy. And they were merciless.

Or rather the effect he had on them was ruthless, relentless, and utterly consuming.

His lips moved on hers, steely and firm, masterfully commanding, demanding in a way that sent hot thrills down her spine. His arm had locked around her, holding her trapped; his hand anchored her head so she was his to devour.

And she didn't care. All she cared about was experiencing more, tasting more, feeling more.

Her lips had somehow parted, letting him fill her mouth, letting his tongue lay claim in a manner she found exciting, thrilling, a dark, hot promise of pleasure.

The physical sensations wreathed her mind, fogged it, hazed her wits. The sensual temptation tugged in a way she couldn't explain.

She wanted. For the first time in her life she felt desire stirring— something more powerful than simple will. Something addictive, that seethed with a demand she felt compelled to sate.

She wanted . . . to kiss him back, to respond in whatever way he wanted, in whatever way would appease and satisfy. Not just him, but her, too. The concept of giving in order to take bloomed in her mind, along with a growing certainty that in this arena, that was how exchanges worked.

Her hands had come to rest against his chest; easing their compulsive grip, she sent them sliding upward, to his shoulders, broad and hard, then farther to his nape, and the silky curls that feathered over her fingers.

She played.

Her touch affected him; he slanted his head and deepened the kiss, his tongue stroking hers in heated persuasion.

A thrill shot through her. Emboldened, she hesitantly kissed him back—tentative, unsure.

His response was a revelation—a wave of passionate desire that seemed to come from his soul, that poured through him and infused the kiss, and rocked her to her toes.

The power, the hunger—the raw need she sensed behind it—should have shocked her to her senses, back into the grip of self-preservatory reason.

Instead, it lured her in.

On. Tempted her into kissing him back more definitely, into letting her tongue tangle with his, into sinking against him.

Into wanting to learn even more.

Through the kiss, through the hard lips pressed to hers, through the hard hands that held her tight against his unyielding body, she sensed a primitive male satisfaction—that she'd permitted, that she'd responded, that she'd invited.

The latter was unwise; even with her wits disengaged, she knew it well enough. Yet the moment, the here and now, held no threat.

No matter how her senses stretched, all she detected was heat and welling pleasure, and, elusively laced through all, underneath and between, a power that was addictive. That called to her at some feminine level she'd never before broached. Never before known was open to her.

Her response to *that* shocked her opened her eyes to the woman within. And her yearnings.

She drew back, broke the kiss on a soft gasp. Stared, stunned, into his eyes.

Burning blue, lit by what she now understood was desire, he stared back.

The expression in his eyes, the way his jaw slowly firmed, told her he'd seen, and understood . . . too much.

With a spurt of fear-induced strength, she wrenched out of his arms and spun around to walk on. She was not going to—absolutely refused to—discuss or even refer to the kiss. Even allude to it.

Not when she felt so shaken. So unlike herself.

So exposed.

So vulnerable.

He didn't say anything. In two strides he'd ranged alongside her, keeping pace easily.

She felt his gaze on her face, but kept her eyes fixed ahead. Head up, she marched on.

They rounded the church and reached a more frequented thoroughfare. Barnaby hailed a hackney. He opened the door and she climbed in without taking his hand.

He followed her inside and shut the door.

Somewhat to her surprise, to her increasing consternation, he slumped on the seat beside her, with enough space between them that she didn't feel crowded. Propping an elbow on the carriage windowsill, he stared out at the passing houses, keeping his thoughts to himself.

Leaving her to hers.

9

He'd parted from her on the steps in Mount Street with what Penelope had interpreted—correctly she was sure—as a warning, in the guise of a promise to meet with her that evening.

Throughout the journey from St. John's Wood, they'd exchanged not a word—not a single observation on that kiss, let alone on what it had revealed.

But they'd thought of it.

In her case, she'd thought of nothing else.

Consequently, here she was, skirting Lady Carlyle's drawing room, loins girded, determination whipped high and bolstered, waiting for him to appear so she could inform him just where she stood on the matter, and how they were going to proceed henceforth.

She wasn't, definitely wasn't, going to indulge in another such kiss.

Regardless of any arguments to the contrary—from either him or her own wretched curiosity—she was adamant, resolved beyond shifting, that she was not going to risk any closer acquaintance with that inner self the kiss had revealed.

While the engagement had demonstrated his interest—his intent— the reality of his motive that she'd transparently severely misjudged more than adequately for her to accept it as real, the aspect of herself that the kiss had exposed was far more disturbing.

Far more alarming.

She'd never known, had never guessed, that beneath her practical and prosaic exterior she harbored a panoply of feminine needs that had, it appeared, lain dormant—until he'd kissed her. Until he'd hauled her into his arms and shown her senses what might be—and simultaneously awoken those latent needs.

They'd risen in response to him, stretched and unfurled, fed on the sensations he'd evoked. He and only him. No other man had affected her in the slightest, yet with Adair she'd sensed the connection from the first—from the instant she'd walked into the lion's den and asked for his help.

If she indulged any further with Barnaby Adair she was perfectly sure those newly awakened needs would become a permanent and potent reality; she knew herself well enough to acknowledge that she never did anything by halves. Those needs would grow and gain a hold on her, one she would have to face and deal with.

And that was a path she wasn't prepared to tread.

Although her habitual drive to know, to learn and understand, remained strong, propelling her forward, in this case it was countered by a consideration powerful enough, disconcerting enough, to make her step back.

To make her accept that there were some things she didn't need to know, where the potential gain wasn't worth the likely price.

She could only explore that inner self and her needs with Barnaby Adair, and she knew what sort of man he was. If she attempted to learn more with him, she might well have to sacrifice something she never could. Her independence. Her free will. The freedom to run her own life.

That was one thing she would never risk, not even put at risk. It wasn't something with which she was willing to gamble.

Courtesy of her peripatetic progress, she'd managed to avoid those among her would-be suitors her ladyship had invited. When she saw Adair's guinea-bright head enter the room, she muttered, "At last," and, deftly avoiding Harlan Rigby's eye, made her way to one corner of the room.

Reaching her goal, she waited for Adair to join her.

He didn't keep her waiting; with what most ladies would no doubt have viewed as flattering speed, he threaded through the guests toward her.

Deciding she didn't need to notice let alone acknowledge the focused intent in his eyes, she nodded in brisk greeting when he halted before her. "I have something I wish to say to you. There's a parlor through there"—with a wave she indicated the archway nearby— "where we can talk in private."

So saying she swung around and swept through the archway.

After a fractional hesitation, and a swift glance around the room, Barnaby followed—as ever at her heels.

The small parlor she led him to was, as she'd intimated, perfect for private conversation. Perfect for seduction.

After that astonishing kiss that afternoon, he would, he felt, have been entirely justified in imagining that she, typically, was taking the lead in organizing for further exploration along those lines.

Of course, he wasn't that stupid.

Given the way she'd drawn back—so abruptly he'd felt as if she'd hauled on a brake—and then immediately fallen to thinking far too hard, as he closed the parlor door he wasn't imagining that she would turn, smile, and walk into his arms.

Halting in the center of the room, she swung to face him, head high, her hands clasped before her.

Her gaze as ever unflinchingly direct, she met his eyes. "I wish to make clear to you that, in the matter of the embrace we shared this afternoon, while I accept that you acted in response to remarks of mine which you clearly saw as goading, and I was equally clearly at fault in my reading of your motives—for which I unreservedly apologize— such an embrace cannot be permitted to occur again."

She drew breath and, chin tilting even higher, continued with her obviously rehearsed speech. "As you know, I came to you for help in rescuing four missing boys, and my devotion is first and always to that task. In order to succeed, you and I must work together, side by side, and neither of us I'm sure would want personal awkwardness to interfere with that work."

Still by the door, he arched a brow at her. "Personal awkwardness?"

Her eyes glinted with latent temper. "As would necessarily ensue should you pursue me, given *I* do not wish to develop any more personal relationship with you."

He studied her for a long moment, then mildly said, "I see." He'd been curious to learn what tack she would take. He'd spent hours trying to speculate, but had eventually decided to let her surprise him. And she had. She'd been both more honest and more pigheaded than he'd expected.

Not that the former was going to help her adhere to the latter, even if, as he now suspected, she wouldn't hesitate to use gentlemanly honor as a weapon to force him to keep his distance.

Much good would such a ploy do her. After that kiss, after all it had revealed, given his current status vis-à-vis her, he doubted there was much in this world that could readily turn him from his path.

He strolled the few steps to stand before her. He studied her eyes. "And if I don't agree?"

She frowned. "There can be no benefit to you in pursuing any personal relationship with me—I would have thought that was obvious. I am *not* looking for marriage, for a husband to ensure a roof over my head—something I can well afford on my own—but into whose keeping I would pass, giving him the right to restrict and control me."

He could appreciate her point. Doing so, however, wasn't going to deter him.

Of his direction with her he no longer harbored the slightest doubt. It wasn't what he would have predicted—or even chosen had he had any choice, but as he didn't . . .

Indeed, he still did not fully comprehend how so much had changed simply because she'd walked into his life. He even saw the ton differently, as if she'd opened his eyes. Walking into Lady Carlyle's drawing room, he'd seen himself with respect to the exalted circle into which he'd been born in a way he never had before.

He was both a part of it, yet not. Despite his protestations he was, still, the man his mother wanted him to be—a man defined by his birthright, by being the third son of the Earl of Cothelstone. He was who he was, and he couldn't deny it. Penelope, her presence, stripped away his assumed aloofness, and exposed the man beneath—and that man was very much a true descendant of his conquering ancestors.

That, however, had never been enough for him—just as for Penelope being the daughter of Viscount Calverton was not enough, and did not define who she was, all of what she was. Of all the females in the ton, she understood what drove him, because the same fundamental motive—to find, take hold of, and shape their own destiny—drove her.

Today, for the first time, it hadn't been him alone going back and forth from the slums to the drawing rooms. She'd been with him, by his side; their time in the lower circles had emphasized what was real and important in their lives—the glitter and sophistication of the ton disguised and screened such things, made them harder to discern. To know. To grasp.

He now knew what he wanted, that she was the lady he had to have by his side. He accepted unreservedly that that was the case.

Looking down into her rich, dark brown eyes, he was intrigued that he was starting to sense, to be sensitive to, not just her thoughts but also her feelings, her emotions. He'd already drawn closer to her than to any other female; their deepening connection was yet another indication that she was, indeed, the one for him.

And they were destined to draw closer still. Much closer. After that kiss, there could be no question, yet he accepted that he was considerably more experienced than she, that she would have no yardstick against which to judge what was growing between them, or to accurately appreciate the significance of milestones already passed.

She was a relative innocent. "Relative" being the operative word; with her intelligence, she wouldn't be intellectually innocent . . . which, he hoped, would give him a weapon he could use. Her curiosity was a tangible thing, a force to be reckoned with—in this instance, possibly one he could exploit.

Penelope frowned even more; his continuing silence while he so steadily considered her bothered her. She had no idea what he was thinking—only that he was. Somewhat contrarily, she didn't feel that boded well; the feeling prodded her to say, "Marriage, I long ago decided, is not for me."

Even as she uttered the words, a warning surfaced in her mind. Portia had lectured her more than once that her directness would land her in difficulties with gentlemen. She'd dismissed the prophecy; to date, her straightforwardness had allowed her to repel untold numbers with brutal efficiency.

With Barnaby Adair, however, she might just have been too direct over the wrong subject. With a gentleman like him, setting herself up as a challenge was very definitely not the way to get him to desist.

"That is to say," she hurriedly put in, even though she hadn't a clue how to regroup, "I—"

He smiled and placed one long, strong finger across her lips. "No, don't. I understand perfectly."

She blinked up at him as he lowered his hand. Was he the exception to every rule? "You do?"

His smile deepened. "I do."

She searched his eyes, then exhaled. "So you won't kiss me again?"

The tenor of his smile changed. "Yes I will. Count on it."

Her jaw dropped; she felt her eyes grow wide. "But—"

A tap on the door had them both glancing that way.

"What the devil?" she muttered, then more loudly called, "Come."

The door opened and a footman entered. He bowed, and offered the salver he carried. "A message for Miss Ashford."

Penelope continued to frown; nothing was progressing as she'd planned. Going forward, she lifted the note from the salver.

The footman was clearly unnerved by her expression. "Lady Calverton insisted I bring it to you directly, miss."

Which answered the question of how he'd known where she was; very little escaped her mother's eagle eyes.

She nodded. "Thank you." Turning from the man, she broke open the plain note. Smoothing out the single sheet, she read the lines within.

Watching her, Barnaby saw the blood drain from her face. "What is it?"

She scanned the note again, her expression utterly stunned. "Mrs. Carter—Jemmie." A second passed, then she raised horror-filled eyes to his face. "Mrs. Carter's been found dead. The doctor found her—he doesn't think she died naturally. He thinks she was smothered."

A chill touched his soul. "And Jemmie?"

She swallowed. "Jemmie's disappeared."

Abruptly she swung around. "I have to go."

He caught her elbow. "*We* have to go." To the footman, he said, "Please convey my compliments to Lady Calverton. Tell her Miss Ashford and I have been called away on urgent business to do with the Foundling House."

The footman bowed. "Immediately, sir."

He departed; Penelope made to follow—Barnaby held her back.

"One moment." He waited until she met his eyes. "We need to tell Stokes immediately—there's no sense going to the Carter house now. It's Stokes we need to alert, then we need to plan how best to search for Jemmie."

For a moment, she stared into his eyes—as if confirming his commitment, matching it against her own, using both to anchor her in a suddenly whirling world—then she drew a tight breath, and nodded. "Yes, you're right. Stokes first—but I'm coming, too."

He made no attempt to dissuade her; given the reason for her prejudice against marriage, in light of his avowed intent it would have been the height of lunacy to argue. Instead, he merely said, "Let's hunt up Lady Carlyle and make our excuses."

Stokes lived in lodgings in Agar Street, just off the Strand. Barnaby had visited often, but as he handed Penelope down he wondered how Stokes would react to having a lady invade his private quarters.

He bore no such reservations about what Penelope would think, that she might feel socially awkward; one thing of which he felt certain was that she would take any situation in her stride.

As he ushered her up the steps and into the building, he reflected that that was another trait that set her apart from other tonnish ladies.

Stokes's rooms were on the first floor. Barnaby knocked; Stokes opened the door in his shirtsleeves and no collar, a comfortable well-worn woolen jacket of the sort gardeners wore slung over his shoulders.

He blinked at them in surprise.

"Inspector Stokes!" Penelope crossed the threshold and grasped Stokes's hands. "A terrible thing has occurred. Mrs. Carter, whom I believe Adair has told you of, has been murdered—and the villains have stolen Jemmie."

In the blink of an eye, Stokes transformed from bemused to alert. He glanced at Barnaby.

Who nodded in confirmation. "Let us inside and we'll tell you the whole."

Stokes stepped back, waving them into his small parlor. Closing the door, he gestured them to the armchairs by the hearth, then crossed to fetch a straight-backed chair from his tiny kitchen.

Setting the chair before the armchairs, he sat. "When did this happen?"

Penelope glanced at Barnaby. "I don't really know—we were at a soiree when the message arrived." She looked back at Stokes. "I gave orders to be informed of any further disappearance regardless of time or where I might be. Mrs. Keggs would have sent a messenger as soon as she heard, but he would have had to travel first to Mount Street, then on to Lady Carlyle's."

"Say an hour for Keggs's message to reach us, and for the news to travel from the East End to Bloomsbury"—Barnaby met Stokes's gaze—"possibly as much as two hours."

Ferreting in her reticule, Penelope pulled out the note and handed it to Stokes. "Apparently the doctor dropped by to check on Mrs. Carter, and found her dead, and Jemmie gone."

Stokes read the note. "It sounds like the doctor is very sure Mrs. Carter didn't die naturally."

"Indeed." Penelope sat forward. "So what should we do?"

Stokes glanced at the clock on the mantelshelf; the hands stood at a quarter to eleven. "There's not a great deal we can achieve tonight, but I'll send word to the local watch house. They'd been keeping an eye on the household, but as none of us imagined Jemmie—or Mrs. Carter—were in any immediate danger, the watch wasn't constant."

Penelope looked pained, but conceded, "There was no way of knowing they would stoop to this."

Stokes inclined his head. "Nevertheless, I'll go into headquarters—I'm close, so that won't take long. We have official messengers—one will take the alert to the Liverpool Street watch house. The doctor will have reported the crime, but interest from Scotland Yard will ensure that the local sergeant immediately starts to gather all the information he can. I'll go there tomorrow and see what he has, and what more I can learn."

Penelope looked at Barnaby. Meeting her eyes, he didn't need any words to know what she was thinking, feeling. But . . . he shook his head. "There's no sense in us going there tonight. We won't be able to learn anything, and in the dark it's possible we may overlook or even destroy some clue."

Her lips compressed; her face looked pinched, but after a moment, she nodded. "Very well. But as you mentioned, we should make plans."

They did, rapidly assessing possible avenues of investigation, people they might question. The logistics of what had to be done were discussed; Stokes undertook to address the more formal aspects, while Barnaby and Penelope would pursue the more personal—the neighbors and locals who might have seen or heard something. Twenty minutes after they'd knocked on Stokes's door, they rose. Stokes grabbed his greatcoat; pulling his door shut, he accompanied them downstairs. They parted on the steps, he striding off toward Scotland Yard while Barnaby helped Penelope into the waiting hackney.

Barnaby shut the door; cool darkness enveloped them. As the carriage rocked into motion, Penelope sighed and leaned back. After a moment she said, "Stokes is good at what he does, isn't he?"

"Excellent." Through the dark, Barnaby reached out and closed his hand about one of hers. The heat of his palm engulfed her fingers, a human warmth in the chill of the night. He squeezed lightly, reassuringly. "Rest assured that this case couldn't be in better hands."

She smiled in the dark. "He's your friend—you would say that."

"True, but ask yourself this: if he wasn't so good, would he still be my friend?"

Her smile deepened. After a moment, she said, "I'm not sure I'm up to dealing with conundrums at present."

Again he squeezed her fingers. "I'm only pointing out the obvious."

Her chest felt tight, yet his nearness—the solid masculine reality of him all but filling the seat beside her—eased and comforted. "Speaking of the obvious . . ."

He followed her thoughts with frightening ease. "We'll have to go back through the Foundling House's records and look at every single boy who fits our schoolmaster's bill, regardless of whether his guardian is close to dying or not."

She felt her face harden. "We can't—absolutely *cannot*—take the chance of another boy being grabbed as Jemmie was."

A long moment passed. Then, as if this time he'd read her fears as well as her thoughts, he said, "We'll get Jemmie back. That I promise you."

She closed her eyes, told herself he was just saying what she needed to hear, but the unwavering resolution in his tone, resonating in his deep voice, made it easy to believe him—to place her faith in him. To believe that together they would get Jemmie back.

She needed to believe that.

A few minutes later, the hackney drew up outside Calverton House. Barnaby opened the door, stepped down, then handed her down. Although her awareness of his touch hadn't abated in the least, she no longer steeled herself against it; indeed, tonight, she welcomed it—drew strength from it—which, in light of their earlier discussion, wasn't a comforting realization.

She pushed it to the back of her mind, and let him escort her up the steps. They paused on the narrow porch; facing him, she offered her hand.

He took it, held it, studied her eyes, her face. "I'll call for you at nine. We'll go first to the Foundling House so you can reassure the staff, then we'll continue to Arnold Circus and spend as long as it takes to learn all we can."

She nodded; he'd earlier convinced her of the need to call in at the Foundling House. "I'll be ready and waiting at nine."

His lips quirked in wry understanding. "Get some sleep." Before she realized what he was about, he raised her fingers to his lips and brushed a kiss—hot and distracting—across the sensitive backs.

Before she had time to assimilate the sensation, and resecure her wits, his other hand captured her face, tipping it up as he stepped closer, bent his head, and pressed his lips to hers.

A gentle kiss this time, one that spun out in sweetness, that extended for just long enough for her to be completely swept away.

Lifting his head, he murmured, the words a wash of heat across her now hungry lips, "Sleep well—and dream of me."

A shiver of anticipation slithered down her spine. She opened her eyes.

Straightening, he reached past her and tugged the bellpull; immediately she heard Leighton's footsteps on the other side of the door.

Barnaby stepped back and saluted her.

Behind her the door opened; with a nod to Leighton, and a last glance for her, Barnaby turned, descended the steps, then strode away into the night.

Leaving her staring after him. Raising a hand, she touched her fingers to her lips, then she swung around and went inside.

10

At eight o'clock the next morning, in the large room on the second floor of his rickety tenement in Weavers Street, deep in the slums east of the north end of Brick Lane, Grimsby in his guise as schoolmaster was preparing to address the latest group of inductees into Grimsby's Burglary School for Orphaned Boys.

Pacing slowly before the seven boys lined up before him, only one short of fulfilling Smythe's order and breaking free of Alert's clutches, Grimsby was pleased. He showed it with an expansive, avuncular smile; he'd long ago learned that boys responded to overt emotions—they quickly learned that when he was happy, they would be happy, too. And then they worked to keep a smile on his face.

Little light penetrated the grimy windows even in summer; today, with fog hanging heavy outside, a gray dimness pervaded the space, yet they were all—the boys, Grimsby, and his assistant, Wally—used to working in poor light. Old straw and the accompanying dust covered the bare plank floor; the dust eddied with every step Grimsby took.

Wally, a quiet, unremarkable sort in his mid-twenties who invariably did exactly as Grimsby told him, stood in the shadows by the stairs. He was of average height, average build, with bland features—a man everyone forgot an instant after seeing him. That, in Grimsby's eyes, was Wally's strength; it was why Smythe had taken Wally with him yesterday to fetch their latest recruit.

There was little furniture in the room, which took up the entire floor. A long narrow trestle at which the boys ate and sometimes worked had been pushed against one wall, the crude benches on which they sat stowed beneath. The unpolished tin bowls and spoons they ate with sat in a dark corner; the straw-filled pallets on which they slept were strewn on the floor of the attic above, which was reached by a wooden ladder.

The aids provided for the boys' education were both primitive and practical. Ropes of various thicknesses dangled from the rafters; a plethora of locks and bolts decorated the wooden walls. A section of iron fencing with spikes at the top rested against one wall; a similar section of bars used to protect windows leaned alongside. Rough wooden frames, all smaller than a man could pass through, lay stacked nearby.

Grimsby surveyed the accoutrements of his trade, then, halting at the center of the line, he looked over his pupils, and beamed. "I've already welcomed some of you to this fine establishment, but today we welcome another into our little group." He focused on the scrawny, brown-haired lad in the middle of the line. "Jemmie here is the second last to join us. There's one more coming—one more place vacant—but he's not here yet."

Grimsby pulled the sides of his woolen coat together; the room was drafty, not that the boys in their thin grimy clothes, or Wally, seemed to notice.

"However," Grimsby continued, "we're going to start your lessons proper from today. The last boy will have to catch up. Now, I've told you—each and every one of you—how lucky you are to get a place here. The authorities have handed you over to us to see to it that you have a trade."

He beamed even more brightly, meeting their wary eyes. None of those he selected were stupid; stupid boys never lasted more than one outing, which made them a waste of his time. "So I'm going to tell you what you'll do. You'll work, eat, and sleep here. You won't go out unless you're with Wally, or later, once you've mastered the basics and are ready fer on-the-job training, with my associate, Mr. Smythe.

"But first, our lessons here will teach you to how to break into houses, how to make your way around the mansions of the nobs in the dark without making a sound, how to slip bolts and pick locks, how to crawl through small spaces, and also how to keep watch. You'll learn how to scale walls, how to deal with dogs. You'll learn everything you need to know to become a burglar's apprentice."

He eyed the line of small watchful faces, and kept his smile genial. "Now, this school doesn't run all the time—only when we have places waiting fer our boys. I don't need to tell you what a piece of luck it is to be chosen to train in a field where there's a job waiting fer you to step into it. You're all orphans—just think of all those other orphans out there, struggling to earn a crust and likely sleeping in the gutter. You've been lucky!"

Leaning closer, smile fading, he met each boy's eyes. "Remember that—that you would have ended in the gutter, just like all the other orphans, if you hadn't been so lucky as to get a place here." He straightened and, features relaxing, nodded at them. "So you work hard, and make sure you're worthy. Now—what do you say to that?"

They shifted, but dutifully chorused, "Yes, Mr. Grimsby."

"Good. Good!" He looked at Wally. "Wally here will start your lessons today—you mark what he says and pay attention and you'll do well. Like I said, once you've grasped the basics, Mr. Smythe—he's a legend in this field—will start taking you out with him on the streets so you get to learn the ropes on the job."

Once again, he surveyed his small troop. "Right now—any questions?"

To his surprise, after a moment of wavering hesitation, their latest recruit tentatively raised his hand.

Grimsby studied him, then nodded. "Yes—what is it?"

The boy—Jemmie, that was it—bit his lips, drew breath, then mumbled, "You said the authorities sent us here to learn how to be burglar's apprentices. But burglary's against the law—why would the authorities send us to learn it?"

Grimsby smiled—he couldn't help it; he'd always approved of boys who could think. "That's a smart question, but the answer, lad, is simple. If there weren't any lads training as burglar's boys, then the burglars couldn't work, or not so much, and then who would the rozzers have to chase? It's a game, see?" He looked at the other faces, well aware the same question had been germinating under each thatch of grimy hair. "It's a game, lads—it's all a game. The rozzers chase us, but they need us. Stands to reason. If we weren't there, they'd be out of a job."

They swallowed the twisted truth whole; Grimsby saw a more certain light enter all seven pairs of eyes. Only natural; they were relieved and reassured that their new life was an honorable one. Yes, there was honor among thieves—at least when they were young.

But as he'd told them, life was a game; they'd learn the truth of that soon enough.

"Well, now." He beamed genially upon them once more. "If that's all, then I'll hand you over to Wally, and he'll start you on your lessons."

As Wally came forward, Grimsby turned to the stairs. "Work hard!" he exhorted the class. "And make me proud to have you here."

"Yes, Mr. Grimsby."

This time the chorus was enthusiastic. Chuckling to himself, Grimsby stumped down the stairs.

"So you didn't see or hear anything last evening—or even during the afternoon?" Penelope wished she could cling to some hope, but the old woman's shaking gray head was the answer she'd expected.

"Nah." The woman lived across the narrow passage, two doors down from the rooms Mrs. Carter and Jemmie had occupied. "I had no inkling anything was wrong." The old woman met Penelope's eyes. "Jemmie would've come and found me if'n he'd needed help. Can't think why he didn't—they haven't been here that long, but me and Maisie Carter got along."

Penelope summoned a half-smile. "I don't think Jemmie had a chance to contact anyone. We think he was whisked away by whoever—"

"Whoever put a pillow over Maisie's face and held it down while she died." The old woman's tone spat venom. Again she met Penelope's eyes. "I heard tell that young man of yours is something to do with the rozzers—not one hisself, of course, but can get them to do things. You get him to make them find out who did this—no need fer any trial, just tip us the wink. We take care of our own around here, we do."

Penelope didn't doubt it; even though she couldn't approve of vigilante action, she fully understood, and shared, the old woman's anger. She'd met the emotion again and again over the past hour she'd spent questioning the inhabitants of the narrow lane.

"We're concentrating on finding and rescuing Jemmie—that has to come first. But when we find him, we'll very likely learn who killed Mrs. Carter." Eyes locked with the old woman's, Penelope made a decision; she nodded curtly. "If the police don't catch him, I'll send word."

The old woman's smile promised retribution. "You do that, dearie, and I can promise we'll take care of the bastard as he deserves."

Penelope stepped back from the woman's doorstep. Looking along the passage, she saw Barnaby talking animatedly to a middle-aged man some way up the lane. Barnaby glanced her way, saw her watching, and beckoned.

Instinct pricking, Penelope started toward him, then she picked up her skirts and hurried. The man Barnaby was speaking with appeared to have stumbled from his bed. He looked tousled and bleary-eyed, but also serious and sober.

Barnaby turned to her as she came up. "Jenks here is a shift worker. He works nights, so he leaves here at three in the afternoon."

Jenks nodded. "Regular as clockwork, or I miss the bell at the factory."

"Yesterday," Barnaby continued, "as he was coming out of his door Jenks saw—just glimpsed—two men going into Mrs. Carter's house."

"Knew she wasn't well, so I thought it were strange." Jenks's face fell. "Wish I'd stopped and asked, now, but I thought p'raps they was friends. Jemmie must'a been there, and there weren't no argy-bargy about them going in."

Penelope glanced at Barnaby, and saw he was waiting for her to ask the question. She turned to Jenks. "What did they look like?"

"The first one, he was big." Jenks looked at Penelope. "I'm big, but he was bigger—not the sort I'd want to face in a fight. Hard and mean, he'd be, but he was dressed neat and proper, and didn't look to be angling to cause any trouble. The second one, well, he was . . . just your average bloke. Brown hair, ordinary clothes." Jenks shrugged. "Nothing special about him."

"Would you know them if you saw them again?" Penelope asked.

"The first one?" Jenks frowned. "Yeah—I'm pretty sure I'd know him. The second . . ." His brow furrowed. "It's strange. I saw him for longer than I did the other, but I reckon I could pass him on the street today and not know him." Jenks met Penelope's eyes and grimaced. "Sorry. I can't tell you more."

"Not at all—you've told us more than anyone else. At least now we know there were two men, and one is identifiable." She smiled. "Thank you. You've given us our first real clue."

Jenks relaxed a fraction more. "Yeah, well, it's no surprise no one else knows anything. If you were going to do what those two did, the middle of the afternoon would be the time to do it. I doubt there'd be more'n a handful of others in this whole block when I leave for work—everyone's out and about their business, not home to see anything that might go on."

Barnaby nodded. "Whoever they were, they knew what they were about."

Penelope reiterated her thanks. Barnaby added his, then they turned and walked back toward Arnold Circus.

"That's it." Barnaby looked along the alley. "I've asked everyone down this side. I kept Jenks until last because they told me he'd be asleep."

"And I've asked everyone on the other side, with no luck." Reaching Mrs. Carter's door, Penelope halted, looked at it and sighed. "What next?" She met Barnaby's eyes. "There must be something else we can do—somewhere else, somehow else we can search for a clue."

He held her gaze for a moment, then raised a brow. "The truth?"

Frowning slightly, she nodded.

"There isn't anything more we can do here. We've spoken with everyone. We've learned what there is to learn. That's all there is. We have to go on—move on to the next chance."

She glanced around, her gaze coming to rest once more on the door behind which Jemmie should have been. "I just feel . . . like I've failed him. And even more her. I told him I'd see him safe and I promised her I would." Looking up, meeting Barnaby's eyes, she read in them complete understanding. "A promise to a dying mother regarding her son's safety. What value can one put on that? I can't—just *can't*—rest with that on my conscience. There has to be more I can do."

His lips twisted, but he neither smiled nor laughed. Taking her arm, he turned her along the alley. "It's not just you involved. I made a promise, too, to Jemmie himself. And yes, I understand, and yes, we have to get him back and put him in the Foundling House where he belongs."

She found herself moving away from the door as he gently propelled her along.

He met her eyes as she glanced up, held her gaze as he said, "I made another promise if you recall—to you—that we will get Jemmie back. That's a promise I intend to keep, just as we'll both keep the promises we made to Jemmie and his mother. But we won't be able to keep any of those promises if we allow ourselves to become distracted through acting simply for the sake of it—to salve our consciences. We need to act, but sensibly, rationally, logically. That's the only way to defeat the blackguards and rescue the innocent."

She studied his eyes, then looked ahead as they emerged into murky daylight and the bustle of Arnold Circus. "You make it sound so straightforward."

He steered her to where their hackney waited. "It is straightforward. What it isn't is easy. It is, however, what we need to do. We have to set aside all emotion and focus on our goal."

Penelope blew out a breath; she would have loved to argue, simply because of the tortured way she felt, but . . . he was right. He swung open the hackney's door and handed her up; settling on the seat, she waited until he sat beside her and the carriage started rolling before saying, "All right. I won't indulge my conscience, at least not by acting impulsively. So what is our next sensible, logical, and rational step?"

Her tone was snippish, but Barnaby was content; while she was sniping at him, she wasn't letting the situation overwhelm her. The lost look in her eyes as she'd stared at the Carters' door had made him feel violent, even more so because he understood how she felt. But he'd been through such times with other investigations; he knew the way forward. "We need to tell Stokes what we've learned. It might not be much, but he'll know how to make the most of it. Jenks's description was meager, but it might make a connection in some sergeant's brain."

It was nearly noon. He'd given the jarvey orders to drive back to Mayfair. They'd called in at the Foundling House earlier, and didn't need to return. "We'll get something to eat, then we can go on to Scotland Yard."

Beside him, Penelope nodded. "And after we've seen Stokes, we really should tell Griselda the news."

Stokes had been visited by exactly the same thought. He arrived at the shop in St. John's Wood High Street just after two o'clock.

This time the girls smiled at him. One immediately bustled back to inform Miss Martin of his presence.

Griselda came to the curtain, a smile on her lips.

He returned the smile, he thought well enough, but she seemed to read his underlying tension. Her expression grew serious; she tilted her head, inviting him with her eyes. "Please—come through."

Passing the girls, he followed her into the kitchen, letting the curtain fall closed behind him. As before, the table was covered with feathers and ribbons; a fashionable bonnet, its decoration half-finished, sat in the center of the space. "I've interrupted you," he said.

She frowned at him. "What's wrong?"

He met her eyes, then glanced back at the curtain. "If you would feel comfortable permitting it, I'd prefer to speak upstairs."

"Of course." She moved around the table to the stairs. "Let's go up."

He followed her up the narrow flight, trying not to focus on her swaying hips, and failing. She led the way into the parlor; going to the armchair that was clearly her favorite, she waved him to its mate.

Dropping into it, he sighed; when he was there, with her, he literally felt as if some amorphous weight lifted from his shoulders. In reply to her raised brows, he said, "I can't remember if Adair and Miss Ashford mentioned they'd found a boy similar to those who'd gone missing, in similar circumstances, but as his mother was by all accounts some way from death's door there seemed little benefit in placing a constant watch on the house."

She shook her head. "What happened?"

Letting his head fall back, he closed his eyes. "Last night we heard the boy's mother had been found dead—murdered—and the boy's disappeared."

She said something beneath her breath he felt sure he wasn't supposed to hear. "In the East End?"

Opening his eyes, he nodded. "Near Arnold Circus." He watched her frown deepen. "Why?"

She glanced at him, then her lips firmed. After a moment, she said, "The East End is in many ways lawless, but they do take care of their own. There are certain boundaries no one crosses, and killing a mother to steal her son—that's one of them. No one's going to be happy with this—if there's any information to be had, it'll be readily given."

"So if we ask, we'll be told?"

She smiled cynically. "The rozzers will get whatever help can be given."

He studied her face. "You don't sound confident that help will be enough."

"Because I'm not. There might be enough information to suggest who took the boy, but finding the villain and getting the boy back will be another matter entirely." After a moment, she said, "There's still five names on your list. It's possible one of those five is the schoolmaster who's snatching the boys. The fastest way I can help you and the others to rescue them is by finding out about those five men."

The bell downstairs jangled. Griselda rose, then cocked her head, listening. Stokes got to his feet.

Griselda glanced at him. "Miss Ashford and Adair."

She went to the top of the stairs and looked down. "Yes, Imogen, I know. Please tell them to come up—they know the way."

A moment later Penelope appeared, followed by Barnaby.

Penelope's eyes widened when she saw Stokes. "There you are! We called at Scotland Yard, but you were out."

Stokes colored faintly. "I spent longer than I expected at Liverpool Street." He glanced at Barnaby. "We've put out an alert to all the watch houses in London, giving Jemmie's description. Soon everyone in the force will know we want him—if he's seen on the streets, there's a chance he'll be picked up."

Barnaby grimaced. "Unfortunately, if he's been snatched for a burglary school he may not be on the streets—not until he's sent out to work."

And once a boy participated in a crime, disentangling him from the legal system would become problematic.

Griselda waved them to sit. They did, all sober, not to say deflated.

Barnaby looked at Stokes. "We spoke with everyone up and down the street. We had one stroke of luck." He explained what Jenks had seen.

Stokes nodded. "It's not much to go on, but it's something. That fits with the time the doctor thinks she was killed, so they most likely are the villains responsible." He thought, then added, "I'll stop by Liverpool Street on my way back and get them to send that description out, too. Neither man may be all that recognizable on his own, but together . . . the description might be more useful than it sounds."

"True," Barnaby said, "but finding the boys is becoming urgent. They have five that we know of, but there may be more—boys we haven't heard about. We can't just wait for information to come in."

"Exactly the point I was making when you arrived." Griselda leaned forward. "I was intending to visit my father tomorrow to see if he'd heard anything more about the five names still on our list. I'll do that first thing, then depending on what he's heard, I'll ask around and see if I can learn anything definite." She looked at Stokes. "If I think I've found the school's location, I'll send word."

"You won't have to send word—I'll be with you." When Griselda opened her mouth, Stokes held up a staying hand. "As I told you before, if you're going out on police business and there's any risk attached—which there definitely is—then I have to be there, too."

Griselda narrowed her eyes, but then inclined her head. "Very well."

"We'll come, too." Penelope pushed up from the depths of the sofa. "We'll get through looking much quicker—"

"No." Barnaby laid a hand on her arm. When she looked at him, he met her eyes. "You have another avenue to pursue." When she looked puzzled, he said, "The files, remember?"

She blinked. "Oh. Yes." She looked at Stokes. "I'd forgotten."

Stokes frowned. "What files?"

"At the Foundling House," Barnaby said. "Remember our earlier thought about setting a trap using some boy who was the right sort and whose guardian was about to die?" When Stokes nodded, he continued, "That plan fell by the wayside because the only boy like that in the files was Jemmie, and it transpired his mother wasn't likely to die for months.

"However"—his tone hardened—"given what's happened with Jemmie, that suggests their need for boys is urgent, enough for them not to blink at bringing ailing guardians' lives to a premature end."

Stokes's expression sharpened. "So if you can find another boy of the right physical sort, with an ailing guardian who's expected to die at some date, there's a chance . . ." He paused, looking inward, then he focused on Penelope. "If you can find a boy like that in the East End, I'll guarantee the police will keep him safe. We'll have a constant watch placed on him—if these villains come calling, we'll have them. Even if I have to do the watching myself."

Penelope saw the commitment blazing in Stokes's eyes; she glanced at Griselda, saw a quieter version infusing her, and suddenly felt a great deal better. She was even prepared to leave the searching to them and Barnaby while she plowed through the mountains of files.

Barnaby sighed. "How many files are there?"

She glanced at him. "You saw the last lot—multiply by ten."

He looked at Stokes. "It might be a better division of labor if I helped Penelope go through the files. If we find a likely candidate, I'll send word."

Stokes met his eyes; after a moment, he nodded. "Yes, you're right. We'll search on the ground, you two search the files."

Penelope narrowed her eyes, first on Stokes, then on Barnaby, and wondered whether it was entirely her imagination that there'd been some other communication in that exchange, one that had run beneath their words.

Regardless, they now had their appointed tasks; leaving Stokes and Griselda making arrangements about where to meet, she and Barnaby went downstairs and out onto the street.

Again they had to walk around the church to find a hackney. As they passed the spot where they'd had their previous afternoon's altercation—and he'd kissed her—a wave of consciousness swept her. It felt like tingles spreading under her skin, leaving her nerve endings tantalized, sensitized.

It helped not at all that a gentleman chose that moment to walk along the same stretch in the opposite direction. As he neared, Barnaby steered her to the side   his large strong hand burning her back, his body a shield between her and the unknown.

She bit her lip and forced herself not to react. That simple touch was an instinctive act, one gentlemen like he performed for ladies such as she. Usually it meant nothing . . . yet to her it did. The courtesy might be a common one, but it wasn't one gentlemen used on her. She didn't normally allow it—because it smacked of protection and she knew where that led.

They continued around the corner, and his hand fell away. Lifting her head, she eased out the breath trapped in her lungs. She wasn't going to say anything, call any attention to the disturbing effect such little attentions from him had on her. While in light of their previous night's discussion she might wonder if he was doing it on purpose, to wear down her resistance, she had no proof that was so—and she would certainly appear irrational if she protested on such grounds.

He raised an arm and summoned a hackney. Waiting beside him, she cast him a sidelong glance. Another reason she wasn't going to say anything was because she needed him to help her rescue Jemmie.

That was her first and most important consideration, one that overrode any missish need to put distance between them. After the events of the last twenty-four hours, cutting off all contact was simply not possible.

When the hackney pulled up and he offered his hand, she calmly placed her fingers in his and allowed him to hand her in.

Sinking onto the padded seat beside her, Barnaby had no difficulty hiding his smile. She might be as transparent as glass, at least over her reaction to him and his touch, but he wasn't such a fool as to take her—or her indomitable will—for granted. She was skittish and so aware; to win her he would need to play the age-old game very carefully.

Luckily, he thrived on challenge.

The carriage rolled swiftly toward Mayfair. After some time, her uncharacteristic silence registered. He glanced at her; her face was half turned toward the window, but what he could see of her expression was serene . . . which meant she was planning something.

"What?"

She looked at him; when she didn't bother asking what he was referring to, he knew he'd read her abstraction correctly.

She considered him, then said, "Jemmie's out there somewhere, alone in a sense, and probably afraid. I'm not inclined to wait until tomorrow to start searching for the next boy they're likely to take. You said it yourself, there's clearly some urgency over getting more boys—every hour we wait is time we can't afford to waste." She met his gaze steadily. "Unfortunately, I'm committed to accompanying my mother to a musicale this evening."

The faint arching of one brow echoed the question in her tone.

Rather than appear too eager—too happy to fall in with her plans—he looked forward, then sighed. "I'll meet you there, and we can slip away. Lord knows they never notice who's there and who isn't once the caterwauling starts, but we'll have to keep an eye on the clock and get back before it ends."

From the corner of his eye, he saw her wave a dismissive hand. "No need." With a sangfroid to match his, she stared out of the window. "I'll develop a headache and claim your escort home. Mama won't make a fuss. I'll make sure she won't check on me when she gets home, either, and Leighton knows to leave the front door on the latch unless he sees me come in."

She turned her head and looked at him. "Once we leave Lady Throgmorton's we can spend all night searching the files."

As offers of how to spend an evening went, he'd had better, but her suggestion would allow him to advance his cause, both with her and in rescuing Jemmie Carter.

He nodded. "Lady Throgmorton's then, at eight o'clock."

By eight forty-five that evening they were sitting in Penelope's office at the Foundling House surrounded by files. Stacks and stacks of them. Barnaby eyed the teetering piles. "There has to be a faster way."

"Unfortunately there isn't."

"What about the files we looked through before—there weren't as many of them."

"*Those* were the files of children in cases where the guardian's death was considered imminent—in Mrs. Carter's case her health improved, but I'd already done the formal visit, which is why I remembered Jemmie."

Seated behind her desk, Penelope surveyed the files—there were over a hundred—that Miss Marsh had gathered and piled on the desk and alongside it. "*These* are the files of all children registered with us as possible candidates to come here at some point in the future. These represent our unculled waiting list. The last lot of files—there were only a few dozen, if you recall—were the accepted and imminent list."

Barnaby picked up the top file from the nearest stack. He started flicking through it. "These files are a lot thinner."

"Because they only contain the initial registration, and at most one note. We haven't yet followed up, got a doctor's report, anything—and I haven't been to visit these families, and neither has Keggs, so we won't have any physical description of the child to help us."

His expression grew wary. "What, exactly, are we searching for here?"

"For a boy between seven and eleven years old. One known as a potential orphan." She ticked the points off on her fingers. "He has to live in the East End. And then we need to check if there's any mention in the note about the guardian. How ill they are, whether they're incapacitated or not." She met his eyes. "I imagine that if they've a choice, these villains will target a guardian they can readily overcome."

"That's a reasonable guess."

"Well, then." She surveyed the files, then looked at him. "Shall we work out a plan of campaign?"

"Please."

"Let's work progressively, taking our points in order   you start, and check each file for whether it's a boy or a girl. Girls set aside, boys pass on to me." Leaning forward, she pointed to the top right corner of the file he'd reopened. "See there? Boy or girl?"

"Boy. One for you." He tossed the file on the desk in front of her and reached for the next.

"I'll check their age and the address." Pulling the file to her, she opened it. "East End or not." She frowned and looked up. "Is it likely they'll extend their reach outside the East End?"

"It's possible"—he dropped the second file to the floor beside his chair—"but only if they can't find a suitable boy on their own patch." He reached for the next file. "Villains tend to stick to specific neighborhoods—like a territory that's somehow their domain for whatever nefarious purpose."

She nodded, and checked the address on the file she had— Paddington. Closing the file, she dropped it to the floor by her chair just as Barnaby slid another her way.

They settled into a silent rhythm as the house quieted around them. When they'd arrived, the older children had been awake, and the staff had been about, overseeing them and tucking the younger ones into bed. The sounds of a bustling family, multiplied significantly, echoed along the corridors. But as the clock on top of the cabinet ticked relentlessly on, all such sounds faded, leaving the dry rustling of paper and the occasional slap of a discarded file the only punctuations in the enfolding silence.

When the clock chimed, signifying the half hour, Penelope glanced up and saw it was half past eleven. With a sigh, she dropped the last of the files to be discarded on the latest pile, then studied, as Barnaby was, the small pile that remained on her blotter.

Reaching out, she riffled the spines. "Fifteen." Fifteen East End boys aged between seven and eleven who were registered as potential foundlings.

Barnaby eyed the discarded files. "I hadn't any notion there would be so many potential orphans." He lifted his gaze to her face. "You can't take in all these."

She shook her head. "We'd like to, but we can't. We have to choose." After a moment, she added, "As it happens, we base our decision on some of the traits these villains look for—quickness of mind, and preferably of body. Size we don't take into account, but knowing we have to choose, we long ago decided that we had to take the children who would make the most of the opportunities we provide."

"And that means quick wits and reasonable health." He reached for the top file of the remaining fifteen. "So now we try to find some indication of the guardian's physical state."

Even with only fifteen files to assess, that took time; they had to read not only what was written, but also to some extent between the lines.

In the end, the pile reduced to three. Three boys they both agreed were the only likely targets among all the files they'd waded through.

Hands folded on her desk, Penelope looked at the three files. "I keep worrying that there will be others, boys who haven't been registered." She raised her eyes to Barnaby's face. "What if the villains go after one of them and leave these boys"—she nodded at the files—"alone?"

He grimaced. "That's a risk we'll have to take. But so far you've lost five of your registered candidates—chances are these boys are, or will become, targets of these villains." He paused, then added, "We have to assume that and go forward with our plan. There are no certainties, but it's the best we can do."

She studied his eyes as if reading his sincerity, then nodded. "You're right." Looking down at the files, she sighed. "There's nothing in these to say if the boys themselves are physically suitable. They might be too big, or clumsy, or . . . I'll have to visit them tomorrow and see."

The clock chimed—one o'clock.

Barnaby rose, rounded the desk, took her hand and drew her to her feet. "We'll go together tomorrow morning, and take a closer look at these three."

Reaching across, he turned down the desk lamp they'd set high to give them light enough to read, then capturing both her hands, he drew her to face him. "We've accomplished all we can for tonight . . . on that front."

She heard his change of direction in his tone. Her eyes widened, searching his. "What . . . ?"

Lips curving, he drew her into his arms, bent his head, and kissed her confusion from her lips. Tasted them, making it clear just what subject he was intent on investigating.

Her. Her lips, her mouth, her tongue.

How she felt in his arms, how she fitted so snugly against him.

He'd anticipated some resistance; instead, all he sensed was a moment of blankness—as if her mind had seized, simply frozen.

Then her lips, already parted when he'd covered them, firmed beneath his—but she didn't try to clamp them shut and deny him; she pressed them more firmly to his and kissed him back.

Definitely—no tentativeness this time. Her sudden change in tack left him mometarily following rather than leading.

Then her hands, braced against his chest, slid up over his shoulders to slip beneath his curls and caress his nape. He had to fight to suppress a shudder, surprised that such a simple touch from her slim fingers on his exposed skin could be so evocative.

But then she stepped into him—and his world quaked.

She pressed against him and yielded her mouth—and he lost touch with his immediate world, transported in a heartbeat to one where his civilized guise was gone and his primitive nature ruled.

He spread his hands on her back, pulled her flush against him. The heat of her response, the offered heat of her mouth, the wanton stroke of her tongue urged him on; he angled his head, laid claim to all she offered, and blatantly, flagrantly, molded her hips to his.

She uttered a soft sound—neither moan, sob, nor gasp but an expression of all three, a sound of encouragement he had no difficulty interpreting; he responded by letting his hands, clamped about her hips, ease and slide down, around, filling his palms with her firm curves. Fingers flexing, he moved her against him, suggestively, provocatively.

And felt her melt.

Felt all resistance, even that telltale tension in her spine, evaporate.

She was his for the taking, and they both knew it.

One small hand slid from his nape to his cheek, pressing along it as she kissed him—every bit as wantonly, as blatantly, as he wished.

Turning, he trapped her against the desk; the edge hit the backs of her thighs. The files littering the expanse were no longer relevant; he reached out to push them away—

Click, click, click.

The clack of heels approaching along the tiled corridor jerked them both back into the world—the one encompassed by her office with its open archway, and the anteroom beyond with its open door.

They broke apart. Barnaby stiffly rounded the desk and dropped into the chair he'd earlier occupied.

Penelope pulled her chair—which had rolled away—back to her desk and sat in it, and grabbed the three files left on her blotter.

She looked up as Mrs. Keggs appeared in the archway.

Mrs. Keggs took in the restacked files, then the three in Penelope's hand. "Well, you have worked like Trojans if you've got through all those. Only three?"

Penelope nodded. "We've just finished." Locating her reticule on the floor by her feet, she picked it up and rose. "And yes, there's only three. I'll have to visit them and see if they're possible targets for these villains." She glanced at the clock. "I'll take the files with me and do that tomorrow."

Barnaby got to his feet.

Mrs. Keggs smiled brightly. "Indeed. You'll be wanting your beds, I've no doubt. I'll lock up after you."

Penelope didn't meet Barnaby's eyes as she walked past him. She paused by the hook on which she'd hung her evening cloak; before she could lift it down, his hand appeared and did so.

Behind her, he shook it out and draped it over her shoulders. "Have you got everything?"

His breath brushed the sensitive skin beneath her ear. Her senses skittered; she grimly hauled them back.

"I believe so." She managed a smile for Mrs. Keggs—her unwitting savior. The three files in one hand, her reticule in the other, her cloak over her shoulders—and Barnaby Adair at her heels—she walked calmly up the long corridor to the foyer, farewelled Mrs. Keggs, then, head high, walked out into the night.

Throughout the subsequent journey back to Mount Street, she remained silent. There was absolutely nothing she could think of to say. She wasn't sure she appreciated his tact in not saying one damned word, either—especially as she sensed he was amused by her silence.

She did, however, have a great deal to think about courtesy of that thoroughly unwise kiss. Not the one he'd given her, initiating the episode, but the one she—witlessly and wantonly—had pressed on him.

That and what had followed were definitely things she needed to analyze.

Exchanging minimal words, they parted at the door in Mount Street, after he'd verified it had, indeed, been left on the latch, allowing her to enter without rousing the household. The last sight she had of him as she closed the door revealed a certain knowing smile on his face; she would have loved to wipe it off, but decided ignoring it was the wiser course.

Lighting the candle left for her on the hall table, she picked it up and trailed up the stairs . . . wondering when her wits were going to return to her enough for her to decide where she now stood with respect to Barnaby Adair.

11

Penelope had expected to spend at least a few hours of what had remained of the night reassessing her position with Barnaby Adair. Instead, the instant her head had made contact with her pillow, she'd fallen deeply asleep. Unfortunately, waking with a smile on her lips hadn't improved her mood.

But it had lent steel to her decision.

She was increasingly certain that all those little touches that might initially have been instinctive were now deliberate. That he knew the effect he had on her and was intentionally playing on her senses.

That he was, in fact, hunting her.

That conclusion had deepened her resolve. After the previous night's kiss—which shouldn't have occurred at all, and how she'd come to be so brainless as to recklessly let herself enjoy it she didn't know—had proved beyond doubt that the only way to deal with him henceforth was to avoid him.

As far as she was able while continuing to work with him on the investigation.

Hurrying down the stairs, juggling the three files while pulling on her gloves, she reflected that at least today she wouldn't have to exercise any great ingenuity to stick to her plan. She'd already taken steps to ensure he wouldn't be with her; she didn't need an escort to look over three boys.

Smiling at Leighton, waiting by the front door to swing it wide, she paused to check her bonnet in the hall mirror. It was barely eight-thirty, far too early for any tonnish gentleman to be up and about, and as she had three addresses to call at, even when he realized she'd left him behind the chances of him correctly guessing which one she was headed for were slim to none.

For today, she was safe. Turning from the mirror, she nodded her thanks to Leighton as he opened the door. Stepping over the threshold, a satisfied smile curving her lips—

She froze, stopped in her tracks by the sight of the bright curly head atop the pair of broad shoulders, from which a modish greatcoat hung, that were presently leaning against the railing above the area steps.

Behind her, Leighton murmured, "Mr. Adair said he was happy to wait outside for you, miss."

So she would have no warning that her plan had been sprung. "Indeed."

The morning was chilly and damp; mist wreathed the street, wisps draping the hackney and its horse by the curb. It would certainly have been warmer to wait indoors.

Eyes narrowing, she went down the steps.

He heard and turned, and smiled—an easy, charming smile that held no hint of triumph. Pushing away from the railing as she reached the pavement, he strolled to the carriage, opened the door, and held out his hand.

Her eyes couldn't get any narrower. She thrust the three files into his hand, grabbed up her skirts, and clambered into the carriage unaided.

If he chuckled, at least she didn't hear it. Dropping onto the seat in the far corner, she quickly arranged her skirts, then looked out of the window.

He climbed in and shut the door; she felt the seat give as he settled beside her.

The carriage started off. She hadn't heard him give the driver any directions; she frowned, glanced at him. "Where are we going?"

He didn't meet her gaze, merely settled his head against the squabs and made himself comfortable. "The driver's from the East End—he knows the area well. We discussed the best route—he'll take us to Gun Street first, then North Tenter, and then around to Black Lion Yard."

It would be childish to sniff disparagingly just because he'd arranged things so well. "I see." Turning her head, she looked out at the passing streetscape, and told herself she shouldn't sulk.

By the time they reached the first address, in Gun Street opposite Spitalfields Market, her irritation had largely evaporated. He'd left her with no excuse to protest, and being with him, simply being near him, tended to erode her resistance.

Regardless, she sternly lectured herself to concentrate on the matter at hand—identifying any other boy who might be at risk from their villains—and to ignore her senses' giddy preoccupation with Barnaby Adair and all his works.

Steeling herself, she let him hand her down at the corner of Gun Street.

Gun was a short street, and within a second of setting eyes on the boy they'd come to see, it was plain he wasn't a candidate for a burglary school. He was squat and heavy-bodied; one glance at his father, consumptive though he was, suggested the boy would only grow larger with every month.

Penelope excused their visit on the grounds of checking details in their file. Barnaby stood by her side as she spent a few minutes easing the father's concern over the Foundling House having questions.

She'd worn a garnet-red pelisse for the excursion; it set off her pure complexion and brought out the red in her sleek dark hair. The gown possessed no frills, no furbelows. While he would have wagered that anything she wore beneath would be silk, he was increasingly intrigued by the question of whether her private garments would be weighed down by the usual ribbons and lace, or if, like the rest of her wardrobe, they would be severely plain.

He wasn't sure which option he would find more arousing; while the former would be a surprise—suggesting she was, beneath her outer screens, much like other ladies—the latter . . . in the same way that her severe gowns somehow emphasized her vivid allure, would severe undergarments also emphasize the . . . glory of what they concealed?

It was a point that understandably exercised his mind.

A sharp prod recalled him to the present; he blinked, and discovered Penelope regarding him with a frown.

"Mr. Nesbit has answered all our questions. It's time to leave."

He smiled. "Yes, of course." With a nod to Nesbit, he followed her from the cramped hovel, and helped her back into the carriage.

Settling beside her on the seat, he continued to smile.

Their next stop, in North Tenter Street, was equally brief.

Back in the carriage, Penelope remarked, "No burglar would ever take such a simpleton as a helper. He'd most likely forget what he was supposed to fetch, and go and wake the housekeeper to ask if she could help him."

The boy hadn't been quite that bad, but he'd been waited on hand and foot all his life by his doting aunt, and no longer believed it was necessary to think for himself.

Barnaby looked out of the window as they made the turn into Leman Street. "That leaves only one more to check."

"Indeed." After a moment, Penelope echoed his thoughts. "I don't know whether to hope this last boy is a likely candidate—which would put him at risk, but also give us a chance to set a trap to catch these villains—or whether I'd rather he was . . . too fat, too slow, too sluggish to interest them, and therefore he and his"—she consulted the file on her lap—"grandmother will not be under any threat at all."

The light glinted off her spectacles as she turned her head and looked at him.

He was tempted to reach for her hand and squeeze it reassuringly—either that or pluck her spectacles from her nose and kiss her senseless, effectively distracting her from such troubling thoughts. Instead, he said, "All we can do is let fate roll her dice, and then deal with whatever turns up."

Black Lion Yard was a small cramped space ringed by a collection of old tenements. The yard, such as it was, was cobbled like a street, but there was no thoroughfare; boxes and crates were haphazardly piled both in the corners and elsewhere across the yard, so anyone entering had to tack and weave to reach their destination.

Their destination was the ground-floor rooms in the building at the center of one side of the yard. Mary Bushel and her grandson Horace—known as Horry—lived there.

Within two minutes of making Horry's acquaintance, both of them knew which way fate's dice had fallen. Horry—small and slight, quick and bright—was unquestionably an outstanding candidate for a burglary school.

When Penelope glanced his way, Barnaby didn't need any words to know what she was thinking. What question she was wordlessly asking. But with Jemmie's disappearance and his mother's too-early death weighing on them both, and on the investigation in general, there was no question over what they should do.

He nodded, a slight but definite movement.

As she had in the previous two instances, she'd excused their visit on the grounds of the Foundling House needing more details for its files. Now she turned back to Horry's grandmother—who, every bit as quick as her grandson, had seen the look he and Penelope had shared. Sudden worry infused Mary's features.

Seeing it, Penelope reached out and placed her hand over Mary's. "There's something we must tell you—but first let me assure you that we will definitely be waiting to take Horry into our care when the time comes."

A large part of Mary's anxiety subsided. "He's a good lad—quick and useful. He's got a good nature—you'll never have any trouble with him."

"I'm sure we won't." Penelope spared a smile for Horry, who, sensing the change in atmosphere, had sidled closer to his grandmother, until he was leaning against her arm where she sat in her chair, his thin hand gripping her bony shoulder. Mary reached up and patted his hand.

Once again meeting Mary's eyes, Penelope said, "Horry is exactly the sort of candidate we at the Foundling House look for. Unfortunately, there are some other men about who also want boys like him—boys who are small, slight, and quick-witted. Good boys who'll do what they're told."

Dawning comprehension narrowed Mary's eyes. After a moment, she said, "I've lived in the East End all me life. I know all the larks—and unless I miss me guess, you're talking of a burglary school."

Penelope nodded. "Yes, that's right." She went on to explain about the four boys who'd gone missing, and then about Jemmie and his mother. Her anger resonated in her voice, something Mary Bushel, sharp as two pins, didn't fail to notice.

But when Penelope mentioned the police, and the notion of having them protect Mary and Horry, Mary's comprehension failed. Astonished, she stared at Penelope, then glanced at Barnaby. "'Garn—you don't mean that. The perlice worrying about folks like us?"

Barnaby met her washed-out blue eyes. "I know it's not what

you're used to around here, but . . ." He paused, realizing that he needed to couch the truth in a way she, and anyone else she asked for advice, would accept. "Think of it this way—this burglary school is training boys, quite a few of them, to burgle . . . which houses?"

Mary blinked. "If they're training boys up, it's usually the houses of the nobs they've got in their sights."

"Precisely. So while Miss Ashford and I might be more concerned over rescuing the missing boys, and making sure no other boys are dragooned into a life of crime, the police are keen to find the villains and shut down the school, so there won't be a string of burglaries in Mayfair to upset the commissioners."

Mary slowly nodded. "Aye—that makes sense."

"And that's why the police will set a watch on this house—both to protect you and Horry, because they don't want more boys going into this school, and also to keep watch for and catch these villains when they come for Horry, as it seems likely they will." Barnaby paused. "It's unusual, I know, but in this case the police's interests and yours are the same. We all want the same things—you and Horry safe, and the villains caught."

Mary nodded again, but then her gaze grew distant. She rocked slightly, then refocused on Barnaby's face. "I don't know about the perlice—I don't know as I'd trust 'em with me and Horry's lives." She held up a hand, halting any comment Barnaby might have thought to make. "However, they can come and keep watch if they please. But fer me peace of mind, I want people I trust about me."

Lifting Horry's hand from her shoulder, she squeezed, then released it. "Get you round next door, Horry, and see if any of the Wills boys are in. Tell 'em I'd like a word."

Horry nodded, cast a glance at Barnaby and Penelope, then quickly went out of the door.

Mary looked at Barnaby and Penelope. "The Wills boys may be rough and ready, but they're honest lads."

Horry returned in less than a minute, two brawny, dark-featured men in tow. Horry went to stand by Mary's shoulder as she nodded in greeting to the newcomers. "Joe, Ned." To Penelope and Barnaby, she said, "These are two of the Wills boys—they're me neighbors. Joe here is the oldest—there's four of 'em, all told."

Joe Wills, taking in Barnaby and Penelope, clearly didn't know what to think. "Horry spun us a bit of a tale, Mary, something about the perlice wanting to come and stop some beggars killing you and snatching him away to do burglaries?"

Clearly Horry had understood the gist of things well enough.

Mary nodded. "Not so much of a tale as it sounds. But I'll let them tell it." She looked to Barnaby and Penelope; the Wills boys followed her lead.

Penelope leapt in. "I'm from the Foundling House in Bloomsbury. Mrs. Bushel here—Mary—has asked us to take Horry in when she passes on."

With the occasional interjection from Mary, Penelope told their tale to the point where they'd learned that Mrs. Carter had been murdered and Jemmie spirited away.

Both Wills boys shifted, and exchanged a dark look.

Barnaby picked up the tale. "As I explained to Mary, despite the usual way of things, in this case the police have a real interest in capturing these villains." Once again he cast the official interest in terms of protecting the "nobs"—it was what the Wills boys would expect; the comprehension in their eyes and the way they nodded as they followed his tale suggested he'd judged their prejudices correctly.

He went on to explain why the police needed to put a close watch on Mary and Horry, "indeed, on Black Lion Yard, so that they can catch these villains when they come for Horry."

Joe Wills's eyes were hard. "You're saying these blackguards might come here and hold a pillow over Mary's face until she's dead, then scarper with Horry?"

Barnaby hesitated, then nodded. "That's precisely what we believe they'll do."

Penelope sat forward. "They think that because with Mary gone Horry will be an orphan, there'll be no one who cares—no one who'll raise a fuss that he's gone. They're assuming—and counting on—Mary and Horry having no friends, at least not nearby. No one who'll pay any attention." She spread her hands. "Well, you can see it, can't you? An old woman in the East End dies and an orphan disappears—who's going to raise a dust?"

Barnaby hid an approving smile. Penelope had judged that well; the Wills boys were all but bristling.

"We will," Joe growled. "Least we would if it were Mary up and dying before her time, and Horry here going missing."

"Yes," Barnaby said, "but the villains don't know that. So far they've snatched five East End boys, and murdered at least one woman, and other than Miss Ashford here and the Foundling House, no one has raised any alarm."

Joe grimaced. "Aye, well—not all places are as tight as we are here." He nodded at Mary. "Like a mum to us, she is. We wouldn't let any blackguard harm her." He glanced at his brother, who nodded, then turned to Barnaby. "No need for the police—we'll keep watch. Day and night. Least we can do."

Barnaby nodded. "Thank you. That will be a big help. But the police will want to watch, too." He glanced at Mary. "As Mary said, there's no harm in them watching as well, but if you and your brothers will stay close, then the police can watch from outside, and concentrate on being able to close in when the villains make their move."

"D'you think they'll do that soon?" Ned asked. "Make their move?"

Barnaby thought of how much longer it would be before the last of the ton quit the capital, balancing that against how long it might take to train a burglar's boy. "They seem in a hurry to get more boys. They might wait a while, just to be safe—maybe a week or so." He met Joe's eyes. "I wouldn't expect them to wait much longer."

"Right then. No great difficulty for us to keep watch for a week or so. One or other of us'll always be in here, within sight of the door." Joe tipped his head to the right. "Walls are thin—a holler from whoever's in here watching will bring the rest of us, and others, too."

Barnaby nodded approvingly. "I'll explain the situation to the officer in charge—an Inspector Stokes from Scotland Yard. He'll come and speak with you"—he included Mary and Horry in his glance—"probably later today, if I can get hold of him."

"An inspector from Scotland Yard?" Joe's real question—what would such a man know of them and the East End?—was echoed in the others' eyes.

"He'll be in charge of the police—he has authority over the local rozzers. Don't worry he won't understand; when you meet him, you'll realize he won't be any problem—not to you or Mary or Horry, at least." Barnaby met Joe's eyes. "Wait until you meet him before you judge."

Joe held his gaze, then nodded. "Fair enough."

The odd thought of what his mother would say if she could see him and Penelope rubbing elbows with East End toughs flitted—distracting and entertaining—through Barnaby's mind.

He glanced at Penelope and raised a brow. "I'd say that at present we can leave Mary and Horry in Joe's and his brothers' capable hands."

Penelope nodded and stood. "Indeed." She offered her hand to Joe. "Thank you."

For a moment, Joe stared at the delicate, gloved hand. Then, blushing, he gently took it in his large paw and briefly shook it, quickly releasing it as if he feared he might damage it.

Behind him, Ned grinned.

Penelope smiled brightly at Ned, then swung to face Mary—thus failing to see the stunned look on Ned's face.

"Take care, please." Penelope patted Mary's hand. "I'm quite keen to have Horry at the Foundling House"—she smiled at Horry encouragingly—"but not before the appointed time."

Mary assured her she'd take care of herself and Horry. Barnaby got the impression the boy wouldn't be going anywhere alone, not until Mary was convinced all threat had passed.

They left the Wills boys discussing their watch with Mary and Horry; steering Penelope out into Black Lion Yard, Barnaby breathed in—and felt truly hopeful for the first time since he'd learned of Mrs. Carter's unnatural demise.

Penelope looked around. "It's a relief to know that Horry at least will be well protected—that we've done all we can, got every possible defense in place."

She glanced at Barnaby as he guided her around the piles of crates, steadying her over the uneven cobbles as they headed for the yard's entrance and the waiting hackney. "The Wills boys are trustworthy, don't you think? They won't . . . oh, go off on a drinking spree and forget about keeping watch over Mary?"

Barnaby shook his head. "Not a chance."

"While I appreciate your certainty, how can you be so sure?"

"You heard them refer to her as 'like a mum' to them?"

"Ye-es. Oh, I see."

"So I don't think we need to worry about Mary or Horry."

"You'll get word to Stokes?"

"I'll hunt him up immediately after I've seen you back to the house."

The next morning, Penelope was working at her desk at the Found-ling House, catching up with myriad details she'd let slide while she'd been searching for the missing boys, when, quite suddenly, a prick-ling sensation ran over her skin.

She looked up—and discovered her nemesis lounging against the archway frame, looking both impossibly elegant and undeniably dan-gerous.

Or so she saw him.

Pen poised above the list she'd been making, with hauteur befit-ting a duchess she raised both brows.

He smiled, not charmingly but intently, and amused with it, for all the world as if he could read the contradictory impulses careening through her.

She had absolutely no idea what she was to do with him, what to make of him and his apparent fixation on her. She was starting to real-ize that the "her" he saw wasn't the same "her" the rest of her tonnish would-be suitors saw. Presumably that was the crux of her difficulty in dealing with him, but how to retreat to any formal distance— especially with the investigation constantly throwing them together— she had no clue.

All she understood, as she saw his lips quirk, then watched him push away from the archway and come prowling into the room, even-tually to subside with his customary ineffable grace into the chair before her desk, was that she really needed to find a solution.

Keeping her expression as uninformative as she could, she stated, coolly, "Good morning. And what can we do for you?"

His untrustworthy smile deepened. "It's more a matter of what I thought to do for you."

"Oh?" Setting down her pen, she folded her hands before her. "And what might that be?"

"I've come to suggest that we circulate notices throughout the East

End, with the names and descriptions of the five missing boys, and offering a reward for information on their whereabouts."

Her reaction was immediate; there was no point trying to hide it. "That's brilliant!" She beamed. Unable to contain her burgeoning enthusiasm, she asked, "How do we go about it?"

He smiled again, but the gesture wasn't in any way threatening. "Simple. You give me a list of the names, with the best descriptions you can muster, and I'll get the notices printed. I know a place that will do them overnight."

A place that owed him no small favor, and would be happy to rebalance their account in however small a way.

Penelope was already pulling out a fresh sheet of paper. "Overnight? I thought there was usually a delay of days at least."

When she glanced at him, he shrugged. "It won't have all that much text, so won't take long to set."

She looked down at the sheet of paper, pen poised in her hand. "How should we word this?"

"List each name, with a description. Then at the bottom write . . ." He dictated the usual form of "Offer of a Reward."

When he concluded with an instruction to contact Inspector Stokes at Scotland Yard, she paused, frowning. "Shouldn't that be me, here, at the Foundling House?"

"No." He was adamant about that, but couched his reply in a tone that suggested it was de rigueur to leave all contact to the police.

While Stokes would certainly prefer that, it was rarely done. However, the notion of a score of East Enders lining up to see Penelope and tell her all they knew—even if they knew nothing—wasn't a scenario he had any wish to contemplate.

Luckily, she accepted his explanation with a shrug, and duly wrote down what he'd told her.

Consulting one of her lists, she filled in the names of the five boys, then rang for Miss Marsh and asked her to fetch Mrs. Keggs. As Miss Marsh departed, Penelope explained, "Keggs was with me when I did the visits. She might remember different aspects of the boys' appearance."

Mrs. Keggs duly arrived. Barnaby set the other chair for her, then retreated to the window, leaving her and Penelope to put together the descriptions.

Hands in his pockets, he stood looking out—watching the children play in the yard, smiling at their antics.

Once again an appreciation of just how much, not only in social terms but in terms of the individual lives of the boys and girls so unrestrainedly enjoying themselves in the yard, the Foundling House achieved rolled through him. And how much of that was directly fashioned, driven, brought to life, and kept in action by Penelope and her indomitable will.

Her independence, her will, were tangible things. Not to be taken lightly, nor to be tampered with, let alone opposed, without due consideration.

That could be—would be—an ongoing and ineradicable source of difficulty for any gentleman who married her. Not insurmountable, yet an issue that would need careful handling. The fruits of her independence, of her indomitable will, were too valuable for any man to quash, to squander. To deny.

The realization slid into his mind, and settled.

Behind him, chair legs scraped. Turning, he saw Mrs. Keggs bustling out.

Penelope was blotting the sheet. "Here you are." She scanned it one last time, then held it out to him. "Five names, descriptions, and an announcement of a reward."

He read through it swiftly. "Excellent." Looking up, he met her eyes. "I'll get this printed up overnight. And then I thought I'd ask Griselda about how best to distribute them throughout the East End."

"Indeed—I'm sure she'll know." Penelope hesitated, but it was part of the investigation after all. "I'll come with you when you pick up the notices—I'd like to see a printer's works—and we can take them directly to Griselda."

His smile was back, playing about his lips, but it wasn't overt, not something she needed to frown at. He inclined his head. "If you wish."

Folding the sheet, he placed it in his pocket. "I'll leave you to your work."

With a graceful half-bow, he turned and walked to the door.

She smelled a rat. She narrowed her eyes on his back—was he hiding something? Planning something? Something without her?

As he reached the archway, she called, "If you have any news to-night, I'll be at Lady Griswald's ball. You'll be able to find me there."

Lifting her pen, she watched as, in the archway, he glanced back. She'd made her announcement matter-of-factly, yet unholy amusement danced in his blue eyes.

And she suddenly, simply, knew. He hadn't asked her where she'd be that evening—because if he had she wouldn't have told him.

His smile deepened. He saluted her. "Excellent. I'll come hunting for you there."

She glared, then looked around for something to throw at him—but by then he was gone.

12

Later that evening, Penelope paced the dark, deserted minstrel's gallery overlooking one end of Lady Griswald's ballroom, and wondered what had possessed her to fall for Adair's trap.

Just the look on his face . . . *insufferable*! And she could just imagine how he would behave once he found her, which was why she was haunting the gallery. If she had any say in the matter, he wasn't going to find her at all.

In the ballroom below, Lady Griswald's party to celebrate her niece's betrothal was in full swing. Ladies and gentlemen were dancing, couples were conversing, dowagers seated on chaises were gossiping for all they were worth. As her ladyship was a close friend of her mother's, Penelope had had no option but to come; she'd done the pretty for half an hour, but the inevitable tension of keeping a constant watch for approaching gilded heads had taken its toll. Rather than snap any more direfully at her would-be suitors, she'd excused herself, swanned past the withdrawing room, and taken refuge in the gallery.

Safe from gentlemen who were entirely too arrogantly certain of themselves.

The problem was, while she might be safe, hiding was only putting off the inevitable—at some point she was going to have to deal with Barnaby Adair.

By falling for his ploy, she'd all but "invited his attention"; if he managed to find her, she'd have little grounds to dismiss him, at least not outright. Which, of course, had been his goal.

Regardless, her problem—how to deal with him—remained, and on that subject she was in a totally uncharacteristic dither.

One part of her mind was convinced that any closer acquaintance with him would be inimical to her future—to her continued independence.

Another part was insatiably curious.

And curiosity was, and always had been, her besetting sin.

Usually, her curiosities were intellectual rather than physical, notable exceptions being waltzing and skating, but Adair stirred a curiosity that was altogether more complex.

She was fascinated by all she was learning of his endeavors, of how he conducted investigations and interacted with Stokes and the police. Through no one but him could she learn of such things—and on that front there was much more she'd yet to learn. While such matters were primarily intellectual, there was a physical side, too; walking the edge of danger when they'd infiltrated the East End in disguise had been exhilarating.

So there were positives to their association, many reasons she wished to continue it, quite aside from rescuing her missing boys.

But it was curiosity of a different sort that fed the ambivalence she felt over him, prompting her to cut off all personal interaction despite her real and burgeoning fascination.

And that was even more out of character. She never backed away from challenging situations, and one part of her, the stronger, dominant, willful part of her, didn't want to back away now.

Reaching the end of the short gallery, she kicked her skirts about and paced back, wrapped in shadows and out of sight of the revelers below.

She'd thought at length over what he inspired in her, what he provoked. It *was* a form of curiosity, which was why she'd felt so comfortable exploring it, why she'd instinctively pursued it.

Emotional curiosity. Something she'd felt for no other soul, certainly for no man. Fascination with such a subject was, unquestionably, an intellectual exercise, yet for her, with him, it also possessed a definite physical side, a sensual side, one she couldn't deny, and— witness her continuing reaction to every little touch—patently couldn't avoid.

And therein lay the crux of her problem.

Unless she was reading the signs entirely wrongly, he wanted her—desired her—in a definitely physical way.

Other men had, or had said they had, but perversely she'd never been the least bit curious about them. But Barnaby Adair made her curious and fascinated, made her wonder about things she'd long ago deemed boring and had dismissed as entirely beneath her notice.

She was noticing now. And that was so strange she didn't know how to react—how to take charge and satisfy her fascination, how to find the answers to her multiplying questions *safely*. Without losing sight of that other reality and risking her future—her ability to continue to exercise her will and lead an independent life. She'd always intended to and still did; nothing whatever had changed on that front.

Halting by the railing, still safely wrapped in gloom, she looked out over the sea of heads and frowned. How long would she need to pace about up there, getting nowhere?

On the thought, a now familiar prickling awareness swept her nape, then spread southward. On a gasp, she whirled, and found a dark, mysterious, dangerous figure directly behind her.

A jolt of anticipation streaked through her. Her heart beat fast, then faster.

She opened her lips to berate him for startling her; before she could get a word out, he seized her waist and swung her around, away from the railing, into deeper shadow.

He stepped closer, hauled her into his arms.

Into a kiss that stole her breath.

Stole her wits.

Fiercely possessive, in no way tentative, he gathered her into his arms. Like steel, they banded her back, pressing her to him. His lips moved commandingly on hers. Hers had already been parted on the protest she'd never uttered; he'd taken advantage and laid claim to her mouth, to her senses.

To sensation, a weapon he wielded with consummate mastery, distracting her, beguiling her, seducing her.

And there was more, this time—more to feel, more to sense, more to learn. More heat, more scintillating pleasure, of a sort that sent thrilling little sparks dancing down her veins to settle beneath her skin, to ignite and burn.

Creating a host of little fires that spread and coalesced, and warmed her.

Heated her.

Until she surrendered to the growing heat, and him, and kissed him back.

She didn't understand why she so wanted to, what drove her to spear her fingers into his silky hair and plunge into a duel of kiss and retreat, of tangling tongues and voracious lips, of pleasure that bloomed and spread and filled her—and him.

She couldn't, in the distant recess of her mind that still functioned, that hadn't yet been suborned into the expanding pleasure of the kiss, comprehend why she felt such a surge of satisfaction at knowing—simply knowing in her soul—that her kiss, and she, brought him pleasure.

Why should that matter to her? It never had with any other man.

Why now? Or was it: why him?

Was it because—could it be because—he desired her? Truly desired her in a way no other man ever had?

She was no witless ninny; she knew what the hard ridge pressing against her stomach was. But he was a man; was that rock-hard bulge any real barometer of his emotions? Of what he felt for her beyond the purely physical?

She'd read extensively, the classics as well as more esoteric texts. When she used the word "desire," she meant something beyond the purely physical—something that transcended the physical, reaching onto that plane where the great emotions ruled.

Was her unconscious, and blatantly ungovernable, attraction to him somehow bound up in desire? Was her attraction a sign that with him, she could, if she chose, explore the elusive conundrums of desire?

Barnaby sensed through the kiss, through the subtle change in her lips, that she'd started to ponder something. But she was heated and pliant in his arms, neither defensive nor resistant, and she'd once again kissed him with a wanton lack of restraint; he was content enough, at least for the moment.

But he was curious, increasingly so, about what held the power to distract her at such a time. In the interests of his continuing campaign, it unquestionably behooved him to find out; given the circumstances, it was almost certainly connected with their exchange.

Drawing unhurriedly back from the honeyed depths of her mouth, reluctantly releasing her lips, he looked down into her face. The shadows cloaked them, but they'd both been in the semidark long enough for their eyes to adjust. He watched, fascinated, as clouds of desire swirled through her dark eyes; they cleared only slowly, her customary incisive, decisive expression only gradually replacing the dazed evidence of delight.

Eventually, she blinked; the expression in her eyes turned to a frown.

He felt his lips curve. "What are you thinking about?"

She studied his face, searched his eyes. "I was wondering . . . about something."

She was normally devastatingly direct. His curiosity only grew. "About what?"

Hands still clasped about his neck, head tilting, she narrowed her eyes fractionally—in undisguised challenge. "If I tell you honestly, will you answer honestly?"

Shifting his hands to her waist, supporting her against him, he didn't need to think. "Yes."

She hesitated a moment, then said, "I was wondering if you truly desire me."

Other women had asked the same thing, on occasions too numerous to count. He'd always understood that when women used the word, they meant far more than men assumed. Consequently, he knew the glib answers, the ways not to answer so he didn't have to lie. In this case, however . . .

And she'd asked for honesty.

He held her dark gaze steadily. "Yes. I do."

Head still tilted, she studied his face. "How do I know you're telling the truth? Men lie about that particular subject all the time."

She was perfectly correct; he had no grounds on which to defend his sex. And it didn't take a genius to see how any argument would go—around in circles.

But demonstrable fact spoke much louder than vows.

Reaching up, he caught one of her hands, and drew it down. All the way down between them, until he curved her palm about his erection.

Her eyes grew enormous.

His smile grew tight. "That doesn't lie."

Her eyes narrowed, but he noticed—very definitely noticed—that she made no move to pull her hand away.

Quite the opposite. The warmth of her palm seeping through his trousers, the light flexing touch of her fingers, instantly became an unsubtle torture that had him questioning his sanity.

It had seemed a good idea at the time.

Jaw clenching, he kept his eyes on hers, and prayed his wouldn't cross.

"I'm not so sure," she murmured, "about that, about its significance. It seems to happen rather often with men—perhaps, in this case, this"—her fingers curled lightly, making him inwardly jerk—"is merely a reflection, an outcome, of our setting, suggestive, illicit, shadowed."

"No." It required massive effort to keep his tone even, as if explaining some logical theory. "Atmosphere doesn't affect it at all. The company, however, does." Ignoring the interest seeping into her eyes, he forced himself to continue, biting the words off through clenching teeth, "And in the present company, *that* happens all the time. Regardless of time and place."

His will was weakening, seduced by the continued heat of her touch; grasping her wrist, he drew her hand away. Releasing it, he drew her nearer, his hands on her back urging her closer; trapped in his eyes, she permitted it. "*That* happens every time I see you. Whenever you're close."

He lowered his head, breathed against her lips as she instinctively tipped her head back, "Especially when you're close."

He covered her lips and kissed her, sensed her continuing question in the way she allowed him to explore, in the way she encouraged him to show her what she wanted to know—more.

Entirely willing, he gathered her more fully into his arms, held her captive, feeding both his senses and hers, building anticipation, letting desire rise up and take hold.

Once it had . . . once she was clinging to his shoulders, fingertips sinking in, once her breathing was rapid, tending ragged, he broke their embrace, swept her into his arms and carried her through the archway at the back of the gallery into the deserted parlor beyond.

He fell into a large armchair with her across his lap, surprising a laugh from her. But the laugh died as he leaned over her. She met his eyes through the dimness—for one pregnant moment studied them—then her lids lowered in blatant invitation; he closed the last inch and his lips covered hers once more.

Her hand slid from his nape to his cheek, cradling . . . as if holding him there while she kissed him back and flagrantly urged him on.

With her mouth, her tongue, with the pressure of her lips, urged him to show her more of desire—of what desire translated to between them. He had no reservations in fulfilling her wish, in letting his hand glide from her jaw, tracing down her throat, over her collarbone to the subtle swell of one breast.

He wasn't hesitant about claiming it; her flesh firmed beneath his palm, her nipple pebbling beneath the fine silk of her bodice. He was tempted, sorely tempted, to slip the tiny pearl buttons free so he could touch and taste her, but a warning, distant but insistent, sounded in his brain.

Trapped in the moment, in their heated, increasingly fiery exchange, in the way she responded, spine bowing, restlessly seeking to learn yet more, it took him a few seconds to recognize and decode the message.

Knowledge is Penelope Ashford's price. If he yielded too much, too quickly . . .

His way forward with her suddenly became a great deal clearer. She was a female for whom knowledge—both facts and even more experience—held a powerful appeal. And in this arena he was entirely willing to teach her anything and everything she wanted to learn.

But like any experienced teacher, he needed to exert some authority—to tempt her with answers to her first question, then tantalize her with the prospect of answering much more.

He needed to stagger her lessons—and ensure she left this one with both reason and eagerness to return for the next.

Beneath his lips, his hand, she was starting to grow demanding, sensing his momentary distraction with his thoughts.

He inwardly smiled, and gave her not what she wished, but more of what she had.

Through the silken screen of her gown he caressed her increasingly intimately, stroking down to her hip, shifting her so he could reach around and capture one firm globe of her bottom, and knead.

Possess. He didn't try to mute his desire—its direction, its goal.

That was what she'd wanted to know. He let it color every touch, every possessive caress.

So that when he ran his hand down the front of her thighs, stroking, assessing, then cupped her through the froth of silk, she gasped and quivered.

Enough. The tactician in his brain stepped forward, reminding him of his aim, his true goal.

He drew back, drew her back.

Penelope understood what he was doing, that he was retreating from showing her more, too much, perhaps, at this point, in this place. Disgruntled but resigned, she followed his lead, letting their kisses grow less ravenous, letting the hunger driving them slowly subside.

It didn't, she noted, die, but, like a banked fire, settled to a smolder. Ready to burst into raging life at a touch.

The right touch. His.

That fact intrigued, as had the entire episode. Her skin felt flushed, her body warm, pleasured and strangely languid, yet ridden by an elusive, expectant urgency she'd yet to fully comprehend.

Their lips parted. He met her eyes as she opened them, studied them for an instant, then he sat up, and helped her up.

Once on her feet, she surveyed her gown, rather surprised to find it in passable state. She wriggled the bodice, brushed down the skirts, and tried—hard—not to dwell on the lingering sensation of his hands as he'd caressed her.

She'd wanted to know, had wordlessly asked, and had learned . . . a bit. Unfortunately, as her returning wits confirmed, not enough to unequivocally answer her burning question about him, about her in relation to him and vice versa.

She frowned, and turned to him as he adjusted his coat sleeves.

Before she could find words to ask, he volunteered, "That's a taste of what desire is, at least between you and me." Through the dimness, he caught her gaze. "If you want to know more, I'll be happy to teach you."

He moved closer, until he stood before her looking down into her face, but he didn't touch her. "However, like all subjects, if you truly want to understand, in depth, with all the ramifications, you have to be eager and willing to learn."

There was a very clear question in those last words. Penelope fought not to let her eyes narrow; she was far too fly to the time of day not to realize what he was doing.

However . . .

She did want to know. A great deal more.

Holding his gaze, she smiled, then swung about and headed for the stairs leading down. "I'll think about it."

Barnaby watched her retreating back through narrowing eyes, then started to follow—as ever in her wake. As she reached the stairs, he said, "The printing works is running our notices tonight—they'll be ready tomorrow morning."

She paused at the head of the stairs. Over her shoulder, she said, "We should discuss with Griselda how to distribute them."

He halted behind her. "I'll call for you in Mount Street at nine o'clock. We can pick up the notices and go on to her shop."

"Excellent." With an inclination of her head, she started down the narrow stairs.

He remained at their head, watching her descend—reminding himself that letting her go was a vital part of his greater plan.

As the wee hours of the night waxed and waned, Penelope tossed and turned in her bed, in her bedroom in Mount Street—such familiar surroundings she couldn't understand why she couldn't clear her mind and fall asleep.

She was such a disciplined thinker, she normally had no difficulty at all.

It was his fault, of course.

He'd set a particularly fascinating hare running in her mind, and she couldn't stop following it.

Sitting up, she thumped her pillow, then flung herself back down and stared at the ceiling.

That he was deliberately tempting her was beyond doubt. As for the price of the knowledge he was dangling, carrotlike, before her, she knew well enough what that was. Yet given she was already twenty-four, and had no desire for marriage, having long ago decided that, with its concordant restrictions, it wouldn't in any way suit her, then what was she keeping her virginity for? In light of what she had now come to regard as her unacceptable ignorance on the subject of desire, let alone passion, it seemed entirely appropriate she trade it—useless thing that it otherwise was—for the knowledge she now craved.

Added to that was the undeniable fact that he was the only male ever to have impinged on her consciousness in such a way—the only man who had ever succeeded in starting that aforementioned hare leaping across the fields of her mind.

Halting her thoughts at that point, she mentally looked over them. Assessed, evaluated. All of the above seemed logically unassailable; her reasoning thus far was sound.

The point that was rendering her too restless to sleep was the next step.

The notion of simply telling him yes, and blithely consigning her education in that sphere to him and his male whims, did not appeal. Not in the least.

She had no great opinion of male brains. Not even his, which seemed superior to the general run. She strongly suspected he did not have, or at least was not aware of it if he had, a logical basis for his desire for her—not beyond desire itself.

No—while she saw no reason not to go forward, albeit on her own terms, she certainly wouldn't be doing so in the misguided expectation that he—a male—would be able to fully elucidate his reasons for desiring her.

Luckily, learning his reasons wasn't her sole intellectual goal. Even more than his reasons, she wanted to know, to understand and comprehend, her own.

She had to know what made her *want*, what it was in his kisses, in his embrace, that stirred her to want so much more. She needed to learn what fueled her own desire.

That was her principal goal.

And Barnaby Adair was the man who could, and would, lead her to it.

The one real danger hadn't, yet, raised its head. Marriage. As long as matrimony remained absent from their equation, all would be well.

She mulled over that point. Considered it from various angles. Accepted that he might feel compelled, having seduced her, as he would see it, to offer for her hand, and even when she refused, continue to insist, seeing the matter as impinging on his honor, a subject over which men of his ilk had a tendency to be particularly pigheaded.

But she knew how to counter that; even if he did try to introduce the baneful prospect of marriage, she felt confident she would be able to prevail, to take a contrary stand and sway him to her way of thinking. If the matter arose, she would explain her views; she was sure he—being a logical, rational man—would understand her stance, and ultimately accept it.

That said . . . her position in any such discussion would be immeasurably strengthened if *she* was the one who instigated their affair. Not acquiesced to but dictated—that was obviously the most sensible way forward for them both. She needed to take charge and define their relationship as an affair, plain and simple, permitting no hint of matrimony to creep in and confuse the issue.

Her mind cleared. That was how it had to be. Obviously.

Lips curving, she sighed; turning onto her side, she snuggled her cheek into her pillow and closed her eyes.

All she needed to do was take control of the situation, and all would be well.

Confident, reassured, she slept.

"I'm so glad I came with you this morning." Penelope stood on the pavement outside Griselda's shop, waiting while Barnaby leaned back into the hackney and retrieved the large box containing their printed notices.

Hefting the box, he nudged the carriage door shut, then nodded to the jarvey. As the hackney pulled away, he turned to Penelope and struggled to hide his smile. From the moment they'd left the printing works off the Edgware Road, she'd entertained him with a steady flow of observations and suppositions.

She fell in beside him as he walked to Griselda's door. "Thank you—it's been a thoroughly informative and useful morning." She glanced at him as, balancing the box on his shoulder, he waved her ahead of him up the steps. "Over the last few years we've been investigating other trades for our orphans. We've had some success with merchants. After meeting Mr. Cole and being shown around his works, I believe we should investigate printing houses as possible places for our boys."

Following her into the shop, he said, "You should speak with Cole—I'm sure he'll be happy to trial some of your lads." Not only was the sister of Viscount Calverton the sort of lady Cole would trip over his toes to assist, but notwithstanding the box on Barnaby's shoulder, the man still owed him.

Nodding, Penelope swept deeper into the shop. "I believe I will." Smiling at the apprentices, she waved them back to their work. "No need to announce us—we'll go through to Miss Martin."

Pushing past the curtain, she halted. Barnaby just managed not to run her down. Griselda wasn't in the kitchen area.

"Up here, Penelope."

Glancing up the narrow stairs, Penelope beamed. "There you are."

She set off up the stairs. Barnaby shrugged the box from his shoulder, then carrying it before him, followed her up.

He emerged into Griselda's parlor to see Penelope shaking hands with Stokes, who was in his "East End" disguise, as was Griselda.

"Perfect." Setting the box on a side table, Barnaby folded back the flaps, pulled out the top sheet, and held it up for Stokes and Griselda to read.

Griselda beside him, Stokes did; he slowly smiled. "Perfect indeed." He took the notice, holding it so he and Griselda could better see. "We were about to head out to follow up the information Mr. Martin and others have gathered on our five remaining potential schoolmasters."

Handing the notice to Griselda, Stokes looked at the box. "How many do you have?"

"Two thousand." Barnaby thrust his hands in his pockets. "Enough to effectively flood the East End. What we need to know is the best way of distributing them—spreading them as far and wide as we can within that area."

"The markets." Griselda looked up from the notice. "We were going there again anyway, but there's no better way to spread these than to leave them with the stallholders. And today's Friday—the Friday and Saturday markets are the busiest. The only other worthwhile places to leave them would be the pubs and taverns, but the markets reach more people—women as well as men."

Stokes nodded. "We'll take them with us today. The sooner we can find the boys the better."

"What have you learned about the other possible schoolmasters?" Penelope looked from Stokes to Griselda. "Anything to suggest one of those names is the man we're after?"

Stokes grimaced. "Nothing definite. The difficulty with these five is that they don't move in wider circles—they keep close to their lairs and interact only with those they must. We think we've got directions for three—Slater, Watts, and Hornby. We'll check those today. The other two—Grimsby and Hughes—we've yet to get any certain news of. However, with both of them, what the local bobbies have got, and Griselda's father, too, are evasive answers, which makes me suspect that both are currrently involved in something illegal. Whether that something is running the school we're seeking is anyone's guess, but if the other three turn out to be law-abiding at present—which us so easily getting their locations makes more likely—then Grimsby and Hughes will become our best bets."

Griselda glanced at Stokes. "After we check the first three, if there's no sign of the boys there, we'll press harder to see what we can turn up on Grimsby and Hughes." She looked at Barnaby. "The problem is that no one knows—or at least is prepared to tell us—what areas they're lurking in, which makes locating them rather like searching for a needle in a massive haystack."

"It's possible the notices might gain us a clue," Barnaby said. "At least point to which area we should focus on."

"What about the Bushels? Mary and Horry?" Penelope looked at Stokes. "Have you visited yet?"

Stokes nodded; he glanced at Barnaby. "Your message reached me in good time—I got to Black Lion Yard late that afternoon. I spoke with Mary Bushel and the Wills boys. Between us, we've worked out a plan that should keep Mary and Horry safe, but leave the door invitingly open, so to speak, in the hope these blackguards will make a move."

Stokes's expression turned feral. "I just hope they do. Between the Willses and the local force, the villains won't find it easy to get out of Black Lion Yard."

Barnaby raised his brows. "I hadn't thought of it, but the yard does lend itself to being an excellent trap."

"Exactly. So Horry and his grandmother are as well protected as they could be, and our trap is in place." Stokes nodded. "Now we need to see if we can get a bead on who we're likely to catch in it."

He picked up the box of notices. "Griselda and I will hand these out as we pass the markets." He glanced at the other three. "We need to learn where this schoolmaster is keeping the boys, and get them out of his clutches, preferably before he sends them out to work."

Barnaby grimaced. "Parliament rises next week. A few days after that and Mayfair will be all but deserted. If our hypothesis of the reason this schoolmaster's training so many boys at once is correct, then we've only got until then to find them."

They all exchanged glances, then Griselda waved to the stairs. "We'd better get going then."

They all trooped down, then out of the shop, leaving the apprentices staring.

Once outside, they headed around the church to find hackneys in the street beyond. Stokes and Griselda took the first, Barnaby and Penelope insisting their task was the more urgent.

Standing on the pavement watching the carriage rattle away to the east, Penelope shifted restlessly.

Beside her, his gaze on the retreating carriage, too, Barnaby said, "If you think of anything you, I, or we can do to learn what we need to learn faster, let me know."

She glanced at his profile. "Do you promise to do the same?"

He looked down at her. "Yes. All right."

"Good." She nodded. "If I think of anything, I'll send word."

13

Everything was in place, yet nothing had happened.

Late that night, wreathed in a thick November fog, Barnaby strolled along St. James and considered the state of their investigation. He'd just left White's after spending a quiet evening in the almost empty, and therefore blissfully silent, club, deeming it wiser to while away the evening there rather than in some ballroom in Penelope's wake—a deliberate ploy to evoke her impatience, leaving her curiosity unappeased, thus prodding her to consider slaking her thirst for knowledge with him. Being the intelligent lady she was, her mind would then follow the obvious path, which would lead her to the conclusion he wished her to reach.

That marrying him would be in her best interests.

That doing so was the route to attaining all the knowledge she might wish on the subject currently—courtesy of their recent interaction—occupying her mind.

He fervently hoped that subject was occupying her mind; other than their investigation—presently stalled—it was the only consideration in his.

Even that—their lack of forward momentum in finding the missing boys—was likely to work in his favor. Stokes and Griselda had distributed the notices, but they'd yet to elicit any response. As for the five names on Stokes's original list, they'd confirmed that Slater and Watts were, if not leading entirely blameless lives, at least not in possession of extraneous boys.

Which left Hornby, Grimsby, and Hughes as their best candidates for the schoolmaster involved, but no avenue had yet yielded any clue as to the latter two's whereabouts.

Otherwise, the trap they'd set in Black Lion Yard two days ago remained primed, but as of this evening, unsprung.

And neither he nor Penelope had managed to think of anything more they could reasonably do to find the missing boys.

So they were waiting.

Patience, he suspected, wasn't her strong suit; it was perfectly possible—even likely—that starved of progress on one front, she would turn her energies toward a different goal.

The notion of said energies being his to guide sent a thrill of expectation through him—something he hadn't felt in a very long time, not since he'd been a green youth.

And perhaps not even then.

Smiling to himself, he turned into Jermyn Street. Swinging his cane, he walked on, ignoring the ever-thickening fog.

The issue of marriage was one he'd avoided, but not because he had any intrinsic dislike or distrust of the state. If truth be known the opposite was true; as the years had rolled by and he'd seen his friends marry, seen the depths of their happiness in their shared lives, he'd grown envious. Yet still he'd been convinced that marriage was not for him, because he'd never met a tonnish female likely to—or even able to—cope with his vocation, his passion for criminal investigations.

Penelope was the sole exception, the lady who broke every rule. She wouldn't just acquiesce to his investigating, she'd actively encourage him. And her intellect was such that, against all the odds, he was looking forward to sharing cases with her—listening to her opinions and suggestions, discussing villains and their traits.

His necessary first step toward what he now saw as his most desirable future was to secure Penelope's hand in marriage. That her brother, Luc, and her family, would find his suit acceptable he had no real doubt; the third son of an earl was a perfectly acceptable match for the daughter of a viscount, and his status and fortune were nothing to sneer at. Gaining her agreement was the only hurdle, and if his stoking of her curiosity and impatience was playing out as planned . . .

Smiling confidently, he twirled his cane. He fully expected her to indicate some interest very soon. He rather thought he should call on her tomorrow.

A discreet black town carriage stood outside the door before his. He noticed it, but pointedly didn't glance that way; he wondered who Elliard, his neighbor, was entertaining that night.

His mind filled with visions of entertaining Penelope. Soon, he assured himself. Very soon. Smiling even more broadly, he swung up the steps to his door, fishing in his waistcoat pocket for his latchkey, glancing down as he did.

Behind him, he heard the black carriage's harness jingle, then the horses' hooves started to clop, the carriage rolling along the street . . .

He froze, premonition snaking down his spine.

He hadn't seen or heard anyone getting into or out of the carriage, no door shutting—why was it suddenly leaving?

He started to turn—in the same instant sensed the onrush of an assault. Whirling, he saw a cloaked figure rushing up the steps, a . . . baton? . . . in one hand.

His brain froze, unable to reconcile what he was seeing. The figure was short, and the cloak covered skirts. And there was a glint of gold beneath the hood, at eye level.

In that split second he recognized his assailant, registered that she'd come from the carriage that had pulled away. He glanced at the departing carriage—then saw, too late, the cosh she raised.

She hit him on the forehead.

Not all that hard, yet enough to make him blink and fall back a step—he half staggered and fetched up against the wall.

Absolutely stunned. Speechless, he stared at her.

She grabbed his coat—apparently mistakenly thinking she'd incapacitated him sufficiently that she needed to stop him falling down.

If he fell at all, it would be from sheer, utter disbelief.

What the devil was she doing?

He blinked again. She tucked the cosh away beneath her cloak, then peered into his face. Apparently reassured he was still compos mentis, she hissed, "Play along!"

What the hell was her script?

One hand still clenched in his coat, she reached out and hammered on his door.

He wondered if he should point out that his latchkey was in his hand, but decided against it. He assumed he was supposed to be incapacitated, so slumped against the wall, eyes half closed.

It wasn't all that hard to summon a pained frown. He could feel a heated throb where she'd hit him; he suspected she'd left a bruise.

Penelope all but jigged with impatience. What was taking his damned man so long?

Then she heard footsteps; a second later, the door opened.

She looked at Barnaby. "Help me! Quickly!" She glanced behind her, down the empty street. "They might come back."

The man frowned. "Who might—" Then he saw Barnaby slumped against the wall. "Oh, my goodness!"

"Exactly." Penelope grabbed Barnaby's arm and dragged it across her shoulders. Slipping her other arm around his waist, she hauled him away from the wall.

She staggered, and only just managed to right herself, and him, before toppling backward down the steps. Lord, he was heavy!

But she could hardly complain when he was doing exactly as she'd asked.

She weaved for an instant before his man—Mostyn, that was it— came to his startled senses and seized his semicomatose master from the other side.

"There now—gently." Mostyn helped her shuffle Barnaby through the open door. "Oh, my heavens!" He stopped, staring at the red mark on Barnaby's forehead.

Penelope cursed under her breath; the man was an old woman! "Shut the door and help me get him upstairs."

She was no longer so certain she hadn't truly injured him; he was leaning very heavily on her. She told herself she hadn't swung the cosh all that hard, but anxiety started to churn in her stomach.

Mostyn rushed to close the door, then reappeared to take Barnaby's other arm.

Barnaby moaned as they headed for the stairs—far too realistically for her peace of mind.

Damn! She had hurt him. Guilt joined the anxiety in a nauseating mix.

"But what happened?" Mostyn asked as they started up the stairs.

She had her story ready. "I convinced him to go out searching for our villains. They waylaid us not far away and coshed him over the head. He took a fearful knock—see the bruise?"

That was all it took; Mostyn tut-tutted and carried on about the dangers his master never seemed to have a care for, how he'd often warned him that something terrible would one day come of his investigating . . . and much more in that vein until Penelope was extremely sorry she'd ever thought up such a tale—adding lashings of more guilt to that already swirling through her. She had to bite her tongue against the urge to caustically defend Barnaby; she had to remember her own role in this drama—that of female accomplice seriously concerned for her white knight's health.

She literally gave thanks when they reached the top of the steep single flight, and could lurch toward, then through, the doorway leading into a sizable room. It took up most of the first floor—a very large bedroom, with a very large bed, plus a small sitting area with a desk and a comfortable armchair angled before the hearth. The fire was cheerily burning, throwing heat and light through the room. A dressing room opened to one side; she glimpsed a bathing chamber beyond.

A pair of tallboys stood against opposing walls, and matching side tables flanked the bed, but it was the bed itself that dominated the room—and fixed her attention.

A four-poster in dark wood with barley-sugar poles, it was hung with figured damask the color of his eyes. The curtains were looped back with tasseled golden cords, revealing a massive expanse of blue satin coverlet, with gold-silk-encased pillows forming a small mountain against the headboard.

In unspoken accord, she and Mostyn teetered toward the bed. Mostyn managed to steer Barnaby—who emitted another dreadful groan—until his back was propped against the nearest pole.

"Miss—if you can steady him there for a moment, I'll ready the bed."

Mostyn warily took his hands from Barnaby, then dove for the head of the bed, but before he could grasp the coverlet and drag it down, Barnaby groaned again, and staggered sideways.

"Oh!" Penelope tried desperately to hold him upright—but then he toppled backward, nearly jerking her off her feet and onto the bed with him as he sprawled on his back across the mattress; it was only because she lost her grip on his coat that she managed to stay on her feet.

Eyes still closed, he winced, then moaned. Weakly, he raised a hand to his head.

Penelope dived to catch his hand. "No—don't touch it. Just lie there and let us get you out of your coat."

He was either an excellent actor, or he really was in pain—she had no idea which.

Thrown entirely off balance, Mostyn fussed and fretted. Penelope shrugged out of her cloak and laid it aside, then rustled back to the bed. Between them, they managed to ease the heavy overcoat off Barnaby's shoulders. The coat beneath, one of Shultz's creations, proved a great deal more difficult to remove; Mostyn had to support Barnaby, holding him upright, while Penelope clambered onto the bed behind him and tugged the tight-fitting garment free.

She shuffled quickly aside as Mostyn let Barnaby back down—to the accompaniment of another excoriating groan.

His waistcoat and cravat were much easier to deal with; she dispensed with those, tugging both free, while Mostyn removed his shoes and stockings.

The instant Mostyn stood again, she snapped, "Fetch some cold water and a cloth."

Mostyn hesitated, but the quite genuine concern ringing in her voice had him moving to the dressing room door. "I'll just be a moment."

Penelope glanced after him; he passed through to the bathing chamber beyond, but with both doors open she didn't dare ask Barnaby if his head really hurt that much, or if he was acting.

The guilt that he might not be, that she really had coshed him harder than she'd intended, contrarily made it easier, when Mostyn returned, to put the next stage of her plan into action.

Taking the basin from him, she set it on one bedside table, briskly wrung out the cloth, then leaned over Barnaby and applied the compress gently to the reddened patch on his wide forehead. The spot wasn't that raised or contused; it was probably just as well she was covering it, especially as Mostyn had moved around the bed to light the candelabra on the other bedside table. The candles flared, then steadied, spilling light over Barnaby as he lay sprawled across the bed.

Without looking directly at Mostyn, she said, "You may go."

It took a moment for her words to penetrate, then he stared at her, stupefied. "I can't do that! It wouldn't be proper."

Slowly, she lifted her gaze and stared—down her nose—at him. "My dear good man." She'd borrowed both words and tone from Lady Osbaldestone, a lady whose ability to lord it over the opposite sex was legendary; she couldn't do better than to borrow from a master. "I do hope"—she kept her voice low, yet her tone was incisive— "that you're not about to suggest there is anything *im*proper in my tending to Mr. Adair in his current injured state, especially as it was in response to a request of mine—indeed, in protecting me—that he was injured?"

Mostyn blinked, frowned.

Before he had a chance to gather any wits, she continued in the same, chilly, impossibly superior tone, "I have two adult brothers, and have tended their hurts often enough." An outright lie; both were much older than she. "I have lived more than twenty-eight years in the haut ton, and never have I heard it sugggested that tending an injured gentleman in a state of incapacitation was in any way considered fast."

Having lied once, she saw no reason not to compound the sin; Mostyn couldn't possibly know how old she was.

Returning her attention to her patient—who had remained silent throughout—she struggled to recall useful terms Mrs. Keggs employed in similar situations, which occurred all too frequently at the Foundling House. "It's very likely he has a concussion."

Alarm flared in Mostyn's eyes. "Mulled wine! My mentor always swore by it." He rushed for the door.

"*No.*" Penelope raised her head and frowned. "He most certainly shouldn't have any hot drinks—and certainly not alcohol. Not wine or brandy. Which shows how much you know." With every evidence of disgust, she waved him away. "I'll sit and watch over him, and keep a cold compress on his injury. When he wakes, I'll ring for you."

"But—" Wide-eyed, Mostyn looked from her to his comatose master.

Penelope sighed, dropped the cloth in the basin, then advanced determinedly on Mostyn—who naturally backed away. "I have no time for this discussion—I need to tend to your master."

She continued to march forward until Mostyn's back hit the door. Halting, planting her hands on her hips, she glared, and lowered her voice to an acid whisper. "All this noise is no doubt hurting his poor head. Now begone!"

Dramatically she pointed to the door.

Mostyn goggled at her, swallowed, cast a last glance at the figure on the bed, then turned, opened the door, and slid through.

He closed it softly behind him.

Disinclined to take chances, Penelope stepped closer and pressed her ear to the panels. She waited until she heard Mostyn's footsteps descending the stairs, then she slid the bolt on the door.

On a huge sigh, she closed her eyes for an instant and leaned her forehead against the panels.

The sound of rustling reached her.

Opening her eyes, turning, she saw Barnaby propped up against the pillows. There was no sign of vagueness in the blue eyes that pinned her.

"What," he asked, "is this all about?"

His diction was precise—no slurring. The relief that swamped her was disconcertingly intense. A spontaneous, delighted smile curving her lips, she started back to the bed. "Good! You aren't really hurt."

He snorted. "After that little tap on the head?"

She grinned even more. "I should have known your skull would be too thick for me to seriously dent it."

"Perhaps, but what—" Barnaby didn't get a chance to finish his question before she answered it.

She'd bounced up to the bed; as he spoke, she bounced onto the coverlet, flung herself into his arms, and kissed him.

Which was all very nice, but he was excruciatingly aware that they were in his bedroom, on his bed—and she'd locked the door. Compounding the problem, it was the middle of the night, and from all he'd witnessed, salvation in the form of Mostyn was unlikely to eventuate anytime soon.

Certainly not soon enough.

Shifting in his arms, she pressed closer, wordlessly inviting. Unable to deny her, he kissed her back; closing his hands about her shoulders, he slid into the warm cavern of her offered mouth and feasted, feeding his senses and hers, letting the pleasure unfold.

She was wearing dark green silk, a conservative, severe gown with black buttons marching from the raised waist to her throat, her long slender arms tightly encased, with even tinier black buttons at her wrists. The semifull skirts thoroughly camouflaged her lower limbs.

With her hair looped back tightly in a sleek chignon, her spectacles perched on her nose, she should have looked forbidding.

Instead, as ever, she looked like forbidden fruit.

The dark silk made her skin glow, porcelain fine, pearlescent pale. His hands moved over her back, consciously possessive; the silk rustled dryly, a sensual sound, one suggesting surrender.

His or hers—he suddenly wasn't sure.

It took effort to draw back from the kiss—in which she'd somehow managed to ensnare him. "Penelope . . ."

Hugely satisfied, she drew back enough to smile beatifically at him, simultaneously relaxing against him, snuggling her breasts against his chest. "I came to inform you that I've made a decision."

"I see." Looking into her dark eyes, aglow with an enthusiasm—an energy—the like of which he hadn't before seen, he wasn't sure he wanted to know the answer, yet felt forced to ask, "What decision?"

She held his gaze, her ripe, luscious lips gently smiling. "The last time we spoke on personal matters, you made an offer—do you recall?"

"I recall very well." His voice sounded gravelly even to his ears.

Her distracting smile deepened. "You said if I wanted to know more, you'd happily teach me, provided I was eager and willing to learn." Head tilting, she studied him, her dark eyes amused; she was enjoying the moment—the culmination of what had clearly been a plan. "I'm here to tell you that I'm both eager and willing—I'm here to ask you to teach me more."

The inevitable effect of her words spread through him, but . . . studying her eyes, her pleased and undeniably eager expression, he confirmed she had indeed skipped a stone or two on his intended path. Agreeing to marry him, for instance.

Of course, he hadn't yet offered for her hand.

Before he could find words to seize the moment, she did.

"I realize a lady of my station is supposed to remain ignorant of such things until she weds, but as I'm firmly and ineradicably opposed to marriage, I had thought I would be condemned to ignorance—which of course isn't at all to my taste. Not on any subject. Which is why I'm so grateful for your offer."

Her expression was one of confident expectation that he would fall in with her plan and educate her ignorance.

His outward expression mild, inwardly he swore. He should have stipulated that she had to marry him, or at least agree to marry him, first—but he hadn't. Could he now renege, renegotiate his offer?

Not easily. She'd told him she wasn't looking for marriage, but . . . *firmly and ineradicably opposed*?

His hands stroked up and down her back, gently soothing—him. Releasing her, putting distance between them wasn't possible; now he had his hands on her, he couldn't get them off. She lay more or less on him; his body craved her warmth, the sensation of her softness, the subtle and arousing assurance of her willingness.

Mentally scrambling, he summoned a mildly intrigued expression, as if he were merely curious about her stance. "Why are you so set against marriage? I thought it was what all young ladies strive for."

Her lips set; she shook her head decisively. "Not me. Just think"—leaning more heavily on his chest, her hip rolling provocatively across his, she freed one hand to gesture—"what allure could marriage possibly hold for me?"

His body, hard and aching from the moment she'd flung herself into his arms, and now throbbing with her hip so warmly wedged against his groin, was only too willing to demonstrate.

But she continued, "What could marriage offer me in compensation for its inevitable cost?"

He frowned. "Cost?"

She smiled, cynical and wry. "My independence. My ability to live my life as I choose, rather than as a husband would prefer." She looked into his eyes. "What gentleman of our class would allow me to freely visit the slums and stews after we were wed?"

He held her gaze steadily—and couldn't answer.

Her tight smile dissolved into one of amusement. She patted his chest. "Don't give yourself a brain sprain—there is no answer. No gentleman who wed me would allow me to do what I feel I must, would allow me to pursue what I see as my life's work. Without that work, what satisfaction would I have? Therefore I will have no wedding."

He looked into her dark eyes, and knew he was going to change her mind. Unfortunately, stating that goal at this time would instantly ensure his failure.

"I . . . see." He forced himself to nod. "I see your point." And he did; rationally, logically, her stance made sense.

It just simply couldn't be. Couldn't continue.

Because he needed her as his wife.

Having her sprawled over him, firm svelte curves a delectable present wrapped in dark green silk, was steadily eroding his capacity to think. Regardless, quite obviously argument wasn't going to save him tonight.

He'd made an offer to teach her more about desire; now she'd taken him up on it, he couldn't draw back. If he did, she wouldn't trust him. No matter what explanation he conjured, she'd feel slighted and rejected; she'd pull back from him, and never let him near her again.

If he mentioned marriage, she'd put up walls and lock him out—and that he couldn't accept. Couldn't allow to happen.

Even worse—much more horrifying still—was the risk that now he'd encouraged it, if he didn't slake her thirst for knowledge in this sphere, she would find someone else—some other man—who would.

Some cad.

Instead of him.

That *definitely* wasn't going to happen.

She was watching him, her eagerness apparent in her eyes, her expression; as he studied it, she tilted her head, arched her brows. "Well?"

The word was unexpectedly sultry, seductive, and provocative—question, challenge, and sheer temptation rolled into one syllable.

He felt it, and the certainty of what he and she were about to do, here in his bed, slide through his consciousness and invade his body, until every muscle seemed to thrum with heat.

Letting his lips slowly curve, his gaze locked in the darkness of hers, he raised a hand to her face and lifted her spectacles from her nose, easing the earpieces free of her hair. Knowing the gesture was a surrender. Sensing it in his bones. "How much can you see without them?"

She blinked, smiled, and scanned his face. "I can see things within five feet quite reasonably, although the detail isn't always as fine as I'd like. Farther away becomes progressively fuzzy."

"In that case . . ." Extending his arm, he set the spectacles on the bedside table. "You won't need these."

She frowned. "Are you sure?"

Looking back at her, he cocked a brow. "Who's teaching whom here?"

She laughed. Bracing her hands on his chest, she tensed to push up and move off him.

His hands on her back, he held her to him, rolled, trapping her beneath him, bent his head and kissed her startled "Oh!" from her lips, then sank into the welcoming warmth of her mouth.

Sank into her.

The immediate response of every muscle he possessed to the sensation of having her beneath him was intense, revealing—and ravenous enough to have him mentally holding his breath while he wrestled his instincts back under his control.

She might have invited him to make love to her—she hadn't invited him to ravish her. A distinction his civilized brain understood, but which his more primitive side—the one she called forth—wasn't so interested in.

Inwardly grim, he reined that less civilized self in; only once he felt confident he had it contained did he allow his hands to move. To slide from beneath her, to grasp her waist, tensing . . . letting his possessiveness taste that much, savor the fact that she was there, committed, his to take.

It was a heady moment; in response, he pressed her lips wide and deepened the kiss, plundering in a languid, leisurely fashion that was a promise of intimacies to come.

Having accepted her script—having once more, entirely unexpectedly, found himself following rather than leading—he had no lingering reservations; he would do as she asked, take the lead and show her more, and introduce her to passion.

To the heat that swelled beneath his hand as he slid it in one slow heavy stroke from her waist, up her silk-clad side, to the swell of her breast.

Penelope gasped through the kiss; he'd caressed her in similar fashion before, yet this time, with the certainty that he wouldn't stop with just the caress blazoned in her mind, his touch seemed more potent, infinitely more powerful.

Every touch was a promise, every sweep of his palm and fingers both an exploration and a claiming.

A delight. Warmth welled, and spilled through her. More definite heat—flames filled with pleasure—flared, grew, and raced through her. Her breasts were soon aching, too tight for the ungiving confinement of silk, her tightly ruched nipples points of sharp delight.

She would have spoken, mentioned her discomfort, but with his mouth locked over hers, with his tongue evocatively tangling with hers, she had neither the chance, the ability, nor the wits to form words.

Words—reasons, rationality, and logic—no longer seemed relevant, not in this world he'd waltzed her into, a world where desire had so swiftly risen she thought she could taste it—sharp, addictive. Compelling.

Trapped under his weight, she pressed her aching flesh into his palm, softly moaned.

He responded, but with an unhurried calm, a lack of urgency that had her own spiraling. Pressing one hand between them, he deftly slipped the buttons closing her bodice free, starting from her throat and slowly progressing down . . . until her bodice gaped and the pressure on her breasts eased.

The loss of discomfiting pressure perversely left her hungry for more, for something more—then he pressed aside the loose halves of her bodice, and through the delicate translucency of her silk chemise, cupped her breast.

She gasped, clung—to the kiss, to him. Her hands had, as usual, locked at his nape. As he weighed, then stroked, then gently kneaded, her hands drifted to his shoulders and gripped. When he brushed his thumb across her engorged nipple, she caught her breath, fingertips sinking deep.

He played, tested, tortured her senses—explored and learned of her, of her responses. Taught her, showed her, what she liked, how much delight could flow from just a simple touch, albeit an illicit one.

His other hand had remained at her waist. Anchoring her, holding her. Now, once more pressing beneath her, it slid down, over her hip, until his large palm cradled her bottom, then slowly cruised over it, assessing, not yet possessing but with the promise that would come. His weight above her, on her, held her down, bore her down, pressing her bottom into that questing hand. Even through the layers of her skirts and petticoats, his touch sent heat, damp and somehow urgent, flushing beneath her skin.

A strange restlessness grew and spread within her. Like the opening of a well, a void, a hunger.

She could taste desire in his kiss, feel it in his touch. Was this passion, rising in response?

Raising his head, breaking their kiss, he looked down at her. His eyes were heavy-lidded, the cerulean blue intense. Then his lips curved in a dangerous smile, and he rolled, taking her with him.

She gasped, grabbed his shoulders, went to push up when he settled on his back, propped high on the pillows, but the weight of his arm across her spine held her to him. Drew her to him so his lips could capture hers again, so he could lure her senses once more into the kiss.

Once she was caught, the cage of his arms eased. Her new position ruffled her senses, leaving them skittering with unaccustomed awareness. Her skirts had rucked up as they'd turned; while there was still silk between them—between her thighs and the sides of his hard body—at the back her skirts had flared out and now lay spread across his legs, leaving her bottom unshielded from the fabric of his trousers, if she were silly enough—wanton enough—to sit back.

For the moment she was content to allow her senses time to grow used to the unexpected position, to the solid, muscled heat of him between her thighs, to the hardness against which the sensitive inner faces of her thighs were pressed.

Then she felt his fingers swiftly undoing the laces down her back.

Barnaby didn't stop until the laces were all undone and the back of her gown lay open to her hips. He let his hands cruise beneath the material, easing it aside, once again finding the filmy silk of her chemise screening her body from his touch.

Impatience rose through him; he tamped it down. Drawing back from the kiss, he urged her up. Reaching down, he drew her knees higher, against his sides, so when she placed her hands on his chest and pushed up, she was straddling him.

Given he was lying against the pillows, propped high, not flat, that left her sitting across his waist, her breasts level with his face.

Exactly where he wanted them.

His lips curved in anticipation as he raised his hands and pushed the shoulders of her gown off and down.

As her sleeves slid down her arms, trapping them, Penelope looked down at his face. He wasn't looking at hers, but at what he'd revealed. His expression was set but rather blank, as if he were holding a great deal within. Controlled. In control. Of himself as well as her. But then she glimpsed his eyes, and the heat—the lust—in them, firing the blue, shocked, delighted, and warmed her.

Some part of her was astonished she didn't feel the slightest stirring of modesty. Quite the opposite. She wanted this, knew she did, and was determined to savor every moment, no matter how shocking.

As she drank in the qualities blazing in his gaze as it slid over the swells of her still partially screened breasts, over the dips, the hollows, the peaks, she felt a subtle sense of triumph grow.

She'd felt something similar before with him—a sense of power that she, her body, could so ensnare him. So capture and hold his attention to the exclusion of all else. Even when his hands shifted and he caught her wrist to slip loose the tiny buttons closing her sleeves, his gaze didn't waver.

Swiftly, wordlessly, he completed the task, then drew the sleeves free of her hands. She drew them clear, then returned her palms once more to his shoulders. As her bodice subsided with a soft rustle in loose folds about her waist, she waited, pleasantly tense with anticipation, to see what next he would do.

She wasn't entirely surprised when he reached for the trailing ends of the bow that held the gathered neckline of her fine chemise closed.

Barnaby tested the tiny cord of flattened silk, rolling it between his fingertips. He'd wondered what she wore beneath her gowns—had fantasized, and she hadn't disappointed.

The chemise was severely simple in style, not a frill or furbelow in sight. But the material was the most fabulously fine, gossamer-weight silk he'd ever encountered; diaphanous, nearly translucent, it whispered over her skin like a lover's caress, bold, wanton, seductive.

The innate sensuality he'd sensed in her from the first was clearly real, no fantasy. The observation racked the tension in his muscles, already taut, one notch more, to a higher degree of readiness.

That was something he didn't truly need; he was already battling impulses more intense, more carnally explicit, than he'd ever experienced. He assumed it was because she was a virgin, that he was the first to see her like this, the first to ever have her, that fueled such rampant, primitive desires.

He drew in a long breath, tightened his grip on a control that was more tenuous than he liked, then raised both hands to her breasts. In worship.

Neither large nor small, they seemed shaped for his palms, for him.

His hands stroked, slowly, over the silk, fondling, caressing. Lightly stroking, circling her peaked nipples until she closed her eyes and shifted, restless, upon him.

He took his time, and savored, noting the rising tension that bowed her spine, that fractured her breathing and had her pressing forward, seeking . . . just one more tantalizing touch.

Her eyes were closed, a line of concentration etched between her brows as she drank in every tiny sensation. Lips curving in a predatory smile, he leaned forward, and licked.

She gasped, swayed, but didn't open her eyes.

The sound sank to his soul. He licked again, then laved the tight bud until her fingertips sank deep in desperation. Only then did he lean closer yet and take the throbbing flesh into his mouth, and suckle.

She moaned, the sound half trapped in her throat; again the simple sound drove him on, to both appease and heighten the ache he'd created. To drive her wild.

Gasping, mentally reeling, Penelope wasn't sure how much more sensation she could bear. He continued feasting at her breasts; screened though they were by her chemise, the lancing pleasure his hot, wet mouth, his raspy tongue pressed on her struck deep, sending heat flaring through her, outward to her fingertips, down to pool low between her thighs.

Until she felt hot, damp, and swollen there, too, until the flesh between her thighs ached and throbbed.

Again, he seemed to know. His hands had left her breasts, fastening about her waist to hold her steady as he gorged on the swollen peaks; now those steadying hands eased their grip, then one after the other pushed up her skirts and petticoats enough to slide beneath.

And grip her bare hips, then slide, slowly, down her naked thighs.

Then, even more slowly, back up.

Courtesy of her position, he could fondle as he wished. He continued to minister to her breasts, pressing unrelenting, distracting delight upon her, keeping her teetering on her knees so she had to grip his shoulders to remain steady.

Although her eyes were closed, as his caresses grew more explicit beneath her skirts, as his long, elegant, too-knowing fingers slipped between her thighs and stroked—and she quivered—she felt the touch of his gaze, burning and hot, searing over her face, then falling to her heaving breasts.

Then he took the peak of one breast into his mouth again, and suckled—more fiercely. She cried out, a short, sharp gasp of pleasure; head back, spine tight, she tried desperately to fill her lungs—failed as she felt his fingers slide through the slickness between her thighs, and slowly, inexorably, penetrate her body.

He eased one finger deep inside her, then stroked. Withdrew to caress again, to touch again, to cup again, then penetrate and stroke once more.

She gasped as sensation blossomed anew, on a wholly different plane. One where the heat expanded, yearning growing within it, tangled and twined, desire and passion seamlessly melding, the flames of one and the heat of the other building to a conflagration.

One he orchestrated.

He gave her just so much, stoking the fires high, only to ease her back from combustion. From the point beyond which she knew she would simply be consumed and die.

Again and again, he took her to the edge; each time the surge of heat increased and battered at her senses. At her mind.

At her will.

Forcing open her eyes, from beneath her heavy lids she glanced down—at him as he suckled at her breast. What she saw in his face was so stark, it shook her mind free for one brief moment of lucidity— to wonder if she knew what she was doing, if she truly understood what she'd invited.

That he wanted her, desired her, she had absolutely no doubt, but that he wanted her to desire him, to want him with the same raw urgency that she sensed building within him, was a revelation.

She suddenly understood the purpose behind his repetitive stimulation, each time taking her senses to new heights, opening her desires to new depths of need.

On the thought, his hand shifted between her thighs and he pressed, worked a second finger in alongside the first, stretching her—blatantly readying her.

She gasped, clung, eyes again shut tight as the world as she knew it grew brighter, tighter, edged by light—but then he drew his fingers from her.

Leaving her with the strangest sensation of hanging in midair.

Before she could return to reality and protest, his hands and mouth left her entirely, then she felt him bunching up her gown.

"Time to get this off."

His voice was so gravelly it took a moment for her to make out the words. She wasn't much help; it was all she could do to follow directions and let him draw the gown off over her head.

He swiftly undid the ties of her petticoats, then they followed her gown—disappearing somewhere off the bed, flung into darkness.

Leaving her on her knees, straddling his waist, clad only in the insubstantial film of her chemise.

The golden light of the candles washed over her; looking, ravenously drinking in every curve, every quintessentially feminine line, Barnaby set his jaw against the urge to rip the delicate material from her.

He wanted—*burned* with a want beyond anything he'd ever known. If he didn't have her soon . . . but she was a virgin; he had to go slowly. Gently. Even if slow and gentle were no longer in his repertoire, not, apparently, when it came to her.

Greedy, rapacious, primitive need clawed his gut, filled his veins.

It was all he could do to, with one hand, reach out and grasp the silken tie he'd earlier fingered, and tug—not rip—just enough to unravel the bow.

"This goes, too."

He could barely recognize his voice, it seemed to come from so deep within him. From the self he kept buried, that she drew forth.

Why she called so unerringly to that more primitive side of him he didn't know; he only knew that she did, that he had to somehow cope with that more primal, raw-emotioned male presence that, ever since he'd got his hands on her, had slowly infused his body and brain.

Unexpectedly, her eyes locked with his. Dark, unfathomable, rich, her eyes promised and lured . . . then she shifted upon him, arms crossing, hands reaching for the hem of the chemise . . .

In one fluid movement, she drew it up, over her head, then, her eyes once more locking with his, she flung the garment away.

He felt more than heard a low growl, realized it was reverberating in his throat.

Moving without conscious thought, his hands grasped her waist, gripped.

It took a massive effort but he set his jaw, hauled back on the reins, and halted his headlong rush to completion. Cut off—denied—the impulse to lift her, slip the buttons on his trouser flap, and release his straining erection so he could pull her down and sink it deep between her thighs.

Later, he promised his primitive self.

Without doubt, that primitive self growled.

Seething, it subsided, once again under his control—allowing him to roll them back to where they'd started, with her on her back beneath him.

But this time she was naked.

Gloriously bare.

All of him—his sophisticated self in complete agreement with his more primitive side—rejoiced. Mentally licked his lips.

He bent his head and kissed her, deeply, thoroughly, reacquainting himself with the wonders of her mouth—ensuring on the way that she was acquiescent, unable to argue, even to talk.

Or so it should have been, but when he drew back and lifted his head, his next goal shining like a beacon through the sensual fog wreathing his mind, he realized she was wriggling, tugging . . .

He blinked and focused on her. She saw, and frowned. "Your shirt."

"What about it?"

She nearly glared. "I'm naked—and you're not. I want . . . you to be."

He nearly glared back, but . . . he did want her to want precisely that. Biting off a muttered curse, he rolled off her; it took exactly ten seconds for him to rid himself of his shirt and trousers.

Then he rolled back, and pinned her.

He looked down into her eyes. "Satisfied?"

Her eyes had grown wide. He wasn't sure how much she'd glimpsed, but that look suggested she'd seen enough. "Ah . . ." Her voice nearly failed. She cleared her throat. "I suppose . . ."

The throaty whisper sawed at his control.

"Don't think about it," he growled, and kissed her again. Deeper, more ravenously, letting his more forceful, ruthless instincts free enough to ensure that this time when he lifted his head, she was in no condition to distract him again.

He hadn't counted on her hands. On her touch.

How such small, fragile feminine hands could exert such power over him he had no clue, but from gripping his sides, as he drew back they skated forward, over his chest—and all he could do was close his eyes and shudder.

And wait, suddenly caught on the sharp hook of expectation, as she spread her fingers and explored, pressing through the wiry hairs to trace the muscle bands, tentatively stroking the flat discs of his nipples before sliding lower, pressing over the ridges of his abdomen— as if she were enthralled.

He was in thrall, effortlessly held immobile as she delicately explored—and razed his control. Cindered it, until only a frazzled strand remained; desperate, he cracked open his lids and looked into her face—saw the fascination etched in her expression, the deepening glow in her eyes.

Fascination, enthrallment, sensual capture—they seemed to affect each other in the same way. To the same degree.

Very possibly in the same vein, to the same end, the same consuming, all-encompassing passion.

The realization shredded what little control he had left; as his more primitive instincts slipped past his guard and insidiously wreathed through him, he groaned, surrendered. Lowering his head, he kissed her again.

Voraciously, as his true nature desired.

Hungrily, as if she were his only succor, the only sweetness that would slake his desires.

He plunged into her mouth and took—and she gave. Far from retreating in the face of his too-aggressive engagement, she eagerly met him, ardently fed him, and—unbelievably—urged him on.

When he next raised his head, it was reeling, filled with the scent, the taste, of her.

Lips parted, she was panting when he edged lower in the bed to sample her breasts again. More aggressively, more fiercely. More possessively.

She permitted it, glorying even while fighting to master the sensations he pressed on her—fighting, he knew, for a degree of control he knew better than to let her seize.

When a soft moan escaped her, when her clenched fingers slackened in his curls, he knew he was safe.

He moved lower still, trailing his lips down the center of her body.

His tongue delved into her navel; Penelope gasped and clutched his head again, too rocked by the novel sensation to even think. Forming thoughts—coherent ones—was far beyond her. Her wits were overrun. He'd used sensation to completely overwhelm them.

All she had left to her was feeling. The most glorious panoply of cresting sensations that built and crashed over her, then washed through her in waves.

Delicious, illicit, dangerous perhaps, yet without thought or reservation she gave herself over to all he offered, all he wished; she'd wanted to know and he was teaching her—more than she'd ever dreamed.

He moved lower still, his hard body sliding down between her legs, forcing her knees apart so he could lie comfortably; she accommodated him without thought. Hot, openmouthed kisses punctuated with gentle nips peppered her stomach; she squirmed, the hot ache inside flickering and flaring.

The sensation of his skin sliding against hers was a curious, surprising, distracting delight. Tougher and rougher, dusted with crinkly abrading hair, stretched over flesh and muscle much harder than her own, his skin played against hers, in comparison so soft and delicate, a primal physical manifestation of his maleness and her femaleness—and the elemental contrasts between.

His lips slid to the crease between thigh and torso, refocusing her attention. With the tip of his tongue, he traced inward, a hot line like an arrow leading to . . .

She inwardly frowned. What . . . ?

His "what next" had her swallowing a shriek.

At the second, more intrusive brush of his lips over her curls, she struggled, then tried to grab his shoulders, but his arm across her waist held her back, down—while his other hand grasped one thigh just above the knee and moved it aside . . .

Opening her so he could look at her there.

Sheer shock held her immobile, her gaze locked on his face—on what she could read in the hard, angular planes. What she could see . . . heaven help her.

Then he bent his head, and set his lips to her flesh.

On a breathless gasp, she shrieked his name, tried desperately to twist away, failed, grabbed his head, fingers locking in his hair, felt her entire body jolt as the sensation of him kissing, then licking—and then, oh God, *sucking*—raced like wildfire through her, a roaring conflagration that melted her nerves and left her a molten puddle of need.

Of hunger burning. Under her skin, through her veins, deep in her body.

She lay back on a moan. Eyes closed, she had no choice but to lie there and let him show her what she'd wished to know—to let the sensations ride her, let them fill her mind and overload her senses.

Let him, and them, sweep her away.

To where desire ruled and passion held sway, to where nothing mattered beyond their heat, and the rapacious, ravenous need that flowed in its wake.

His tongue lapped, stroked, his lips caressed, and the heat within her coalesced. With every touch, the fire burned brighter. Tighter. More intense.

Until it became her all, the one thing that in that instant mattered.

A true consuming. A real surrender.

But the fiery tension only grew more intense. Until she couldn't breathe. Until the strands of desire, all fire and heat, wrapped about her so tightly she felt she'd implode.

Then with his tongue he mimicked what he'd earlier done with his finger, a slow, languid penetration and retreat.

And she shattered.

Fractured into a million shards of heat and light and glory.

She gasped, rode the moment—greedily absorbing all she could. But the brightness faded, leaving her dazed, yet strangely empty. Oddly expectant, as if there should be more.

Every muscle in her body felt liquefied, all tension released, yet . . . still she hungered.

Opening her eyes, she looked down at him. He'd lifted his head, and was watching her.

He studied her eyes, then shifted, rising like some powerful god over her.

Raising one hand, she set her palm to his chest, stroked lightly. Even through the gentle touch she could feel the steely tension coiled within him. Feeling entirely too powerful—knowing that tension was because of her, was born of desire for her—she found the strength to arch her brows. "Is that it?"

She knew perfectly well it wasn't.

From under heavy lids, his eyes met hers. He'd set her thighs wide; now he wedged his hips between. She felt the broad head of his erection seek, and find, her entrance; it hovered there, and she quivered.

Bracing his forearms on the pillows, caging her head, he bent his and found her lips—took her mouth in a slow, deep, soul-stealing kiss that once again had her wits whirling, that when he finally lifted his head left her breathless.

From a distance of mere inches, Barnaby met her gaze. "That was the prelude. *This*"—he thrust slowly, powerfully, and steadily, deep into her slick heat—"is the beginning of the main event."

He felt the restriction of her maidenhead, tested it, then withdrew and thrust sharply, more powerfully, breaching the barrier and riding deep into her luscious body.

Shock lanced through her; her features pinched, reflecting pain.

Inwardly cursing, he held still, jaw clenched with the effort to deny his raging impulses—his primitive side that wanted immediately to plunder and ravish unrestrained; despite having been more than ready, she was small—and he wasn't.

Head bowing, muscles bunching and flickering, his breathing harsh in his ears, he fought to give her time to adjust.

She did. In tortuous increments. As if unsure how far she should go, how far it was safe to relax. Her muscles unclenched in stages.

Gritting his teeth, he gave her as long as he could, then looked at her—met her eyes. "You're all right."

Not a question. She blinked up at him, her eyes dark, lustrous pools in the candlelight. Their expression grew briefly distant, as if she were checking the validity of his statement, then she refocused on him. And there was wonder in her eyes. "Yes. You're right." Her lips curved. The last of her panicked tension evaporated.

Tension of a different sort returned to fill the void, and called to him. To every instinct he possessed.

The sudden glow in her eyes, the subtle deepening of her sirenlike smile, the way her hand slid up to cradle his nape, the way she met his gaze—inviting, alluring, a female who sensed her worth—said she knew it, knew the effect she had on him, knew exactly what he wanted to do—and approved. Wholeheartedly.

On a groan, he surrendered to her urging and lowered his lips to hers.

And gave them both what they wanted.

He took her mouth in a soul-deep kiss, anchoring them. Then he withdrew and thrust again, whirling them into a landscape he knew well, one of sensual pleasure. He kept them there with each slow, measured thrust, every deep, forceful penetration.

As when they waltzed, she followed his lead. Her body undulated beneath his, complementing, matching, receiving, taking, giving.

The pleasure swelled, welled, swirled through them as they danced, growing ever hotter, ever more insistent, ever more intense.

He refused to rush, and wonder of wonders she didn't press him to; rather, she matched him, readily rode with him, her curiosity and delight apparent in every gasp, every encouraging murmur, every evocative touch of her fingers on his skin.

Wherever she touched, he burned, but that was nothing—no comparison to—the fiery heat of her sheath. It gripped him, drew him in; scalding and wet, she took him in and plainly gloried in the act.

Beneath him, she writhed; as the tempo inevitably increased, she clutched, nails digging in as she held tight and urged him—drove him—on.

He dragged in a shuddering breath and complied. The sensations that surrounded him, her lush body, her passion, her readily offered desire, colored his familiar landscape more brightly, more intensely, than it had ever been before.

Every movement, every touch, of his body and hers, every exchange seemed more laden with feeling. Tactile sensation, true, yet it carried something deeper, something finer—something other.

Some intangible part of them both. As if on this familiar landscape they'd somehow shifted onto some higher plane and were communing at a more elemental level.

He couldn't think about it, define it, now. His mind was too awash with whatever he was feeling. The intensity alone, the heightened sensations, battered at his mind.

He wouldn't have believed it if he'd been told—that she, an innocent no matter how well read, could so easily and completely and utterly engage with him, with his sensual side, one so very experienced—more, with the primitive passions he normally suppressed, normally kept on a tight leash so he wouldn't shock his partner.

She—patently—saw no purpose in any leash. As their passions rose higher, as locked together, arms banding, hands grasping, they rode the moment wildly, far from falling back from him, she only grew more demanding.

Until he simply surrendered, let the leashes fall, and let them both revel in his—and her—unfettered desire.

She gasped; without direction, she lifted her legs and wrapped them about his hips, and took him deeper. Urged him deeper still.

Until he felt as if he touched the very sun.

On a smothered scream, she shattered.

And took him with her, her contractions calling on his climax, her powerful, unrestrained release unchaining his, setting it—for what in that glorious instant felt like the first time in his life—totally and utterly free.

In the instant he emptied himself into her, he felt like he'd given her his soul.

Uncounted heartbeats later, he cracked open his eyes and looked down—at her, sprawled beneath him, eyes closed, features passion-blank, except for the glorious smile curving her lips.

He felt his own lips curve in similar sated delight. He withdrew and collapsed beside her, reaching for her to hold her close.

As satiation spread its soft wings about them, he prayed that if he had indeed surrendered his soul, she would agree, at some point soon, to reciprocate and surrender hers.

14

If it hadn't been for a feline altercation on a nearby wall, it might have fallen to Mostyn to wake them.

Even as, alerted to the encroaching dawn, Barnaby hurried Penelope—who didn't want to wake up, and wanted even less to leave his bed—to do both, and dress, and let him lead her downstairs, even as he let them both out of the front door and set out to walk her home, some small part of him was disappointed he hadn't learned how his stultifyingly correct gentleman's gentleman would have coped.

The chill of predawn penetrated his greatcoat. His brain growing more alert, he decided it was just as well he'd acted on instinct and got Penelope away; he wasn't at all sure that, had Mostyn encountered her in his bed, his henchman wouldn't have felt moved to write to his, Barnaby's, mother.

And that would definitely not do.

Not because his mother might disapprove; what he feared—to his toes—was that she might decide he needed help and descend to offer hers.

Just the thought was enough to make him shudder.

He glanced at Penelope. Her arm linked with his, she was matching his stride—shortened to accommodate hers—but her thoughts were clearly far away. Despite the remarkable vigor of their coupling, she seemed unaffected, untroubled. Indeed, if she'd had her way they would still be in his bed, exploring further.

She'd actually pouted when he'd insisted they had to leave.

Her lips weren't pouting now. They were relaxed, rosy red, as luscious as ever.

A few paces later, he realized he was staring, fantasizing again. Shaking the salacious images from his head, he faced forward, and focused his thoughts on where they now were, where he wished them to be, and how to get from one point to the other.

Which, as it happened, was also the route to converting his salacious fantasies to realities.

Concentrating wasn't all that hard.

They'd decided against bothering trying to find a hackney; at this hour, it was likely to be just as fast to walk to Mount Street. In the small hours between the end of one day and the start of the next, there were few people on the streets of Mayfair, either on foot or in carriages.

The night was dark, moonless, at least beneath the November clouds. Although all was quiet, the silence wasn't absolute; the sleeping rumble of the huge city at night, a blanket of distant, muffled sounds, enveloped them.

They were both used to such city silence; unperturbed, they walked along, wreathed in the drifting fog, both busy with their thoughts.

He had little idea what she might be pondering, or even if she was truly thinking at all. Regardless, he'd been left in no doubt of her response to the night's developments, which was, in its way, comforting. He didn't have to wonder if she'd enjoyed it, or if she would be interested in continuing their liaison; she'd already made her views on those matters absolutely clear.

Thinking back . . . he recalled where they'd been before she'd appeared on his doorstep. Or at least where *he'd* thought they'd been. He'd thought the next move in their game was his. She, clearly, had been following different rules.

Indeed, now he came to think of it, he didn't know—had no idea—what had prompted her to call on him, let alone in such an eccentric fashion, cosh in hand.

He glanced at her, eyes narrowing as he pieced together what he knew: that she must have come in her brother's town carriage—the plain black carriage that had pulled away just before she'd rushed at him—and instructed the coachman to leave her on the street, Jermyn Street at close to midnight. And the coachman had obeyed.

She was a menace; God only knew what potential dangers might have lurked.

"It occurs to me." He paused until, alerted by the cool steel in his tone, she glanced at him; he caught her eyes. "That your brother clearly fails to exercise sufficient authority, let alone control, over you. Being let out of a carriage in Jermyn Street late at night, rushing up to me wielding a cosh—you had no idea what might have happened. Someone might have seen you, and rushed to my assistance—*I* might have seen you sooner and struck out with my cane." The thought made him feel ill. He scowled at her. "Your brother has no business letting you run amok."

She studied his eyes, then humphed and looked ahead. "Rubbish. My plan worked perfectly well. And as for Luc—he's the very best of brothers. Even if he is sometimes priggish and stupidly overprotective. He's always insisted that we could go our own ways, make our own decisions on how to live our lives. He's allowed us to—even encouraged us to—make our own choices, and because of that you are not allowed to say so much as one word against him."

He eyed the tip of her nose, which had risen significantly higher; he continued to frown. "That's a . . . rather unconventional attitude. I've met Luc. He doesn't seem the sort to be so lenient."

"You mean he's the sort who ought to have locked his four sisters in some tower—or at least confined us to Calverton Chase—to be allowed out only after our weddings?"

"To attend your weddings, but not before. Something along those lines."

She smiled. "I daresay he would have been like that—you're correct in thinking that's more his true nature—but Luc himself was almost forced to marry to rescue the family fortunes years ago. He didn't—he couldn't—so he worked like the devil at finances and rescued us that way, and then Amelia proposed to him and he'd always wanted to marry her, so everything turned out perfectly in the end, but only because he stuck to his guns and did what he felt he should, not what society thought he ought."

Barnaby's frown remained. "Don't you mean he proposed to Amelia?"

"No. She proposed." They walked on a few paces, then she added, breaking into his bemusement, "If you must know, that was where I got the idea of rescuing you on your doorstep in order to end in your bedroom with you, alone. Amelia waylaid Luc one night as he was coming home."

He stared at her. "Did she hit him with a cosh, too?"

She shook her head. "She didn't have to. Luc was five sheets to the wind at the time, after celebrating freeing the family from debt."

"Three sheets."

"What?"

"It's three sheets to the wind." Looking ahead, he paced on. "That's the saying."

"I know. But Luc was definitely five sheets, or so Amelia says. He collapsed at her feet."

Barnaby decided he now knew more than he needed to about Luc and his wife. Yet the man he knew as Viscount Calverton . . . had as sharp and shrewd a brain . . . as his sister. And according to Penelope, who could be trusted to know the truth, Luc had always wanted to marry Amelia. So when Amelia had proposed . . .

Calverton, Barnaby decided, was a lucky dog.

Not having to go down on bended knee and beg, not even metaphorically.

Indeed . . . now he thought of it, having a lady propose marriage had a great deal to recommend it—specifically and importantly because it excused the gentleman involved from having to declare his lovelorn state.

The more he considered that, the more he saw it as a highly significant, indeed strategic, benefit—especially if the lady involved was Penelope.

As they left Berkeley Square and turned into Mount Street, he glanced at her face—serene, confident, the face of a lady who knew what she wanted and, as she'd had demonstrated on several occasions, that night being the most recent, wasn't in the least reluctant to act to satisfy her needs.

Recalling his earlier assessment of where they now were, and where he wanted them to be, as, fingers tightening about her elbow, he turned with her up the Calverton House steps, it seemed that, courtesy of her most recent plan, he'd just discovered the very best way to realize his ultimate goal.

• • •

"Thank you, Mrs. Epps. I'll let my da know." With a smile, Griselda disengaged from the old lady who'd claimed her attention to ask about her widowed father.

Playing his part, Stokes grunted—a universal male "about time" sound—cast Mrs. Epps a frowning nod, and hand locked about Griselda's elbow, hauled her away.

Five paces on, Griselda smiled. "Thank you. I thought I'd never get free."

"So did I." Continuing to frown, Stokes scanned the street along which they were walking. Although the original cobbled width was reasonable, the houses had encroached in myriad ways, deep over-hangs above, enclosed and extended porches at street level; with the crates and boxes piled outside various abodes, the route was now little more than a winding passage. "You're sure it's this way?"

Griselda threw him another of her amused glances. "Yes, I am." Looking ahead, she added, "It's not that long ago that I used to live in the area."

He snorted. "It has to be at least . . . ten years."

Her smile grew. "How tactful of you. It's sixteen. I left at fifteen to start my apprenticeship, but I've visited often enough so I've never completely lost touch—let alone lost my sense of direction."

Stokes humphed; just as well—in the close, winding streets, with the smog above blocking the sun, he was having difficulty knowing which way was which. But he'd finally learned her age—fifteen plus sixteen equaled thirty-one—a few years older than he'd thought her. Which was excellent, given he was thirty-nine.

They were trudging away from the city, Aldgate and Whitechapel at their backs, Stepney ahead of them, in pursuit of one Arnold Hornby. On Friday, after distributing the printed notices among the stallholders of both Petticoat Lane and Brick Lane, they'd "visited" the addresses they'd been given for Slater, then Watts, in each case watching long enough to be sure neither man was involved in any-thing illegal.

Stokes had considered interviewing Slater and Watts, but the risk that even if they knew nothing they'd mention the interest the police had in whatever school was currently running, thus indirectly alerting the schoolmaster, who would then shift his school and hide the boys, was too great.

"And," Griselda had said, "we've still got names to chase."

Which was what they were doing today, Saturday—chasing down Arnold Hornby.

They seemed to be trudging awfully far, into increasingly dangerous territory. He glanced at Griselda, but if she was uncomfortable or growing nervous, she gave no sign; even though they were both once more in disguise, in the slums into which they were heading, they were starting to stand out as too well dressed.

But she kept walking confidently on. He strode beside her, at her shoulder, constantly scanning, alert, and growing ever more tense as the potential for danger increased.

He was very aware that had he been alone, he wouldn't have felt anywhere near the same tension.

They reached a fork. Without hesitation, she took the lane on the left, still heading away from London.

"I thought," he grumbled, "that the East End was defined as within hearing of Bow Bells."

She chuckled. "It is—but that depends on how the wind is blowing."

After a moment, she added, "It's not far now. Just beyond that next alley on the left."

He glanced ahead. "The building with the green door?"

She nodded. "And how convenient—there's a tavern directly opposite."

He took her arm and they made for the tavern, barely glancing at the green-doored hovel. Lowering his head, Stokes murmured in Griselda's ear, "We might be able to learn all we need while we eat."

She inclined her head in acknowledgment, and let him steer her inside.

There were three bruisers lurking at a table toward the rear, but otherwise the small tavern was empty. It was nearing midday; presumably others would soon arrive. A table stood before the front window. The wooden shutters had been set wide, giving an unimpeded view of the residence opposite. Griselda headed for that table; Stokes followed.

There were rough chairs; he nearly pulled one out for her but stopped himself in time. She claimed a chair and sat, facing the window. He pulled out the one beside her, angled it half toward her and sat, draping his arm along the back of her chair. It was a gesture that screamed his view of her as his. He glanced at the bruisers in the shadows to make sure they'd got his message. They shifted their gazes away.

Satisfied, he turned to Griselda and the view beyond the window.

She leaned toward him, patted the arm he'd rested on the table, and whispered, "No need to scare the locals."

He met her amused eyes, then humphed and looked across the road. He left his arm where it was.

A wan waitress came out from the rear; barely beyond girlhood, she asked what they wanted. Beyond growling an order for a pint pot of ale, he left the girl to Griselda. Somewhat to his surprise, she didn't angle for information but confined herself to ordering food for them both.

When the girl went off, he turned to Griselda and raised a brow.

She grimaced lightly. "She was looking at my clothes. We may as well eat and give her time to decide we're no threat."

He grunted and looked away. Reflecting that through most of the days they'd spent together, she must have heard more grunts than anything else from him, he cast about, then ventured, "She's right—you don't belong here."

He looked at her.

She inclined her head. After a moment, her gaze on the green door, she said, "I left. I knew if I stayed there was a good chance I'd turn out like her"—with her head she indicated the waitress—"with no real hope of anything better."

"So you worked, and left, and worked still harder to establish yourself outside the East End."

She nodded, lips curving. "And I succeeded. So now"—she glanced at him, met his eyes—"I'm betwixt and between—not of the East End any longer, yet I don't belong anywhere else, either."

He saw beyond her easy smile. "I know how that feels."

She raised her brows, not disbelieving so much as curious. "Do you?"

He held her gaze. "I'm not exactly a gentleman, yet I'm not your average rozzer, either."

She smiled. "I'd noticed." She studied him, then asked, "So where do you hail from? And how did that—being betwixt and between like me—come about?"

He gazed at the green door. "I was born in Colchester. My father was a merchant, my mother a clergyman's daughter. I was an only child, as my mother had been. My grandfather—her father—took an interest in me, and had me educated at the local grammar school."

Looking back, he met Griselda's eyes. "That's where the 'almost a gentleman' part comes from, and that sets me apart from most of those in the force. I'm not one of the higher-ups, but I'm not one of the men, either." He held her gaze. "I'm not a gentleman."

Her expression was serious as she studied his eyes, but then her lips curved; she leaned confidingly closer. "Just as well—I don't know that I'd feel all that comfortable sitting here with a gentleman."

The girl came out bearing a tray with their meal—two bowls of surprisingly appetizing stew and bread, a trifle hard but edible. The aroma of the stew gave Griselda a chance to compliment the girl sincerely. She thawed somewhat, but again Griselda let her go.

Stokes told himself to trust her instincts. He applied himself to his bowl and kept his gaze on the green door.

He and Griselda had finished their meal and were sitting waiting patiently for the waitress to come back when the green door opened and a blowsy brunette in her twenties stepped out. Leaving the door ajar, she strode for the tavern.

Hands on hips, she stopped just inside the door. "Here—Maida! Get me five pints, there's a dear."

Maida, the waitress, ducked her head and disappeared into the rear. She returned minutes later bearing a wooden tray with five brimming pint pots balanced on it.

"Ta." The brunette hefted the tray. "Put it on our tab. Arnold'll be around later to settle."

Maida bobbed her head again. Standing in the doorway wiping her hands on a rag, she watched the brunette cross the narrow street and go in through the green door. It shut behind her.

"A bit of action across the way?" Griselda murmured.

Maida glanced at her, and pulled a face. "You could say that." She looked back at the green door. "Wonder how many they have in there this morning." She glanced back at Griselda. "Johns, I mean."

Griselda's brows rose. "That's the way of it, is it?"

"Aye." Maida settled her weight, disposed to chat. "There's three of them there—girls, that is. Poor old Arnold. I thought, when he said they were his nieces come to stay, he was spinning a yarn, but I've heard them have at him. Reckon they must be related. Poor old codger—if he's getting rent money from them, he'll be lucky. But the girls are doing all right, and they're good enough neighbors, all in all."

"No nephews?" Stokes asked, as if he were merely curious. Discussing all manner of crime was, after all, normal East End gossip.

"Nah." Maida shifted. "Not much of that this way—more the toffs who go fer that sort of thing and we're too far from their playgrounds. Mind you, I'm sure Arnold wouldn't mind having some male in the house to share the load—those girls keep him in there most of the time. He may be old, but he's a hulking sort—good protection. And if he's their uncle, what's he to do? Got him all tied up, those girls have, no mistake."

Griselda frowned, as if remembering. "My old da used to know an Arnold somewhere round here—used to be a bit of a fence, in that game anyway. What was his name?" She stared at Stokes as if searching for inspiration, then her face lit. She looked at Maida. "Ormsby— that was it. Arnold Ormsby."

"Hornby," Maida corrected. "Aye, that's our Arnold. He was in that game, but he ain't in it now. Farthest he gets from his house is in here. Moans about the old days and how he's lost all his contacts and how's a man to get along." She shrugged. "Unless his nieces leave, he's got no hope—they've got first call on his time, seems."

And that, Stokes judged, was all they were likely to get from Maida. He caught Griselda's eye. "We'd better get on."

She nodded. He stood, waited for her to do the same, then dropped a few coins on the table. Turning, he flipped a sixpence at Maida. "Thanks, love. It was good grub."

Moving faster than a hornet, Maida's hand snagged the sixpence out of the air. She grinned and nodded as they passed her. "Aye, well—stop by again sometime."

Griselda smiled and waved.

Stokes caught her arm and steered her determinedly back toward

WHERE THE HEART LEADS223

the city and civilization as he knew it, the words "not in this lifetime" ringing in his mind.

Penelope lurked in Lady Carnegie's drawing room, pretending to listen to the political discussions going on about her. Her ladyship's November dinner was a major event in political circles, one of the last before Parliament rose and most members retreated to their far-flung estates for the winter.

For them, tonight was their chance to rally for the last surge of activity in the houses.

For her, tonight figured as a gilt-edged opportunity to learn more.

Barnaby would have been invited. Quite aside from being his father's son—and the earl had his finger in numerous political pies—his connection with Peel and the police force made him a sought-after source of information for those present tonight; they would far rather question him—one of their own—than any of Peel's official deputies.

Regardless, in this company, she could disappear for a few hours and not be missed, and after the initial round of questioning in the drawing room prior to going in to dinner, Barnaby, too, should be ranked as excusable.

Smiling encouragingly at Lord Molyneaux, who was holding forth on the new reform laws, Penelope went over her plans, and her expectations. Last night had been a good first step in learning of desire, of what hers encompassed, what fueled it, but it was plain that, however enthralling the previous night's endeavors, she'd only scratched the surface.

In the wake of last night, a small host of questions had suggested themselves, popping into her head at odd moments through the day, distracting her. Step by step whipping her curiosity to new heights.

To gain any degree of satisfaction, she was going to have to learn more.

Without being obvious, she scanned the crowd again. And inwardly frowned. If Barnaby had decided not to attend, she would simply have to hunt him down.

She still had her cosh.

As if her mental threat had summoned him, he walked through the open doorway, Lord Nettlefold at his elbow. He paused to greet Lady Carnegie; whatever he said made her ladyship laugh. She patted his cheek, and waved him on. Nettlefold followed, intent on continuing a conversation with Barnaby.

Halting, Barnaby let Nettlefold talk to him while he scanned the room. His blue gaze swept over the various groups—until it reached her, and landed on her face.

She allowed her gaze to meet his for an instant, then she turned to respond to Lord Molyneaux. From the corner of her eye, she saw Barnaby remain where he was, turning to speak with Nettlefold.

Good. Nettlefold was one of the few present of their generation; in the past, he'd shown a diffident but definite tendency to see her presence at such events as declaring her a potentially eligible *parti*. In reality she was there to keep abreast of any legislative maneuverings that might impact on the Foundling House, and also to keep in touch with past and potential donors.

She really didn't want to spend her evening hinting Nettlefold away.

Barnaby apparently agreed with her; only after he and Nettlefold had concluded their conversation and parted did he make his way, in fits and starts via various other groups, to her side.

Eventually he arrived, and took the hand she offered him. A medley of emotions washed over her as his fingers closed on hers; relief of a sort that he was there, that she would indeed be learning more that night, welling expectation over what tonight's lesson would encompass, and a frisson of something more acute, arising from a suprisingly clear tactile memory of his hands on her breasts, on her hips, between her thighs.

She flicked open her fan and plied it. "Good evening, sir."

She waited while he and Lord Molyneaux exchanged greetings. Thankfully, the police force wasn't one of Molyneaux's interests.

Lord Carnegie, their host, came up at that moment, keen to have a word with Molyneaux. With smiles, the four parted; setting her hand on his arm, Barnaby guided Penelope to a spot closer to the wall, out of the immediate circle of the conversing groups.

He met her eyes, read the determination that burned in the dark depths. "We can't slip away yet."

"Of course not." She glanced over the rest of the guests. "After dinner. You know what they're like once the gentlemen are well primed. They won't miss us for at least a few hours."

"Your mother's here?" He hadn't sighted her.

"No. She cried off. She sometimes does."

"So you're here unchaperoned?" He was faintly amazed. He glanced at her, recalling. "And I know perfectly well you're not twenty-eight."

She shrugged, nose elevating. "Your Mostyn is an old woman—adding a few years made it easier to calm him."

He snorted. "He was totally confounded when he learned I'd miraculously recovered enough to take you home."

She shrugged again, signifying it mattered not at all to her. "I'm here as the administrator of the Foundling House, not as Miss Penelope Ashford. That's why the hostesses—most of whom have known me from birth—think nothing of it if I appear without Mama."

He raised his brows, but had to admit that having no one specifically keeping an eye on her would make it considerably easier and safer to slip away from this sort of gathering; it was far less crowded than a ball, and therefore not so easy to believe that members of the company would be lost from sight for any length of time while actually remaining in the drawing room. "After dinner then, once we return to the drawing room."

She was right; the discussions would go on for hours, and would only grow more heated, holding the attention of the company even more avidly than now.

"You haven't heard anything from Stokes, have you?"

His gaze on the company, he shook his head. "No—I would have sent word if I had."

She nodded, then said, "There's a lovely parlor on the other side of the house." She glanced up at him. "While I have no experience from which to judge, I would imagine it to be perfect for . . . consideration of that subject we both wish to explore."

His lips twitched. After a moment, he inclined his head. "Very well. But until then, behave."

"Of course." With a haughty glance at him, she left his side and swanned off to join Mrs. Henderson's group.

He watched her until she'd merged with that circle, then went off to join one of his own, allowing the other men present to pose the questions they wished to ask on the current state of the police force. His father was in town, but attending a cabinet dinner tonight; he would drop by later, but until then, Barnaby was in large measure his surrogate. If he wanted to slip away with Penelope and keep his absence unnoticed, he needed to satisfy all queries first.

While he moved from group to group, applying himself to that task, another part of his mind tried to think ahead, to plan how tonight's engagement should go.

Unfortunately, while his goal—to marry her—was now clear, and his route to achieving that—convincing her that marrying him would have more benefits than risks—obvious, that very route dictated that, in large measure, he had to let her direct their interaction.

He needed her, of her own accord, to reach the conclusion that she had nothing to fear in marrying him, that as her husband he wouldn't curtail her independence, let alone seek to control her. If he was lucky, once she'd made up her mind she would act and propose; that shouldn't be too difficult to arrange. Given she'd instigated their liaison, it seemed only fair that she be the one to bring it to its appropriate end.

To attain that ultimate prize, however, he had to show himself willing to indulge her in allowing her to take the dominant role. Once again, he had to let her lead, and relegate himself to following.

The concept wasn't one that, until her, he'd ever contemplated, and not even his sophisticated self approved of it, much less that more primitive side that, when it came to her, dominated in his mind.

However . . . as they went into dinner, and he found himself seated on the opposite side of the table to her, he realized he was simply going to have to grit his teeth and bear it.

Grit his teeth and remind himself of the ultimate benefits.

The dinner was an extended one, with much conversation during courses, but eventually the last was removed. As was common at such gatherings, the men did not remain at the table but followed the ladies back to the drawing room, where port and brandy were served to lubricate the vocal cords for further discussion.

Shaking his head at a footman offering him brandy, Barnaby made his way to Penelope's side. By the time he reached her, she'd dismissed the gentleman who'd partnered her at the table. As was customary, the lamps had been turned low, allowing shadows to cloak sections of the room; often the discussions held in this later stage were sensitive, and those undertaking them preferred to keep their expressions masked from potential observers.

The shadow Penelope had chosen for her own hid the expectant anticipation glowing in her eyes from all but him.

For which he was grateful. Lady Carnegie was a close friend of his mother's and very far from blind.

Taking Penelope's hand, he set it on his sleeve. "Where's this parlor?"

Penelope gestured to a side door. "We can reach it through there."

He steered her the few paces to the door, concealed by the angle of a minor wall in the irregularly shaped room. Opening the door, he ushered her through, then followed, shutting it behind him.

The corridor was unlit, but enough moonlight seeped in through uncurtained windows to allow them to see. As she led the way down it, Penelope's instincts prodded, increasingly insistent; something wasn't quite right. Wasn't quite believable.

Halfway down the corridor, she halted and turned to face the looming presence at her heels.

Through the soft gloom, she studied his face, confirming, affirming, defining what, exactly, didn't add up.

Studying her face in return, he arched one brow in arrogant query.

Underscoring her instincts' accuracy.

She narrowed her eyes. "You're being far too . . . *amenable* over this. You are not the sort to follow meekly at any lady's heels."

A second ticked by, then he said, "When the lady is heading in the direction I wish to go, there's little point in arguing over who's in the lead."

She frowned. After a moment, she asked, "Does that mean that if I choose to go in a direction you don't wish to, you won't follow?"

The line of his lips subtly altered, more a warning than a smile. "No—it means that if you attempt to go in a direction that has no value, I'll . . . redirect you."

Brows rising, she held his gaze. "*Redirect* me?"

He met her gaze steadily, and made no reply. Leaving her no longer so certain she was, as she'd assumed, in charge of their affair, controlling it by defining when they would meet, and what aspects she was interested in pursuing.

If he *allowed* her to be in charge . . . did that count as being in charge? Especially if he could, at any time, rescind his follower status and take control?

She blinked, no longer so sure where they stood—her or him—in relation to each other.

After a moment more of searching his blue eyes, and gaining no further insight, she waved down the corridor. "And tonight?"

His lips curved a fraction more; graceful yet intent, he inclined his head. "Lead on."

She turned and did, awareness slithering down her spine. Odd. Exciting. She was in charge—he would let her retain control—as long as her direction suited him.

Which left her with the challenge of "suiting him," a challenge she was, at this point, apparently meeting.

Reaching the parlor, she opened the door and walked in. She glanced around, confirming it was as she'd recalled, a square room overlooking the deserted side garden, comfortably furnished with two well-padded sofas angled before the hearth, an armchair, and numerous side tables. A bureau stood against one wall, and a harp occupied one shadowed corner.

No lamp or candle had been left burning; the room hadn't been prepared for guests. But moonlight, soft and pervasive, streamed in, a gentle illumination that, at least to her, seemed more conducive to their purpose.

Halting between the sofas, she turned; he'd paused just inside the door. She spread her arms. "Is this suitable?"

He'd been scanning the room. Now he looked at her. In the silence, she heard the lock on the door click. Leaving the door, he slowly walked toward her. "That depends on what you have in mind."

More. But exactly what, and how . . . she met his eyes as he halted before her. "I'm aware that ladies and gentlemen of our station frequently indulge in encounters at events such as this, in rooms such as this." That was one of the reasons she was keen to try it, to experience whatever illicit thrill was associated with such an encounter. To learn what more it might teach her of desire.

His gaze had lowered to her lips. She wondered if he was imagining kissing her.

Boldly stepping closer, she raised her hands, pressed them to his chest, then slid them slowly up, over his shoulders, moving closer yet so her breasts brushed his chest as she linked her hands at his nape. "I thought . . ."

His gaze was fixed on her lips. His hands rose to grasp her waist, fingers flexing as he gripped, and held her.

Running the tip of her tongue over her lips, she watched his eyes track the movement. Felt deliciously sinful—deliciously sirenlike and in control as she continued, "That perhaps we might play it by ear, so to speak, and see where desire leads us."

His eyes rose, at last, to meet hers. To search them briefly, then his lips curved. "What," he murmured, his breath a warm wash over her lips as he bent his head, "an excellent idea."

She stretched up as he bent; their lips met—she couldn't have said who kissed whom. From the first touch, the engagement was intent, fiery, and entirely mutual, driven by the desire that, somewhat to her surprise, seemed to flare all but instantly, from spark to flame to raging inferno.

Stronger than before, more certain, more powerful, it spread beneath her skin, and left her sensually gasping.

Desire wasn't pleasure but the need for it, not delight but the hunger that craved it.

Within minutes their kiss had become a wanton duel of deliberate incitement—a contest to see who could more deeply, more completely, evoke the other's passions. While he was unquestionably more experienced, she had enthusiasm, eagerness, and the blind faith in her own invincibility that was the hallmark of the innocent.

Mouths melded, lips locked, tongues tangling and claiming, he plundered while she taunted, and the flames between them roared.

Neither won. She wasn't even sure such a concept applied, not in this sort of contest.

Her body was heated, breasts swollen and aching within the restrictive confines of her bodice, long before he stepped back, taking her with him; without breaking the kiss, he sank back and down, onto one of the sofas, lifting her, then setting her on her knees, one on either side of his thighs, so she could lean into him and continue their heated kiss.

While his hands rose and pandered to her needs, swiftly unbuttoning her bodice so it gaped, then with a flick of his long fingers dispensing with her chemise so his hand could make contact with her flushed skin and ease her.

Soothe her, and excite her.

The duality in his touch was plain to her, even through the distracting fire of the kiss. When his fingers found her nipple and traced, then tweaked, she gasped as pleasure radiated through her, but escalating hunger swam in its wake.

For every touch he gave her, she wanted many more. Every brief burst of pleasure, of delight, only deepened her craving.

She reached for the buttons closing his shirt.

He stopped her, his hand closing over hers. He drew back from the kiss, only a bare inch, just enough to inform her, his voice a dark rumble, "No—we have to return to the drawing room. You wanted this type of encounter—you have to play by the rules."

In control, yet not. She licked her swollen lips. "What are these rules?"

"We remain more or less fully clothed."

She blinked. "Can we?"

"Easily."

He proceeded to show her how. How, with her as she was on her knees before him, he could arrange her skirt and petticoats, spreading the back free over his legs, tugging the fronts from beneath her knees, leaving the silk skirt relatively uncrushed, the froth of her petticoats no longer between them—leaving the sensitive inner faces of her thighs riding against the fine wool of his trousers and the steely muscles beneath.

The faint abrading every time they shifted, however slightly, felt unexpectedly erotic.

She'd barely absorbed that when he pushed up the front of her skirts and slid his hands beneath. And touched her.

Sensation stabbed through her, a delicious spike. On a moan, she closed her eyes, felt her spine weaken. He leaned forward and captured her lips, took her mouth in a slow, languorous claiming while beneath her skirts he traced, explored, fondled, and caressed.

Touched and stroked until she burned with a now familiar longing.

His hands were magic, pure magic on her skin. Strong palms intimately sculpted her curves, powerful, too-knowing fingers caressed and stroked, penetrated and retreated, until she was afire, until she thought she'd go mad with wanting.

She didn't have the strength to pull back from the kiss and issue an order. Her hands were locked on his shoulders, gripping in near desperation; easing the grip of one, she slid it to his throat, found his earlobe, and pinched.

He drew back from the kiss. "What?" His voice was a gravelly rumble.

"Now!" She closed her eyes and shuddered as his fingers slid deep and stroked inside her. "Not *that*," she hissed. "You!"

For a moment, she thought she was going to have to drag her lids open and glare, and somehow take matters into her own hands . . . the notion was attractive—very—but courtesy of their position and her already too-fraught state, she doubted she could—certainly not in the sense of giving the moment its due, and properly learning from it.

But thankfully he comprehended that she was beyond being denied. She felt more than heard his irritatingly arrogant chuckle, but as he promptly shifted, one hand going to the buttons of his trousers, she decided to ignore it.

Then the rigid rod of his erection sprang free, effectively claiming her entire attention. He guided the blunt head to her entrance; his hand on her hip tightened, she realized how it would work, and eagerly, enthusiastically—with untold relief—embraced the moment and sank down.

Slowly.

The sensation of him filling her, stetching her, all under her control, flooded her mind. With him only an inch in, she drew a huge breath, and opened her eyes.

She had to see his face, had to watch as, inch by slow inch, she eased him into her body, enclosing him—taking him.

Not being taken.

The difference, she realized, eyes locked on his, her senses and all she was locked on the sensation of their joining, was profound.

Barnaby felt it. To his marrow. He'd never felt the like, not in all his years of similar experiences. He couldn't count the times he'd been in a situation just like this; he'd never been backward in accepting the diversions the bored matrons of the ton had always been so ready to offer him.

But with not one of them had it been like this.

Not one of them had been her.

It was a battle to keep his eyes open, to focus on her face as she slowly, deliberately, took him in, encasing him in a slick, scalding heat that threatened to cinder every civilized instinct he possessed.

There was nothing civilized about the way he felt—the powerful gloating triumph that flooded him, that hardened every muscle and flexed in greedy anticipation.

She. Was. His.

Despite the steady awareness, the intelligence and will that watched him from the depths of her dark eyes, regardless of that, of anything she thought, he saw the moment as an elemental surrender.

A sensual sacrifice.

One in which she pandered to his desires and willingly set herself to sate his hunger.

His potent, unrelenting hunger for her.

It only seemed to grow with every day that passed, had escalated dramatically since the previous night.

She reached the end of her long downward slide, then shifted, pressing lower still to take him all.

Then she smiled.

In the dim light, the gesture was veiled in mystery, a quintessentially female smile. It deepened fractionally; still holding his gaze, she started to rise.

Smothering a groan, he closed his eyes; he understood what she wanted, what she wished . . . he didn't know if he was strong enough to give it to her.

He tried. Tried to lock his body into submission, to stop himself from taking control, so she could ride him as she wished, and experiment.

She rose up and, once again slowly, slid down, exploring as she did, contracting the muscles of her sheath about his hard length, feeling him.

The sensation was more potent than if she'd used her hands.

Eyes shut, he concentrated on not reacting, tried to blot out the barrage of tactile sensations she pressed on him—largely failed. His fingers sank deep, gripping almost desperately, locking about her hips; he'd leave bruises, but he knew without thinking that she would prefer bruises to him taking control. To him denying her the freedom to explore and learn.

But he could only go so far.

Could only endure so much of the delicious torture.

Releasing one of her hips, he cupped her nape and hauled her forward—into a bruising kiss.

She didn't recoil, but met him—every bit as hungry as he.

Not good.

Control—his or hers—became a moot point. A thing of the past, past and forgotten.

Not in all his years, in his countless engagements, had he ever found himself immersed in such heat. Engulfed in such an elemental conflagration. It seared through them both, like a wave reared and crashed, broke through them and swept them away.

Into a raging tide of need, of hungry, desperate yearning. More powerful, so much more needy, greedy, so much more passion-racked that he was lost—as lost as she—equally at its mercy.

Entirely beyond control.

Lost in the realm of a deeper need, a more fundamental, more primitive hunger.

They both gasped, clung, kissed as if their lives hung in the balance. Joined, their bodies slick beneath her skirts, as if reaching the promised paradise was an absolute requirement for continued existence.

And then they were there.

She shattered with a cry, muted by their kiss; in reply, release swept him, fracturing and scattering his wits, cracking his awareness, leaving it open. Receptive.

To the powerful surge of feeling that came in release's wake.

That filled him, gilding satiation in a way he'd never before felt.

Burgeoning to fill his chest as, replete, a small delighted smile curving her lips, she collapsed against him, into his arms, and he closed them about her.

Untold minutes later, he sat cradling her in his arms, one hand stroking her nape and back, soothing not just her, but himself.

The warm weight of her slumped around him, her sheath a hot glove about his semiturgid erection, he wanted nothing more in that moment but to hold her, and feel complete.

Feel, for the first time in his life, what completeness could be.

It wasn't simply a physical sensation. Admittedly his palate had grown jaded with the years, making her innocent delight an intoxicating elixir, yet the joy and untainted pleasure they shared seemed somehow finer, more refined, a culminating experience he'd been unknowingly searching for all his life.

She was what he'd been searching for all his adult life.

His arms tightened about her; having found her, he had no intention of ever letting her go. On that, both his sophisticated self and his more primitive nature were in complete accord.

Leaning his jaw against the sleek silk of her hair, he breathed in—the musk of their lovemaking was overlaid by a scent that was purely her, a fragrance of lilacs and rose, of soft female and indomitable will. How willpower could have a scent he didn't know, but to him it definitely had a place in the bouquet that was her.

She stirred, still loose-limbed, relaxed to her toes. He dropped a gentle kiss on her hair. "We have time. No rush."

She humphed, and slumped again. "Good."

The word, almost purred, conveyed pleasured content beyond description. He smiled, more than pleased to hear that in her tone. To know it was there because of what they'd shared.

At long last he understood, fully and completely, why his friends—Gerrard Debbington, Dillon Caxton, and Charlie Morwellan—had all changed their minds about marriage. At one time, albeit for widely differing reasons, the four of them had been firmly set against the wedded state. Yet with the right lady, as each of the other three had found, marriage—to have and to hold from that day forth, forevermore—was for them the true path, their real destinies.

Penelope Ashford was the right lady for him. She was his destiny.

That had, to him, been proved beyond doubt. He'd been feeling restless, dissatisfied with his lot; since she'd walked into his life, restlessness and dissatisfaction had been banished. She was the missing piece in the jigsaw of his life; with her in place, his life would form a cohesive whole.

He no longer even contemplated a life without her; that was not in the cards. So . . .

The best, possibly the only, way to ensure she agreed to wed him was to subtly lead her to decide, of her own will, that being his wife was her destiny. That decision had to be freely reached; he might encourage, demonstrate the benefits, persuade—but he couldn't push. Even less could he dictate. And as the evening's endeavors had illustrated, allowing her to pursue her own route to that decision meant letting her follow her own script.

Unfortunately—as she'd just demonstrated—her script might require actions, even sacrifices, on his part that were more than he was accustomed to, more than he felt all that comfortable making. Letting her take him rather than the other way about had shaken him; it had required more strength than he'd known he possessed to even indulge her as far as he had.

If he wanted to be able to let her follow her own road . . . he was going to have to limit the byways.

Or, perhaps, to subtly suggest avenues she might wish to explore—ones that left him in control.

Eyes narrowing, gaze unfocused, he considered. Under her skirts, his hands cupped her naked bottom, porcelain curves he'd glimpsed the night before but hadn't had time to visually savor.

He could easily envision an interlude that pandered to that and associated whims.

Perhaps, with her, what he needed to do was not minimize his control, but rather make her crave it, desire and invite it, by casting that as a natural part of the game—as indeed it was.

Curiosity, after all, was her major motivation.

All he had to do was interest her in the right things.

15

'Ere, 'Orace? You seen this?"

Grimsby came shuffling from the back of his shop, blinking owlishly at Booth, a jack-of-all-trades who occasionally brought him knickknacks to sell. "What?"

Booth set a printed notice on the counter. "This. Saw it in the market yesterday—lots being passed around. 'Eard about it, too, in the pub last night." Booth stared hard at Grimsby. "Thought you'd want to know."

Frowning, Grimsby picked up the notice. As he read, he felt the color drain from his face. When he saw the announcement of a reward, his hand shook; he quickly set the notice back down.

Booth had been watching him closely. "Just thought I'd tip you the wink, 'Orace. We go back a long ways—old friends need to look out for each other, right?"

Grimsby forced himself to nod. "Aye, Booth—that we do. Thank ye fer this. I don't know nothing about it, o'course."

Booth grinned. "No more'n I do, 'Orace." He saluted Grimsby. "I'll be seeing you around, then. Bye."

Grimsby nodded in farewell, but his mind was elsewhere. While Booth made his way out of the shop, he picked up the notice and read it again.

Then, "*Wally!*"

The roar brought Wally thumping down the stairs. He scanned the shop, then looked at Grimsby. "What's up, boss?"

"This." With one grimy fingernail, Grimsby poked the notice across the counter. His tone was disgusted. "Who'd 've thought hoity-toity Scotland bloody Yard would take an interest in East End brats!" Leaving Wally perusing the notice, he stomped around the counter. "It ain't right, I tell you."

Which was the point that exercised him the most. In Grimsby's experience, such unnatural occurrences, things that stepped beyond the normal order of life, never boded well.

Wally straightened. "I . . . er, did hear a few whispers at the tavern last night—didn't know it was about this, but I heard people were asking around after boys."

Wally's diffident tone and his avoidance of Grimsby's eye didn't escape Grimsby. With a snarl, he caught Wally's ear and cruelly twisted. "What else did you hear?"

Wally hopped and wriggled. "Ow!"

Grimsby twisted a little more and leaned closer. "Were they, by any chance, asking who might be running a burglary school hereabouts?"

Wally's silence was answer enough.

Grimsby lowered his voice. "Did anyone say anything?"

Wally tried to shake his head and winced painfully. "No! No one was saying anything at all. They was just wondering about the people asking, and why, is all."

Grimsby pulled a face; he let Wally go. "Get back to the boys."

With a careful glance at him, Wally turned and went, rubbing his abused ear.

Returning to the counter, Grimsby stood looking down at the notice. The names and descriptions didn't worry him; the boys hadn't left the house, and now wouldn't, except at night. And all urchins looked the same in the dark.

It was the reward that bothered him. No one had said anything *yet,* but someone, sometime, somewhere, would. There were those in the neighborhood who would sell their mother for the whiff of a solid coin.

He read the announcement again, and drew a little comfort from the reward being specifically for information about the boys, not about any burglary school. As the boys hadn't been seen, not even by his nearest neighbors, he wasn't, he felt, staring at the prospect of being fingered by the locals just yet.

But the boys needed to be out on the streets for the latter part of their training. Normally, Wally would have first taken them out during the day to wander around Mayfair, growing accustomed to the layout of the wider streets, learning about possible places to hide, like basement areas and the steps leading to them. Such spots didn't exist in the East End; good burglar's boys needed to know the lay of the land they worked.

Now all that part of their training would have to be done at night, and Wally would be no use for that. Smythe would have to do it all. And even then . . .

No matter how set on his plan he was, Grimsby couldn't imagine Alert would want to risk the whole thing blowing up in his face.

Yet by his reckoning, they were only a week or so away from concluding their business. Despite the pricking of his thumbs, Grimsby felt reluctant to pull back—especially not with Alert holding a sword over his head.

And there was Smythe to consider, too.

Grimsby glanced again at the notice. Had he been acting on his own, he'd turn the boys out, let them find their way home, and wash his hands of the whole business. He was too old for prison, let alone transportation.

But Alert would be a problem. He was a toff, and arrogant with it.

Smythe, on the other hand, knew the ropes.

That afternoon, Penelope lolled in Barnaby's big bed, and couldn't remember ever being so content. So at peace.

Outside the windows, the gray November afternoon was quiet, dull and subdued. It was Sunday; there was little activity on the streets, a nippy breeze carrying the scent of winter keeping even the more hardy within doors.

The room was cozy, warmed by the fire burning cheerily in the hearth opposite the end of the bed. Slumped on the pillows, she snuggled under the covers, warmed to her bones and similarly relaxed, all of which owed little to the fire. The bed curtains had been loosened; although only partially drawn, they created a sense of enclosure, transforming the bed with its deep, cushioning mattress and numerous soft pillows into a cave of secret pleasures and illicit delight.

It was the pleasures and delight that had melted her bones.

After an early luncheon she'd told her mother she was going to deal with Foundling House business, then had taken a hackney to Jermyn Street. While they'd been readjusting their clothes in Lady Carnegie's parlor the previous night, Barnaby had mentioned that Mostyn had Sunday afternoons off. Barnaby had therefore opened the door to her knock—ready to welcome her, and entertain her.

Thoroughly.

"Here."

She turned to see him standing by the bed—gloriously naked— offering her a glass of sherry. Smiling in transparent appreciation, she freed one arm and reached for the glass. "Thank you." She could do with the restorative; it was early yet and, as she'd learned the previous evening—and had had confirmed over the last hour—she still had a great deal to learn.

To experience and absorb, not least about herself—how she reacted to his patently expert lovemaking and, more important, why.

She'd had no idea the activity would prove so enthralling. So engrossing. So demanding not just physically but in ways she didn't fully comprehend.

Certainly there was more than physical communion involved.

And that only intrigued her all the more.

She sipped, from beneath lowered lashes watched as, after checking the state of the fire, he prowled back to the bed.

Picking up his glass from the bedside table, he lifted the covers and climbed in beside her. His weight bowed the bed; the nearness of his hard body, always so warm, the promise inherent in his naked presence beside her, no barriers of any sort between, sent tendrils of anticipation snaking through her.

Now that she had a much better idea of what that promise entailed, the anticipation had only grown sharper and sweeter. She sipped, and savored.

Closing her eyes, she mentally stretched, reached, assessed. Her body thrummed gently, all but purring; her mind was an unusually calm sea. She truly couldn't recall any time in her life she'd felt so completely satisfied in the moment, so truly content. Even though frustration over their lack of progress in finding her missing boys irked and worried her, in this moment the frustration and worry were distant. Beyond the bed curtains, outside this room.

Within this room, within the private confines of his bed, she'd experienced not just pleasure and delight, but in their wake a deeper, more powerful sense of peace.

Beside her, Barnaby sank against the pillows, sipped his wine, and eyed her profile. She was thinking; he couldn't guess the subject, although judging from her serene expression it wasn't their case. They'd dealt with what little there was to discuss concerning the investigation before he'd got her up the stairs. With no news, no progress, no possible useful activity to occupy them, she'd been gratifyingly eager to fall in with his plans for their mutual distraction.

With his latest, more subtle direction in mind, he'd allowed his natural, dominant side to show—not completely, just enough to intrigue and challenge her; after an initial moment of surprise, he'd been rewarded with her complete and utter attention.

Exactly as he'd hoped, her curiosity had stirred.

He'd waltzed her into the room, kicked the door shut, then proceeded to waltz her to the bed, stripping her as they went.

She'd responded with gratifying eagerness, although at one point her insistence on divesting him of his shirt had caused a moment of confusion—at least for him. He hadn't expected her to filch the reins back, but she had. Even though he'd retrieved them again, later she'd wanted them back; passing control back and forth—sharing it, switching from leading to following and then back again—wasn't what he was used to, but he'd managed to adjust.

By the time he'd had her spread naked across his bed, all he'd been able to think about was sinking his by-then throbbing staff into her luscious body. As she'd been similarly urgent and insistent, wantonly writhing, seductively beckoning, he'd done just that, setting aside his wish to spend considerably longer exploring her naked curves.

In daylight. At length.

He glanced at her, sipped, and promised himself he would. Soon.

All in all, he'd judged her correctly: knowledge was indeed her price. In this sphere, it was a currency in which, compared to her, he had bottomless coffers.

Unsurprisingly, she was more adventurous than the norm. Ladies of the ton tended to invite, instigate, and then acquiesce; she did the first two, but not the third—she actively engaged, expected to contribute if not equally then nevertheless definitely to the outcome, to defining the landscape through which their passions took them, and at what rate and by what route they scaled the peak.

She was keen, applied herself to the task, and was steadily learning.

And while he preferred to remain firmly in charge, he was starting to suspect that he might enjoy at least some of the benefits of occasionally sharing the reins.

Sipping the crisp amontillado, he shifted his gaze to the fire, evaluating where on his path to a wedding they now were.

A step or two further along than they had been last night.

It was, perhaps, time to seed a few more notions into her receptive and fertile mind.

Draining his glass, he reached out and set it on the bedside table, then turned to her, stretching out beside her.

Her lids cracked open; he caught the glint of her dark eyes beneath the lush curve of her lashes.

Picking up her hand from where it lay on the covers, he lifted her fingers to his lips and kissed—then drew her arm up and placed her hand on the pillows above her head.

He had her complete attention, but didn't meet her eyes. Sliding his arm beneath the covers, he set his fingers to one side of her throat, lightly tracing the curve from just beneath her ear to her collarbone.

She tensed fractionally, watching. He raised his hand to repeat the caress, easing back the covers as he did, then he leaned in and set his lips to trace the same line, and her breath shivered.

He shifted and repeated the caress on her other side; she tilted her head to give him better access, lips lightly curving as she sighed.

Moving on, he subjected her shoulders to the same exploring touch, first with his fingers, then with his lips and tongue.

The covers had dropped to lie just above her breasts. Sliding his hand beneath the edge, he closed it about one breast. He didn't try to hide his possessiveness, simply closed his fingers about the firm mound and claimed. Then he set his fingers stroking, circling the tightening nipple until it was taut, then catching and rolling it between finger and thumb.

Her breathing broke, fractured.

Leaning closer, with the back of his hand he nudged the covers aside so he could examine the flesh he was fondling. View it, study it; then he bent his head and slowly licked.

She sucked in a breath.

He settled to taste her—to fill his senses with the arousing taste of her after he'd already had her once. Twice would come, but only after he'd had his fill and satisfied his craving to explore every fascinating inch of her.

With his eyes, his tongue, his hands.

A subtle branding that she would allow because she'd never experienced it before. A branding he fully intended to deepen and reinforce the sensual link between them, making her even more unquestionably his in her mind as well as his own.

Her skin was impossibly white and fine. When cool, it felt like the most delicate alabaster, smooth yet warming to the touch; flushed as it now was, her breasts swollen and peaked, the evidence of his claiming apparent, it felt like peach silk.

Satisfied he'd adequately explored one breast, he edged the covers lower and moved on to the other. She trembled as he took possession— interesting considering how intimate they'd already been. When, after a thorough study, he suckled her fiercely, she gasped, spine bowing, her head pressing back into the pillows.

The hand holding the sherry glass wavered; reaching up, he slipped the stem from her weakening grasp; reaching farther, he set the glass down on the bedside table. The click of the base on the wood echoed in the room, an unequivocal statement of intent.

One Penelope heard. As he drew back from her breast, she reached for him. To her surprise he caught her hand; without shifting his gaze from her flushed and swollen breasts, he drew her hand up over her head, setting it alongside the other in the pillows.

"Leave them there." His voice was a raspy growl, deep and dictatorial. "Just lie back and let me . . . worship you."

She hesitated, studying his face, trying to determine what it was she saw there—something harder, more powerful than she'd yet encountered. Curious, she acquiesced. And tried—unsuccessfully—to cling to her earlier calm as he—with a species of deliberation that was peculiarly exciting—continued his study of her, of her body and how she responded to his caresses.

When a particularly artful drift of his fingertips down her belly made her quiver, he murmured, "You like that."

She didn't bother to nod. He didn't even check for her answer—his words had been a statement of fact. Being passive for any length of time felt strange, yet in this case . . . worship, he'd said, and in a curious way there was reverence involved, even if he could have said "take you," or "claim you," and been equally accurate.

The way he interacted with her fascinated and intrigued her.

He worked his way steadily down her body. Initially he would reach beneath the bedclothes to caress and fondle, then he would push the covers down, revealing the area on which he was presently concentrating to his gaze. He would study, examine, assess—then he would lower his head and taste.

The covers fell progressively lower, exposing more and more of her to his detailed examination. He didn't ask permission, not even wordlessly, just continued his exploration as if he had an unquestioned right.

As if she'd ceded it to him.

Had she?

She honestly wasn't sure—and was even less sure that she cared.

His hands . . . she'd earlier labeled his touch magic. Closing her eyes as beneath the covers one hard palm swept down over her hip, she struggled against a shiver. She wasn't cold—in the aftermath of his attentions, her flesh glowed—but the drift of sensations his fingers sent spreading beneath her skin was exquisite, sliding over her nerves, leaving them sensitized and eager—so eager—for more.

To feel more.

It was a type of tactile stimulation she'd never experienced before, one that seemed to open her pores to absorbing so much more, to heightening her senses so that his next touch, however light, registered as so much more.

So much more laden with feeling, with meaning. With intent.

She drank it all in as beneath the covers his hand moved down and his fingers flirted teasingly with the curls at the apex of her thighs.

A moment later, his fingers slid lower still, and pressed between her thighs to stroke, fondle, caress.

Eventually the covers slid to her knees.

What followed was rather more than she'd bargained for—more intense, progressively more intimate—but she was unable to call a halt, not even demand a pause to catch her breath ... because she didn't have breath left to do so, not once her tightening lungs had seized.

As they did when, the covers long gone, he parted her thighs, setting her legs well apart so he could, as he had everywhere else, examine her, then with his fingers explore, stroking, caressing—noting in a gravelly rumble what she liked, distracting her with the sound, then focusing her mind with his words—just as he demonstrated again.

She was long beyond protesting when he bent his head to sample her. To taste her, to lick and lightly suckle, until she was wild.

Until, writhing and heated, she sobbed and begged. And this time, she knew what for.

Like an emperor granting a slave her wish, he gave it to her, his wicked tongue sending her soaring over that bright edge and into pleasured oblivion.

An oblivion more pleasured, more deeply sated, than she'd previously known. She sank beneath the wave of satiation, welcomed it, and let it wash through her.

Barnaby watched her face—watched as her climax washed through her and wiped all her tension away. With a sigh she let go, sank back against the pillows, her tensed muscles unraveling, her expression relaxed, her features blank, except for her lips, which, as he watched, lightly curved.

Inwardly smiling, he drew back onto his knees, grasped her hips, and turned her over.

She flopped over readily, slumping on her stomach, settling her cheek on the pillow. Lips curving in anticipation, he eased her feet apart, and knelt between.

He started with her ankles, lifting each to explore, caress, then nibble. He didn't touch her soles in case she was ticklish; the last thing he wished at this point was to jerk her to full awareness too fast.

The swell of her calves, the backs of her knees, the long upward sweep of her thighs, he paid dutiful homage to all, and she sighed and let him.

Let him trace the globes of her bottom, kiss and lick his way over their swell and the indentations at the base of her spine. He spread his fingers across the back of her waist, then ran his hands upward, with his lips and tongue tracing the line of her spine, pausing to examine her shoulder blades, until eventually he reached her nape.

Pressing aside the hair he'd earlier released, he touched, caressed, then set his lips to the sensitive skin, and lowered his body to hers.

Covering her.

He nipped, then set his teeth to the tendon at the side of her throat as he pressed his hands into the mattress, sliding them beneath her so he could fill them with her breasts. Closing his hands, he kneaded, then found her nipples and tweaked.

His erection, hot and as hard as iron, rested, throbbing, between the globes of her luscious bottom. From the tension that had flooded her, infusing her limbs as he released her right breast and reached down to lift her right leg, grasping her knee, drawing it up and wide, opening her to him, she'd guessed what he intended even though he doubted she knew exactly how—he could imagine her brain buzzing with questions, ones she thankfully had neither breath nor time to pose.

He made sure of the latter, releasing her knee, drawing back and reaching between them to position the blunt head of his erection at her entrance. Immediately he eased into her—just a little, just enough to answer her first questions.

Shifting so that his weight was more on one arm and he was no longer squashing her into the bed, he returned his hand to its position at her breast, claiming it anew. His weight kept her pinned, kept her other breast pressed to his other palm. Lowering his head, he caught her earlobe and nipped, then pressed his lips to the sensitive skin beneath as he flexed his spine—and slowly, deliberately slowly, savoring every inch, sank into her.

Beneath him she shuddered. Her eyes were closed; concentration had claimed her features.

He pushed deeper, feeling her body give and let him in, then embrace him. She closed around him tightly, wrapping his erection in slick, scalding heat.

His breath tangled in his lungs, strangled in his throat.

Then she moved beneath him, pressing back, instinctively seeking more. Opening a fraction more for him.

He seized the invitation and thrust deep, hard, and heard her whimper—not in pain but in pleasure. The sound slid through him, sank in and set its claws, fraying his reins so he had to stop and close his eyes and hold his breath, until he had some measure of control again.

When he did, he slowly withdrew, then thrust powerfully in again.

Again she caught her breath on a sob.

His lips cruising just beneath her ear, he murmured, "You like that, too."

Her only answer was a tiny but blatantly demanding wriggle of her bottom.

He laughed, a short guttural sound, and obliged. Drawing back again, he settled to ride her—slowly, each thrust measured both for power and depth, exquisitely tuned to enhance her pleasure. She writhed and begged, tried to urge him to go faster; he didn't listen, just adhered to his plan, all the time wielding an absolute control he knew better than to let her weaken.

He would much rather have had her on her knees before him, naked, her lush derriere pressed to his groin as he thrust into her welcoming heat, but that, he'd realized, would be going too fast.

She might well have welcomed the novel position, and he was starting to suspect she was unlikely to be shocked—not to the point of retreating—no matter how forcefully he took her, but he had to remember his purpose, his plan. He couldn't answer her questions all at once; he had to leave the heavier-gauge ammunition in his locker, at least for now.

Just as well—God only knew what she might provoke if she tried to take the reins from him in any more dominant position. Even now, although he had her trapped and more or less at his mercy, she fought him for control, squirming beneath him, and when that didn't work, using the muscles of her sheath to distract and control him.

He gritted his teeth and increased the pace, using his weight to subdue her and thrusting deep, kneading her breasts as he did—until she climaxed on a scream—the first he'd wrung from her.

The sound snapped his reins; on a groan he buried himself to the hilt within her, again and again, until release poured through him on a searing tide, and swept him, his conscious mind, before it, flooding him with bone deep pleasure as he let go and pumped his seed into her.

Racked, shattered, he collapsed on top of her, too weak, too exhausted, too sated to move.

As soon as he could summon the requisite strength, he rolled to the side, holding her to him, resettling her against him, her back to his chest.

His hands now loose about her breasts, he could track the swell of her ribs as she fought to regain her breath.

After a moment, she lifted one arm, reached back, and ran her hand down his flank, a gentle, patting, stroking motion that testified to her thoughts—her thanks.

He nuzzled her nape in response, his own form of wordless thanks.

But as soon as he'd caught his breath, he murmured, "So that's what you could enjoy whenever the mood strikes you."

Her answering chuckle was the definition of sultry. "Whenever? Surely I'd need you to achieve the desired result."

"True." That was precisely what he wanted her to realize. Lifting his head, he set his lips to her ear. "But as I'm here . . ."

With one hand he resumed fondling her breast, while he skated the other down, splaying it across her lower belly and pressing lightly as he moved suggestively behind her—reminding her that he was still inside her. Recalling the pleasure she'd derived from that.

As if she needed reminding. Suppressing an altogether unnecessary shudder—he patently didn't need further encouraging—Penelope was finding it hard to believe that she'd lived so long without comprehending that pleasure this deep, this warm and satisfying, existed. That with the right male, she could indulge to this extent, to where glory seemed to sing through her veins. That the simple joy of intimacy could be so intense.

With the right male; presumably that was why she'd never before felt inclined to explore in this direction. Barnaby Adair was different— to her, different in so many ways. She didn't think him weak or unintelligent, not even less intelligent than herself—and she felt a secret thrill at his size relative to her. He was so much bigger, hard, stronger, yet they seemed to fit together, not just intimately but in other ways, too; she'd grown used to having him, a wall of masculinity, hovering at her shoulder.

Which was quite a turnaround, given her usual reaction to large hovering males.

"It's rather remarkable, when you consider it"—his voice, relaxed and deep, floated past her ear; she sensed he was speaking as much to himself as to her—"that we deal so well together." His fingers drifted across her breast. "Not just in bed but beyond it—in society, and even through our investigations."

He paused, then went on, his tone pondering, "I actually enjoy talking with you—and that, I have to confess, isn't the norm. Your mind doesn't revolve about fashions, or weddings, or babies—not that I imagine you never think of those things, but you don't feel compelled to discuss such matters with me, and instead have other ideas, other concerns, ones I can share."

Penelope stared unseeing across the room, conscious not just of the warmth of his body cradling hers, of his hand idly stroking her breast, but of that other warmth that dervied from shared thoughts, shared endeavors.

"You're not, thank heaven, shocked by my work." He paused, then went on, "Then again, I'm not shocked by yours."

She chuckled, then said, "We do seem to be rather complementary."

He shifted behind her, reminding her of that. "As you say."

She laughed at his dry tone, but her thoughts—driven by his— claimed her. They did seem to have a natural meeting of minds, one she—and it seemed he, too—had found with no other. They were from the same select social circle, one whose strictures neither he nor she felt overly bound by, yet that similar background made it easier for them to understand each other, how the other would react in any situation.

A slow swell of warm pleasure rolled up and through her, and she realized he was moving, very gently, within her. Realized he'd got his second wind, so to speak.

She glanced at the window; even though it appeared fuzzy, the light had faded even more. Ignoring the passion already wreathing through her, she forced herself to say, "I have to leave. We don't have time."

Her disappointment colored her tone.

In response, his hands tightened, holding her in place; he withdrew, but then thrust more forcefully in again, surprising a shivering gasp from her.

"We have time." He withdrew and thrust again, hands gripping more definitely, anchoring her before him. "And *then* you can leave."

A lick of delight slid up her spine. Her lips curved, but she forced out a sigh. "If you insist."

He did, delighting her thoroughly once again before he allowed her up, allowed her to dress, then escorted her home to Mount Street.

Smythe appeared in Grimsby's rooms late on Sunday night. Grimsby looked up—and Smythe was there, filling the doorway to his private chamber.

"Gawd almighty!" Trapped in his ancient armchair, Grimsby clapped a hand to his heart. "Give a bloke some warning, or you'll likely be the death of me."

Smythe's lips twitched; walking in, he snagged an old straight-backed chair, swung it around so the back was facing Grimsby, then sat. "So—what's the problem?"

Grimsby pulled a face. He'd left a message at the Prince's Dog tavern, the only known way to contact Smythe. He had no idea when Smythe would get the message, much less when he would comply. "We've a spot of bother." Shifting to reach into the pocket of his old coat, Grimsby hauled out the printed notice and handed it to Smythe. "Rozzers have got the word out."

Smythe took the notice and read it. When he reached the announcement of the reward, his brows rose.

Grimsby nodded. "Aye—I didn't like that part, either." He went on to relate how he'd learned of the notice, and what Wally had told him. "So it's too dangerous to take the boys out to train, leastways not during the day. I'm not about to ask Wally to do it—last thing we need is the rozzers catching him with two of them, and then coming around here and nabbing the lot of them."

Smythe was gazing into the distance. He nodded.

Grimsby waited, eyeing him, unwilling with Smythe to push.

Eventually, Smythe murmured, "You're right. No sense risking the whole, and I've no wish to be caught with the little beggars, either." He refocused on Grimsby. "That said, I'm not inclined to let a prime job like this lapse—and I'll warrant you're not, either, not with Alert's interest in you."

Grimsby scowled. "You got that right. He'll hold me to it no matter what. But with lads only partially trained, you're bound to lose some—well, that's why we have so many to begin with, but still." He nodded at the notice in Smythe's hand. "I'm thinking you should show him that, just so he can't later say he didn't know, or didn't understand what it means, that we can't fully train the boys as expected."

Smythe studied the notice again, then rose. "I'll do that." Tucking the notice into his pocket, he looked at Grimsby. "Who knows? Alert may have some idea—or some way of learning—who set the rozzers onto his game."

Grimsby shrugged; he didn't get up as Smythe walked out. He listened to Smythe's heavy footsteps descend the stairs, then heard the shop door shut.

Blowing out a breath, Grimsby wondered if he'd imagined it—Smythe's unvoiced suggestion that if Alert learned who was stirring up the rozzers, interfering with his game, he would make that person regret it.

Then Grimsby thought of Alert—and decided he wasn't imagining at all.

An hour later, Penelope settled down to sleep. She closed her eyes. She was in her own bed, in her own room in Calverton House in Mount Street, the same room in which she'd fallen asleep for fully half her life. Yet tonight she felt something was missing.

Something warm, hard, and masculine curving along her back.

She sighed. In lieu of his presence, she let her mind drift back over her blissful—bliss-filled—afternoon. Spending the entire afternoon in bed with Barnaby Adair had proved a very satisfying experience.

A horizon-expanding experience; she'd certainly learned more about desire, about how he evoked hers, about how she responded. And how he responded to her.

Lips spontaneously curving, she reflected that she was learning in leaps and bounds. And what she'd learned . . . was starting, to her surprise, to reshape her view of life.

She hadn't anticipated any such thing. Hadn't considered it possible that desire, the pursuit of it, the study of it, would lead to any fundamental rethinking on her part. Her views had been set in stone, immutable—or so she'd thought. Now . . .

Despite the stubborn streak that made it difficult to admit a change of mind, inside, in her mind, she had far fewer reservations over considering changing her stance—considering if her life might be better if she did. After her blissful afternoon, it was difficult not to question whether she'd been overhasty in thinking she didn't, and never would, want some relationship with a man—even a long-term one. She knew she didn't *need* such a relationship to be happy and satisfied with her lot, but the question wasn't whether she needed it, but whether she wanted it. Whether such a relationship might offer benefits sufficient to tempt her to risk it.

Benefits such as the deep-seated contentment that still rode her veins. That was something she'd never felt before, but the glow was so rich, so warming, so addictive, she knew that if the chance offered, she'd opt to keep it in her life.

She didn't entirely understand its source; it was part physical intimacy, part a different level of sharing, part the joy of being close—that closely joined—with another being with a mind so like her own. A male who understood her far better than her own sex ever had.

He understood her wants and needs—understood her desires, both the physical and intellectual, better than she did. And he seemed to truly revel in exploring those desires, his complementary ones, and her body.

All of which contributed to the pleasure he conjured, the pleasure she felt when she lay in his arms.

All of which was so very much greater than she'd ever imagined could be.

Her initial notion of indulging until she learned all, then calmly walking away, no longer fitted.

She had to reevaluate.

To reconsider her plan and change it. But change it to what? That was the bigger question. How far in altering her position should she go—was it safe, in her best interests, to go?

Did she even have a choice—long-term liaison or marriage?

There were numerous long-term liaisons in the ton, but none involved ladies of her age and social standing. Given who she was, and who he was, any attempt at a long-standing affair was going to be seriously messy, at least until she reached an age where society deemed her truly on the shelf. In her case, that would be at least twenty-eight—four years more.

She tried to imagine breaking their liaison and then waiting four years before resuming it . . . the notion was risible, on more than one count.

Which left her with one option. Marrying him.

Considering the prospect, she still couldn't see that marriage per se had anything to recommend it, not to her; the potential risks far outweighed the likely benefits. The reasons for her long-standing rejection remained sound.

However, when she added Barnaby Adair to the scales, the result was far less clear.

Marriage to Barnaby Adair. Could that be her destiny?

For long minutes she stared at the ceiling and tried to imagine, to pose and answer questions, to see how such a marriage might work. They were both considered eccentric already; while a union between them was guaranteed not to conform to the customary pattern, the ton wouldn't expect it to.

Marriage to Barnaby Adair might *possibly* be a union she could live within; being *his* wife would most likely not impinge heavily on her freedoms, as being the wife of any other gentleman would.

Provided, of course, that he was amenable, both in allowing her, once she was his wife, the freedom to be herself, and, of course, in wanting to marry her.

Would he be amenable?

How could she learn if he was?

Many minutes later, when sleep finally crept over her, those questions were still circling, unanswered, in her brain.

16

Late the next night, Smythe once again darkened the French door of the back parlor of the town house in St. John's Wood Terrace.

As before, Alert was waiting in the shadows of the unlit room. He waved Smythe in. "Well?" There was a sharpness in his tone Smythe didn't fail to notice. "What, might I ask, is the purpose of this visit?"

Smythe showed no emotion as he walked closer, all but looming over Alert as he sat, comfortably at ease in the armchair. "This." Pulling a folded sheet from his pocket, he presented it.

Alert let a moment pass, then took the single sheet. Spreading it open, he swung to the fire. Even by the poor light, just a glance was enough to take in the printed characters, and recognize the format. The word "reward" fairly leapt off the page.

Ensuring his face remained devoid of emotion, he assessed his options, then crumpled the sheet and tossed it onto the glowing embers. It caught, flared. In the sudden rosy light, he glanced at Smythe. "Inconvenient, but not of any great import, I would have thought."

A clear warning not to allow it to be of any import slid beneath his smooth tones. Smythe shrugged. "Only insofar as we can't risk training the little beggars by day."

"So train them by night. Is that a problem?"

Smythe grimaced. "Not so easy."

"But it can be done?"

"Aye."

"Then do it that way." Alert paused, his gaze on Smythe's face, then said, "This caper is too important—too lucrative—for us to simply give it up because of a minor threat. I take it you now have all the boys you need?"

"All bar one."

"Get that last one."

Smythe shifted. "We've got seven."

"You told me you need eight to do the job as I wish."

Smythe nodded. "To do that many houses all in one night I'll need eight to be sure. But if we do the same houses over two nights—"

"No." Alert didn't raise his voice, but his tone made the word final. "I told you—I know how the police operate. If we do all in one night, we'll run absolutely no risk—the chances are they won't even know we've been in and out until sometime next year. That's the way it has to be. You need eight boys, then get eight boys. Don't think to do this caper halfheartedly."

He let a moment tick by, then asked, "Will you—or should I say our mutual friend Grimsby—find your last boy, or do I need to rethink our connection?"

Smythe's lip curled. "We'll get the boy."

Alert smiled. "Good. The ton will start fleeing the capital later this week. If there are rumblings developing, we should move earlier rather than later. When can you be ready?"

Smythe considered. "A week, eight days."

Alert nodded a dismissal. "In that case, we'll have nothing to worry about. All will go forward as planned."

Smythe looked at him, then nodded back. "I'll tell Grimsby."

Alert watched Smythe go to the door and slip noiselessly out, shutting it behind him. He continued looking that way, fingers lightly drumming on the chair arm, then he turned his head and looked at the ashes littering the red glow of the embers—all that was left of the notice.

The *printed* notice.

Five minutes ticked past, then Alert smoothly rose, went to the French door and opened it. He stepped through, looked about, then closed the door behind him, slipped a key into the outside lock and turned it. Then he walked away in the opposite direction to the one in which Smythe had gone.

• • •

The following afternoon, Inspector Basil Stokes of Scotland Yard paced back and forth above a shop filled with feminine fripperies. He'd been pacing for what seemed like hours—an eternity; outside the day was waning, the light fading. The girls downstairs had told him their mistress had left that morning, dressed in her "old clothes." For the umpteenth time, Stokes cursed beneath his breath; if she didn't return soon he was going to—

The irritating tinkle of the bell on the front door halted him in his tracks. Scowling, listening even though, after numerous frustrations, he fully expected to hear some female inquire about the right shade of velvet ribbon to match her pelisse, he waited . . . and finally, *finally*, heard the voice he'd been aching to hear.

His relief was real but fleeting, drowned beneath emotions much more powerful.

Scowling ferociously, he stalked to the head of the stairs. He was waiting there, hands on hips, when, after reassuring her apprentices and setting them back to work, Griselda—in her down-at-heels East End disguise—came hurrying up.

Looking up, she saw his face, blinked, and slowed, but then, lips setting firmly, she continued up. "Inspector Stokes—I wasn't expecting you."

"Obviously." Jaw clenched, he fought to keep his voice low. "*Where the devil have you been?*"

Griselda blinked at him, studied him for a fraught moment—and bit back her instinctive reply: that that was none of his damned business. She did not appreciate being browbeaten by a towering, glowering hulk, in her own parlor, no less, but . . .

After a further moment of studying the storm roiling in his gray eyes, she instead—with entirely unfeigned curiosity—inquired, "Why do you want to know?"

He stared at her while the silence stretched . . . it seemed that with her perfectly reasonable question she'd pulled the rug out from under his temper, but then he glared. "Why? *Why?* You go out dressed like that"—he waved at her attire—"alone, and wander about the East End, and then you ask *why* I've been pacing about this damned room for the last hour imagining all manner of ghastly fates befalling you, torturing myself with images of you in the hands of one of our blackguards?"

He paused. Realizing his tirade had been rhetorical—buying himself time—she nodded. "Yes. Exactly. Why have you been doing that?"

He blinked at her. His anger—even the pretense of it—faded from his eyes. "Because . . ." His voice died. He raised one hand; she wasn't even sure he knew he did it. His fingers hovered by her cheek, close, but not touching. As if afraid to touch. Briefly he searched her eyes, as if he might find his answer there, then, failing, he swore softly and moved.

Caught her by the shoulders and hauled her to him, crushed her to him as he covered her lips with his.

She mentally gasped, grabbed his shoulder and clung, her fingers closing tightly in his coat as she hung on for dear life.

It was like being pulled into a whirlpool—of wants and needs, of desire and yearning.

And he called to her, effortlessly drew her until she was kissing him back, until she sank against him and gave him her mouth. And the turbulence within him eased.

Slackened as he controlled it, until instead of walking on the edge of a maelstrom, she found herself waltzing into pleasure.

The simple pleasure of a kiss tinged with something deeper, laced with banked desire, sweetened by caring.

Long minutes later, he lifted his head; he waited until she opened her eyes and met his to say, "*That's* why."

Further words were superfluous.

She blinked, struggling to reorient herself in a world that had canted. "Ah . . ." It was her turn to lose the power of speech. She could feel the heat in her cheeks, knew they'd be rosy.

Slowly, his lips curved—gently, reassuringly. "As you haven't yet slapped me, I take it you aren't . . . averse to my interest."

She blushed even harder, but forced her tongue to work. "No—I'm not . . . averse to any interest you might have."

His distracting smile deepened. "Good."

She wriggled and carefully eased out of his arms; he let her go, but reluctantly.

"Now," he said, once more assuming a stern façade, "if you could answer my initial question?"

Griselda turned and walked to her favorite chair; she sat, frowning, trying to recall.

He sighed and sat in the armchair opposite. "Where the devil have you been?"

"Oh." She brightened. "Yes. I went into the East End. I stopped by to see my father, then looked in on the Bushels—Black Lion Yard is more or less on my way."

"How are they faring, the Bushels? And were the Wills boys there?"

She nodded. "Mary and Horry are well, although Mary is growing a trifle obstreperous over having to stay indoors. Two of the Wills boys were there. They were playing dice and teaching Horry. After that, I went on to visit old Edie, the button lady in Petticoat Lane. She promised to see if she could roust out old Grimsby, but she says he's like a crab—sticks close to home. She hasn't seen him in years, and hasn't been able to find anyone who has."

"So Grimsby remains on our list—the last of the names your father gave us." Stokes grimaced. "Unfortunately, that's no guarantee he's the one who has the boys."

"No." Dejected, Griselda shook her head. "There *must be* some way we can get word of them. Five boys. Surely someone must have seen them, heard them—noticed them."

"Our notices are out there." Stokes understood her frustration. "We'll have to be patient, and see if the promise of a reward shakes loose any useful information."

"Nothing as yet?"

He shook his head. After a moment of broodingly studying her, he shifted forward; reaching out, he took her hands, one in each of his. With his thumbs, he stroked her fingers, but kept his eyes on hers. "I realize you feel safe in the East End, that it's your home, and you need to go back to see your father. But . . ." He paused, lips compressing, but pride wouldn't keep him warm at nights. "Please, when you do go that way, can you tell me first? Or if that's not possible, at least leave a note—of where you're going and when you'll be back?"

He closed his lips on the urge to give more directions, even to order. Hoped, prayed, that she would read the reason behind his request in his eyes.

After a moment she smiled softly, then cast a glance toward the head of the stairs. "I suppose, in the interests of preserving my rug, so you don't wear a track in it, I could do that."

Relief poured through him; he was sure it showed in his answering smile. "Thank you."

He continued to hold her hands. Continued to hold her gaze. She continued to return his steady regard.

They both opened their lips to speak—just as the bell below tinkled.

Both looked to the stairs, listened.

Penelope's clear tones drifted up from below, assuring Imogen and Jane that "we know the way."

Stokes met Griselda's eyes. "Later."

She held his gaze for one last moment, then nodded. "Yes. Later. After all this is over and we have time to think."

He nodded his agreement, released her hands, and rose as Penelope's dark head appeared on the stairs.

Looking up, Penelope saw them. She smiled. "Hello. Any news?"

Stokes shook his head. He looked at Barnaby as he followed Penelope to the sofa. "You?"

Barnaby grimaced. "Nary a whisper of any sort from anywhere."

Penelope dropped onto the sofa, a disgruntled expression on her face. Entirely unnecessarily she informed them, "Patience isn't my strong suit."

Griselda smiled commisseratingly. "I used to think it was mine, but over this . . ."

"What's worse," Barnaby said, "is that we're running out of time. Parliament rises at the end of this week."

Silence greeted that announcement. Griselda broke it. "It's time to shut the shop. Anyone for tea?"

The others all expressed an interest. Griselda went downstairs. Barnaby and Stokes fell to discussing one of the political intrigues currently affecting the police. Penelope listened to them, and the sounds of Griselda farewelling her apprentices, then locking the front door and pulling down the blinds.

She stood. "I'm going to help Griselda with the tea."

The men nodded absentmindedly; she made her way down the stairs and into the little kitchen.

Setting the kettle on the stove, Griselda looked up and smiled. She nodded to a tin on the table. "I've shortbread—you could set it out."

Penelope opened the tin, then looked around for a plate. Griselda handed one to her, then reached to a high shelf for a tray.

She blew dust from it, then wiped it with a cloth. Setting it on the table, she grinned. "I don't have much company."

Placing the plate neatly piled with biscuits on the tray, Penelope glanced up at her. "Neither do I, if it comes to that."

"Oh?" Griselda hesitated, then said, "I thought all ton ladies visited each other all the time. Morning teas, afternoon teas, high teas."

"Lots of teas," Penelope conceded. "But I only attend in my mother's train, and although ladies call on her, they never call on me."

Griselda tilted her head. "Why?"

Picking up a shortbread, Penelope nibbled. "Because I don't have any real friends among the younger ladies. The older ladies, yes, but they expect me to call on them, of course." Without waiting for Griselda to ask, she continued, "I think I scare them—the younger ladies, I mean."

Griselda grinned. "I can see how that might be."

"Hmm . . . perhaps." Penelope focused on her. "But I don't scare you."

Griselda looked at her, then shook her head. "No, you don't."

Penelope smiled. "Good." She waved the remnant of her biscuit. "These are excellent, by the way."

Griselda smiled, and the kettle chose that moment to sing.

They busied themselves filling the pot and collecting mugs, then Griselda hefted the tray, Penelope carried the biscuit plate, and they returned to the parlor above.

Supplied with tea and biscuits, the men left politics and policing and the talk returned to the one topic that exercised all their minds. They ate, drank, and racked their brains for some avenue they'd yet to pursue, some brilliant way to locate the boys that they'd failed to see—but there was nothing.

"Nothing," Penelope reiterated; she sounded disgusted. "We've notices out. We've offered a reward. We've people looking. We have a trap set." She glowered at the teapot. "You'd think something would *happen*."

None of the others had anything to add; they sat, sipped, sharing her disgruntlement.

Griselda glanced around the small circle, conscious of how easy in one another's company they'd all grown in a short time. Never in her wildest dreams would she have imagined sitting in her small parlor entertaining the third son of an earl, the daughter of a viscount, and an inspector from Scotland Yard. Yet here they all were, linked by common cause . . . and friendship.

A friendship that had grown and deepened, that had come to be because they all shared one trait—a liking for justice, for seeing justice served. They differed in many ways, but that they all shared—it linked them and always would.

She felt Stokes's gray gaze. She met his eyes—held them for an instant, glorying in the connection, in what she could see and feel, then, knowing she'd blush if she looked too long, she looked down and sipped.

The conversation grew intermittent, desultory.

The tea had grown cold; she was contemplating refreshing the pot when a heavy pounding rattled her front door.

They all looked up. Then Stokes and Barnaby were on their feet, heading for the stairs. Penelope set down her mug and followed. Griselda brought up the rear.

The pounding didn't stop. Stokes reached the door first. He threw the bolts and hauled it wide.

The young boy who'd been thumping jumped back, eyes flaring wide.

Stokes pinned him with a hard stare. "What's going on?"

When that just elicited a frightened stare, he tried to soften his tone. "Who did you want to see?"

"Me, obviously." Griselda pushed past him. She recognized the lad. "Barry—what's happened?"

Reassured, relieved, the boy came closer. "Me brothers said fer you to come right away, miss—t' Black Lion Yard. Some beggar tried to kill Horry's gran'ma."

The four crowding the front door exchanged one glance, then

Penelope fled to fetch her coat, Barnaby at her heels. Griselda turned back to Barry Wills. "Wait here—we'll be with you in an instant."

It was evening by the time they reached Black Lion Yard. Leaving the hackney at the entrance, they hurried across the cobbles, dodging the crates and boxes to reach Mary Bushel's home.

Stokes led the way in. None of them knew what they would find, but all were relieved to see Mary hale and whole in her chair by the fire, flanked by two burly Wills boys.

Both Wills brothers and the small room looked the worse for wear. Barnaby recognized Joe, now sporting a developing black eye and a split lip.

Joe nodded in greeting. "The blackguards came." He glanced at Mary, satisfaction in his eyes. "Didn't get Mary nor Horry, either." He looked at Stokes, and grimaced. "But we couldn't hold them— they got away."

Stokes looked grim, but nodded. "Mary's and Horry's safety comes first. What happened? Start at the beginning."

Joe glanced at Mary.

She looked up at him, perched on the arm of her chair, then reached out and patted his hand. "You tell it, dearie."

Joe nodded and faced them. "Ted and me were here keeping watch. Ted saw them coming—saw the way they looked around as they came. So he and I took Horry out back"—with his head he indicated a curtained doorway—"and listened and watched from there."

"They knocked," Mary put in, "polite as you please. Said they were from the bailiff."

"There were two of them?" Stokes clarified.

Mary nodded. "One was a big bruiser, the other just your average bloke."

Barnaby caught Stokes's eye; the description fitted the pair who'd taken Jemmie.

Mary went on, "Asked about me health, and about Horry, where he was. I got annoyed—well, anyone would—and told them they ought to leave. But they didn't. The big one picked up that cushion there, and . . ." Her gaze on the cushion, her voice faded away.

Joe put his arm around Mary's shoulders. He looked at Stokes. "He was going to smother Mary with the cushion. Held it in his hands and came toward her. That's when we came out."

Mary sniffed. "A right to-do it was, wrestling, crashing about."

Stokes frowned. He looked at Joe and his brother. "How did they get away? There's two of you, and three bobbies were outside."

Joe looked sheepish. "We thought they'd fight. That they'd try to get through us to Mary and Horry. Only they didn't. The instant they realized we were set on protecting them, and Horry blew the whistle you gave him, they scarpered. And Smythe's a big man— you'd need more than two to hold him. He shook us off, pushed the other bloke out, and then went through your bobbies like nine-pins."

"Smythe." Barnaby couldn't keep the excitement from his voice. "You know him?"

Joe nodded. "That's why I wasn't all that bothered about him getting away. Least we know who he is."

"What's he like, this Smythe?" Stokes asked.

"He's a cracksman by trade, and word is he's not a man to cross." Joe frowned. "Never heard tell that he was one to get blood on his hands—cracksmen generally don't—but he sure as eggs was going to snuff out Mary."

"By cracksman, you mean burglar," Barnaby said. "Does he use boys?"

Joe nodded. "High-class burglar—he definitely uses boys."

"Do you know where he gets them from?"

Joe shook his head. "Smythe's a loner—most of the best cracksmen are. He gets his boys from schoolmasters in the slums, but he'll take them from whoever's got them. I've heard tell he's right fussy about his boys, but again, good cracksmen are. What makes them good, I suppose."

Ted, his brother, shifted. When everyone looked at him, he colored and ducked his head. Glancing at his brother, he said, "The other bloke—he works for Grimsby. Most like Smythe's getting his boys from ole Grimsby, else why'd he have Grimsby's lad with him to do the snatching?"

Joe was as stunned as the rest of them. "You know the bloke?"

Ted nodded. "Wally. Works for Grimsby."

Joe shook his head. He looked at Stokes. "I wouldn't know the geezer again if I saw him."

Grim-faced, Stokes nodded. "We've heard he's like that—ordinary."

"Aye, he's that," Ted said. "He's not all that clever, but he knows to follow orders. Been with Grimsby for years."

"Well—there you are then." Joe looked at them all. "It's Grimsby you're after—everyone knows he runs schools now and then."

"Where," Stokes asked, the intensity of the hunt in his voice, "can we find Grimsby?"

"More to the point"—Penelope spoke for the first time—"where can we find his school?"

Come into my parlor, said the spider to the fly. The old saying threaded through Grimsby's mind as he stepped through the French door into Alert's parlor. As always, the room was wreathed in shadows. With the clouds heavy in the sky, there was little light to illuminate the room; he could just make out Alert, sitting in his usual armchair by the hearth.

Mentally cursing the man, Grimsby lumbered forward, Smythe at his back. They ranged before Alert, who remained seated, as he always did.

Neither he nor Smythe needed better light to know Alert was furious, although he hid it well.

"What happened?" Alert's flat tones cut through the silence.

Smythe told him, baldly and succinctly. He concluded with the most pertinent point. "They were waiting for us."

When Alert didn't respond, just sat there looking up at them, Grimsby shifted. "We have to back off. The rozzers know of your game. They're onto it. If you don't want to walk away, then at least put the business on hold until the interest dies down."

Alert studied him, but said nothing.

"Look." Grimsby tried to find words to convey the situation in all its danger. "There's those notices out there now, and people have heard about a reward. Next thing we know this boy and his grandma have protection—*local* protection—and bobbies on the watch, too. This has become too hot to handle." Expression hardening, he reiterated, "We need to back off."

The man they knew as Alert slowly shook his head. "No." He held their gazes and waited, letting the absolute finality of his refusal sink in. Unbeknown to them, he'd suffered a visit from his blood-sucking cent-per-cent earlier in the evening—just to remind him that reneging on his promise to repay wouldn't be a wise idea.

He'd assured the man that all was in place. Even if it was he who said so, his plan was brilliant. It would succeed. He'd be free of his debts once and for all; by the turn of the year, he'd have the fortune he'd for years pretended he had.

"We'll go ahead"—he looked at Smythe—"with the seven boys we have. As you've botched getting the eighth, you'll make do with seven."

Smythe gave no sign of agreement or disagreement. Which was good enough for Alert. Smythe wasn't his principal source of concern.

He looked at Grimsby. "You will continue to train and house the boys. You'll have them ready for Smythe. He'll complete their training as necessary. And in a few days, we'll make our move. All you have to do is play your part for a few more days." He let his voice soften. "That's all you need do to ensure you never hear from me again—never hear a whisper about what I know."

What he knew would see Grimsby transported, and, as Grimsby knew, he could make it happen. And he would if Grimsby didn't dance to his tune.

He wasn't at all surprised to see Grimsby's lips thin, but the man offered no further argument.

Shifting his gaze to Smythe, he arched a brow. "Any comments?"

Smythe stared back at him, then shook his head. "I'll do the job—jobs—with seven, then. They're not going to be as well trained as I'd like, but . . ." He shrugged. "With luck, we'll get by."

"Good." That was exactly what Alert had wanted to hear. Smythe, thank God, knew how to keep him happy.

Smythe tipped his head toward the door. "I've the most promising two with me tonight. I'll take them out on the streets, teach them how to move about the lanes and houses, how to get into and out of the mansions and to find their way around inside. I've found two empty houses in Mayfair. I'll train them there."

Alert let his approbation show. "Excellent. So despite this minor hiccup, we're on track. Our scheme goes forward as planned."

He looked from one to the other. "Any more questions?"

They shook their heads.

"Well, then." With a smile, he waved to the door. "Good luck, gentlemen."

He waited until Smythe had stepped outside and Grimsby was about to follow before saying, in quite a different tone, "Take care, Grimsby."

Grimsby glanced back at him, then turned and followed Smythe out, pulling the door shut behind him.

Alert sat in the dark and—for the umpteenth time—went over his plan. It was sound. It was necessary. In the silent dark, his need was very clear, the pressure to succeed tangible, real.

He didn't like to consider failure, but an escape route was an essential part of any careful plan. Sitting back, he looked around, then up, and smiled.

Even if the entire scheme went arse-over-tit, he would escape detection. He'd have to leave London to avoid the cent-per-cent, but he'd still be free.

Judging that sufficient time had elapsed, he rose and let himself out through the French door, carefully locking it behind him. An acquaintance, Riggs, scion of a noble house, owned the town house; Riggs's mistress, who lived there, was, most helpfully, addicted to laudanum. Riggs, of course, had left London for the delights of the country weeks ago, leaving his town house as the perfect place for the man known as Alert to indulge his alter ego.

As he walked away into the night, he smiled. If the scheme did, indeed, go all to pieces, there was nothing to connect him with it. No way whatever to trace any of it back to him.

17

For what Penelope understood was the very first time, the new police force and the denizens of the East End worked shoulder to shoulder to locate Grimsby and his burglary school.

Joe Wills and his brothers got the word out, telling their mates, ensuring that the request and the purpose behind it, the attack on Mary, the story of Jemmie and his murdered mother, percolated through the area.

It was a densely populated enclave; local word of mouth was more powerful even than printed notices offering a reward.

The information they'd been searching for finally came in late that night. Both Penelope and Griselda had flatly refused to return to their respective homes; Penelope unbent enough to send a note to Calverton House, but otherwise refused to budge. She and Griselda sat in chairs in Stokes's office and waited alongside the men. Their men. Neither needed any discussion to know that was how things stood.

Joe Wills was shown in just before midnight. He looked uneasy to be surrounded by police, but even as a sergeant ushered him in, triumph glowed in his eyes.

Penelope saw it. She rose. "You found them."

Joe grinned at her and ducked his head. He nodded to Griselda, then looked at Stokes and Barnaby, now also standing, behind Stokes's desk. "Someone had the bright idea to look in Grimsby Street."

Stokes looked at him disbelievingly. "He lives in Grimsby Street?"

"Nah. But the street's named after his granddad, so seemed likely someone round there might know where he'd sloped off to. Sure enough, his old auntie still lives there—she told us he has a place in Weavers Street. It's not far from Grimsby Street.

"We went around there and checked it out quiet like. It was easy to find once we knew where to look—he's lived there for years." Joe met Stokes's eyes. "I left Ned, Ted, and some of our mates watching the place. It's got two floors above, and attics above that. The neighbors we spoke with didn't know anything about boys, but if they're kept indoors on the upper floors, there's no reason they'd be seen. They—the neighbors—did know that Wally lives there, along with Grimsby."

Stokes was scribbling. "So there's at least two men inside the house."

"Aye." Joe grimaced. "Don't know about Smythe. The neighbors know him enough to recognize, but far as they know he ain't there, and doesn't normally stay there."

"Good. It's Grimsby and the boys we want first. Smythe can come later." Stokes looked up at the sergeant hovering in the doorway. "Miller—tell Coates I'll need all the men he can spare."

The sergeant straightened. "Now, sir?"

Stokes glanced at the clock. "To be assembled downstairs in an hour. I want a cordon around the building before we go in."

The next hours flew in a frenzy of organization, one in which, for once, Penelope had no role. Reduced to the status of observer, she sat quietly beside Griselda and watched—with nearly as keen an interest as her companion—Stokes in action.

When Barnaby strolled over and arched a brow, she deigned to be impressed. "I had no idea the police were—could be—so efficient."

He glanced back at Stokes, seated at his desk surrounded by subordinates, all concentrating on a map as they placed their forces. Joe stood at Stokes's shoulder; Stokes deferred to him frequently, checking that the area was in fact as the map said. Barnaby smiled. "Not all of them, sadly, are. Stokes is different." Looking back, he met Griselda's eyes. "In my opinion, he's the best of the bunch."

Griselda nodded, and transferred her gaze once more to Stokes.

Penelope studied Barnaby's face. "How much longer before we go?" For her, that was the only remaining question.

Barnaby glanced at Stokes again. "I'd say within the hour."

By the time they reached Weavers Street it was edging toward dawn. A small army had quietly encircled the area; more bobbies hugged the shadows up and down the street. Weavers Street had two arms; Grimsby's house was in the center of the shorter stretch. A run-down, sagging, largely timber structure, it looked little different from its neighbors; two alleys, barely wide enough for a man, ran down both sides.

It was cold and damp. Fog had rolled in through the night, and now hung low; the close-packed houses kept the wind out, so there was nothing to stir, let alone help lift the dense veils; Penelope could barely see Grimsby's front door from where she stood beneath the overhang of a rude porch directly across the narrow street.

Peering at the building through the murky gloom, she could just make out shutters, all closed. There wouldn't be glass in any windows; she hoped the men gathering in the street continued to do so silently.

Stokes and Barnaby had circled the house, checking all exits. From what she'd gathered from their murmured conversation—they were the only two allowed to speak—they believed all escape routes were now blocked.

Feeling expectation rise, Penelope glanced around. The ranks of the bobbies had been swelled by local men. Farther back in the gloom hung women; despite the hour, they'd thrown shawls about their shoulders and come out to watch. Most would be mothers with sons of their own; while their men openly glowered, it was the silent inten-sity in the women's shadowed eyes that made Penelope shiver.

Griselda, beside her, arched a brow at her.

Penelope leaned close and whispered, "If Grimsby has an ounce of self-preservatory sense, he'll give himself up to Stokes." She glanced at the locals.

Following her gaze, Griselda nodded. "The East End takes care of its own."

Barnaby materialized from the fog before them. "We're about to go in. You're to stay here until Sergeant Miller fetches you—he'll come and get you, and escort you inside as soon as the boys are freed." He looked directly at Penelope. "If you don't stay here until Miller comes, I'll never, ever, tell you anything about any of my investiga-tions again."

His lips set in a grim line; even through the gloom, she felt the force of his blue gaze.

Without waiting for any assent, he turned on his heel and stalked off through the fog.

Beside Penelope, Griselda shifted. "Never ever?" she murmured.

Penelope shrugged.

Even though there'd been no general announcement, excitement spread through the watching crowd.

There was a brief flurry of activity about Grimsby's door; Barnaby was in the thick of it, with Stokes by his side. Then the door swung inward revealing a yawning black cavern. Grabbing a lantern, Stokes unshielded it and led the way inside.

"Police!"

The sudden noise was deafening as bobbies piled through the door. Stokes and Barnaby were lost in the wave. Penelope weaved, trying to see, but a cordon of bobbies lined up outside the door, keeping everyone else out; they blocked her view.

More lights flared on the ground floor, then a faint glow appeared on the first floor. Grabbing Griselda's arm, Penelope pointed. "They're going upstairs." The glow came from deep within the building, distant from the shuttered windows facing the front.

In the front corner of the first floor, another light, smaller and much closer to the windows, bloomed.

"I'll bet that's Grimsby," Griselda said.

One of the shutters on that corner swung open; a large round head topped with scraggly gray hair poked out.

The onlookers promptly jeered.

"Come on down here, Grimsby."

"Killing old women."

"We'll show you what's what."

Those and other chants rose through the fog.

Grimsby—it had to be he—goggled. With a weak, "*Strewth!*" he slammed the shutter closed.

The crowd jeered more loudly, baying for his blood.

A series of thuds and thumps emanated from the house, along with shouts that were impossible to make out.

Penelope jigged. She wanted—*needed*—to know what was going on. Where were the boys?

The glow of the lantern had reached the second floor. For long moments, it remained on that level. The glow strengthened as more lanterns joined the first.

Penelope peered at the boards just below the roofline. Joe Wills had said there were attics, but there were no windows to be seen from the front. There didn't seem to be any dormers on the sides, either. She jogged Griselda's elbow. "There's no windows for the attics."

Griselda glanced up. "It'll just be the space under the roof. No windows. Probably no proper floor either, and no walls or ceiling—just the underside of the shingles."

Penelope shivered. Then she clutched Griselda's arm and pointed upward again. The lantern bearers—Stokes and Barnaby, she'd wager—had at last found their way into the attics. Light shone through the cracks between the boards and through the ill-fitting shingles. "They're there."

For the next five minutes, she prayed that all the boys would be safe, and that all five would be there. She was about to risk never ever knowing anything about Barnaby's investigations again when Miller came and rescued her. He conducted her and Griselda through the crowd gathering in the street, then through the police cordon and into the house.

If it could be called a house; it appeared more like a warehouse filled to the rafters with junk. Penelope and Griselda halted in what little space there was, midway between the door and the stairs, just as the first boy was led down.

Penelope anxiously counted heads as one by one boys trooped down the stairs. *Five!* She smiled brilliantly, ecstatic with relief.

In the dim light, the boys milled, looking around, confused, clutching blankets around bony shoulders. Imperiously, she called, "This way, boys!"

Her tone and manner, perfected over the years, had an instant effect. The boys' heads came up; she beckoned, and three quickly headed her way. The other two followed more slowly.

The first three lined up before her. "Excellent." She studied their faces, recognizing all three—the first three boys who'd been filched from under the Foundling House's nose.

One, Fred Hachett, blinked large brown eyes up at her. "You're the lady from the house. M'mum said you was supposed to fetch me, but ole Grimsby came instead."

"Indeed—he stole you." Penelope continued to smile, but the gesture now had an edge. "And so we're taking you back, and sending him to prison."

The boys glanced around at the bobbies pushing past, most heading out now the boys had been found and the villains caught.

"Were all these rozzers 'ere for us then?" one of the others asked.

Penelope racked her brain, and came up with a name. "Yes, Dan, they were. We've been hunting for you for weeks."

The boys exchanged glances, as if impressed with their worth.

"Right, now." Penelope beamed at the boys; she could barely believe that after all their searching, they had them back safe and sound. "We'll be taking you to the Foundling House directly." She shifted to catch the eyes of the last two boys, who continued to hang back.

Abruptly her heart sank. Sickeningly.

They should have been Dick and Jemmie. But they weren't.

Seeing her staring, they ducked their heads.

After a moment, one peeked at her from under a grimy fringe. "What about us, then, miss? Tommy here and me—we weren't s'pposed to go to any house."

Penelope blinked; she struggled to think through the emotions careening around her mind. "No, but . . . you're orphans now, aren't you?"

Tommy and his friend exchanged glances, then nodded.

"In that case, you can come along, too. We can work out the details later, but there's no need for you to go out on the streets. You can come along with Fred, Dan, and Ben, and we'll get you all an excellent breakfast and a warm bed."

The promise of food guaranteed the boys' willingness to be transported wherever she wished.

She dragged in a huge breath. "But first, tell me . . . were there any other boys with you here? Ones who should have gone to the Foundling House?"

"You mean Dick and Jemmie." Eyes now bright, eager to help, Fred nodded. "They're here—leastways they *were*, but they went out with Smythe yesterday evening and they ain't come back."

Leaving the five boys with Griselda, with strict orders to wait for her, Penelope ducked around milling bobbies and made her way to the stairs. She reached the foot as Miller came down. "I have to speak with Stokes and Adair—it's urgent."

Miller took in her tense expression. He glanced back up the stairs. "They're coming down now, miss."

Together with Miller, Penelope retreated to the room's center as two heavily built bobbies appeared, leading an ordinary-looking man with his wrists in shackles.

Wally—she assumed it was he—looked confused. His hair stood on end, his clothes were rumpled; an expression of complete incomprehension filled his plain face. He gave the bobbies no trouble; they herded him to the side so others could come down the stairs.

Another two bobbies descended, this time leading a much older man. Grimsby. The heavy-jowled, large round head with its scraggly twists of lank gray hair Penelope had already seen. It sat atop hunched shoulders and a sunken chest. Grimsby might once have cut an imposing figure, but now he was old, weighed down with the years. Despite that, shrewd cunning glinted in his eyes as they darted about, taking in the boys and Griselda, the other bobbies, Miller—and Penelope.

She made him frown. Grimsby couldn't place her.

Stokes and Barnaby were the last down the stairs.

The bobbies led Grimsby to the center of the cleared space, then halted him, turning him to face Stokes. Under Miller's direction, more lanterns were gathered and perched about the area, flooding it with light.

Penelope grasped the moment; stepping forward, she caught Barnaby's eye, touched Stokes's sleeve to get his attention. Once both had turned to her, she spoke quietly. "Dick and Jemmie, the last two boys taken, aren't here." Both men immediately looked over at the boys. "Yes, there are five, but two aren't ones we knew about. According to the others, Dick and Jemmie were here, but Smythe took them out yesterday, and hasn't yet returned them."

Stokes swore beneath his breath. He exchanged a glance with Barnaby, who also looked grim. "If Smythe is half as good as he's said to be, he won't come within blocks of this place again."

"And if he needs boys," Barnaby said, "he'll hang on to the two he has—he won't let them go."

"*Damn!*" Stokes gave voice to their frustration. After a moment, he said, "Let's see what we can learn from Grimsby."

"Try Wally first." Penelope glanced at the younger man. "He's . . . simpler."

Not precisely simple, but she was fairly certain Wally wasn't dealing from a full pack. Turning from her and Barnaby, Stokes faced his prisoners. Sliding her hand into Barnaby's, Penelope squeezed, then releasing him, made her way quietly back to the boys; she didn't want them to feel deserted again.

After a moment's hesitation, Barnaby followed her.

For some moments, Stokes stared impassively at Grimsby, then considered Wally. Eventually, he said, "Wally, isn't it?" When, a puzzled frown on his face, Wally nodded, Stokes asked, "Who told you to kill Mrs. Carter?"

Wally's frown deepened. He shook his head. "I didn't kill no one. Who's Mrs. Carter?"

It was transparently obvious that Wally was telling the truth. "You took the boy, Jemmie, from his mother—she was Mrs. Carter."

Wally nodded, his face clearing. "Aye—I fetched Jemmie away. Went with Smythe to fetch him. His ma weren't well, but she was alive when we left."

"When you left." Stokes paused, then ventured, "So you and Jemmie left . . ."

Wally nodded. "Smythe told me to take Jemmie out so he could speak private like with Jemmie's ma, then when he came out he said she'd said Jemmie should come along with us because she was feeling poorly and needed to rest."

"I see. And yesterday you went with Smythe to Black Lion Yard."

Again Wally nodded. "Aye. We was supposed to fetch another boy—his grandma was ailing." Wally's frown returned. "But it all went wrong. We was only wanting to take the boy to put him into Mr. Grimsby's school here, so he'd have a trade when he grew up, but people there didn't understand."

It wasn't the people of Black Lion Yard who hadn't understood. Stokes looked at Barnaby, standing beside Penelope. Barnaby tilted his head toward the boys, and mouthed, "Smythe."

Refocusing on Wally, Stokes asked, "Do you know where Smythe stays—he has two of the boys, hasn't he?"

"Aye. He took Dick and Jemmie out to train on the streets last night. Said they're the sharpest two." Wally's brow furrowed even more as he realized. "He hasn't brought them back though—well, don't suppose he will, not with all you rozzers about. But I don't know where he hangs his hat. The boss might know." He looked at Grimsby.

Who looked thoroughly disgusted. "No, I don't know. Smythe's not one to hand out cards, much less invite me around for a glass or two of an evening. Keeps to himself with a vengeance, he does."

Barnaby had expected no less. He glanced at Penelope, gently squeezed the fingers she'd once again slipped into his hand.

Stokes turned to Grimsby. "You've been around long enough to know the ropes, Grimsby. You've been running a school here, training boys to assist with burglaries. No judge is going to look kindly on that. You'll be spending the rest of your unnatural life behind bars. You won't see daylight again."

Grimsby's disgust deepened. "Yeah, I know. So . . ." He eyed Stokes speculatively. "If I agree to help by telling all I know, what's me options?"

Stokes's smile was the epitome of cynical. "If—and I stress if—you can convince me you've bared your soul, and what you have assists us in our investigations, then I'll speak to the judge. A more lenient sentence is the most you can expect. Transportation instead of a cell."

Grimsby pulled a face. "I'm too old for long sea journeys."

"Better than spending the rest of your life in the dark, so I've heard." Stokes shrugged. "Regardless, in your case, that's the best I can do."

Grimsby screwed up his face, then heaved a huge sigh. "All right. But damn it, I *warned* them—Smythe and Alert both—once I saw that blasted notice. Told them the game was getting too hot, but would they listen? No. No respect for age and experience. And so now *I'm* the one ends behind bars when all I'm doing is teaching nippers a few tricks. *I'm* not the one leading them astray."

"Don't you dare try to pretend that you're not an evil old man preying on the innocence of young boys."

Penelope's voice sliced through the closeness, vibrating with so much fury it literally shocked. Everyone fell silent.

Grimsby stared at her—met her eyes across the space—paled, and edged back toward the two burly bobbies.

Stokes cleared his throat. "Indeed. I couldn't have put it better."

Grimsby sent a shocked look his way. "Who's she?" he whispered hoarsely.

"She, and the gentleman beside her, have a close interest in this matter, and between them are probably related to any of the judges you're likely to meet." Stokes held Grimsby's increasingly horrified gaze. "I think that's your cue to leave aside the excuses and tell us what we want to know."

Flustered, Grismby waved his shackled hands. "Happy to tell you all I know. I said so."

Stokes didn't smile. "Who's Alert?"

"This toff who's got some plan to rob places."

"Houses in Mayfair."

"Yes. He wanted a cracksman, so I put him onto Smythe, but I don't know anything about their arrangements."

"You don't know anything about the planned burglaries?" Stokes looked skeptical.

"I don't! Alert plays his cards slap up against his chest—cool beggar, he is. And Smythe's as close as a clam about any job he does. All I know is Smythe decided he needed eight boys. Eight! I ain't never heard of a cracksman needing eight boys all at once, but that's what Smythe said he wanted."

"And you were happy to supply him, of course."

Grimsby looked grumpy. "No, as a matter of fact. Eight is hard to get—especially with Smythe being so particular. Wouldn't have done it, even for him, except . . ."

When Grimsby shot him a look, Stokes filled in the gap. "Smythe had something on you, some lever to pressure you into doing what he wanted."

"Not Smythe. Alert."

Stokes frowned. "How did a toff brush up against the likes of you, let alone get some hold over you?"

Grimsby grimaced. "Happened a few years ago. I was going through a bad patch. Tried a little jemmying on me own. I used to have a flair for it in me youth. Broke into a place—and walked into Alert in the dark. Coshed me, he did. When I came around, he had me trussed tight—he gave me a choice, tell him all about who I was, what I did, how I did it, and so on, and he wouldn't hand me over to the rozzers. Like I was his entertainment for the evening. I fingered him for one of those nobs who likes to rub shoulders with us hoi polloi, likes to think of themselves as in the know, so I told him everything." Grimsby shook his head at his own naïveté. "Didn't seem any great risk at the time. I mean, he was a toff—a gentleman. What would he care about me and what I told him?"

"But he remembered."

Grimsby passed a hand over his face. "Aye, all too well." He paused, then went on, "He said if I provided Smythe with the boys he wanted, he'd forget he'd ever met me."

"And you believed him?'

"What choice did I have?" Grimsby glanced around, disgusted again. "And here I am anyway, in the arms of the rozzers."

Leaving Penelope's side, Barnaby joined Stokes. "You say Alert is a toff—describe him."

Grimsby eyed him, then said, "Not as tall as you. Brown hair—darkish and straight. Middling to heavy weight. I've never seen him in good light, so can't say much more than that."

"Clothes?" Barnaby asked.

"Good quality—Mayfair quality."

"Have you met with him recently?" Stokes asked.

Grimsby nodded. "In a house in St. John's Wood. We meet in the back parlor. He sends a message to Smythe if he wants us there, or if we need a meet, Smythe leaves a note at some tavern—I don't know where."

"Does Smythe know all of Alert's plan?" Barnaby asked.

"Not as of yesterday. When he came to fetch the boys he was grumbling about Alert being so cagey about naming the targets. Smythe likes to do a fair amount of reconnoitering before he goes in. Smythe knows more'n I do, but he doesn't know it all. Not yet."

Stokes frowned. "This house you meet in—it's his?"

Grimsby pulled a "how should I know" face. "I assume it is. He's always right at home there, comfy and relaxed."

"What's the address?" Stokes asked.

"Number 32, St. John's Wood Terrace. We always go round the back, to the parlor doors to the garden. There's a lane running be-hind."

Barnaby had been studying Grimsby. "You say Smythe wanting

eight boys is unusual. Why do you think he wants so many?" When Grimsby shrugged, Barnaby let his tone harden. "Guess."

Grimsby held his gaze for a moment, then said, "If I had to guess, I'd say Alert's plan was to hit more'n eight houses all at once—all in one night. That way you rozzers wouldn't have any chance to get in his way."

Head rising, Barnaby envisioned it, combined the prospect with what Grimsby had already let fall. "You said targets. Specific targets. So Alert is planning to send Smythe to burgle specific houses that he—Alert—has selected in Mayfair, more than eight of them, all in one night." He refocused on Grimsby. "Is that his plan?"

"That's as much as I can *guess*," Grimsby said. "Which houses, I have no clue."

Stokes eyed Grimsby assessingly, then asked, "Is there anything else—anything at all—you can tell us?"

"Especially about Alert," Barnaby added.

Grimsby went to shake his head, then stopped. "One thing—don't know if it's real or just me imagination, but on more than one occasion, Alert said he knows how the police operate. He stressed it—he was always telling us to leave worrying about the rozzers to him."

Stokes frowned. He glanced at Barnaby.

Barnaby returned his gaze; no more than Stokes did he like the sound of that. Softly, he said, "A gentleman who feels confident in knowing how the police operate."

Stokes turned back to Grimsby. "This house in St. John's Wood Terrace. I think it's time we paid your Mr. Alert a visit."

"There's no 'Mr. Alert' living in St. John's Wood Terrace." Griselda's voice had everyone glancing her way. She colored, but looked steadily at Stokes. "I know that stretch. I'm not sure who lives in number 32, but I'm certain their name's not Alert."

Stokes nodded. "Hardly surprising—he'll be using an alias."

Beside him, Barnaby murmured, "But he's using his own house?"

That was hard to swallow, but clearly they had to visit St. John's Wood Terrace to learn what they could. Stokes gave orders for Wally to be taken to Scotland Yard. Sergeant Miller, Grimsby, and his two guards would go with them to St. John's Wood.

While hackneys were being summoned and the other bobbies

given orders to return to their watch houses, Barnaby and Stokes crossed to where Penelope and Griselda were marshaling the five boys.

Penelope looked up as they neared. Her expression declared she was torn between the duty she felt to see the boys safe and settled at the Foundling House and her determination to catch the villains. The news that Alert was a gentleman would only have driven her resolve to new heights—as it had with Barnaby.

Halting by her side, he met her eyes, and waited for her decision, far too wise in her ways to even hint which way he felt it should go.

She wrinkled her nose at him. "I'll take the boys to the Foundling House."

He nodded. "I'll go with Stokes."

Stokes indicated two constables standing by the door. "Johns and Matthews will see you safely to the Foundling House. They've got a hackney waiting."

Penelope murmured her thanks and started ushering the boys out. The five were still round-eyed, staring at the police, noting the shackles on Grimsby and Wally. Drinking it all in so they could later describe the scene to others—their ticket to importance at least for a few days.

Barnaby helped her to get the boys in the carriage, then took her hand and assisted her up. She paused on the step and looked back at him. He smiled. "I'll come and tell you all later."

She squeezed his fingers. "Thank you. I'll be dying of curiosity until then."

He released her. Stepping back, he shut the carriage door.

Griselda came bustling up to look in through the window. "I'm going with them. I'll see you later. I promise to tell you all, including what he"—she tipped her head at Barnaby—"leaves out."

Penelope laughed and sat back. The two bobbies had already clambered up. The jarvey cracked his whip and the horse started plodding—taking her and her five charges to the Foundling House, where they all belonged.

"Is this it?" Pointing to the door of number 32, St. John's Wood Terrace, Stokes looked at Grimsby.

"Aye." Grimsby nodded. "Never came to the front—he always had us come and go through the back lane. But this is the one, right enough."

Stokes marched up the steps and plied the knocker with an authoritative beat.

After a moment, footsteps approached. The door opened, revealing an older maid in cap and apron. "Yes?"

"Inspector Stokes, Scotland Yard. I'd like to speak with Mr. Alert."

The maid frowned. "There's no Mr. Alert here—you must have the wrong address." Eyeing the small crowd gathered on the pavement with open disapproval, she started to close the door.

"One moment." Stokes's tone halted her. "I'll need to speak with your employer. Please fetch him."

The maid eyed the rabble behind him—and turned up her nose. "Her. And it's far too early. It's barely eight—hardly a decent hour—"

She broke off, staring at Stokes and the notebook he'd hauled from his greatcoat pocket.

He glanced up at her, pencil poised. "Your name, miss?"

She primmed her lips, then, "Very well. Wait here—I'll fetch Miss Walker."

She turned and shut the door, allowing Stokes a small smile.

Barnaby joined him on the steps; they leaned on the railings to either side of the porch. "Ten minutes," Barnaby said. "At least."

Stokes shrugged. "She might make it in five."

Eight minutes later the door opened again, but as the vision revealed was rather scantily clad in a lacy robe, Barnaby felt he'd been closer to the mark. The woman's face was fashionably pale, but there were dark smudges under her eyes. She took in Stokes—slowly—then looked her fill at Barnaby before returning her gaze to Stokes's face. "Yes?"

"You're the mistress here?" Stokes colored faintly; judging by the woman's attire, the question stood an excellent chance of being ambiguous.

She raised impressively arched brows, but nodded. "I am."

When she volunteered nothing more, just looked at him expectantly, Stokes went on, "I'm looking for a Mr. Alert."

The woman didn't reply, waiting for Stokes to explain a connection, then realizing, she said, "There's no one of that name here. Indeed, I can't say I've ever heard the name."

From Grimsby came a muttered, "Strewth. Knew I should never have trusted the shifty beggar even that much."

Stokes glanced back at Grimsby. "If you're still certain this is the house . . . ?" When Grimsby gave an emphatic nod and grumbled "I am," Stokes went on, "Then we're still left with one question."

Turning, he looked at Miss Walker; her maid had reappeared, peering over her shoulder. "A gentleman calling himself Mr. Alert has been using your back parlor to meet with this man"—he waved at Grimsby—"and one other, on a number of occasions in recent weeks. I would like to know how that came to be."

The confusion on Miss Walker's face was clearly genuine. "Well, I'm sure I don't know how that could be." She glanced at her maid. "We haven't had any . . . incidents, have we? No instances of the parlor garden doors being left unlocked?"

The maid shook her head, but she was now frowning.

Barnaby and Stokes both saw it. Stokes asked, "What is it?"

The maid glanced at her mistress, then said, "The armchair by the hearth in the back parlor. Someone's been sitting there, on and off. I straighten the parlor before I leave at nights, and sometimes the cushion is dented the next morning."

Stokes looked his puzzlement. "But Miss Walker . . . ?"

Miss Walker turned an interesting shade of pink. "I . . . ah . . ." She darted a glance at her maid, then confessed, "I'm usually in bed by the time Hannah leaves, and I sleep rather heavily."

Hannah nodded. "*Very* heavily." There was disapproval in her eyes, but no hint of prevarication.

Barnaby understood, as did Stokes, that they were telling them that Miss Walker was, as many like her were, addicted to laudanum. Once in bed, dosed, she wouldn't hear an artillery shell exploding in the street.

"Perhaps," Barnaby suggested, "this man, Mr. Alert, might be known to your . . . benefactor."

Stokes took the hint. "Who owns this house, Miss Walker?"

But Miss Walker was now alarmed. She tilted her chin. "I'm sure that's none of your business. He isn't here, and you don't need to bother him over a matter like this."

"He may be able to help us," Stokes stated. "And this is a matter of murder."

Barnaby inwardly groaned. Mentioning murder predictably didn't help. Miss Walker and the maid were now thoroughly frightened and refused point-blank to reveal anything at all.

There was a shuffling on the pavement, then Griselda joined them; she tugged Stokes's sleeve.

When he looked at her, she said, "Riggs. The gentleman who owns this house is the Honorable Carlton Riggs." She glanced past Stokes. "He comes into the shop sometimes to buy bonnets and gloves for Miss Walker."

Stokes looked back at Miss Walker and raised a brow. She colored, but then nodded. "Yes. Carlton Riggs owns this house—he has for years, for longer than I've known him."

Stokes inclined his head. "And where is Mr. Riggs now?"

Miss Walker blinked at him, then glanced at Barnaby. She clearly recognized him as one of the ton. "Well, he's on holidays, isn't he?" She looked back at Stokes. "It's the off-season for town. He went up north to his family's house three weeks ago."

The cemetery that ran alongside the St. John's Wood church was a dark and gloomy place at the best of times. At eleven o'clock on a foggy November night, the moldering monuments interspersed with old gnarled trees cast more than enough shadow to conceal two men.

Smythe stood under the biggest tree, in the middle of the plot, and watched Alert stroll casually, with the aura of an eccentric gentleman out to take the air, toward him.

He had to give the man points; he was cool under fire. As was their custom, Smythe had left a message with the bartender at the Crown and Anchor in Fleet Street, but this time his message had been rather more than his usual few words. He'd asked for an urgent and immediate meeting, and warned Alert in no uncertain terms against going to their usual place—the parlor in number 32, St. John's Wood Terrace, a few blocks to the north—nominating the cemetery instead.

As he'd expected, Alert had been intelligent enough to heed his warning. As he'd also anticipated, he wasn't happy about it.

Halting before Smythe, Alert snapped, "You'd better have a damned good reason for asking for this meeting."

"I have," Smythe growled.

Alert glanced across the cemetery. "And why the devil can't we meet at the house?"

"Because the house, in fact the whole street, is crawling with rozzers just waiting for you and me to show our faces."

Despite the poor light, Smythe sensed Alert's start, but he didn't immediately respond.

When he did, his voice was even, flat—deadly. "What happened?"

Smythe told him what he knew—that Grimsby's school had been raided and they'd lost Grimsby, Wally, and five of the boys. Smythe was quietly furious on his own account—the opportunity to pull off a whole string of burglaries of the caliber Alert had described didn't come around but once in a lifetime; quite aside from the money, he would have made his name, which would have kept him in good standing for the rest of his life. He was angry, but his fury was nothing compared to Alert's.

Not that Alert did anything more than take two paces away and rest a fist on the edge of a gravestone. It was the rage that screamed in every line of his body, in the stiff, brittle tension that rode him, the violence he contained, that he battled to suppress, that set the very air—and Smythe's instincts—quivering.

And set him thinking. Such fury suggested Alert was quite possibly desperate to have the buglaries done.

Which, in Smythe's view, augered well. For him.

He couldn't do the burglaries without the information Alert had thus far withheld, but perhaps Alert would now be more amenable to running the enterprise Smythe's way.

"Do you have any idea who—" Fury vibrated through Alert's voice; he cut himself off and drew a huge breath. "No. That doesn't matter. We can't allow ourselves to be distracted—"

Again he broke off. Swinging around, he took three strides in another direction, then halted, lifted his head and breathed deeply again, then he swung to face Smythe. "Yes, it does matter. Or might matter. Do you have any idea who or what brought the police down on Grimsby's head?"

"Could've been anyone. Remember that notice? We were on borrowed time as it was."

Alert grimaced. "I didn't realize it might happen so fast. We only needed another week." He fell to pacing again, but this time with less heat. "Were you there when they grabbed Grimsby?"

"For a bit. I didn't hang around, especially as I had two of the boys with me. I got there just after the rozzers had gone in—I only stayed long enough to be certain what was happening. I left before they brought Grimsby out."

Alert frowned. "Was there anyone else there with the police?"

"I didn't see anyone . . . well, except for the lady from the Foundling House. I expect she was there for the boys."

"Lady?" The man known as Alert halted. "Describe her."

Smythe was observant; his quick description was enough to identify the lady. Who was indeed a lady. Penelope Ashford. Damn that meddling shrew! Her brother should have sent her to a convent years ago.

But Calverton hadn't, which had left her free to interfere with his grand plan. To jeopardize it. He certainly wouldn't put it past the infernal female to have been behind the raid on Grimsby's school.

His earlier fury tugged at his mind, along with the fear that fueled it. He'd had another visit from his cent-per-cent, but this time, rather than catch him at one of his haunts, the damned usurer had come to the house! To his place of work!

The message couldn't have been plainer; if he didn't clear his debt as promised, he'd be ruined. And the depth, breadth, and completeness of that ruin had now assumed epic proportions.

Under the tree, Smythe shifted, drawing his attention. "Like I said, I've two of the boys with me—or rather I've left them locked up tight. As it happens, they're the best two by far, even though they're the ones Grimsby had for the least time. They're nimble and quick, and I can keep them in line well enough. I'll need to teach them more—much more if we want to use them to do your jobs—because now we'll need to get them clean away every time."

Their original plan had involved leaving the boy used for each house inside the house once he'd passed out the lifted item; the boy would have orders to wait for an hour before attempting to leave—usually the most dangerous stage and the one where the boys were most likely to be caught—but by then Smythe, Alert, and the liberated items would be long gone.

Alert grimaced; Smythe had explained his procedures well enough for him to understand that with only two boys they couldn't afford to lose them. He grunted. "I suppose, with only two, if you lose one, the other—seeing his own fate demonstrated—would run away rather than keep working."

"Precisely. The boys need to be clever or they're no use to me, but if they are . . ." Smythe shrugged. "These two are clever, but at heart they're still East End boys. They'll do what I tell them, as long as they feel safe enough."

Alert paced. "How long will you need to train them well enough to use?"

"Now I've only got the two to concentrate on . . . four days."

"Once they're fully trained, will you be able to do the eight houses all on one night, as we'd planned?"

"No. No chance. Even four in one night is pushing it with only two boys. They get tired, they make mistakes, and you lose all your work."

Alert thought it over, balancing Smythe's concerns against his own knowledge of how the police would react once they learned of the burglaries. Any of the burglaries, the thefts he'd planned.

Drawing in a huge breath, he stopped pacing and faced Smythe. "Two nights. We can't stretch it over more. Four houses on each of two nights. We can order the houses so the more difficult are at the end of the list. That way your boys can grow more experienced with the easier houses before having to face the more demanding—we're less likely to lose them that way, and if we do, it'll be toward the end of our game."

Smythe considered, weighing the pros and cons—the most weighty being that he wanted to do the jobs—then nodded. "All right. We'll do the eight over two nights."

"Good." Alert paused, then said, "We'll meet here, three nights from now. Until then, keep yourself and those boys out of sight."

An entirely unnecessary reminder; Smythe suppressed his instinctive reaction and evenly said, "That might not work, depending on when you want to do the jobs." When Alert frowned, he continued, "I told you before—I need at least three days to study the houses. Given we're doing so many, even if they're in the same area, I'd prefer longer, but if I have to I'll do the scouting in three days. But I won't go in unless I've had at least that long."

Alert hesitated, then his hand went to his pocket. Smythe stilled, but it was only a piece of paper Alert pulled out.

He looked at it, then held it out. "These are the houses, but the families are still in residence. Once they leave, and we're ready to do the job, I'll give you the list of the items we need to lift from each house, as well as details of where in each house the item to be lifted is located."

Taking the list, Smythe glanced at it, but it was too dark to make out the words. Folding it, he put it in his pocket. "Still just the one item from each house?"

"Yes." Alert's gaze sharpened on his face. "As I explained at the outset, with these particular items, one from each house is all we need. You'll be rich beyond your wildest imaginings with just one—eight items all told. And"—his voice lowered, becoming more steely, more threatening—"there are reasons why, in these instances, only that one item must be taken. To indiscriminately filch anything else will risk . . . the entire game."

Smythe shrugged. "Whatever you say, I'll check out these houses and train the boys—then once the coast is clear, just give me your list of items and we'll do the deed."

Alert studied him for a moment, then nodded. "Good. I'll see you here three nights from now."

With that, he turned and walked out of the cemetery.

Smythe remained under the tree and watched until Alert disappeared among the monuments. Smiling to himself, Smythe set off in a different direction.

He patted his pocket, reassured by the crackle of paper inside. He'd been waiting to get something on Alert—something that would identify the man; he didn't like doing business with people he didn't know, especially when they were toffs. When things went wrong, toffs had a habit of pointing at the lower orders and claiming complete innocence. Not that Smythe expected to be caught, but having a little something up his sleeve to either ensure Alert's silence, or alternatively to trade if things got sticky, was always reassuring.

Now he had the list of houses—houses Alert knew contained a very valuable item, and more, that he knew well enough to describe that item and where it was located in detail.

"And how would you know that, my fine gentleman?" Grinning, Smythe answered the question. "Because you're a regular visitor to every one of those houses."

Eight houses. If he ever needed to identify Alert, a list of eight houses with which the man was intimately familiar would, Smythe felt sure, do the trick.

18

Investigations are often like pulling teeth." Barnaby reached for another crumpet from the tray before Griselda's parlor fire. "Painful and slow."

Munching on her own crumpet, Penelope swallowed, then humphed. "A slow torture, you mean."

Barnaby grimaced, but didn't deny it.

Three days had passed since they'd raided Grimsby's school; despite the best efforts of everyone involved, they hadn't heard so much as a whisper about Smythe and the boys he'd spirited away. Jemmie and Dick were still out there somewhere, hence their somber mood.

Griselda slipped from her chair and retrieved the teapot she'd left on the hearth. Prosaically, she refilled their mugs. "How are the boys settling in at the Foundling House?"

"They're doing very well." Penelope had spent most of the previous two days smoothing the boys' way and dealing with the formalities of assuming the guardianship of the two extra boys they'd found. "Of course, being rescued in a police raid on a notorious East End burglary school means they've become heroes of sorts, but one can scarcely begrudge them their moment, and it has made finding their feet among the other boys easier."

It was Saturday afternoon. She'd come to ask Griselda if she'd heard anything from her East End contacts, which, unfortunately, she hadn't. They'd settled in to console themselves with tea and crumpets by the fire in her parlor, then Barnaby had arrived; he'd looked for her first in Mount Street, and been redirected to St. John's Wood by the redoubtable, unruffleable Leighton.

The day after the raid, he—Barnaby—had hied off to Leicester-shire to speak with the Honorable Carlton Riggs, in the hope Riggs might know who Alert was. As both Barnaby and Griselda knew Riggs by sight, they'd known he wasn't Alert himself—Alert was, apparently, very fair-haired.

All very well, but instead of immediately and comprehensively satisfying her and Griselda's curiosity the instant he'd appeared, on spying the crumpets Barnaby had declared himself in dire need of sustenance, refusing to say a word about his findings until his hunger was assuaged.

Which had led her to make a tart comment on the wretched slow-ness of their investigation, which had resulted in his comment about pulling teeth.

Curled up in one corner of the sofa, she watched him polish off the crumpet. "That's your second." She narrowed her eyes at him. "You aren't going to faint—so talk."

His lips curved in a teasing smile. He reached for his mug, sipped, then sat back in the other corner of the sofa.

She looked at him expectantly; drawing breath, he opened his mouth—only to close it as a sharp knocking sounded on the front door.

Penelope closed her eyes and groaned, then quickly opened them and sat up. "That must be Stokes." Griselda went past her to the stairs. "Perhaps he's learned something." She glared at Barnaby. "Something useful."

If he'd made any advance, he would have been eager to share it.

Stokes climbed the stairs two at a time, then came to an abrupt halt at the top as he saw them. Penelope smiled and waved. Smiling herself, Griselda welcomed him, then led him to join them.

Subsiding into the armchair opposite Griselda's, Stokes accepted the mug she offered him. He reached to snag a crumpet, but Penelope shot from the sofa and grabbed the plate. Stokes looked at her in sur-prise as she retreated to the sofa, shielding the plate within one arm. She caught his eye. "Report first. Then you can eat."

Stokes looked from her to Barnaby, then shook his head. He sipped his tea, then sighed. "You may as well hand over that plate. I've noth-ing to report—nothing positive anyway."

Penelope sighed, too, and stood again to put the plate back down on the hearth within Stokes's reach. "Nothing?"

"Not a peep. Smythe has gone to ground. He's not been seen at any of his regular haunts. The locals are helping as much as they can. We found where he'd been staying, but he's moved—God knows where to." Stokes helped himself to a crumpet.

"The watch on the house in St. John's Wood Terrace," Griselda prompted. "Have they seen anyone?"

Stokes shook his head. He chewed, then swallowed. "No one's been near the place. All I can think of is that Smythe must have been somewhere outside in Weavers Street—he saw us take Grimsby and knew Grimsby would tell us about the house. Smythe knows how to contact Alert, so Smythe warned him off and went into hiding, taking the boys with him."

Stokes looked at Barnaby. "Did Riggs have any clue?" He didn't sound hopeful.

Which proved just as well.

"Not the slightest inkling." Barnaby's voice altered, slipping into mimickry. "Indeed, the notion that someone was using the back parlor of his love nest to meet with criminals in the dead of night positively *appalled* him."

Penelope snorted.

"Exactly." Barnaby inclined his head. "Riggs was *that* sort—pompous and blustering. I asked who else knew about the house, which of his friends he'd entertained there. The list was too long to contemplate. He's had the place for over a decade and never made any secret of it to his male acquaintance. And of course, that means their gentlemen's gentlemen, and his man's friends, and various other servants, and so on and so forth—which is to say, there's absolutely no way forward via Riggs."

They didn't all sigh, but it felt like it. A general moroseness settled over the room, until Griselda glanced around and said, "Buck up. We'll keep looking. And the one good piece of news is that if we've heard nary a whisper about Smythe, that means he's actively hiding, which means he's most likely still looking to use the boys for his burglaries, which means he'll keep them safe and well fed. By all accounts, he's one to keep his tools in prime condition."

Penelope blinked. "So he'll take good care of them because it's in his own best interests?"

"Exactly. So there's no sense imagining they're in danger of being knocked about, or spending their nights shivering under a bridge somewhere. Smythe will most likely take better care of them than Grimsby. He wanted eight, but now he's only got two—he's not going to risk them."

Both Barnaby and Stokes slowly sat up; both were frowning.

"He's still planning to do these burglaries, isn't he? The ones with Alert." Stokes looked at Barnaby. "I assumed he'd give it up after we raided the school."

Barnaby nodded. "I assumed the same. But as Griselda so sagely points out, he hasn't given up the plan—because if he had, he'd just let the boys go, and with so many in the East End eager to claim that reward, we'd have heard of it by now. And he would let them go—they're no threat to him yet, and entirely unnecessary baggage—unless he has a use for them, and the only use would be . . ." Eyes lighting, he raised his cup in a toast. "The game is still on."

Stokes leaned forward, hands clasped between his knees. "So what's his plan—which houses, and why?"

"It's not Smythe doing the planning, at least not the where, when, or what for. That's all coming from Alert. He's providing the details, Smythe is providing the expertise. And Alert, we know, is a gentleman."

Penelope raised her brows, wondering what that last fact might imply.

After a moment Barnaby continued, "I've been thinking about what Grimsby said about Smythe needing so many boys because he was to hit a whole string of houses in one night." He looked at Stokes. "That's not Smythe's—or any burglar's—usual modus operandi. The 'all in one night' is being dictated by Alert. But *why*? Why would a gentleman insist on a series of burglaries being done all in one night?"

Stokes stared back at him. Eventually he offered, "The only thing I can think of, as Grimsby also said, is that they'll get no trouble from the police if the whole series—and one assumes there has to be some reason behind doing a series of burglaries in the first place—is done in one night. Once a burglary is discovered, it takes a day, more usually two, to organize more men on patrol, that sort of thing."

Barnaby nodded. "Which leaves us with two points. One—correct me if I err, but increased police patrols and so on would only happen if the houses burgled are in Mayfair." When Stokes nodded, Barnaby continued, "That confirms what we've suspected given Smythe's need for burglary boys—that these burglaries are of a series of houses in Mayfair. *However,* to my second point, his insistence on the burglaries being done all in one night suggests that once the burglaries—even one of them—are discovered, the outcry will be significant, enough to make any further burglaries in Mayfair too risky."

Stokes's face blanked. "Hell."

"Indeed." Barnaby nodded. "The only scenario that makes sense of Alert's plan—a string of houses in Mayfair that must be burgled all in one night—is that the items to be stolen are *extremely* valuable."

Stokes focused on Barnaby. "Any chance of us getting the word out through the ton—putting households on alert? Possibly identifying households that have extremely valuable items of the sort a boy could lift?"

Barnaby looked at him, then glanced at the window and the louring sky beyond. "As to your first question, Parliament rose on Thursday. It's now late Saturday afternoon." He met Stokes's eyes. "We're too late for any general alert—most ton families will have left town by now. More than that, in the current political climate I don't think it would be wise for Peel to suggest, however obliquely, that the police weren't able to protect the mansions of Mayfair from the depredations of one burglar."

Stokes pulled a horrendous face and looked away.

"As for identifying households containing smallish items that are extremely valuable," Penelope said, "the entire ton is littered with such things. Every house in Mayfair would have at least one, and in many cases more than one." She grimaced, looking from Stokes to Griselda, then back again. "I know it seems absurd, but generally those things have been in our families for generations. We don't think of them as valuable, but as Great-aunt Mary's vase that she got from her Parisian admirer. That sort of thing. The vase might be priceless Limoges, but that's not why it's sitting on the corner table, and it's not how we think of, or remember, it."

"She's right." Barnaby met Stokes's gaze. "Forget any idea of identifying which houses." He grimaced. "While we might now know the sort of item Alert is after, that sadly doesn't get us much further."

After a moment, Stokes said, "Perhaps not. But there is one other thing." He looked at Barnaby. "If, as seems certain, Alert's plan was designed to avoid police interference, then Alert, whoever he is—"

"Knows a damned sight more than the average gentleman about the workings of the Metropolitan Police." Barnaby nodded. "Indeed."

After a moment, he went on, "We can't find Smythe, and we can't identify the houses he's targeting well enough to set any trap. By my reckoning, that leaves us with only one avenue worth exploring."

Stokes nodded. "We go after Alert."

She'd told herself it was frustration, disappointment, and simple impatience with the investigation that had driven her to seek distraction— but the truth was, she'd missed him.

Later that night, Penelope lay propped in Barnaby's big bed. He lay beside her, on his back, one arm crooked above his head. The glow of candlelight fell over them. She let her gaze wander, and smiled with, she had to admit, possessive delight.

For the moment at least he was hers, all hers, and she knew it.

Reaching out, she laid one hand on his chest, then slowly slid it down—over the heavy muscle bands, down over his ridged abdomen to the indentation of his navel, then lower, to that part of him that always seemed eager for her touch. That despite their recent couplings, still grew beneath her hand.

The fact sent a sense of power shivering through her.

Not that the rest of him—all of him—hadn't been glad to see her. Even though they'd made no assignation, when she'd knocked on his door earlier that night, he'd been waiting to open it; Mostyn had been nowhere in sight. He'd escorted her upstairs to his bedroom and locked the door behind them—all with an intent alacrity that had warmed her. That had set her heart pounding, set her senses stretching in anticipation.

She'd turned into his arms—all but flung herself at him—and simply let her hunger free. Let it burn. For him. And he'd reciprocated. They'd wrestled, as they always did, control first his, then hers, then his again. He'd finally pinned her, naked, beneath him on the bed, and joined with her in a frenzy that had left them both wrung out, deliciously sated.

Content again.

It had seemed that he'd missed her, too.

That had been the first time. The second . . . she had an excellent memory; she could recall in vivid detail the various positions described in the esoteric texts she and Portia had studied years before in their drive to educate themselves on all aspects of life. Those texts had been quite illuminating.

And clearly accurate. When she'd risen up on her hands and knees and asked whether they could try it that way, he'd been stunned—for all of a heartbeat. Then he'd been behind her, and inside her, joining with her through long, deep, excruciatingly controlled thrusts; he'd demonstrated very thoroughly just why that position had featured in most texts.

Afterward, they'd collapsed in a tangled heap, mutually sated to their toes.

Now . . . after the heady glow of aftermath had faded, she'd been left with a pervasive warmth, her body thrumming with a steady, purring content and a quiet joy she hadn't known it was possible to feel.

She was lightly, gently, stroking his chest, fascinated as always by the contrasts. Her hand looked so tiny, so puny, against the muscled, inherently powerful expanse; he was hard to her soft, heavy to her slight, large to her small—yet they seemed, in so many ways, complementary.

And not just physically.

On the surface, interludes such as this were all about satisfying physical cravings, yet before and beneath, what gave rise to the cravings in the first place and what, in achieving true satiation, was the more powerful and dominant hunger assuaged, was very definitely not physical. At least not for her.

And, she was starting to believe, not for him, either.

Possessiveness, protectiveness, need, and care were all part of what now lay between them, and at least within the confines of his bed acknowledged as such—there in his touch, investing his loving and hers—evidence of an emotional connection that was only growing stronger and more profound with every day that passed.

After spending the last three days apart, the notion of losing that connection, of ending it . . . suffice it to say that her mind was assessing ways and means of ensuring that connection continued indefinitely.

She was aware he was watching her, studying her face from beneath heavy lids. Shifting her head on the pillows, she met his blue, blue gaze; after a moment, she arched a brow.

He smiled. Raising one hand to her cheek, he brushed back a lock of hair, setting it behind her ear. "Stokes and I will start first thing tomorrow . . ." He glanced at the window. "Today. But unless we're lucky, it'll take time to identify Alert—if we even can. And time is a commodity that for us is limited."

She turned on her side so she could look into his face. "If you can't find Alert before the burglaries take place, we won't be able to rescue the boys before they're . . . implicated."

Barnaby grimaced. "As long as we rescue them before Alert's plan is complete, we'll be able to argue them free of the courts, but if his plan is successful, once it's over and done and time passes, the boys will be held to be as criminally responsible as Smythe and Alert." After a moment, he went on, "There's also the not insignificant consideration that if Alert's plan is successful, the police force is going to be severely discredited, and Peel and the commissioners are going to have the devil of a time defending its existence."

He met Penelope's eyes. "There are many who would be perfectly happy to see the force disbanded."

She humphed disapprovingly and lay back. Staring at the ceiling, she asked, "What sort of person could Alert be? Where are you and Stokes going to start?"

Perfectly content with the conversation's direction, he settled to tell her. He'd deliberately distracted her, and himself, by mentioning the investigation; there were only two subjects currently in his mind, and the way the moment between them had been evolving, the weight of it just before he'd spoken . . . the temptation had been great and burgeoning, but he didn't want to risk speaking of that other subject too soon.

Not before she'd made up her own mind and reached the conclusion he'd already reached.

Interviewing Carlton Riggs had been a God-given excuse he'd seized with both hands. Riggs's family estate was in Leicestershire, not all that far from Calverton Chase. After questioning Riggs, he'd declined an invitation to stay the night, and had instead driven across to drop in on Luc, Viscount Calverton, Penelope's elder brother and guardian.

Luc and his wife, Amelia, had welcomed him; they'd met him on numerous social occasions within their wider family, and Luc had interacted with him on a previous investigation. Luckily, with three children demanding Amelia's attention, it hadn't been difficult to engineer time alone with Luc in his study.

He'd lost no time declaring his hand and making a formal offer for Penelope's. After swallowing his surprise, after shaking his head in disbelief, then commenting that Barnaby was the last man he'd have expected to lose his head—which comment had prompted Luc to ask just how well Barnaby knew his sister, to which Barnaby had tersely replied, "Too well," which had led to a moment of tension—Luc, by that time narrow-eyed, very much the shrewd, sharp gentleman-with-four-sisters, had nodded, and given his permission for Barnaby to pay his addresses to Penelope—if she would let him.

Barnaby knew well enough not to take that last for granted—even with her lying naked and sated beside him in his bed.

But at least he no longer felt guilty about having her lying naked and sated beside him in his bed. Her being in that state might have come about through her own very deliberate instigation, yet he'd been waiting, ready, and very willing to accommodate her.

"Stokes and I . . . we'll probably start by making a list of all gentlemen known to be associated with the police. The commissioners and their staffs, and those involved with the force through other authorities, like the Home Office and the Water Police."

"Hmm." Her eyes narrowed in thought. "Given what we've assumed is his plan, Alert must be someone who not only knows other gentlemen of the ton—through his club, for instance—but who visits their homes. How else could he know which houses he wants to target?" She met Barnaby's eyes. "So Alert must be someone with a certain social standing."

He frowned, nodded. "You're right. Once we have our list, we can use that to refine it, to eliminate those not likely." After a moment, he added, "Very few clerks would have the social entrée Alert must have. We'll have to see who turns up in our net."

19

The next day was Sunday. In the morning, Barnaby and Stokes met at his office and made a good start on their list. Penelope's observation eliminated a good few names without further examination; others—such as the commissioners and many on their staffs—Barnaby was going to have to inquire into more closely.

But Sunday afternoon wasn't a good time to go trawling through the ton. Leaving Stokes to his own devices—which he suspected would involve a visit to St. John's Wood High Street—Barnaby returned to Jermyn Street—to discover Penelope waiting, not patiently, in his parlor.

They didn't remain in the parlor for long.

The afternoon was fading into November twilight when, after a delightful, calming, and somehow reassuring afternoon of lovemaking interspersed with games of chess, Penelope followed Barnaby down the stairs and through the door at the back of his hall to the rear door of his lodgings.

On learning that she'd come in her brother's town carriage and it was waiting for her farther along the street, Barnaby had gone out and ordered her coachman to bring the carriage into the lane behind the house. Even in the gathering dusk of a November Sunday, Jermyn Street, the premier haunt of the ton's bachelors, was sure to have someone walking along. Someone to see her being helped into her carriage at that telltale hour, someone who might recognize her and talk.

She understood perfectly well why Barnaby had ordered the carriage to pull up in the lane. While she might be fairly cavalier with her reputation, that he was anything but made her feel cared for, rather than annoyed.

Being cared for was one of the emotional benefits of their interaction she was starting to grow quite fond of; she'd caught herself excusing behavior on his part, accepting and tolerating possessive or protective acts that from any other gentleman would have earned a harsh rebuke. With Barnaby, she found herself smiling with fond affection, both inwardly and outwardly.

The changes he and their relationship were making in her were a trifle unsettling. She didn't readily suffer fools, or any impinging on her will or her directions, yet with him . . . she felt not softer but less rigid, less defensive, and therefore willing and able to accommodate him within certain bounds. Within some structure she'd yet to define; she'd yet to decide whether their relationship would be—could be—compatible with marriage.

Whether marriage to Barnaby Adair might work.

Whether marriage to him was her true destiny.

Reaching the rear door, he glanced back at her. "Wait here while I check." Opening the door, he stepped out, partially closing it behind him, protecting her from the gust of chilly wind that tried to barrel into the house, and from any potentially curious eyes.

She contemplated the half-open door, and the calmness that held her. Her frustration with the investigation—her impatience, and the hurdles that seemed so insurmountable she had to consider that despite all they did they might not be able to rescue Dick and Jemmie—would normally have had her pacing and railing.

Uselessly, but she would still have railed, both silently and vociferously in turn. Which would have been a great waste of energy, and most likely would have given her a headache.

Instead, she'd come to Barnaby, and now felt calm and somehow stronger. Better able to deal with whatever demands the investigation made of her, more confident that, somehow, they—he, she, Stokes, and Griselda—would triumph.

That confidence had no firm basis, yet still it buoyed her, giving her hope and the resolve to go on.

Barnaby returned, pushing the door wider to offer his hand.

She smiled, placed her fingers in his—still felt that special thrill as his fingers closed around hers—and let him draw her over the threshold.

The carriage was waiting. She turned to farewell Barnaby. A distracted frown in his eyes, he reached for the hood of her cloak and lifted it over her loosely pinned hair; half of her pins still lay scattered about his bedroom floor.

Smiling, she raised a hand and laid her palm briefly against his cheek. "Thank you." For an afternoon that had meant more to her than she'd known any interlude could, for taking care of her and her complex needs unasked, spontaneously.

He caught her hand, kissed her fingers. "The instant Stokes or I learn anything relevant, I'll come and tell you."

She nodded. She was about to turn away when a movement in the corridor behind Barnaby caught her eye.

It was Mostyn. He must have returned early from his afternoon off. Like any experienced gentleman's gentleman, he made himself scarce when she was with Barnaby; he'd come out of the kitchen unaware they were at the rear door. He saw them, froze, then, after a moment's hesitation, to her considerable surprise—she was perfectly aware he didn't approve of her—he bowed. A very correct acknowledgment untainted by any hint of disrespect.

Before she could react, Barnaby, unaware of her distraction, grasped her arm and urged her to the carriage. Turning, she followed his direction.

Opening the carriage door, he helped her in. "Let me know if you hear—or think—of anything pertinent."

"I will." As he shut the door, she glanced back, but could no longer see into the corridor. "Good-bye."

Barnaby stepped back and saluted her, then signaled to her coachman. With a jingle of the harness, the carriage pulled away.

The following afternoon, Penelope was sitting on the chaise in old Lady Harris's drawing room, sipping tea and pretending to listen to the babble of conversations about her, when the select gathering of some of the ton's most influential ladies—those still in town because their husbands held senior posts within the government and were therefore not yet free to retreat to the country—was disrupted in spectacular fashion by the entrance of a policeman.

Few of the ladies had met one before. Consequently, Silas, Lady Harris's butler's announcement—"A member of the constabulary has called, ma'am"—was greeted with a profound silence little else could have achieved.

The constable, a middle-aged man in a tightly fitting uniform who had followed in the imposing Silas's wake, looked taken aback by the stares directed his way. But when Lady Harris in her sweet bemused way inquired as to his business, he collected himself and looked around the room. "I'm here to fetch Miss Ashford."

Penelope set down her cup and rose. "I'm Miss Ashford. I take it Inspector Stokes sent you?"

The constable frowned. "No, miss. I'm here because the ladies at the Foundling House said as you were the one in charge. My sergeant just executed a warrant against the house. You're wanted there to answer questions."

Penelope stared at him.

The constable waved to the door. "If you'll come along with me, miss?"

She went, leaving considerable consternation in her wake—and not a small amount of gossip. Her mother would smooth things over—as far as was possible—but Penelope gave thanks she was not the sort of young lady to be easily affected by the ton's opinion; her life and her happiness, thankfully, were not dependant on the ton's approbation.

The hackney the constable had had waiting pulled up outside the Foundling House. She forced herself to let the constable descend first and hold the door for her; such little things emphasized her rank, something she would very likely need to wield in dealing with the constable's sergeant.

She swept into the house, consciously drawing on the quiet superiority her mother and the Lady Harrises of the world used to command. Stripping off her gloves, she cast a critical glance around. "Where's your sergeant?"

"This way, miss."

"Ma'am." She allowed the constable to precede her down the long corridor.

He cast a puzzled glance over his shoulder. "Begging your pardon, miss?"

"*Ma'am*. Given my age, and that I run the Foundling House, a position of some responsibility, then regardless of marital status, the correct form of address is 'ma'am.'" It never hurt to keep potentially annoying people in their places, and while the constable had yet to do anything to spark her ire, she doubted his sergeant—he who had executed a warrant on the Foundling House—would prove so innocuous, but the master would likely take his tone from his servant's.

"Oh." Frowning, the constable worked to digest the lesson.

They found the sergeant, one hip propped against the desk in her office, watching two constables searching through the tall cabinets that stood against one wall; one swift glance at her desk showed they'd already searched there. Two constables were likewise pawing through the files in the row of cabinets in the anteroom, much to Miss Marsh's evident distress.

Sizing up the sergeant in one sharp glance, and not liking what she saw—he was a swaggering braggart, she felt sure—Penelope swept around the desk, set her reticule upon it, and sat in her chair, pulling it up to the desk.

Reasserting control.

"I have been told you have a warrant, Sergeant." She'd yet to meet the man's eye, instead looking over her desk with a faint frown, as if noting the changes due to their search; she extended a hand, imperiously waggling her fingers. "If I could see it?"

Predictably, the man frowned; from the corner of her eye, she watched as he reluctantly straightened away from her desk. He glanced at his three subordinates; as she'd guessed, he spent a moment longer assessing the reaction of the constable who'd fetched her, before, regrettably, making the wrong decision. He hiked up his belt, and pugnaciously declared, "I don't know as that's proper. We're here in pursuit of the law, doing our job to ferret out—"

"The warrant, Sergeant." Her words cut coldly. Looking up, she met his gaze, this time reaching for the haughty arrogance of Lady Osbaldestone and the Duchesses of St. Ives—both the Dowager and Honoria; in dealing with such situations, those three were role models par excellence. "I believe that as the representative of the owners of this place, as well as in my capacity as administrator, that prior to any search being instituted, *proper* procedure dictates that I, the effective owner and occupier of the premises, should have been shown the warrant. Is that not correct?"

She was guessing, but she'd discussed police procedures with Barnaby and that sounded right.

From the way he shifted, and the glances he threw his three constables—the two searching had slowed, then stopped their rifling through the files, waiting—the sergeant suspected she was right, too.

Again, she held out her hand commandingly. "The warrant, if you please."

With a great show of reluctance, he reached into his coat and drew out a folded sheet.

Penelope took it, unfolded it. "How one is supposed to cooperate when one isn't even permitted to know *what* this nonsense is about . . ."

Her patter was designed to give her time to absorb the details of the warrant, but her voice faded, then died as, taking in the action for which the warrant was sworn—a search of all files and administrative papers of the Foundling House—she moved on to the reason behind the search. *"What?"*

All four men in the room straightened.

Staring at the warrant, literally unable to believe her eyes, Penelope declared, *"This is outrageous!"* Her tone set new benchmarks for feminine outrage.

When she glanced up, the sergeant took a step back. "Yes," he said, suddenly sounding anything but sure. "Outrageous it is, miss—which is why we're here. Can't have you selling boys to the burglary schools, now can we?"

Penelope made a heroic effort to hang on to her temper; to be accused of the very thing she'd been spending the last weeks fighting against . . . "What the devil put such a bacon-brained notion into your collective heads?"

Although her voice hadn't risen, the heat in her tone was enough to scorch.

Demonstrating a supreme disregard for self-preservation, the sergeant looked smug. He pulled another paper from his pocket and handed it to her. "Scotland Yard's been circulating these. They sent one with the order to search your files. Well, easy enough to put two and two together."

Holding the warrant in one hand, Penelope stared at the second paper—one of their notices describing the missing boys and offering a reward. "I drafted this notice. The reward, if any is ever claimed, will come from the Foundling House. The notice was printed by a Mr. Cole in his printing works in the Edgware Road, as a favor for Mr. Barnaby Adair, son of the Earl of Cothelstone, who is one of the commissioners overseeing the police force. Inspector Basil Stokes, of Scotland Yard, distributed the notices with a friend."

Raising her gaze to the hapless sergeant's face, with dreadful calm she continued, "I fail to see what, in those circumstances, you consider as in any way supporting or excusing, or even explaining *this*." She brandished the warrant. "Would you care to enlighten me, Sergeant?"

The stupid man tried. At length, in a variey of ways.

The search had come to a complete halt, all attention diverted to the battle of wills occurring over Penelope's desk. Mrs. Keggs bustled in at one point, waiting only for a pause and an inquiring glance from Penelope to inform her that all classes had been suspended by order of the sergeant, and all teachers had been summoned to the office and were now gathered in the corridor.

That resulted in another incredulous *"What?"* from Penelope, and the opening of a second front in her verbal stoush with the sergeant. Only by threatening to hold him personally accountable for any damage or hurt caused by or inflicted on any of the children left so thoroughly unsupervised by his edict did she eventually force him to back down and allow the teachers to return to their classes.

She was still trying to establish what the sergeant was searching for—given the strange circumstances she wasn't prepared to simply sit back and allow the search to continue; who knew what might have somehow been slipped into the office files and left there to be found?—when Englehart came in and took up a position at her back.

When she paused in her harangue and sent a questioning look his way, he smiled reassuringly. "I gave my boys some exercises that will keep them busy for some time. I rather thought"—he lifted his gaze to the sergeant's face—"that having a senior clerk from a respected law firm present as a witness might be wise."

His expression had assumed the impassivity of all good legal personnel. Penelope nodded. "Indeed." She turned back to the sergeant.

In the end, she sent for Stokes. The sergeant continued to insist that it was Scotland Yard that had ordered the search. "In that case," she snapped, all patience long gone, "the inspector will support you, and the search will go ahead. But until I hear confirmation of this nonsensical order from someone directly associated with Scotland Yard, you and your men will touch not one thing in this place."

Folding her arms, she sat back in her chair, and waited.

She didn't invite the sergeant or his constables to sit; given the turmoil of her feelings, she felt she was letting them off lightly.

It took some time to fetch Stokes; the light was fading by the time she glimpsed him coming through the front gate.

A minute later, he stood beside her desk, looking from the warrant to the copy of their notice, then back again.

Frowning, he looked at the sergeant, now standing to attention before the desk. "I, myself, am in charge of the case of these missing boys, Sergeant. No order regarding the case would be issued by Scotland Yard without my knowledge, indeed, without my signature." He held up the warrant. "I have no knowledge whatever of any order regarding the Foundling House."

The sergeant blinked; his expression blanked. "But . . . I saw the order myself, sir. Came in last night in the satchel from the Yard."

"I see." Stokes's frown didn't ease. After a moment, he glanced at Penelope. "My apologies, Miss Ashford, to you and your staff. There appears to be someone playing games with our investigation."

He looked at the sergeant. "I accept, Sergeant, that you were only following orders. However, those orders were false. Indeed, fake. I'll return with you to"—he glanced at the warrant—"Holborn and explain to your superiors. I'd like a word with them, to see if they can shed any light on these spurious orders."

The sergeant's face had fallen, but in the circumstances he was happy to leave. He waited for Stokes to lead the way out; he started to follow, but then, with grudging respect, paused to nod to Penelope. "My apologies, too, Miss Ashford."

Penelope met his eyes, then inclined her head in acceptance.

The police presence withdrew in Stokes's wake.

It took another hour of calming and reassuring to settle the house and its occupants back into their regular routine. By the time she finally returned to her office, Penelope felt wrung out.

Miss Marsh was waiting in the anteroom. "I checked all the files—the ones in your office, too. I couldn't find anything amiss."

"Thank you." Penelope smiled tiredly. "That's one less thing to worry about."

Miss Marsh smiled shyly; she seemed about to say something, then apparently thought better of it. Bidding Penelope a good night, she left.

Glancing out the window, Penelope saw that evening had drawn in. It was already dark, the yellow flare of street lamps shining like moons through the encroaching fog.

Another day had gone by and they'd got no further; instead, she felt drained after dealing with the vexatious sergeant and his unfounded charges.

Walking into her office, she sighed—and saw Barnaby standing by her desk.

He opened his arms—without a word, she walked into them and let them close around her. Leaning her head against his chest, she sighed again. "It's been an awful day." After a moment, she asked, "How did you know to come?"

"Stokes sent word." He hugged her, then released her and urged her to sit in her chair. Pulling one of the other chairs around the desk, he set it near hers and sat close, studying her face. "Stokes's message was brief—just that there'd been some bother here arising out of a falsely sworn warrant. I want you to tell me everything you can remember about the warrant and anything else the constables here said."

"There was a sergeant in charge." She sat back and described the warrant, and how their notice had been put with it to lend the accusation credence.

"The sergeant said the notice was sent *with* the order for the search?"

She cast her mind back, then nodded. "Yes. Specifically with. He took it as an explanation for the search."

After a moment, she said, "I didn't want to risk taking the high moral ground and letting them search, just in case there was something in the files to be found." She caught his eye. "Something none of us here knew about."

Taking her hand, he gently squeezed. "That was good thinking. Did I hear Miss Marsh say she hadn't found anything?"

Penelope nodded.

"Regardless, you were wise not to take the risk. This was distressing enough—had someone planted some evidence of something nefarious, the scandal could have seriously damaged the standing of the Foundling House."

And her reputation. Barnaby studied her face, the unrelenting stubborness that masked her tiredness. "How did you learn of the search? Where were you?"

She grimaced and told him. "Despite there being so few ladies still in residence, the news that the Foundling House was the subject of a warrant will be all over town come morning."

"No it won't. Not if we act appropriately tonight. What did you have planned for this evening?"

Frowning, she took a moment to recall. "Lady Forsythe's dinner. I have to go because some of our major donors will be there. Mama was already promised to an old friend, Lady Mitchell—this is their last chance to get together before winter, so I'll be going to Lady Forsythe's alone."

Barnaby thought, then said, "I have an idea."

"What?"

He glanced at her, and smiled. "First, I need to speak with your mother."

Penelope was too tired to argue, to demand to be told; she uncharacteristically surrendered and let him take her home. It was an odd hour when they arrived in Mount Street—six o'clock; Minerva, the Dowager Viscountess Calverton, received them in her dressing room.

She listened patiently and sympathetically while Penelope related the outcome of her return to the Foundling House and the saga of the warrant.

"And now," Penelope concluded, "I have to appear at Lady Forsythe's and attempt to scotch the inevitable rumors."

"Which," Barnaby cut in, "is a point where I believe I can help." He spoke directly to Minerva. "Neither Inspector Stokes nor I am inclined to dismiss this false order as merely vexatious. We believe that our villain has attempted to use the police to his own ends, to strike back at Penelope and the Foundling House because they've largely thwarted his plans, at the very least made them much harder to carry out."

He paused, then went on, "To take that one step further, it's possible the villain, whoever he is, specifically intended to harm Penelope. Most ladies wouldn't have known to stand firm against the warrant, let alone known to contact Stokes. But as someone who lives within the ton, as our villain assuredly does, would know, rumors can cause a great deal of harm within our circle. With a view to ensuring that we quash all possible rumors before they gain hold, I believe it would be wise for me to accompany Penelope to Lady Forsythe's this evening. Even if Penelope denounces the warrant as having no validity, some may remain unconvinced, if not of her innocence then that all at the Foundling House is aboveboard. However, if I, with my known connections with the police, were to denounce the warrant as being falsely laid, few would not accept that as fact, absolving both Penelope and the Foundling House from all suspicion."

Minerva smiled warmly. "Thank you, Mr. Adair—that's a very kind offer, and one I, for one, would gladly accept." She turned her dark eyes on her daughter. "Penelope?"

Penelope had been studying Barnaby, a considering expression on her face; she shook free of her absorption and nodded. "Yes. I have to admit I'll feel much happier having some support in facing this down."

Barnaby noticed Minerva's blink, her surprise, quickly masked, at Penelope's ready acceptance of his assistance, and his escort.

"Well," Minerva said, "in that case I'll send a note to Amarantha Forsythe and beg her indulgence in adding you to her table at such short notice." She smiled. "Not that she won't be thrilled. At this time of year there are so few of us present, adding another leaf will be no trouble, and if I drop a hint of the reason for your presence, Mr. Adair, I guarantee she'll be delighted to welcome you."

Barnaby bowed. "Thank you, ma'am."

Minerva's dark eyes caught his; hers twinkled. "Indeed. I was just reading a letter from my son, conveying a few matters of interest from Leicestershire."

Penelope perked up. "What did Luc say?"

Barnaby inwardly swore, prayed . . .

Minerva's smile deepened a fraction. She glanced at her daughter. "Just the usual family matters, dear—and, of course, a strict injunction to watch over you."

"Oh." Penelope immediately lost interest. She glanced at the clock. "Look at the time. I have to get ready."

Barnaby rose as she did. He caught Minerva's eyes, held them for an instant, then bowed, a touch lower than the norm. "I'll take good care of Miss Ashford, ma'am. You may count on that."

Minerva nodded graciously. "Oh, I do, Mr. Adair. I do."

Somewhat relieved, Barnaby escaped in Penelope's train. He took his leave of her in the hall, and went off to get ready himself.

"It was true, wasn't it? What you told Mama?"

Much later that night, after they'd attended Lady Forsythe's dinner and slain all rumors with the truth, Penelope lay snuggled in Barnaby's arms, the shadowed billows of his bed a warm and comforting resting place, his arms and body even more so.

She'd never felt so safe and protected—had never previously wanted to feel so. Never previously appreciated the feeling. Even now, with the villainous Mr. Alert trying to maliciously damage her reputation, she doubted she would have found comfort, been able to take comfort, from any other man.

Barnaby Adair, third son of an earl, investigator of tonnish crimes, was different. Very different.

He didn't, for instance, need any further words to understand to what she was alluding. To know what her mind was dwelling on.

He moved his head and pressed a kiss to her temple. "Sadly, yes. I think Alert took a specific tilt at you, not just at the Foundling House. If you think of it in those terms, his message is plain: if you hurt me, I'll hurt you."

After a moment of frowning into the dark, she asked, "But how did he do it? We've realized he knows a lot about how the police operate, but to falsify orders from Scotland Yard? Surely there can't be many people who could do that."

"One would hope not." Without hesitation, Barnaby went on, "I spoke with Stokes before I came to fetch you for dinner. He and I will go to the Holborn watch house tomorrow and retrieve the original order sent from Scotland Yard—he was too late to get hold of it this evening. We'll trace it back to whoever issued it, if we can."

"He'll have covered his tracks, surely?"

"I would assume our backtracking will come to a halt at some point short of a single identity, but we might get far enough to greatly reduce the number of potential suspects."

Warm and snug, with the dramas of the day dealt with and all possible damage nullified, Penelope discovered she could view the events with a greater detachment. Wriggling around in Barnaby's arms, she rose up and leaned on his chest so she could look into his face. "How ironic if, in taking a tilt at me, Alert opened up an avenue through which you and Stokes could unmask him."

His hands cruising upward from her thighs, over her bottom, to glide, artfully caressing, up her sides, Barnaby raised his brows. "Ironic. And appropriate."

Sliding more fully over him, she smiled down into his eyes. "Have I thanked you for standing beside me tonight, through all the tedious questions?"

"I believe you did mention it once or twice—but that was, as it were, in the heat of the moment. I don't think I heard."

"Ah . . ." Sirenlike, she slid her body side to side over his, delighting in the instantaneous hardening of his powerfully muscled frame. Hers, all hers. "Perhaps," she purred, "I should thank you again. More definitely. To make sure you remember that I did."

Barnaby stared into the dark mysterious depths of her eyes. "Perhaps you ought."

She did. With a devastating thoroughness, an unswerving, unwavering commitment that had him shuddering, reduced to blind need.

After the first time she'd suggested a new position, he'd realized her intellectual curiosity had extended to this sphere, too; she was forever eager to explore, to learn more about things she'd clearly studied but had never experienced. Even so, as his hands fisted in her hair and he fought to breathe, her devotion to knowing all, experiencing all, was not something to be taken lightly.

No more than her hot mouth; initially untutored, she'd quickly learned how to drive him wild. How to, with excruciating exactitude, shred his control so he was wholly and completely in her power.

Her lips, those gloriously lush, ripe lips he'd fantasized about from the first, had become a wicked reality, pandering to his senses, caressing him with a wanton joy that sank to his bones. Being the absolute focus of her supremely sexual attentions cast a net over him, and held him effortlessly, made him her willing slave.

He gasped, spine bowing as she took him deep, as her small hands played, possessed.

Being hers, all hers, was in that moment all he wanted. Everything he wanted.

And when the heat and the passion, the fierce need that gripped them both became too much, she rose up and took him in, sheathed him in her body and rode him with a slow delicious languor that forced full awareness of every single sensation upon them both.

She had a will to match his, maintaining that slow pace even when their bodies, their ravenous senses, clamored for more. Hands spread on his chest, arms braced, she closed her eyes and rode him, steady and sure, deliberate and determined. Devoted, beyond question, to his delight and her own.

To pleasure—pleasuring him, and taking pleasure in doing so.

He watched her as she did, watched the concentration, the fierce intentness in her face. Even as the sight rocked him, held him in thrall, he felt enough—knew and acknowledged his own feelings enough—to understand that in his devotion to her, his need of her, he'd stepped far beyond the merely physical. As she tightened about him and made his world quake, he closed his eyes and prayed that, like him, sating their physical needs was no longer enough, prayed that, like him, she was learning that devotedly pandering to those other linked needs, of a different caliber on a different plane, brought an even deeper, more profound satisfaction.

She slowed even more, her control stretching thin; he sensed it in the flexing of her fingers on his chest as she struggled to rein their rampaging desires in. She still moved upon him, confident and assured, yet wanting more, fighting to stretch the moment out for one last while.

From beneath his lashes, he caught the glint of her dark eyes beneath her heavy lids; she was watching him as he watched her, drinking in the sight of him as under her control passion built and gripped him ever more tightly. She rode on again, more forcefully now, more definite; determined and divine, she drove him and herself steadily on.

But he had no intention of surrendering so easily, not in this. When the pressure built, when the hot tide started to rise and threatened to sweep through him, he fought to hold it back. His hands were at her waist, fingers curved over her hips, gripping and savoring the evidence of her body accepting his, taking him deep; releasing one hand, he slid it up her spine, drew her closer as he leaned up, and set his tongue and lips to her breast.

He licked, laved, then took the tight peak into his mouth and suckled, gently at first, then steadily more strongly as she gasped, tightened about him, and rode on.

Faster, tighter, hotter, wetter.

When the end came it shattered them both.

Sundered them from the mortal plane, leaving them drifting in a golden void of indescribable pleasure.

Together, sated, at peace.

She chuckled as she collapsed on his chest. Smiling, he closed his arms around her and held her close.

When it came time for Penelope to leave, they discovered it was raining. Leaving her at the front door, Barnaby took an umbrella and went to summon her carriage, waiting farther down the street; the coachman was no doubt dozing inside.

Wrapping her cloak tightly about her, Penelope stared out at the dark night. Then, over the patter of the rain, she heard a footstep—behind her.

She turned. In the faint light of the single candle Barnaby had left on the hall table, she saw Mostyn shrugging into his coat as he came hurrying from the nether regions.

He saw her, slowed, then halted.

Even in the poor light, she saw him blush.

"Ah . . . I heard the door . . ." Collecting himself, he drew breath, drew himself up, and bowed. "Pray excuse me, ma'am." He colored more definitely. "Miss."

He hesitated as if unsure whether to leave her; puzzled by what she sensed from the man, she did as she usually did and took the bull by the horns.

"Mostyn, I realize the situation is somewhat awkward, however . . . I'm confused. When I first called on your master—incidentally he's down the street fetching my carriage, too far away to hear—when we first met I was under the impression you disapproved of me. Yet you've now seen me leaving in illicit fashion twice, and—do correct me if I'm wrong, Mostyn, but instead of growing more disapproving, you seem to have unbent toward me." She frowned, curious not censorious. "Why is that? Why are you now more approving rather than less?"

As she spoke, Mostyn had looked increasingly conscious, which only strengthened her desire to understand. He didn't immediately reply, but she waited.

Eventually, shifting closer to where he could see out of the door, he cleared his throat. "I've worked for the master since he first came on the town. I know his ways." Having confirmed said master was nowhere in sight, Mostyn met Penelope's eyes. "He's never brought any other lady here." He colored again, but went on, "No other female of any degree. So when I saw you . . . well . . ."

Penelope caught his drift; she felt her expression blank. "Ah. I see." She looked away, out of the door—hoping to see Barnaby striding back. He still wasn't visible. She nodded. "Thank you, Mostyn. I understand."

The man thought she and Barnaby . . .

In some ways Mostyn knew his master better than she.

Her mind in a whirl, she waited for Mostyn to leave her.

He hovered beside her, a pace deeper into the hall. After a moment, he cleared his throat again. "May I say, ma'am—miss—that I hope my conjecture isn't unwelcome, nor that it's amiss."

His sincerity touched her. She turned to look at him. "No." She drew breath and went on, "No, Mostyn, your conjecture isn't unwelcome at all."

The sound of Barnaby's approaching footsteps reached them. She inclined her head to Mostyn, and turned to face the door, murmuring, "As for it being amiss, we'll have to see."

"Indeed, ma'am. I'll hope to hear good news soon. I'll bid you a good night."

From the corner of her eye, she saw Mostyn bow, then silently withdraw, merging into the shadows at the rear of the hall.

Barnaby materialized out of the driving rain, and came quickly up the steps. She drew her cloak tighter and went out to meet him as her carriage rolled quietly up.

20

There was no way we could tell the order was fake, sir." The captain of the Holborn watch house leaned across the plain table and poked at the order he'd received from Scotland Yard. "It's on the right form, all filled out properly and signed, just like always."

The order sat in the center of the table. Barnaby, seated opposite the captain, Stokes beside him, studied it, as did the sergeant who'd executed the subsequent warrant to search the Foundling House.

"It certainly appears genuine," Stokes allowed. "Unfortunately, the signature isn't that of anyone at the Yard, or indeed, on the force."

The captain grimaced. "Aye, well, we couldn't have known that. If we checked with the Yard to see if every signature on every order was genuine, we'd never have time to carry the orders out."

Stokes nodded. "You're right. Which is what our villain counted on." He picked up the order, folding it.

The sergeant was frowning. "If I could ask, sir, who could this villain be, to be able to get hold of an order form and know just how to fill it out, and then get it sent to us in the official bag?"

Stokes smiled tightly. "That's what I, and Mr. Adair, intend to find out."

Leaving the watch house, Barnaby and Stokes emerged from Procter Street and turned into the mid-morning bustle of High Holborn. Halting at the curb, looking about for a hackney, Barnaby asked, "What was the signature? I didn't see it well enough to make out."

Stokes grunted. "Grimsby."

Barnaby turned to stare at him. After a moment, he looked away. "Our Mr. Alert has a sense of humor."

"He's playing with us."

"Obviously." Seeing a hackney approaching, Barnaby hailed it; the driver acknowledged him with a wave of his whip. While they waited for the carriage to tack through the press of traffic, he asked, "Tell me about this official bag. Is that how the orders get sent out to the different watch houses?"

Stokes nodded. "The orders associated with any major crime come from the officer in charge of the case at the Yard. Any officer has a stack of the forms—there's a stack in a drawer of my desk."

"So laying hands on a form wouldn't be difficult."

"No. Once filled out and signed, the forms get put in official dispatch pouches—leather satchels that hang in the dispatch office. There's one for each watch house."

"So this business of the fake order takes Alert's connection with the police one step further—he has to be someone with access to Scotland Yard, who knows the ropes well enough to fake an order and get it sent out with no one the wiser."

Stokes grunted as the hackney rocked to a halt before them. "There's one thing more—the dispatch office is never unmanned. There's always at least a sergeant there, and usually one or more runners ready to take urgent orders out."

"Oh-ho! So Alert is someone the dispatch sergeants are used to seeing put orders into the bags—he has to be someone who has access in the normal way of things. It has to be part of his usual job."

"Exactly." Stokes opened the hackney door. "Which is why we're heading straight to the dispatch office."

Barnaby climbed into the carriage. Stokes looked up at the jarvey, "Scotland Yard. As fast as you can."

While Barnaby and Stokes rattled through the traffic, at the Foundling House Penelope was applying herself to ensuring that in the aftermath of the police raid, everything was once again running smoothly.

Mrs. Keggs and the staff had rallied magnificently; even Miss

Marsh, normally so timid, looked determined and resolute as she tidied the files the constables had disarranged.

"Ham-fisted louts." She clucked her tongue as Penelope swept through the anteroom. "Couldn't even leave things in order."

Penelope felt her lips twitch. She continued into her office. She was impressed by how strongly the staff, and even the older children, had reacted to the implied threat of the police raid. How firmly they'd stood against any panic, and refused to believe anything ill of the place—more, had strongly resented the implication that anything whatever was wrong with how the house—and she as its administrator—conducted its business.

Sinking into her chair, she entirely unexpectedly felt some good had come from the raid. The house had been in existence for five years; clearly in those five years they'd succeeded in becoming the sort of institution that those who worked in, and those who lived within, valued—enough to fight for.

She wouldn't have known that—how much the staff and the children valued what they'd achieved—if it hadn't been for the raid.

And now that everything was back to normal, all was calm and peaceful in this part of her world. All it lacked was Dick and Jemmie. Once she had them back, her life—this aspect of it—would be full and complete.

Whole.

Sitting back in her chair, she swiveled it and stared out at the gray day. A fine drizzle had set in; the children had stayed inside, warm and dry in the dining hall.

Her life—the question of its wholeness, its completeness—filled her mind. All she felt, all she thought, was progressively leading her down one particular path, one she'd never thought she'd tread. Mostyn's unexpected revelations added another layer—raised another question.

While she was increasingly certain of what she was thinking, what was Barnaby thinking?

She'd thought—assumed—she'd known, but in light of Mostyn's more informed observations, she was no longer so sure.

Of one thing she *was* certain: Barnaby Adair was every bit as intelligent, as quick-witted and clever as she. He'd proved surprisingly insightful when it came to her thoughts, her reactions. On more than one occasion he'd responded to her wishes without her making them known—sometimes even before she'd consciously been aware of them.

But . . . regardless of all she sensed between them, did she truly want to accept the risk inherent in following the path her instincts even more than her thoughts were pushing her down?

She stared out at the gray day as the minutes stretched, then with a sigh, turned back to her desk and forced her mind to business.

Despite all, she had reservations—questions to which she didn't yet have answers, and didn't, yet, know how to get them. Despite the compulsion of instincts and feelings, and even rational thought, her careful, logical side felt uncomfortable—unable to go on until those questions had been resolved.

How to resolve them was the issue.

Pulling a stack of official guardianship papers onto her blotter, she picked up the first and started to read.

The Dispatch Office in Scotland Yard was located on the ground floor, off a corridor from the front foyer heading toward the rear. Barnaby followed Stokes through the swinging double doors.

Pausing in the center of the room, he looked around and saw what Stokes meant; the dispatch sergeant, seated behind a long counter that filled the wall opposite the doors, and his minions working at raised desks behind him, couldn't miss seeing anyone who entered.

The walls to either side were lined with wooden pegs four rows high; a leather satchel hung from each peg. Above each peg was a plaque inscribed with the name of one of the London watch houses. Following Stokes to the counter, Barnaby noted there were even dispatch satchels for Birmingham, Manchester, Liverpool—all the major towns across England.

The sergeant behind the counter, a veteran, greeted Stokes with an easy smile and a nod. "Morning, sir. How can we help you?"

"Good morning, Jenkins." Stokes showed him the order that had been sent to Holborn, explaining it was a fake.

"Holborn." Jenkins pointed to a section of pegs about ten feet from the counter. "That's just along there—second row from the top."

Given the distance between the door and the satchel in question, and its proximity to the desk, the notion that someone had surreptitiously crept in and slipped the order into the Holborn satchel unnoticed was instantly untenable.

"Right, then." Stokes turned back to Jenkins. "Who has access to the satchels? List all the types of people you normally see coming in here, placing orders—or papers of any kind—in those satchels."

Jenkins considered, then said, "There aren't that many, when all's said and done. There's the duty sergeants, and the watch sergeants—four each of them. The inspectors like yourself, and their senior investigators, the superintendent, and the governors—the commissioners—although of course they don't come in themselves. It's their secretaries we see popping in and out." The sergeant's eyes narrowed as he looked down the room. He lowered his voice. "Like Mr. Cameron there."

Both Stokes and Barnaby heard the creak of the door as it swung closed. Looking around, they saw a man both knew by sight sauntering up the room. Douglas Cameron, Lord Huntingdon's private secretary, was an arrogant sort; it showed in his long-legged walk, and the angle at which he held his head, the elevation of his long nose and pinched nostrils making him appear always to be smelling something noxious.

As if unaware of their presence, Cameron strolled to the satchel for Birmingham, on the opposite side of the room from the Holborn satchel and closer to the counter. Lifting the flap, he slid a folded sheet inside, then dropped the flap, and turned to face them.

He could hardly miss the fact they'd all been watching him. His hard hazel gaze passed over Jenkins and Stokes without a flicker of recognition; they, clearly, were beneath his notice. His gaze reached Barnaby, and stopped. Coolly, Cameron nodded. "Adair. Slumming again?"

Barnaby smiled tightly. "As you see."

With a faint lift of his brows, Cameron inclined his head and strolled out, every bit as unhurriedly as he'd strolled in.

"Stuck-up bastard," Barnaby muttered, turning back to the counter.

Lips twitching, Jenkins looked down, shuffling some papers. "Won't get much argument on that score from anyone here, sir."

Barnaby sighed. "Sadly, being a stuck-up bastard isn't any reason to imagine Cameron might be our man."

Stokes grunted in assent. He nodded to the sergeant. "Thank you, Jenkins." He hesitated, then said, "On the off chance, could you ask around among the dispatchers, just in case anyone noticed anything odd, anyone not normally in here stopping by, for whatever reason?"

Jenkins nodded. "I'll do that, sir."

Barnaby and Stokes left the Dispatch Office and climbed the stairs to Stokes's domain. Once inside, Stokes pointedly closed the door, something he rarely did, then circled his desk to drop into the chair behind it. Barnaby was already sprawled in one of the chairs facing the desk, a frown denoting deep thought on his face.

Stokes eyed it for several moments, then asked, "What do you think? Can we afford to discount people from the force itself—all those who aren't gentlemen?"

Barnaby met his eyes. "I think we're on solid ground concluding that Alert is a gentleman. Accepting that as fact, then, given he's been meeting with Grimsby and Smythe, I believe we can safely assume it was he, himself, who walked into the Dispatch Office and put that fake order in the Holborn satchel."

Stokes nodded. "Dealing with Smythe directly, face-to-face, is the biggest risk he's taken, and by all accounts he took it without the slightest reservation. He's never tried to distance himself from proceedings—why start with this, relatively minor, event?"

"More, it's a tangential act, not part of his main plan. Striking back at Penelope and the Foundling House was the act of a confident man, not one in a panic, or frightened of exposure. He's sure of himself, supremely confident—I can't see him bothering to get someone else to slip the order into the Holborn bag. Why complicate things?'

"And potentially have someone who might, if questions were asked, remember and volunteer his name?"

"Exactly." Barnaby nodded decisively. "We delete all nongentlemen from Jenkins's list. How many does that leave?"

Stokes was writing. "Aside from our friend Cameron, there's Jury, Partridge, Wallis, Andrews, Passel, Worthington, and Fenwick." He frowned. "There are a few more in the governors' offices, assistants whose names I don't know. But I can get them."

"Excellent." Sitting up, Barnaby looked at the list. "As our next step, I think we should see what we can learn about these gentlemen's finances."

Starting on a duplicate list, Stokes glanced at him. "You'll have to do most of that. I can check the pawnbrokers, but if it's gambling debts . . ."

Barnaby nodded. "I'll take care of it." He smiled and stood. "I know just who to ask."

"Good." Stokes handed him the copy of the list of names and rose. "Go and ask. I'll do the same." Following Barnaby out of the door, he added, "Time's running out on us—we need to find those boys."

That evening saw Penelope at another dinner, this one even more formal than Lady Forsythe's. Lady Carlingford was an astute political hostess; her guests included a number of donors who contributed to the Foundling House's coffers, making Penelope's attendance essential.

She arrived with her mother; after greeting Lady Carlingford, they circulated among the guests, gathered in groups in her ladyship's drawing room.

Penelope had parted from her mother, and was speaking with Lord Barford when Barnaby appeared beside her. Surprised, pleased, she gave him her hand. He greeted her suavely, then, tucking her hand in his arm, smiled at Lord Barford and asked him how his hunters were faring; his lordship was a keen rider to hounds.

In parting, his lordship assured her the Foundling House could count on his continuing support. "Don't forget to remember me to your brother, m'dear. Best hound I ever had, the bitch I got from him."

Smiling in reply, Penelope allowed Barnaby to steer her toward the next group. "I didn't expect to see you here." She glanced up at him.

The smile in his eyes warmed her. "M'father's left town. I often stand in for him at gatherings such as this, especially when it's to do with the police force, rather than his other concerns."

"Your eldest brother isn't interested in politics?"

"Not of the sort that involves the police. But anyway, both the other two, along with their wives, and my sister and her husband, are already at Cothelstone."

She thought about that as they chatted briefly with Mrs. Worley. When they moved on, she said, "Your mother must be expecting you home. Will you be leaving town soon?"

He nodded to Lady Wishdale, an urbane smile on his lips. "That depends."

"On our investigation?"

He met her eyes. "In part." He hesitated, then added, "On that, and on when you depart."

Their gazes locked—then Penelope was forced to look forward as Lady Parkdale swept up to them.

"My dears!" her ladyship exclaimed. "So *lovely* to see you both."

As for all her gossipy avidity, Lady Parkdale was a major donor to the Foundling House, and Penelope bore with her dramatic utterances and arch glances with good grace.

"At least she's never malicious," Barnaby murmured as, having parted from her exuberant ladyship, they moved on.

Penelope smiled in companionable understanding.

Barnaby continued to steer her around the guests, continued to stand by her side and field questions from the men about Peel's force and its workings. He knew everyone there, the ladies as well as the gentlemen; for all it masqueraded as a social gathering, the evening was, at its core, a serious affair.

In truth, he found such "entertainments" more to his liking than purely frivolous events; as he guided Penelope from one group to the next, he got the distinct impression that in that—as in so many things—they were as one.

Both of them were socially adept, and had more than enough wit to hold their own in the most demanding circles. And both preferred to have to use said wits while conversing; they enjoyed the challenge, the weightier repartee that in this setting, in this company, was the accepted norm.

He seized a moment between groups to tell her of their day's endeavors, and Stokes's subsequent decision to request permission to put more constables on the beat in Mayfair. "Unfortunately, Stokes holds out little hope. Equally unfortunately, learning the financial status of gentlemen isn't something that can be accomplished in a few days."

She was frowning. "There's that man the Cynsters and my brother use whenever they need to do financial investigations."

"Montague. I saw him this afternoon. He's agreed to learn what he can about the gentlemen on our list, but until we narrow the field, it's not feasible to do any in-depth searching."

"Hmm." He'd told her the names on their list. She shook her head. "I must admit I've never met any of them—but if they're in the habit of frequenting gambling hells, our paths would be unlikely to cross."

He thought of her in a gambling hell, and made no reply.

When they went in to dinner, he sent a special smile his hostess's way on discovering he and Penelope were paired. They sat side by side and traded quips and pointed banter in between entertaining their other partners. At one point, glancing up the table, he caught Lady Calverton's eye. Smiling in patent approval, Penelope's mother raised her glass to him in an unobtrusive toast.

He inclined his head in acknowledgment, then lifted his own glass. Under cover of taking a sip, he glanced at Penelope—and wondered if she, like he, saw just how very compatible they were.

Too soon, the ladies rose and left the gentlemen to pass the port and discuss the state of the nation—the bills that hadn't made it through Parliament during the autumn session, and the expectations for the legislative calendar in the coming year.

Penelope took the opportunity of the gentlemen's absence to speak with all the ladies who, as administrator of the Foundling House, she should. Some were donors in their own right, while others were responsible for arranging their husband's generosity. Still others were valuable contacts in other respects, such as Lady Paignton, patroness of a service—the Athena Agency—that placed young women as maids, governesses, and the like in ton households. The agency was much patronized by the matrons of the haut ton. As many of the Foundling House's female charges left to make their way as maids of one sort or another, Penelope had known Lady Paignton for years.

An attractive matron with dark red hair, Lady Paignton smiled as Penelope joined her. "My husband is no doubt grilling Mr. Adair about this latest initiative of Peel's. Now we've taken to spending so much time in the country, he's taking his role as magistrate very seriously. There's been talk, I gather, of setting up constables and watch houses in the larger towns."

"So I believe." The Paigntons had four children, two boys and two girls. Penelope said, "I met your eldest daughter a few weeks ago. I gather she takes an active interest in the agency."

"Indeed." Lady Paignton smiled fondly. "She's determined to eventually take over the reins. Quite gratifying, really . . . ah, here come the men, back at last." Her ladyship met Penelope's eyes. "Do tell your people to continue to send any girls they deem suitable our way. We've been very happy with the girls the house has sent us."

Smiling, Penelope inclined her head. "I'll remind them."

They parted; she watched as Lady Paignton swept up to a tall, well-set-up gentleman, extremely distinguished with silver wings in his dark hair. He was the first of the gentlemen to reappear in the drawing room. Viscount Paignton was one of the major landowners in Devon and had become increasingly influential, especially in Home Office affairs.

She hadn't intended to visually eavesdrop, but the light in Lord Paignton's eyes—a mixture of pride, joy, and happiness as he looked on his wife—was impossible to miss.

Impossible to mistake.

Entirely unexpectedly, Penelope was struck by a sudden, very specific yearning—that a man would, one day, look at her with just such a light in his eyes. Not the rather innocent and naïve light, the untested light one saw in a newly married couple's eyes, but that deeper, mature, and abiding glow that spoke of an enduring love.

She blinked and looked away, and wondered where that thought—that want—had come from, from where within her it had suddenly sprung.

Lady Curtin paused beside her. "So very heartening, my dear, to see Adair dancing attendance on you." Before Penelope could correct her—Barnaby was there in lieu of his father—her ladyship rolled on, "I'm an old friend of Dulcie, his mother, and I have to tell you that boy—well, man as he now is—has driven her to distraction with his absolute refusal to engage with marriageable females, let alone properly look about him for a wife. The way he avoids ton females—well, the marriageable sort anyway—you'd think they carried the plague! According to Dulcie, he's elevated avoidance to an art form. Why, even when he appears as Cothelstone's deputy, as he has tonight, he usually refuses utterly to play the game."

Finally pausing to draw a longer breath, Lady Curtin studied her. "You aren't quite the normal run of young ladies, yet regardless you're entirely eligible. If an odd kick to your gallop is what's needed to fix his attention, then so be it—I know Dulcie will swoon at your feet."

With a brisk pat on Penelope's wrist, Lady Curtin swept on.

Leaving Penelope slightly dazed.

Unbidden, her gaze traveled to the doorway through which more gentlemen were ambling, those at the rear still caught in discussions. At the very back of the crowd, she saw a gilded head, bent to catch what Lord Carlingford was saying.

Alone for the moment on the other side of the room, she seized the chance to study him. To consider . . . her recent thoughts, Lady Curtin's revelations, Lady Parkdale's arch comments, the light in Lord Paignton's eyes.

Barnaby didn't look at her like that . . . but could he?

If she followed the path her heart was increasingly urging her down, would he, one day in the future?

He parted from Lord Carlingford; scanning the room, he saw her, smiled, and started toward her.

She watched him approach, his attention fixed on her. Recalled she'd heard Lady Curtin's comments echoed by others; the Honorable Barnaby Adair did not dance attendance on marriageable females.

Except her.

He smiled, reclaimed her hand and laid it on his sleeve. "I've said all I wish to about the police tonight. Have you any others you wish to speak with?"

Deciding to be wise, she smiled and directed him to Lord Fitchett.

Tonight she had to leave with her mother, which was, perhaps, just as well. She needed to think about Barnaby Adair. And thinking about him in a rational, logical manner was difficult, not to say impossible, while in his arms.

The man who called himself Mr. Alert stood in the shadows beneath the old tree at the center of the cemetery at the corner of St. John's

Wood High Street. The fog clung close as a shroud; he heard Smythe approaching long before the man came into view, slipping between two large gravestones to reach the tree.

Eyes screened beneath the brim of an old cap pulled low over his forehead, Smythe halted and scanned the darkness under the tree.

Alert smiled to himself. "I'm here."

Smythe ducked beneath the canopy. "It's a poor night for walking—a much better night for burgling."

"I daresay tomorrow night will be the same. Are you ready?"

"Aye. The boys are as ready as I can make them, leastways in so short a time. Lucky they're quick and sharp enough to know it's in their best interests to work hard."

"Good." Pulling a set of folded papers from his pocket, Alert handed it to Smythe. "These are the details of the items to be lifted from the first four houses, in the order in which I want the burglaries performed. You don't need to read any of it now. I've described each item, well enough so any fool could recognize it. Also noted is the location, in detail, of the item inside the house, not just where it will be found but what doors and locks might be in the way. There's nothing the merest child couldn't handle in the way of locks."

Unfolding the pages, Smythe tilted them so they caught what light there was. He couldn't read anything, but could see the wealth of detail provided.

"As we discussed," Alert went on, "I'll be driving a small, black town carriage, unmarked, around the streets. I'll be dressed as a coachman. I'll rendezvous with you at the corner noted at the bottom of each description, close by each house, and relieve you of the item lifted. None are too big for the boys to get out of each house, but all are unwieldy enough that you won't want to chance walking any great distance with them."

Smythe's head came up. "And you'll hand over the down payment for each item as we deliver it?"

Alert nodded. "Then once I've passed the items onto buyers, and they've paid me, you'll get the rest of your share. As agreed."

"Good." Smythe stuffed the folded papers into the pocket of his heavy coat.

"One thing." Alert's voice grew cold. "As we also agreed, you are to ensure no other items are lifted from those particular houses by your boys. Once we've sold our items and have our cash, you can go back if you wish, but—and I can't stress this enough—only the item I've listed must be lifted from each house at this time."

Smythe nodded. "I agreed to that at the outset—I haven't forgotten. We'll run the job as you wish. But what about the police? You said you'd check."

"Indeed. And I have. There will be no extra police on the beat tomorrow night."

"And what about the second night—assuming you're still set on doing your other four houses on the following night?"

"Yes—that can't change. The explanation is complicated, but we can't risk anything more than two nights."

Smythe studied Alert for a moment, then nodded. "All right—but what about the police on the second night?"

Again Alert's voice grew arrogantly cold. "Now you see why I wanted all eight houses done on a single night. There is, of course, a chance—a possibility, no more—that the police will be alerted and move to increase patrols in Mayfair. However, they're unlikely to move fast enough to trouble us seriously on the second night. A third night would be foolhardly, but the second night will be only marginally more dangerous than the first.

"In addition, I've learned who's driving the police interest in our scheme. I've taken steps to ensure they won't be free to meddle in our activities on the second night. Through the first night, they'll remain blissfully ignorant—even now that we've had to reorganize to two nights, if luck is with us they won't even know we've struck until months from now."

Smythe studied him through the gloom. "So we won't be bothered—not by anyone?"

"Even if they're alerted, the most likely scenario is one we'll be able to work around." Alert straightened; confidence infused his voice. "I'll have the details of any extra forces out and about on the second night. And as for our interferring busybodies"—he smiled, a flash of white teeth in the darkness—"I've organized a distraction for them."

21

As I feared"—Stokes slumped into what had become his usual armchair in Griselda's parlor—"my request to put more constables on the beat in Mayfair fell on deaf ears."

The others—Penelope and Barnaby on the sofa, Griselda in her chair—grimaced. They'd made no plans to meet that afternoon, but once her duties at the Foundling House had been completed, impatient and at loose ends, Penelope had come to call in the faint hope Griselda might have heard something from her East End friends—a hope Griselda, shutting her shop early, had dashed.

Barnaby had arrived shortly afterward; Stokes had been ten minutes behind him.

After a moment, Stokes went on, frustration ringing in his tone, "If I had some real threat—some proof of it—I'd get action without delay. However, the very fact that to us makes the burglaries much more likely, namely the absence of tonnish households from town and the resulting empty mansions, works against us in calling for more police on the streets—all the superintendents see is that with hardly any nobs in town, there's little chance of some tonnish head being cracked during a burglary, ergo, no need for any but the lightest police presence."

Accepting the mug of tea Griselda handed him, Stokes sipped, then rather glumly looked at Penelope. "When we were discussing Alert's plan, you mentioned that those not of the ton might not appreciate how many things of great value were left lying around in Mayfair mansions." He grimaced. "You were right. My superintendent simply can't imagine it. And none of the governors I know—like Barnaby's father—are still in town."

Stokes sighed. "I tried. I outlined what we believe Alert's plan to be, but the higher-ups think I'm being fanciful."

"Much as it suits us not at all, your superintendents are right—at least from their point of view." Barnaby slumped back in his corner of the sofa. "We have no proof—everything we're saying is conjecture and speculation."

Griselda shook her head. "Missing boys and murder aren't speculation."

"Exactly." Penelope's voice was a great deal more decisive, not to say belligerent. "I don't care about snuffboxes, or vases, or whatever Alert plans to steal, but we have to rescue those boys. If the police won't patrol the streets of Mayfair, we'll have to."

As one Stokes and Barnaby sat up. "No."

They'd spoken as one, too. Penelope looked from one to the other, a frown darkening her face. "But—"

"No." Barnaby trapped her gaze. "We cannot go wandering the streets at night in the hope of running into Smythe and Alert." *And instead running into God knew who else.* Pushing the image of Penelope stalking down dark deserted streets, cobbled mews, and dank lanes behind houses from his mind, he spoke quickly. "We'll have to think of some other way to approach this—for instance, looking at how Alert plans to sell the stolen items." He glanced at Stokes. "If these items are extremely valuable, they'll most likely be rare and highly identifiable. The usual sellers of nicked goods know better than to touch such things."

"True." Stokes frowned. "So how . . . ?"

"He must have something organized. I wonder . . ." It took a moment for the notion to clarify in Barnaby's mind. "Could Alert be stealing on demand, as it were? Could he be stealing specific items that people he knew of wanted, and were ready to pay for if he delivered them?"

He looked at Stokes, who shrugged.

"Could be. But as we don't know the items, that doesn't get us much further."

But it had distracted Penelope from her notion of marching around Mayfair's streets; with any luck, she was now thinking of who might be Alert's "buyers." Barnaby was congratulating himself on having diverted her train of thought when Griselda spoke—demonstrating that she, at least, hadn't been diverted at all.

"Regardless, we'll need to avoid cornering Smythe while he has the boys with him." Griselda met Penelope's eyes. "When experienced burglars like him are on the streets, they keep their boys on leashes, so if we stumble upon Smythe on his way to a house, or from one, he'll have hostages. And he'll use them. He might not have been known as a killer before, but he smothered Jemmie's mother, and went after Horry's grandmother. If we corner him while he's got the boys tied to him . . ."

Penelope grimaced. She flopped back on the sofa. "You're right. Damn it. But we have to do *something* to get those boys back!"

No one had any suggestion to make. Barnaby glanced around their small circle. While Penelope and Griselda were primarily focused on rescuing the boys, with foiling any burglaries a very secondary concern, the reverse was true for Stokes. For him, the burglaries posed a professional threat, not solely to him but to the entire police force; to him, rescuing the boys was part of preventing the burglaries and catching Alert.

For himself . . . Barnaby felt both needs keenly; he wanted to rescue the boys for Penelope's and the boys' sakes, wanted to foil Alert's plans for Stokes and the police force in general. For the greater good of the general populace; for the first time, he could see himself more directly serving a wider cause. Could better appreciate what drove his father to give so much time to politics; for years he'd thought it merely an escape from his mother's constant social round.

He stirred, and looked at Penelope. "Come—I'll escort you home." He glanced at the others. "For the moment, there's nothing we can do. If anyone thinks of anything, or learns anything . . ."

Stokes rose as he did. "We'll send out a bugle call."

That evening, despite a great deal of inner railing, Penelope dutifully dressed in her best winter evening gown, an austere example of the modiste's art in heavy silk the color of dark garnets, and accompanied her mother to dinner with Lord Montford.

His lordship was a reclusive gentleman and a great philanthropist.

He'd expressed an interest in the Foundling House, and was keen to speak further with her and her mother; that was the principal reason for the dinner.

Shown into his lordship's rooms off Piccadilly, she was greeted by Lord Montford, a rotund gentleman of genial good humor. She liked him instantly, replying to his polite inquiry into her health with genuine attention.

After greeting her mother, Lord Montford ushered them into his drawing room. "I believe you're acquainted with my other guests."

The twinkle in his eyes warned her an instant before she looked across the room and saw Barnaby uncoiling his long length from a chair. Lord and Lady Hancock were the only other guests; she and her mother knew them well.

Penelope was unsurprised when the older four gathered in a group, discussing children, grandchildren, and hunting, leaving her to Barnaby to entertain, and vice versa. She eyed him speculatively. "Have you known his lordship for long?"

He smiled. "He's an old friend of the pater's." He looked down at her. "Do you do a lot of this? Talking to donors, soliciting funds?"

"Not usually. Portia handles most of the fund-raising—she's good with people, as you put it, soliciting funds. But now she's in the country, she's landed me with these meetings, those held at this time of year. She'll return to town for the Season next spring, and will take back the fund-raising reins then, but meanwhile"—she spread her hands—"here I am."

Barnaby smiled. "You underestimate yourself. You can be very persuasive when you wish to be." When she let her passion for her work show.

She glanced at Lord Montford. "Any hints?"

"Just be yourself." He hesitated, then added, "He's very shrewd—much more so than he appears."

"I thought that might be the case."

They joined the others as Montford's butler announced that dinner was served. They went into the cozy dining room; despite the ambience created by costly furnishings, the room was conducive to more intimate, relaxed interaction. From the first, conversation flowed easily on all sides.

Penelope was seated at Lord Montford's right, with Barnaby beside her. Lady Hancock was on Lord Montford's other side, with Penelope's mother at the end of the table, opposite their host, with Lord Hancock between the two ladies. The Hancocks were already donors to the Foundling House; they and Lady Calverton became engrossed in discussing other subjects—leaving Lord Montford free to interrogate Penelope about the Foundling House.

Barnaby sat back and watched her deal with Montford; she avoided the trap of answering his questions too lightly, instead giving him the benefit of her considerable intelligence—something Montford, no fool, responded to. Indeed, watching Montford grow increasingly fascinated—both with the Foundling House's programs and Penelope and her role in them—he realized that being admitted into Penelope's intellectual confidence was a subtle honor. She patently did not consider many people, men especially, to be up to her considerable mental weight.

The thought made him smile. He watched her unknowingly seduce Montford, who, although most likely aware of it, was perfectly happy to be seduced in such a way.

When dessert arrived, Montford, transparently satisfied with all he'd learned about the Foundling House, directed the conversation to the police force and the recent and pending political manuevers affecting it, effectively turning the spotlight on Barnaby.

Somewhat to his surprise, Penelope followed Montford's lead, holding her own in what became an in-depth review of policing proposals, and the personalities and prejudices affecting the likely outcomes.

By the time they strolled back into the drawing room, they were engrossed. The topic carried them through the next hour, but after the tea had been served and consumed, the evening drew to a reluctant close.

Montford turned to Penelope. "My dear, I'll send a draft to the house tomorrow, but in addition, once we all return in the new year I'd like to call on you and discuss further options. I prefer to fund specific programs—practical ones that will achieve long-term gains. I'd like to consider some educational and training programs—perhaps more innovative ones—for specific funding."

Delighted, Penelope gave him her hand. "You will always be welcome at the Foundling House, my lord. I'll give some thought to possible programs in the interim."

Taking her hand in both of his, Montford patted it. "You—and your sisters, too—are a credit to your mother." Releasing her hand, smiling sincerely, he looked at Barnaby. "I have to say I find it heartening to discover a young couple such as yourselves, from families and circumstances where you've never had to—and will never have to—worry about your next meal, so devoted to helping others less fortunate. You"—he nodded at Penelope—"through your work with the Foundling House. And you"—he turned his gaze on Barnaby—"through your work with the police, through solving crimes and apprehending criminals regardless of the cut of their coats."

Smiling genially upon them, his next words were clearly intended as a benediction. "You make a remarkable couple—and I warn you, I fully expect to be invited to the wedding."

"John?"

Lord Montford turned away to attend Lady Hancock, and so missed the moment of complete and utter silence that followed his remark.

Barnaby glanced at Penelope. She glanced at him, but their gazes didn't, as they usually did, lock.

He didn't know what to say, couldn't think of anything; his brain had seized. She seemed similarly afflicted.

That they'd both been reduced to speechlessness—helplessness—by the single word "wedding" . . . that had to mean something.

Just what, he got no time to investigate. A loud rapping on the front door sent Montford's butler striding for it.

He returned a moment later, po-faced, to offer his salver and the folded note upon it to Barnaby. "An urgent message from Scotland Yard, sir."

Barnaby took the note, opened it, and read, in Stokes's bold hand: *The game is on.*

Shoving the note into his pocket, he nodded briefly to the others, then turned to Montford. "My apologies, my lord, but I must go."

"Of course, my boy." Montford clapped him on the shoulder, turning with him toward the hall. "The evening is at an end, anyway—Godspeed."

In the front hall, Montford shook his hand and released him without further questions.

Predictably Penelope wasn't so inclined. She'd followed at his heels and now caught his sleeve. "What's happened?"

Halting, Barnaby looked down at her, wondered if she realized how revealing her attitude, her question—and his inevitable response—would be to Montford and the others, who'd followed them from the drawing room and were now watching, too.

Not that it mattered. Seeing the worry and concern that had flared to life and now swam so clearly in the depths of her dark eyes, he couldn't not answer. He closed his hand over hers on his sleeve. "I don't know. Stokes wrote that the game was on—nothing more." He tipped his head toward the door. "The messenger will know where he is. I'll go and find out what's happened." He hesitated, then added, "If there's anything pertinent, I'll come and tell you tomorrow morning."

She seemed to realize that was all he could do. Pressing her lips together—he suspected to hold back unwise words—she nodded. "Thank you."

Drawing her hand from beneath his, she stepped back.

He bowed to her, and to the others behind her, then he turned and walked out of the door.

"Be careful with that thing!" Smythe hissed. He followed on Jemmie's and Dick's heels as they manuevered the heavy, ornate clock they'd just lifted from the fourth and last house on Alert's list for that night up the area steps.

Much taller than the boys, the instant his head cleared the street, he hissed again. "Hold up!"

The boys staggered to a halt; he could hear their panicked, increasingly labored breathing. Ignoring it, he scanned the street. Rozzers or passersby; with the heavy clock as booty he didn't want to run into anyone. The dark street seemed empty, the street flares burning low, their light diffused by the thick fog that had helpfully returned.

He strained his ears, but heard nothing. Not even the distant clop of a horse's hooves, but the street was a long one, the corner some distance away. He glanced at the boys. He hoped Alert was waiting. "Right then—move."

The boys staggered up the last steps, then angled the clock—all gilt, fancy dials, and ornate hands—through the gate at the top of the area steps. Smythe held it back until they got through, then joined them, resetting the latch.

He nodded down the street. "That way." His words were a thin whisper, but the boys heard and set off, eager to set the heavy clock down.

As at each of the previous three houses they'd hit, the unmarked black carriage was waiting around the corner.

Jemmie looked up, peering through the murky dark. The same man was on the box. He looked down, not at them but at the clock they were struggling with, and smiled. He nodded to Smythe. "Good work." Reaching down, he handed Smythe a pouch.

Without being told, the boys lugged the clock to the back of the carriage. Smythe followed. He opened the boot. There was a blanket waiting to wrap the clock in. Jemmie and Dick juggled the clock while Smythe swathed it in the blanket, then Smythe loaded the bundle into the boot, between the bundle that was the vase they'd nicked from the first house, and the tightly wrapped statue they'd taken from the third. The painting they'd lifted from the wall of the second house's library sat at the back of the boot.

Relieved of their burden, for an instant free of restraint, Jemmie looked at Dick, but before he could catch his friend's eye and give the signal to run, Smythe shut the boot and dropped a heavy hand on each of their shoulders.

Jemmie bit back a curse and hung his head. As under Smythe's guiding hand he trudged alongside Dick to the side of the carriage, he told himself—as he had for days, a week even—that a time would come.

When it did, he and Dick would run.

Unfortunately, the devil would be snapping at their heels; he held no illusions about Smythe. He would kill them if he caught them; they had to make sure that when they made their bid for freedom, they got clean away.

Smythe halted them beside the front of the carriage. "So we're done for tonight. You got the list for tomorrow?"

The man nodded. "I'll need to go over it with you." He tipped his head toward the carriage. "Climb in. I'll drive to somewhere we can talk."

Smythe nudged the boys back and opened the carriage door. "Get in." Once the boys had scrambled up, he joined them. Jemmie squished himself into the far corner of the seat; Dick did the same on the seat opposite. Smythe shut the door and dropped onto the seat beside Jemmie. The instant he did, the coach shifted and rolled off.

The driver drove slowly, as if his horse were plodding home. They left the big houses behind, then large trees appeared outside, enveloping the carriage in even deeper gloom.

A little way along, the carriage slowed, then halted. Smythe reached for the door handle, then paused; through the dimness he studied them. They heard the sounds of the driver climbing down. "Stay there," Smythe growled.

He climbed out, shutting the door behind him.

Jemmie looked at Dick, then they both sat up and peered out of the windows beside them. The scene that met their eyes wasn't encouraging; the trees the carriage had stopped beneath bordered a wide vista of open space. They'd left the worst of the fog behind; here it was little more than a veil, letting moonlight bathe the expanse, leaving them with nowhere to hide. To two urchins born and bred in the slums, the wide-open spaces weren't comforting. If they ran, Smythe would hear them leave the carriage. He'd be able to see them, and run them down. He'd catch them for certain.

Disappointed, Jemmie looked across at Dick. Lips tight, he shook his head. Swallowing his fear, he looked at the windows on the other side of the carriage; through them, he could see Smythe's shoulders, and those of the gentleman. They'd heard him speak; they knew he was a nob.

The pair had moved a few steps from the carriage; heads bent, their backs to the carriage, they were poring over something, presumably the list they'd wanted to discuss.

Exchanging another glance with Dick, Jemmie slid noiselessly from his seat and crept to that side of the carriage, ducking down by the door so he couldn't be seen. A second later, Dick joined him.

Heads resting against the door panel, they heard the gentleman explaining where a particular statue would be. From what followed, it seemed they were to burgle more houses the next night. At one point, Dick, eyes wide, looked at Jemmie and mouthed, "Four more?"

Jemmie nodded. Then they heard Smythe ask, "What about the police?"

The gentleman replied. His voice was lower, more mellow; they couldn't catch all his words. They did hear him say, "If any of your thefts tonight are reported, there might be more police on the streets tomorrow night. However, I'll know where they'll be, and they won't be near the houses we're interested in. Don't worry. You'll have a clear field. And as I said, those most interested in our activities will be distracted."

The man listened to Smythe's answering growl, then said, "If you pull off your end of things as well as you did tonight, all will go perfectly."

Hearing the note of finality in that cultured voice, the boys flashed each other frightened looks and scurried back to their corners, wedging themselves into their former positions as Smythe yanked open the door.

He surveyed them, then snarled, "Come out—we're leaving."

The boys scrambled out of the carriage. The instant they did, Smythe snagged a leading rein through a harness loop on the rope holding up each boy's baggy pants. Once both were secure, he shook the reins. "Come on—let's go."

They set off walking. Neither boy was silly enough to turn his head and look back at the carriage. They trudged on, over the open expanse, into the chilly night.

"I can't believe it!" Stokes paced back and forth in his office at Scotland Yard.

From his position lounging against the side of Stokes's desk, Barnaby watched him. Sergeant Miller hovered in the open doorway.

"There's no way to tell who else has been burgled!" Stokes flung up his hands. "Damn it—it's going to be hard enough to prove they've been burgled at all"—he flung a hand toward the door—"even when the staff are sure they have been."

Barnaby cocked a brow at Miller. "The old butler is sure the urn was there?"

Miller nodded.

"*But,*" Stokes said, his tone vicious, "he can't be certain his master hasn't sold it. He—the old butler-cum-caretaker—knows it was a fabulously valuable piece that many others had admired, so it's possible his master sold it the day before leaving town and forgot to mention it. So we're going to have to check with the marquess first, before we put out any hue and cry for a thief. And the marquess is currently in Scotland for the shooting."

Halting, Stokes drew in a huge breath, struggling to master his temper.

Impassively, Barnaby stated the obvious to spare Stokes the aggravation. "It'll be days, more like a week, before we know."

Stokes nodded tersely, his features like stone. "And by then . . . we'll have no chance at all of recovering even such an identifiable piece." Rounding his desk, he dropped into his chair. He stared across the room. "The truth is, if the caretaker hadn't been the ex-butler, it's unlikely he'd have known anything was gone. The marquess would have returned in February or March, and *then* we'd have heard about it."

Relinquishing his position against the desk, Barnaby moved to one of the chairs facing it. He glanced at Miller. "The caretaker didn't see anything useful?"

Miller shook his head. "He lives in the basement rather than the attics, or he wouldn't have known anything at all. He's old and sleeps poorly. He heard light footsteps pattering overhead, so he went up to look. He saw nothing amiss, but then thought he may as well check the windows. He found one unlocked, yet he's sure he'd locked it. He didn't worry because the window was barred, so he relocked it and headed back to bed. But he passed his master's study on the way. He leaves the doors open when he's in the house alone, so he can glance into rooms easily. When he looked in tonight, he knew something was wrong. Took him a while to realize that the holland cover on the table was lying flat where it should have been peaked over this Chinese urn that as far as he knows should have been there, but isn't anymore."

Stokes groaned. He stared at his desk. After a moment, he asked without looking up, "Has the superintendent sent that note to the marquess yet?"

His voice had lowered. Barnaby looked around, and saw Miller glance along the corridor.

"Looks like he's still writing it," Miller reported, voice lower, too.

Stokes sighed. He waved Miller in the direction he'd looked. "Go and make sure it's sent off express. We have to cover ourselves at least that much."

Once Miller had gone, Barnaby said, "From which comment I take it your superiors are still unwilling to admit they might have a series of extremely upsetting burglaries being committed right now, under their noses?"

Stokes nodded. "They don't want to believe it. The thought sends them into a panic, and they don't know what to do—and the truth is there's precious little we *can* do, short of flooding Mayfair with constables, which is not only impractical but would cause a panic of its own."

Heaving a huge sigh, Stokes sat back. He met Barnaby's eyes. "The truth is we—the police force—are facing a political nightmare."

He didn't need to elaborate; if anything Barnaby could see the ramifications even better than Stokes. The police were going to appear inept fools, unable to protect the property of wealthy Londoners from the depredations of a single clever thief. In the current political climate, that was a setback the still youthful and evolving force didn't need. Holding Stokes's gaze, Barnaby flatly stated, "There has to be something we can do."

Wrapped in her cloak, Penelope climbed the steps to Barnaby's front door. Her brother's carriage dallied by the curb even though she'd given the coachman—an ally of long standing—instructions to drive home to the mews behind Mount Street; he'd go once he saw her safely within doors. Steeling herself, she eyed the door, then raised a hand and rapped smartly.

Mostyn opened the door. His eyes widened.

"Good evening, Mostyn. Has your master returned yet?"

"Ah . . . no, ma'am." Mostyn fell back, giving way as she walked in.

"Close the door. It's chilly outside." She pulled off her gloves and put back the hood of her cloak while he complied. When he turned to face her, she continued, "Your master and I were at Lord Montford's when he—Adair—was called away urgently on some matter pertaining to our current investigation." Turning, she walked toward the parlor. "I have to wait here for him to return."

A statement of fact, one Mostyn didn't question. He hurried to open the parlor door; she swept in and he followed. "Tea, ma'am?"

The fire was burning brightly. She walked to stand before it, warming her hands. "No, thank you, Mostyn." She glanced around, then moved to the chair she'd occupied weeks before, when she'd first come to ask for Barnaby's help. "I'll just sit here by the fire, and wait."

Sinking into the chair, she looked at Mostyn. "Please do retire—he may be quite late."

Mostyn hesitated, but then bowed. "Very good, ma'am."

He quietly withdrew, leaving the door ajar so she could see into the hall.

She listened to Mostyn's footsteps fading, then, with a sigh, settled deeper into the chair and closed her eyes; she wasn't content, but at least she was where she needed to be. She had no idea how long it might be before Barnaby came home, but she'd told Mostyn the un-varnished truth: she had to wait for him to return. She had to be there to see that he'd come to no harm—there was no point attempting to sleep until she knew he was safe.

The powerful, flaring need had hit her the instant he'd passed out of her sight at Lord Montford's, in the moment she'd realized she had no notion what he was going out to face. *The game is on.* Who knew what Stokes had meant by that? They might, at that very moment, be chasing that devil Alert through alleyways and slums, out across the docks, dodging who knew what dangers.

Equally, they might be sitting in Stokes's office, but how could she tell?

In the face of her need to know he was safe, the notion of falling asleep had been laughable. She'd traveled home with her mother, tipped her coachman the wink, waited for the house to quiet, then had slipped out the back door and into the mews.

She knew on some distant rational level that she was very likely worrying over nothing.

That didn't change anything; the worry was still there. Potent, powerful, forceful enough to ensure she accepted that this was where she had to be—waiting for him to come home so she could see with her own eyes that he was unharmed.

She didn't bother pondering why she felt so. The reason was no longer in question; it simply was. Undeniable, and obvious, as Lord Montford had made abundantly clear.

She would have to deal with that reason soon, but for tonight . . . it was enough to see him home safe and sound. The rest, the reason, could wait . . . for now.

It was the dead of night when Barnaby let himself in through his front door. He and Stokes had waited at Scotland Yard, hoping some other burglary would be reported, but none had been. Eventually accepting that nothing further would be known until morning, they'd left for their respective beds.

Sliding the bolt home, he headed for the stairs. The parlor door had been left open; he glanced in—and halted.

In the red glow of the dying fire, she was little more than a shapeless bundle in the chair, her face hidden, tucked to one side. But he knew it was she—knew it in his bones through some primitive sense that would recognize her anywhere, no matter the lack of detail.

Silently he went in, crossing to stand before the chair.

In that moment, he couldn't put a name to what he felt, to the emotions that swelled, welled, and poured through him. He held still, made no sound, let the moment stretch, savoring it, hoarding the feelings, and the emotions, greedily holding them to his heart.

No one had ever waited up for him; no one had ever been there waiting when he came home at night, often tired and dejected, disappointed, sometimes disillusioned. And of all the people in the world, she was the one he wanted to be there, to be waiting for his return. She was the one in whose arms, for him, comfort lay.

His first impulse was to scoop her into his arms and carry her upstairs to his bed. But then he thought of why she was there.

After a moment, he crouched down, found her hands amid the folds of her cloak, lightly chafed them. "Penelope? Wake up, sweetheart."

She roused at the sound of his voice. Eyes blinking, then opening wide, she stared at him, then flung herself into his arms. "You're all right!" She hugged him violently.

He laughed and caught her; rocked back on his heels, rather than sprawl on the rug he rose, drawing her with him.

The instant her feet touched the floor, she pulled back and looked him over; it took a second to realize she was checking for damage.

He smiled and tugged her back into his arms. "I'm unhurt—there wasn't any action. I've been at Scotland Yard all night."

She stared into his face. "So what happened?"

He looked down at her, then stooped, swung her up in his arms, turned and sat in the armchair, settling her on his lap.

She made herself comfortable, leaning against his arm so she could see his face. "So?"

He told her everything. He even described Stokes's frustration. She made him recount every tiny fact he'd learned of the single burglary reported, then with him hypothesized as to what had occurred—how one of the boys must have slipped in and out through the bars, taking the urn.

She frowned. "It must have been a small urn."

"It was. Stokes and I questioned the caretaker before he left. He described the urn—from the sound of it it wasn't just any Chinese urn, but a very old one made of carved ivory. God only knows how much it might be worth."

After a moment, she said, "He's targeted collector's pieces, hasn't he?"

He nodded. "Which fits with the idea of him thieving on demand—stealing specific items he knows certain individuals want and will pay for, without asking difficult questions about how he got them."

She grimaced. "Sadly, when it comes to the more avid collectors, there are quite a few unscrupulous enough to fit the bill."

He didn't reply. They'd covered all the known facts; no matter the urgency they both felt over finding the two missing boys, there was nothing else—no other avenue—for them to explore that night.

Not in terms of the investigation.

He could tell she was thinking, still mulling over all he'd told her. Absentmindedly she rubbed her cheek against his chest. The simple, unconscious caress sent warmth, not just of desire but of a deeper need, swirling through him.

She was quiet, at ease, at peace in his arms.

The opportunity was there if he wished to grasp it, yet . . . the moment still felt so special, so novel and quietly glorious, he couldn't bring himself to disrupt it, to cut it short.

After Lord Montford's comment, after her coming here—after his reaction to finding her waiting for him—there was no question of what lay between them. He'd wanted her to speak, to suggest that they marry, thus absolving him of having to, yet his need to have her as his wife and what drove that need, while still featuring in his mind as a vulnerability, was no longer something he sought to hide . . . or more accurately, hiding it was no longer reason enough to keep him from seizing what he needed, what he wanted, what he had to have.

If she didn't speak soon, he would.

But here, tonight, was not the time.

They were both tired, and the morrow looked set to make demands on them both. Tonight they needed respite—they needed what they would find in each other's arms. Pleasure, and an oblivion that healed.

Carefully, he stood, lifting her securely in his arms. He started for the door. "Is your poor coachman waiting outside?"

Penelope rested her head on his shoulder, her arms loosely circling his neck. "No. I sent him home. We'll have to find a hackney later." As he turned toward the stairs, she smiled and murmured, "Much later—at dawn."

22

Penelope spent the next morning struggling to concentrate on running the Foundling House. There was nothing on her plate that was unusual, and issues such as which supplier to use for the next order for towels were not demanding enough to pull her mind from the treadmill of her thoughts.

When she'd discovered Dick missing, she'd felt in some way personally responsible. Logically she knew no blame attached to her, yet still she'd felt as if somehow she should have prevented it.

Losing Jemmie had only intensified the feeling. In murdering his mother and taking the boy, Smythe and Grimsby—and by extension Alert—had struck directly at her. At that point, the investigation had become very personal.

Now, with so many avenues exhausted or closed to them for one reason or another, a species of frustration laced with dread rode her, consuming her mind.

They had to—simply had to—find and rescue Jemmie and Dick.

Yet rack her brain though she might, she couldn't think of anything they could do, couldn't see any way forward.

"Any news of those two boys, ma'am?"

She looked up, finding a smile, albeit a brief one, for Mrs. Keggs. "Unfortunately not."

That redoubtable matron sighed and shook her gray head. "It's a worry—two innocents like that in the hands of a murderer."

"Indeed." Knowing she had to for the sake of staff morale, Penelope summoned a confident expression. "We—myself, Mr. Adair,

Inspector Stokes, and others—are doing all we can to locate Dick and Jemmie."

"Aye, and it's a relief to know they haven't been forgotten." Mrs. Keggs clasped her hands. "We'll all be praying you succeed, and soon."

With a nod, Mrs. Keggs departed.

All confidence fading, Penelope grimaced at the empty doorway. "As will I, Keggs. As will I." Praying, it seemed, was all she could do.

"I can't think of anything." Stokes, pacing across his office, shot a sharp glance at Barnaby, perched once again on the edge of his desk. "Can you?"

Barnaby shook his head. "We've been through it a hundred times. Smythe has the boys, and unless the Almighty decides to take a hand we've no prospect of locating him in the short term."

"And the short term is all we've got."

"Indeed. Alert . . . now we have a better feeling for the game he's playing, I'm more confident we'll identify him—in time." Barnaby's voice hardened. "Again, it's 'in time.' Montague sent a message this morning—he's checked enough to learn that every one of our eleven gentlemen suspects is in debt to some degree. Given their ages, and that they're all bachelors, that's not particularly surprising. However, how significant that debt might be will depend on their individual circumstances, and that Montague hasn't yet had time to assess. He says that'll take days, at least."

Stokes grimaced. "None of my contacts has come up with any hint of any of the eleven being involved in shady dealings."

Barnaby shook his head. "I don't think Alert will have stooped to petty crime, or even associated with criminals in the past. He's clever and careful, even if he is growing increasingly cocky."

Stokes grunted, still pacing. "He has the right to feel cocky. So far, he's trumped us at every turn."

Barnaby made no reply. For the first time in his investigative career he was truly stumped, at least on the subject of locating the boys. Alert he would pursue and eventually catch, but rescuing the boys . . .

He'd made a promise to Jemmie's mother, and to the boy himself. Losing Jemmie—having the boy snatched away so that he couldn't fulfill his promises—lay like a leaden weight on his soul, on his honor.

On top of that, the loss of Dick and Jemmie was making Penelope fret, more than he'd dreamed possible.

Like him, she didn't deal well with failure.

And this time failure was staring them in the face.

Stokes continued to pace. For all of them, being forced to wait without anything to do, knowing the boys were out there somewhere, was eating at their nerves. And time was running out. Now the boys had burgled houses alongside Smythe, he, knowing they were being looked for, might well view them as potential threats.

Now that Alert had executed his plan and pulled off his burglaries, even if they'd only learned of one . . .

Abruptly Barnaby refocused on Stokes. "Could Smythe have done eight burglaries in one night?"

Halting, Stokes blinked at him. "With two boys? No."

"No? Definitely no?"

Stokes saw what he meant. His face lit. "No, damn it—it's not physically possible. Which means if Alert is adhering to his original series of eight burglaries—"

"And why wouldn't he be, given his scheme appears to be working perfectly?"

Stokes nodded. "Then he has . . . at least three more burglaries to do."

"Five's the maximum in one night?"

"Four's more like it. Especially if he's having to use boys for them all, which according to Grimsby is the case."

"So Alert's series of burglaries are currently a work in progress. He's not finished—which means we have at least one more night, and possibly four more burglaries during which they might be caught."

Stokes grimaced. "I wouldn't count on Smythe making a mistake."

"It doesn't have to be him."

Stokes raised his brows. "The boys?"

"There's always a chance. And if there's a chance, there's hope." Barnaby thought for a minute, then stood and picked his coat up off the chair. "I'm going to see a man about another sort of chance."

• • •

"That's all he told you? And you let him go?" Penelope looked at Stokes with transparent disgust.

Stokes shrugged and reached for another pikelet. "He'll tell me if anything useful comes from whatever hare he's gone to chase. Meanwhile, with more burglaries pending, I've enough to think about."

Penelope humphed. They—she, Stokes, and Griselda—were once again gathered in Griselda's parlor. Today, Griselda had made pikelets, which Penelope hadn't had since she'd been in the nursery. It was comforting to sit curled on Griselda's sofa, a mug of tea in her hand, and nibble and sip.

And share her despondency.

"Joe and Ned Wills dropped by this morning," Griselda said. "No news, but they said the whole East End has its eyes and ears open. Once Smythe lets the boys go, we'll have them within hours."

Stokes sighed. "He won't."

"He won't let them go?" Penelope stared at him.

His expression grim, Stokes shook his head. "He knows we're searching for them. He'll either keep them and use them in more burglaries, or he'll get rid of them in such a way that they won't pose any threat to him. Perhaps take them to Deptford or Rotherhithe, make them apprentices, or cabin boys on coal haulers. He'll get money for handing them over, and at the same time ensure they won't be telling tales to anyone who'll listen any time soon."

A knock on the street door took Griselda downstairs; she returned with Barnaby in her wake.

To Penelope, he seemed more intent than she'd expected. He helped himself to three pikelets and Griselda handed him a mug of tea. He sipped as she said, "We were just discussing what Smythe will do with the boys. Stokes thinks he might put them out as apprentices."

She glanced at Stokes. "You don't think he'll kill them?" The nightmare that lurked in the back of her mind.

Stokes met her gaze steadily. "I can't say he won't. If he feels they pose a real threat to him, he might." He looked at Barnaby. "Where have you been?"

Barnaby lowered his mug. "Checking with Lord Winslow—he's

one of the law lords. If it can be proved the boys, as minors operating under an adult's thumb, were forced to burgle houses against their wishes—and we can prove that by personal testimonies including mine and that of Miss Ashford here—then they'll be excused the crime and can bear witness against their oppressor."

Stokes's expression grew grimmer. "So if we find them, they will indeed pose a threat to Smythe."

Barnaby nodded. He met Penelope's eyes. "They'll be regarded as innocent, *if* we can find them. But we need to find them soon, and get them out of Smythe's hands. He might not know what 'under duress' means, that the boys can testify against him without implicating themselves, but they know too much and, like Grimsby, Smythe will know all about making bargains with the police—he'll assume the boys will be encouraged to tell all they know in return for lighter sentences." Sober, he held her gaze. "Which means that whichever way Smythe thinks about it, once Alert's burglaries are over, Jemmie and Dick are very real threats to him."

That summation, its implication, settled like a grim reality upon them.

They went over all they knew yet again. Unfortunately, knowing more burglaries would take place didn't help in doing anything about them, or in locating Smythe and his charges.

"Alert really has tied this up tight." Stokes set down his mug. "He's anticipated what we, the police, will do, and from the first worked around us."

They'd talked themselves to a standstill again. Penelope glanced out the window and saw that the dull day had closed in to an even duller evening. She sighed; setting down her mug, she rose. "I have to go. I've another fund-raising dinner tonight."

Barnaby scanned her face. Setting down his mug, he rose, too. "I'll see you home."

Again they had to walk past the church with its cemetery alongside to reach the main road and find a hackney. Once in the carriage rattling toward Mount Street, Barnaby studied Penelope's profile, then closed his hand about one of hers, lifted it to his lips and lightly kissed her fingers.

She shot him a sidelong, questioning glance.

He smiled. "Where's this dinner?"

"Lord Abingdon's, in Park Place." She sighed, looking forward. "Portia arranges all these affairs—and then goes off to the country with Simon and leaves me to attend them!" She paused, then went on, "I've never missed her so much as I do now. I hate having to concentrate on social niceties, on polite conversation, when there's something so much more important to attend to."

Soothingly stroking her fingers, he said, "In reality there's nothing we can do tonight. We have no idea when Alert will attempt his next burglaries, whether he'll spread them out over more than one night— we don't even know how many more of the eight Smythe has yet to do. If Alert is well connected with the police, he'll know they aren't going to act until they hear back from the marquess about that urn. And even then what are they going to do? From the police's point of view— the governors' and Peel's—it's a devilishly difficult situation."

She put her head back against the squabs. "I know. And Lord Abingdon is a kindly sort who helps us on several fronts. I can't truly begrudge him the evening." After a moment, she added, "Unfortunately, Mama can't attend—she heard this morning that an old friend is failing and has gone off to Essex to see her before we have to leave for the Chase."

Time was running out on more than one front. "I know Abingdon quite well. I helped him resolve a minor difficulty some years ago." He caught her eyes when she looked at him. "I'll escort you tonight, if you like."

She looked at him for a long moment, studying his eyes, his face, then her lips lightly curved. "Yes. I'd like."

He smiled. Raising her hand, he kissed her fingers again. "I'll come for you at . . . what? Seven?"

Her smile deepening, she nodded. "Seven."

At eleven o'clock that night, after a pleasant dinner with Lord Abingdon and two friends who, like his lordship, were interested in philanthropic works, Barnaby and Penelope descended the steps of his lordship's town house to discover the fog had blown away, leaving the night crisp and clear.

"If I stare hard enough I can even see the stars." Penelope tucked her hand in the crook of Barnaby's elbow. "Let's not bother with a hackney—it'll be nice to walk."

Barnaby glanced down at her as they started along the pavement. "We'll have to cross half of Mayfair to reach Mount Street. You're not, by any chance, hoping to run into Smythe along the way?"

Her brows rose. "Strange to say, that idea hadn't crossed my mind." She met his gaze; her lips were curved. "I wasn't thinking of walking to Mount Street. Jermyn Street's much closer."

It was. He blinked. "Your mother . . ."

"Is in Essex."

They reached Arlington Street; turning the corner, they continued strolling. "I feel I ought to point out that in the interests of propriety you shouldn't be seen strolling down Jermyn Street on a gentleman's arm at night."

"Nonsense. In this cloak, with my hood up, no one will recognize me."

He wasn't sure why he was arguing; he was entirely content to have her come home with him—exactly as if they were already married, or at least an affianced couple—but . . . "Mostyn will be shocked."

She snorted. "I could demand to see your menus for the week and all Mostyn would do is bow, murmur 'Yes, ma'am,' and hurry to fetch them."

He blinked. It took a moment to digest all those few words conveyed. In the end, he said, "He addresses you as 'ma'am'?"

She shrugged. "Many do."

Many wasn't Mostyn, his terribly correct gentleman's gentleman. "I see." They'd reached the corner of Bent Street. Without further argument, Barnaby turned them along it.

He glanced at her face; beneath her lighthearted, almost playful expression he could detect a certain determination. Given the unresolved state of their relationship, he suspected he'd be wise to graciously give way. And see where she was taking them.

It might very well be where he wanted to go.

Penelope was indeed plotting and planning—rehearsing suitable phrases with which to introduce the subject of marriage once they'd reached his house. In the parlor would be preferable; easier to talk there—less distraction, there being no bed.

She'd assumed any discussion of their relationship, of how it had evolved from the initial purely professional connection to something so much more, to the point that they now, as they had over the last two nights, appeared to all others as a couple, connected in that indefinable way that marked two people who were, or should be, married, would be better put off until after they'd rescued Dick and Jemmie.

But with Smythe proving so elusive . . . what was the point in waiting? In putting off the inevitable?

Especially when, as they'd proved time and again over the last week, the inevitable held significant benefits for them both.

She couldn't believe that the reality of their relationship wasn't as clear to him as it was to her. She *could* believe, quite easily given her accumulated experience of gentlemen of his ilk, that he would vacillate over speaking—that even he would shy from declaring his heart.

She had no such reservations—was prey to no such hesitation. She felt perfectly able, and willing, to broach that particular subject.

But first they had to reach his parlor. She chatted blithely about this and that—curious about the gentlemen's clubs she barely glimpsed as he whisked her across St. James—then they were strolling down Jermyn Street.

She felt her nerves tighten as his door came into view. He guided her up the steps, then released her to reach into his pocket for his key.

Hearing footsteps approaching on the other side of the door, she swung to face it.

Barnaby looked up as the door opened and Mostyn stood there, filling the doorway.

Before he could blink, Penelope swept in. Mostyn gave way, bowing respectfully.

"Tea, please, Mostyn. In the parlor."

Tone and attitude were perfectly gauged; she was behaving exactly as if she were his wife. Leaving him gawping on the doorstep.

She glanced briefly back at him, then turned toward the parlor. "Your master and I have matters to discuss."

What matters? Brows rising along with welling hope, Barnaby took a step forward.

"Hist!"

Hist? Still on his front step, Barnaby turned and saw a man waiting by the area railings. The man beckoned, furtively glancing around.

Puzzled, Barnaby walked to the edge of the wide top step. "What is it?"

"You're Mr. Adair?"

"Yes."

"I was sent with a message, sir. Urgent like." The man beckoned again.

Frowning, Barnaby stepped down. One step gave him a better perspective on the street. Abruptly he halted, staring through the darkness, premonition prickling across his nape. Seeing three—he glanced the other way—no, four—men hanging back in the shadows to either side of his house, he started to step back.

They saw—and flung themselves at him.

He caught the first with a kick to the chest, throwing him against the side railings, but before he could recover the others swarmed up the steps and over him. He downed another with a blow to the gut, but the others pressed up and in, hemming him in so he couldn't move enough to get any force behind his blows.

They were trying to grab him, to wrestle him down the steps. To subdue and take him, but not to harm him. No knives, thank God.

He was wrestling with one, simultaneously trying to block the others from getting behind him to push, when he sensed someone else at his back. The heavy head of his grandfather's cane appeared over his shoulder, striking at the head of the man he was wrestling with.

Mostyn had flung himself into the breach.

His attacker yelled as the blows connected; two others tried to intervene, but the cane slashed first one way, then the other, and they fell back.

The cane returned to hit the man still holding Barnaby; he put up a hand to protect his head—loosening his grip.

In the same instant, smaller hands clutched the back of Barnaby's coat, steadying him—then hauling back with surprising strength.

A strength he used to help him wrench free of the man's desperate hold.

With a hoarse bellow the man ignored the thumping cane, flung himself forward, lower to the step, and seized Barnaby's flapping coat again. He got a good handful and tried to tumble Barnaby down the steps, but with Penelope's added weight to anchor him, Barnaby set his feet and wrenched his coat free, then whirled and pushed Penelope back over the threshold, gathered Mostyn—still slashing mightily with the cane—and bundled him back, too.

Flinging himself after them, he just had time before the wrestler picked himself up and his friends joined him, hurling themselves up the steps, to slam the door in their faces.

They hit the door with significant force.

Leaning against it, Barnaby reached up and threw the bolts. Mostyn quickly took care of the lower set.

The door shook under a fresh assault.

Mostyn rushed to add his weight to Barnaby's. The pounding continued. Mostyn put their combined incredulity into words. "This is *Jermyn Street,* for heaven's sake! Don't they know?"

"It appears they don't care." Grim-faced, Barnaby fished in his waistcoat pocket. He pulled out a police whistle on a ribbon. Still struggling to bolster the shaking door, he held it out to Penelope. "The parlor window."

Wide-eyed, she grabbed the whistle and rushed into the parlor.

In the warmly lit parlor, Penelope flung back the curtains, unlatched the casement window, swung it wide, dragged in a huge breath, leaned out as far as she dared over the area steps, put her lips to the whistle, and blew with all her might.

The shrill sound was enough to shatter eardrums.

She looked to see what effect it had had on the men pounding on the door—with a squeak, she ducked back just in time to avoid the brick that came sailing through the window.

Outrage welled. Furious, she dragged in a breath.

"Penelope?"

Eyes narrowed, she cast a dark glance at the window, then whirled and raced out into the hall. "I'm all right." The pounding on the door resumed. Barnaby and Mostyn pressed hard against the shuddering panels. "I'm going upstairs."

Grabbing her skirts, she held them up and took the stairs at a run. Racing into Barnaby's bedroom, she rushed to the window overlooking the street, flung wide the curtains, wrestled with the sash. Eventually pushing it up, she hiked herself up onto the wide sill, leaned out, glanced down at the men below, then put the whistle to her lips again.

She blew and blew.

The men looked up, swore, and shook their fists at her, but she was beyond their reach.

She grew giddy and stopped blowing, but by then she could see movement down the street. The sound of running footsteps—many heavy pounding footsteps—rolled up out of the night as constables of the watch converged from all directions.

With grim satisfaction, she watched as Barnaby's attackers turned to face the police.

What followed puzzled her.

The attackers didn't flee, as she felt attackers should. Instead, they flung themselves at the watch. In seconds, a melee had erupted, filling the street. More constables ran up—and, she noticed, a few more from the other side slid from the shadows to join the fight.

"How odd." It was as if the attackers' real target hadn't been Barnaby at all, but the police . . .

Stepping away from the window, she stared unseeing across the room. "Oh, my God!"

Grabbing up her skirts, she raced for the door. She flung herself recklessly down the stairs.

The much-abused front door stood open. She ran out—and uttered a prayer of relief when she found Barnaby on the front step rather than in the heaving jumble of bodies that continued to swell, jamming the street.

As she had done, he was frowning at the melee as if he couldn't work it out.

She grabbed his arm and hauled him around to face her. "It's a diversion!" She had to all but scream to be heard over the grunts and shouts.

He blinked at her. "What?"

"A *diversion!*" She swung out an arm, encompassing the crowd. "Look at all the police here—all the watch constables from around about. They're here—so they can't be on the beats they're supposed to be patrolling."

Understanding lit his blue eyes. "They're doing more burglaries tonight."

"Yes!" She literally jigged with impatience. "We have to go and look!"

"I *know* it's drawing a long bow, I *know* it's potentially dangerous, but we can't just sit at home and wait and wonder." Penelope marched along at Barnaby's side, scanning the houses they passed.

Although she'd kept her voice low, her words rang with a determination Barnaby couldn't—didn't have it in him—to dispute; he was no more inclined to passive patience than she.

It had been impossible to break up the melee. He'd waded in and collared a young constable; dragging the lad free, he'd sent him hotfoot to Scotland Yard with a message for Stokes. He had no idea whether Sergeant Miller would be on duty, or anyone else he could count on to act. And he had even less idea where Stokes might be; he had a sneaking suspicion his friend might be in St. John's Wood, in which case he was too far away to be of any material help.

So here they were, just the two of them, wandering Mayfair's streets.

December was around the corner, as evidenced by the crisp chill in the air; like the mansions they passed, the streets were largely deserted. An occasional hackney or town carriage clopped past. It was after midnight; the few couples still in town would have returned from their evening's engagements and be tucked up in bed, while the tonnish bachelors wouldn't yet have left their clubs.

These were the hours during which burglars struck.

They'd walked up Berkeley Street, and around the square, then down Bolton Street. They were presently walking up Clarges Street. Reaching the corner where it intersected with the mews, they turned left toward Queen Street. Ahead of them, a black carriage slowly rolled across the end of the mews, going up Queen Street.

Penelope frowned. "I could have sworn I saw that carriage before."

Barnaby grunted.

Penelope didn't say more. The carriage was a small black town carriage, the sort every major household had sitting in their stables, their second carriage. Why it had stuck in her head—why she was so convinced she'd seen that particular carriage earlier . . . she remembered where. They'd been crossing the northwest corner of Berkeley Square when the carriage had cut across Mount Street a block ahead of them, trundling in that same slow manner up Carlos Place.

She'd turned her head and looked at it; the angle of her view of the horse, carriage, and coachman on the box had been exactly the same as it had been a few minutes ago.

But why such a sight—to her, in this area, such a common sight— should so nag at her, why the certainty that it was the same carriage should be so insistently fixed in her brain, she had no clue. She puzzled over it as they walked quietly along, carefully scanning shadows, glancing down area steps, but came to no conclusion.

Reaching Queen Street, they hesitated, then Barnaby tugged her to the left. Settling her hand more comfortably in his arm, she strolled beside him. In another season, anyone seeing them would have thought them an affianced couple taking a long stroll the better to spend time in each other's company. With winter in the air, such a reason was unlikely, but their slow, ambling progress gave them plenty of time to examine the houses they passed.

Just like the couple she saw walking along the other side of Curzon Street.

Reaching the corner where Queen met Curzon, she stared, then tugged on Barnaby's arm. When he glanced her way, she pointed across and down Curzon Street.

He looked, then snorted.

In unspoken accord, they crossed to the southern side of the street and waited until the other couple strolled up.

Stokes looked shamefaced. He shrugged. "We couldn't think of anything else to do."

"Hostages or not, we couldn't sit at home and do nothing at all," Griselda stated.

"Anyway," Stokes said, "I take it from your presence here you felt the same."

"Actually"—Barnaby glanced at Penelope—"our presence here is more a response to direct action."

Stokes was instantly alert. "What happened?"

Barnaby described the "diversion."

"We sent a message," Penelope said, "but if you've been out walking, they wouldn't know where to find you."

Stokes nodded. "But we're here now—and you're right. They *must* be doing more houses tonight." He glanced around. "And most likely in this area."

"Given the diversion was in Jermyn Streeet," Barnaby said, "which beats in Mayfair are most likely to be currently deserted?"

Stokes saw his point. He waved to the south. "If we take Piccadilly as the southern boundary, then all the way to the Circus, then up Regent Street"—he pointed to the east—"up as far as Conduit Street. From there, across Bond Street to Bruton Street, along the top of Berkeley Square . . . and as your rooms are at this end of Jermyn Street, then they've probably come running from as far north as Hill Street, and probably"—he turned to look back along Curzon Street—"from all the areas out to Park Lane."

"So we're standing more or less in the middle of the deserted patch?" Penelope asked.

Jaw firming, Stokes nodded. "Depending on where in the beat they were, but I haven't seen any constables since we headed this way."

"We haven't seen any, either," Barnaby said, looking around, "but then we started from where they've all gone."

Stokes swore beneath his breath. "Let's divide the area and split up."

He and Barnaby put their heads together and sorted out routes. Stokes nodded. "We'll meet up again on the south side of Berkeley Square, unless either of us sights the beggars. You've got your whistle?"

Penelope patted her pocket. "I have it."

Barnaby retook her hand. He nodded a farewell to Griselda, then met Stokes's eyes. "If either of us see a bobby, or even a hackney, we should send word to the Yard and get them to send more men this way."

Stokes saluted and reached for Griselda's arm.

Barnaby and Penelope turned to head east along Curzon Street. Before they'd taken even one step a shrill shriek cut through the night and froze them.

Stokes was immediately beside them, searching the night. "Where?"

None of them was sure.

Then a second shriek split the silence. Penelope pointed ahead, to the left. "There! Half Moon Street."

Picking up her skirts, she ran. In a few strides, Barnaby and Stokes had outstripped her; Griselda appeared at her shoulder.

The shrieking had grown to a continuous wail, escalating in volume the closer they got to the intersection.

Barnaby and Stokes were a few paces from Half Moon Street when the shrieking reached new heights and two small figures came pelting around the corner.

Running at full speed, they streaked past both men before either could react.

Farther back, Penelope skidded to a halt. Now that their shrieks weren't distorted by the houses, she could hear they were calling for help.

"Dick?" One pale face looked up. She recognized the other. "Jemmie!"

Barely able to believe her eyes, she waved them to where she'd stopped with Griselda beside her.

Jemmie swerved to come to her, but Dick hung back in the middle of the road, eyes wild and staring, glancing back at the way they'd come, ready to dart off again. Jemmie noticed. "It's the miss from the Foundling House."

Dick looked at her again; the relief that flooded his face was almost painful to see. He shot over to join Jemmie.

Both boys grabbed her hands, one each, squeezing, jigging in their nervousness. "Please, miss—*please* save us!"

"Of course." Penelope bent and hugged them both. Crouching down, she drew Jemmie closer as Griselda also crouched, enfolding Dick in a protective embrace.

Barnaby and Stokes came walking back to them. Both were large men; with their features shadowed and unrecognizable, they were an intimidating sight. Penelope wasn't surprised when both boys shrank back against her and Griselda. "It's all right." She smiled at them reassuringly. "We're here. But what are we saving you from?"

The words had barely left her lips when a roar erupted, once again shattering the night. They all looked up. Barnaby and Stokes swung about, instinctively ranging themselves between the women and the boys and the oncoming danger.

A huge figure shot out of Half Moon Street, swearing and cursing, charging straight for them.

"Him!" the boys shrieked.

The ogre looked up and saw them—saw Stokes and Barnaby directly ahead of him. He swore, skidded to a halt, scrambled around, and fled in the opposite direction.

Barnaby and Stokes were already after him.

That sliding halt had cost the man too much ground; Barnaby was on him before he'd gone a block, Stokes just behind. In less than a minute they had the villain flat on his face on the cobbles. Barnaby sat on him while Stokes tied his arms and hands, then hobbled his ankles with the reins they'd found attached to his belt.

"I do like a criminal who comes prepared." Stokes hauled the man to his feet. He looked into his face, then smiled. "Mr. Smythe, I presume."

Smythe snarled.

23

Who is Alert?" Stokes paced slowly before the chair on which Smythe sat slumped. They'd brought him to Barnaby's rooms; not only had Jermyn Street been a lot nearer than Scotland Yard, but as Barnaby had been quick to point out, with Alert, whoever he was, connected with the police force, it was far preferable to keep the cards that had at long last fallen into their hands very close to their chests.

Even if Alert knew that something had gone wrong, even if he knew they had Smythe, the less he knew of what they learned from Smythe, the better.

They'd tied Smythe to the chair. He couldn't break free, and wasn't trying to. He'd tested his bonds once; finding them secure, he hadn't wasted effort trying to break them again.

He might be a massive hulk, a burglar and very likely a murderer, too, but he wasn't stupid; Stokes had every confidence Smythe would eventually tell them all he knew. He'd want something in return, but he had nothing to gain by keeping Alert's secrets.

They'd set Smythe's chair in the center of the room, facing the hearth; Stokes paced in the clear space before it. Penelope and Griselda were seated in the armchairs to either side of the now brightly burning fire. Barnaby stood beside Penelope's chair, one arm braced on the mantelshelf.

Dick and Jemmie were seated at a small table along one wall, wolfing down huge sandwiches Mostyn had produced. Mostyn hovered beside them, as interested as they in the scene being enacted in the room's center.

Stokes wasn't surprised when Smythe didn't immediately answer his question—Smythe was still thinking, his head bowed to his chest.

What surprised them both was Jemmie's reply. "He's a gentl'man—a nob. He's the one as planned all the burglaries. And he took all the things we stole from the houses."

Stokes turned to Jemmie; even Smythe lifted his head and looked at him. "You saw him?"

Jemmie squirmed. "Not to reckernize—it was always dark, and he wore a hat and muffler, pretending to be a coachman."

"The coachman!" Penelope sat up. "That's it!" She looked at Stokes. "I saw a carriage rolling slowly along while we were walking—I saw the same carriage *three times* tonight. The last time was as we started back down Bolton Street with the boys and Smythe—the carriage rolled along behind us, along Curzon Street. I couldn't get the sight of it out of my mind—there was something odd about it—and now I know what. I know what coachmen look like when they're on the box—they hunch a little. This man sat bolt upright. He was dressed like a coachman, but he wasn't a coachman—he was a gentleman pretending to be a coachman."

She looked at Jemmie and Dick. "Was that where the things you took from the other houses tonight went—into that carriage?"

Both boys nodded. "That's how it was set up," Jemmie said. "After we left every house, the carriage and Mr. Alert were waiting at the corner to take the thing from us."

Dick piped up, "Alert would give Smythe a purse, a down payment they called it, after we put each thing in the carriage's boot."

"Smythe was supposed to get more money later," Jemmie added. "After Alert sold the things."

Stokes glanced at Smythe, and could almost hear the wheels turning in his brain. If he waited much longer, the boys might divulge enough for them to guess Alert's identity, leaving him with nothing to bargain with.

Smythe felt Stokes's gaze and looked back at him.

Stokes arched a brow. "Any thoughts?" When Smythe hesitated, he went on, "At present, you'll be charged with burglary, murder, and attempted murder. You're going to hang, Smythe, all because of your association with Alert and his schemes. As matters stand, he's got all except one of the items he wanted, and he looks set to get clean away, leaving you to face the wrath of the courts when it's finally realized just what you stole."

Smythe shifted. "I might have stolen things, but it was on Alert's behalf. Pretty obvious it's not my normal job—whoever heard of taking just one thing once you get in a house?" He looked down. "And I didn't murder anyone."

Stokes studied him, then asked, "What about Mrs. Carter?"

Smythe didn't look up. "You can't prove anything."

"Be that as it may"—Stokes's tone was granite hard—"we have witnesses aplenty that you tried to kill Mary Bushel in Black Lion Yard."

Smythe snorted. "But I didn't, did I?" He paused, then went on, still talking to Stokes's boots, "Murdering people's not what I'm good at. I'm an ace cracksman. If it hadn't been for bloody Alert insisting on doing this caper—all eight houses—*his* way, I'd never have even thought of murder."

Stokes let the silence stretch, then prompted, "So?"

Smythe finally looked up at Stokes. "If I give you all I know about Alert—and it's enough for you to identify him—what'll my charges be?"

After another long moment, Stokes replied, "If what you give us proves enough to identify Alert, and you agree to testify against him if need be, we'll keep the charges at burglary and attempted murder. If we could prove murder, you'd go to the gallows. Without it, and a recommendation on the grounds of cooperation, it'll be transportation." Stokes paused, then said, "Your choice."

Smythe snorted. "I'll take transportation."

"So who is Alert?"

Smythe glanced down. "There's a hidden pocket in this coat—in the lining off the left side seam, thigh level." Stokes crouched down, feeling through the coat. "There's three lists in there."

Stokes found the folded papers and drew them out. Rising, he smoothed them, then held them up to read. Leaving the hearth, Barnaby joined him.

"Those are the lists Alert gave me. The first is a list of the houses . . ." Smythe talked them through Alert's plan, describing their meetings, recounting what they'd said. As he went through the burglaries, the four of the previous night as well as the three they'd completed that night, Stokes and Barnaby cross-referenced the lists—the street addresses of the houses burgled and the items taken.

At one point Barnaby stopped and swore.

Stokes glanced at him. Smythe stopped speaking.

"What?" Stokes asked.

Grimly, Barnaby pointed to one address—that of the first house burgled that night. "That's Cothelstone House."

"Your father's house?"

Barnaby nodded. He took the descriptions of items to be filched and located the relevant entry. "Silver figurine of lady on the table in the library window . . . good Lord!" He met Stokes's eyes.

Stokes raised a brow. "It's valuable, I take it. How much are we talking about?"

Barnaby shook his head. "It's worth . . . I have no clue of the figure. The word generally used in reference to that statue is 'priceless.' Literally priceless."

He looked again through the items listed. "We're not talking a small fortune here. If these other items are of the same caliber, Alert is setting himself up to rival the richest in the land."

Stokes shook his head. "You're telling me this statue—in the house of one of the peers overseeing the police, in a house *you* regularly visit—was sitting there on a table just waiting for some enterprising thief to make off with it?"

Barnaby glanced at him, then shrugged. "You'll have to take that up with m'mother, but I warn you you're unlikely to have much success. God knows the pater's been after her to lock it away for years—he gave up decades ago. As Penelope pointed out, these things have been around us since birth, and we don't even notice them all that much anymore."

"Until someone nicks them." Stokes looked disgusted. He turned back to Smythe. "So everything went smoothly, Alert picking up each piece in the carriage after every house, until the last. What went wrong?"

Smythe scowled and looked at the boys. "I'm not clear on that myself. Best you ask them."

Stokes turned to Dick and Jemmie. "The last house. What happened—how did you two break away?"

The boys exchanged glances, then Jemmie said, "The first night,

Smythe didn't tell us where in the houses we had to go until we got to each house. So we couldn't plan when to make our move. But later that night, after the first four houses, Alert took us up in his carriage, all three of us, and then stopped at a park somewhere to talk to Smythe about tonight's houses. They left Dick and me in the carriage, but we listened."

"We heard that one of us would have to go through the kitchen at the third house—that turned out to be me," Dick said. "We arranged that whichever of us it was, we'd pick up a knife sharp enough to saw through the reins." He nodded to the reins Smythe had been carrying, which now hobbled the big man's feet. "He used them to keep hold of us when we were going between houses, and if one of us was left outside, he'd tie us to a fence or a post with them."

"We also heard that the last house tonight would be only one of us," Jemmie went on. "We was supposed to take a small picture off the wall in an upstairs room. Smythe put me in the scullery window at the back, and waited there for me to come out. Because I had to go upstairs, I knew he'd wait a while before getting suspicious—I went out the front door instead. But the front door bolt screeched."

"I was nearly done cutting through the reins when he came out," Dick said. "But Smythe heard the screech and guessed what it was. Jemmie helped me get free, but then we saw Smythe coming up the side of the house. We ran."

"You did very well," Penelope said, approval and admiration in her tone.

Smythe grunted. He looked back at Stokes. "So that's it—all I can tell you. You find a gent who knows all those houses, enough to know all the details written down there—where the things were and exactly how to get to them—you bring him to me, and I'll tell you if he's your man."

Stokes studied Smythe for a long moment. "You'll recognize him, but then it's your word against his. Is there anyone else who knows him?"

"Grimsby," Smythe said. "He's seen him more than I have."

Stokes grimaced. "Unfortunately, gaol didn't agree with Grimsby. He had a heart attack. He's dead. He can't help us."

Smythe glanced down and softly swore. Then he looked across at the boys.

Stokes, following his gaze, asked, "Boys, think hard—did you see Alert, anything about him, well enough to recognize if you saw him again?"

Both boys screwed up their faces, but then shook their heads.

Stokes sighed. He was turning back to Smythe when Jemmie said, "We *heard* him well enough to know him again, though."

Penelope beamed at them. "Excellent!" She caught Stokes's eye. "That's good enough, isn't it?"

He thought, then nodded. "It should be."

"So"—Barnaby had been concentrating on the lists—"all we need now—" He broke off at the sound of someone rapping on the door.

It was a polite *rat-a-tat-tat*. Barnaby looked at Mostyn, who with a bow went to answer it.

Mostyn left the parlor door ajar. Nobody spoke, the adults waiting to see who it was, the boys too busy polishing off their sandwiches to care.

The latch on the front door clicked; a second later, a rumbling voice, too indistinct to make out, greeted Mostyn.

Mostyn's reply was clearer. "My lord! We . . . er, weren't expecting you."

"I daresay, Mostyn, but here I am," an urbane voice declared. "And here's my hat, too. Now where is that son of mine?"

The parlor door swung open and the Earl of Cothelstone calmly walked in. He surveyed the company, and smiled benignly. "Barnaby, dear boy—you seem to have quite a gathering here."

Barnaby blinked. "Papa . . ." He broke off, frowning. "I thought you'd gone north."

"So did I." The earl sighed. "Unfortunately your mother decided I'd left something in London she was set on me bringing home, so she dispatched me back to fetch it."

The light in the earl's eyes as they rested on his son informed everyone what the countess's "something" was.

Smiling genially, the earl turned his attention to the others in the room, then raised his brows at Barnaby.

"Ah . . ." Barnaby had a sense of matters spinning out of his control. "You know Stokes, of course." The earl exchanged a nod with Stokes, whom he knew quite well. Barnaby turned to Penelope. "Allow me to present Miss Penelope Ashford."

Penelope rose, bobbed a curtsy, then shook hands with the earl. "My lord. It's a pleasure to meet you."

"And you, my dear. And you." Clasping her hand between both of his, the earl patted it. He smiled delightedly upon her. "I'm acquainted with your brother. He often mentions you."

Penelope smiled and returned a polite reply.

A sinking feeling assailed Barnaby. His father knew. How, he didn't know, but if his father knew . . . so did his mother. He inwardly swore. He managed to breathe a trifle easier when his father—at long last—released Penelope and turned to Griselda.

Barnaby made the introduction, then steered his father to the boys, giving him enough of their story to explain their presence.

"Brave lads!" The earl nodded approvingly, then turned to survey Smythe. "And this is our villain, I take it?"

"More his henchman." Eager to keep his father's attention away from Penelope, Barnaby handed him one of Alert's lists. He was about to explain what it was when Penelope touched his arm.

With a nod, she directed his attention to the boys, both yawning. "Perhaps Mostyn can take them to the kitchen for some milk, and then find them some beds. I can take them to the Foundling House tomorrow."

Mostyn nodded his understanding. Gathering up the boys, he herded them from the room.

Barnaby turned back to his father, to find him frowning at the list.

"What are you doing with one of Cameron's infernal lists?" His father looked at him. "What's this about?"

For one instant, Barnaby felt sure he'd misheard. "*Cameron's* list?"

His father shook the list he'd given him—the one of the houses to be burgled. "This. I know Cameron wrote it." He looked at the sheet again. "It might be block capitals, but I'd recognize his style anywhere. As Huntingdon's secretary, Cameron writes up our agendas and minutes, all neatly laid out just like this." Puzzled, the earl looked at Barnaby. "What is this? I recognize our address, of course, and the others—this looks like one of Huntingdon's rounds."

Recalled from exchanging a stunned look with Stokes, Barnaby frowned. "Huntingdon's rounds?"

The earl snorted. "You need to pay more attention to politics. Huntingdon is extremely conscientious and regularly visits the power brokers in the party in his parliamentary capacity. Very dedicated, Huntingdon."

"And Cameron goes with him?" Stokes asked.

The earl shrugged. "Not every time but often, yes. If there's any business to be discussed, Cameron would be there to take notes."

Stokes caught Barnaby's eye. "All the stolen items were from libraries or studies—did you notice?"

Barnaby nodded.

The earl lost patience. "*What* stolen items?"

Barnaby handed him the rest of the sheets. "These items—the ones our principal villain arranged for Smythe to collect for him."

The earl took the papers and studied them. It didn't take him long to see the implications, especially when he came to the object stolen from his own house. "Your mother's great-aunt's statue?"

He looked up at Barnaby, who nodded. "Along with everything else."

There was nothing at all genial about the earl now. "He got them all?"

"All except the last, but he hasn't yet had time to dispose of them. And now, thanks to you and Smythe combined, we know who he is."

The earl smiled, this time predatorially. "Excellent."

It was Penelope who asked the most pertinent question. "Where does Cameron live?"

The earl knew. "He lives with his lordship at Huntingdon House."

Assured by the earl that Lord Huntingdon would still be up and about to receive them even though it was close to two o'clock, they all trooped around to Huntingdon House, which was luckily situated in nearby Dover Street.

Stokes pulled two constables from their patrol in St. James and put them in charge of Smythe, who Lord Cothelstone declared needed to come, too, so it was quite a procession that marched through the

doors of Huntingdon House. But Huntingdon's butler drew himself
up, and handled the matter with aplomb. Leaving the earl, a frequent
visitor, to see himself and Barnaby into Lord Huntingdon's presence
in his study, the butler bowed Penelope, Griselda, and Stokes into the
drawing room, then whisked the boys, Mostyn, the constables, and
Smythe to a set of straight-backed chairs lined up along the corridor
leading from the front hall.

Within five minutes the butler was back, to conduct them all into
his master's sanctum.

Huntingdon, a large, heavyset gentleman, was no fool. He listened
without emotion as Barnaby and Stokes outlined the case as they
knew it against the man Smythe and the boys had known as Mr.
Alert, now believed to be his lordship's private secretary, Douglas
Cameron.

When told that Smythe and the boys could identify Alert, Smythe
by sight, the boys by his voice, Huntingdon studied all three carefully,
then nodded. "Very well. Your story otherwise strains belief, but those
lists are damning. That *is* his hand, and those *are* houses he has visited
frequently in my train. I see no reason not to put Cameron to the test.
If by some twist of fate he's innocent, no harm will be done."

Barnaby inclined his head. "Thank you, my lord."

"However"—Huntingdon held up one finger—"we will do this
correctly." So saying, his lordship made his dispositions, directing
everyone as to where they should stand, and what they should do.

Two doors, one on either side of the long study, led to adjoining
rooms; a large oriental screen stood before each door. Huntingdon
sent the two constables and Smythe to stand behind one screen. He
dispatched Penelope, Griselda, and both boys to the room beyond the
other screen.

"I want you to bring the boys out only when you receive word
from me. Adair's man will stand by the main door here, and when I
give him the signal, he'll go out into the hall and around to tell you to
enter. I want you to keep the boys behind the screen, where they can
hear us, but not see us." Huntingdon fixed Penelope with his weighty
gaze. "I rely on you, Miss Ashford, to tell me if the boys correctly
identify Cameron as the man they heard giving Smythe instructions.
You'll know from my lead when to step out and tell me."

Penelope nodded. "Yes, sir." She gathered the boys; together with Griselda they went into the next room.

When everything was arranged to Huntingdon's liking, with the earl and Barnaby standing behind the desk to his right, and Stokes by the wall to his left, Huntingdon rang for his butler and instructed him to fetch Cameron. "And Fergus—no word to him regarding who is here."

The butler looked offended. "Naturally not, my lord."

Huntingdon glanced at Stokes, then at Barnaby. "Gentlemen, while I appreciate your interest in this, I will conduct this interview. I would take it kindly if, regardless of whatever Cameron may say, you maintain your silence."

Stokes looked unhappy, but nodded. Barnaby agreed more readily; he approved of his lordship's tactics, and saw no reason not to leave the interrogation in his clearly capable hands.

A minute ticked by, then the door opened and Cameron entered.

Barnaby studied him. His hair, an average brown, fashionably cut, was slightly ruffled, and there was a faint flush on his pale cheeks; Huntingdon had earlier stated that he hadn't asked Cameron to hold himself available that evening, and Fergus had confirmed that Cameron had been out since nine, returning only recently.

He was as well dressed as usual, not a cuff out of place; after an infinitesimal hesitation, excusable given the unexpected company, he closed the door and walked forward, surveying them with his usual arrogant air, significantly more deferential when it came to Barnaby's father and Huntingdon.

Barnaby noted that, along with Cameron's more evenhanded attitude toward himself. The man was supremely conscious of the lines of class; he treated everyone he considered beneath him with dismissive arrogance, all those above him—like Huntingdon and the earl—with toadying deference, while those he considered his equals—such as Barnaby—he acknowledged with an unruffled air. In Barnaby's experience, only those *not* secure in their place in the world expended so much effort reinforcing it.

Cameron halted a pace before the desk. Like any good secretary, his expression revealed nothing, not even curiosity. "Yes, my lord?"

"Cameron." Clasping his large hands on his blotter, Huntingdon fixed him with a level look. "These gentlemen have come to me with a disturbing tale. It seems they believe you have been involved . . ."

Huntingdon gave an expert summary of their case, omitting all unnecessary details, concentrating on the outcomes and conclusions.

Watching Cameron carefully, Barnaby thought he paled at mention of the lists, but that might have simply been his flush slowly fading.

Regardless, Barnaby—and he was quite sure Stokes, his father, and Huntingdon, too—had Cameron's guilt confirmed within minutes.

The man didn't react; even though Huntingdon's initial statement had told him *he* was suspected of being behind the crimes Huntingdon subsequently described, Cameron maintained his aloof composure. An innocent man, no matter his control, would have at least shown some sign of surprise, shock—at least perturbation—on being informed he was suspected of such acts.

Instead, Cameron simply waited patiently until Huntingdon reached the end of his recitation, concluding with, "Well, sir? Can you enlighten us as to the accuracy of this tale?"

Then Cameron smiled, an easy, gentlemanly smile inviting his lordship, and the earl, too, to join him in the joke. "My lord, this entire tale is nothing more than fabrication, at least as regards my supposed involvement." A wave of his hand dismissed the notion, along with the lists lying by Huntingdon's blotter. "I have no idea why suspicion has fallen on me, but I assure you I had nothing whatever to do with this . . . series of burglaries." He made the last words sound like an act he couldn't conceivably have been thought to perform—like cleaning out a fireplace.

With that, he simply stood there, the expectation, the absolute belief that Huntingdon would accept his word and dismiss the charges evident in his expression, his stance, his whole attitude.

Barnaby suddenly understood. Cameron, driving the coach, had seen them with Smythe, but he hadn't, even then, imagined they'd identify him. He hadn't remembered the lists, or hadn't thought anyone who might see them would recognize his style. He'd come to the study prepared to face down the worst accusations he'd thought might eventuate—vague ones not backed by any strong evidence—placing complete, overweening confidence in his position among the ton being sufficient to deflect any such charges.

Things weren't as he'd assumed, but now he was there all he could do was play out his scripted role. He had no other defense.

Looking down, Barnaby murmured, "It's a performance. He thinks he knows the rules."

He'd spoken quietly, but his father and Huntingdon would have heard, and they'd know what rules he meant.

Huntingdon studied Cameron, then unclasped his hands and eased back in his chair. "Come now, Cameron. You'll have to do better than that."

Anger flashed through Cameron's eyes. He was used to reading his employer; he now saw that, contrary to his expectations, Huntingdon wasn't going to join him in waving away the "fanciful" tale, let alone close ranks, gentleman siding with gentleman. "My lord." Cameron spread his hands. "I don't know what to say. I have no knowledge of these events."

From his position behind the desk, from the corner of his eye Barnaby saw movement behind the screen as Penelope and Griselda silently ushered the boys back in; Mostyn had unobtrusively left the room a few minutes before.

Cameron drew breath. "Indeed, I have to say I'm a little surprised to find myself a target of such allegations." His eyes flicked to Stokes. "One can only surmise that the investigating officers are at a loss for a culprit, and imagine that pointing a finger at one of their betters will cause sufficient consternation that their failure to protect the ton from such depredations will be overlooked."

A muscle leapt in Stokes's jaw; a slight flush tinted his cheekbones, but other than that, he didn't respond to the taunt, but continued to watch Cameron with a steady regard that somehow still managed to convey his contempt.

Cameron's eyes narrowed, but he couldn't say more on that front; turning from Stokes, he looked at his employer, and realized his words hadn't yet succeeded in deflecting the charge.

But Huntingdon appeared to be considering his suggestion. "Indeed?" His tone was encouraging, inviting Cameron to elaborate.

Cameron glanced at Barnaby, then met Huntingdon's eyes. "I'm also aware that, for some, solving crimes such as this, and pinning the blame on members of the upper class, has become something of a passion. One that carries a certain notoriety—even fame. Such considerations can cloud judgment when they're indulged to the point of obsession." Cameron allowed his lips to curve. "An addiction of sorts, if you will."

"Oh?" Huntingdon's response was cool.

Barnaby looked down to hide a smile; Cameron had just stepped over an invisible line. A gentleman did not make that sort of allegation about another gentleman other than in private.

"In short, my lord"—Cameron's voice hardened—"I suspect that these allegations, accusations, call them what you will, have been laid at my door as a matter of expediency. I don't imagine there was any truly personal aspect to the choice of me as scapegoat, but merely that I fit the bill as a suspect who, by virtue of my station and position as your secretary, will deflect attention from the woeful lack of evidence."

Looking up, Barnaby saw Cameron's now hard gaze fixed on Huntingdon's face. He had to give Cameron credit; had it been anyone with less backbone than Huntingdon, that last jibe—a reminder that should Cameron be charged, Huntingdon's personal standing would suffer—would have seen him walking free, at least of this room at this time.

Whatever he thought he saw in Huntingdon's face had Cameron's confidence returning. His expression eased. With a polite half-bow, he asked, "Will there be anything else, my lord?"

He'd misjudged Huntingdon badly. Once again clasping his hands on his blotter, Huntingdon fixed Cameron with a heavy look. "Indeed, there will. You have singularly failed to explain how lists of houses and items stolen from them, laid out in your distinctive style, came to be in the possession of the burglar who admits stealing the items. While you claim to know nothing about these lists, I myself can confirm that you've frequently visited every house listed, and that you're familiar with the libraries and studies therein, enough to have certain knowledge of the items stolen. Very few gentlemen would have such knowledge, not of *all* these houses. Likewise, you are one of the few with knowledge and access sufficient to have falsified the police order against the Foundling House.

"While lists composed in your peculiar style, your familiarity with the houses involved, and your ability to falsify police orders might individually be dismissed as circumstantial, taken together, they are highly suggestive. However, as you maintain you're entirely innocent, you can have no objection to allowing the burglar"—Huntingdon beckoned Smythe out from behind the screen—"to take a look at you and confirm whether or not you're the man for whom he's been working."

That Cameron had prepared for. Calmly, he turned and faced Smythe.

Smythe took one long look at him and snarled, "That's him. He called himself Mr. Alert."

Cameron merely raised his brows, then turned back to Huntingdon. "My lord!" His expression and tone were incredulous. "Surely you can't be intending to place any faith in the word of a man like this? He'd say anything." Gaze flicking to Stokes, Cameron added, "I daresay he's been offered an incentive to do so. No court would convict on his word."

Gravely, Huntingdon nodded. "Perhaps not. However, there are other witnesses." He looked to the other side of the room. "Miss Ashford?"

Penelope came out from behind the other screen. Hands clasped before her, she addressed his lordship. "Both boys reacted instantly to Cameron's voice. There can be no doubt that he was the man they overheard giving Smythe instructions"—she looked at Cameron—"of which houses to burgle and what to steal from each."

Cameron stared at her.

"Two innocent boys who are under no compulsion or threat, and therefore have no reason to lie." Huntingdon paused, then asked, "What say you now, Cameron?"

Cameron hauled his gaze from Penelope and her condemnatory stare—and glanced at his lordship.

All trace of the gentleman had vanished.

Barnaby swore and started around the desk.

Cameron didn't react like a gentleman; he lunged for Penelope.

Stunned, disbelieving, she found herself seized by the arms. Wild-eyed, Cameron swung her before him; he slung one arm across her shoulders, locking her against him. And brandished a knife before her face.

She focused on it; a chill slid down her spine. Cameron had to be insane. The knife looked sharp.

"Stay back!" Cameron shifted so his back was to the wall.

She could feel his head turning this way and that. Could feel the nervousness—the near panic—pouring off him.

"*Back*, I said! Or I'll slice open her cheek."

His hand shifted; the knife with its glinting edge was suddenly very close to her face.

Icy fear trickled down her spine. He was too strong for her to break from his hold, especially not with the knife so close. He'd widened his stance—she couldn't even kick his legs.

Hauling in a breath, she forced her gaze from the knife. She looked at the others; their faces were a blur. Then her gaze reached Barnaby and locked on his face, her focus sharpening.

He was pale, his face drawn, features tense. He stood poised beside the desk, held back by Cameron's threat.

He was watching Cameron, and her, closely; when Cameron glanced around the room, checking the others, Barnaby trapped her gaze—and opened his mouth and bit down.

She blinked, realized; pressing her head back against Cameron's chest, she focused on the hand holding the knife before her face. Because she was so short, the hand was in front of her mouth.

Opening her mouth wide, she sank her teeth into Cameron's hand.

He yelped.

Closing her eyes, she bit down as hard as she could and locked her jaw.

He yelled. He tried to pull his hand away, but couldn't. With that hand immobilized, he couldn't use the knife.

With her jaw in the way, he couldn't release it.

He flung this way and that, howling, furiously trying to dislodge her; for one crazy moment they waltzed around, but she refused to let go.

With a huge effort, he flung her away. The momentum forced her to release him; she sailed across the room and collided with Stokes and the earl. They went down in a tangle, tripping the two constables who'd rushed up to help.

Scrambling free of the melee, on her hands and knees, Penelope looked across the room and saw Cameron using the knife to keep Barnaby at bay. Huntingdon was on his feet, but he couldn't get around his desk without distracting Barnaby.

And from the look on Cameron's face, he was just waiting for a chance to slice Barnaby up.

Time slowed.

The knife flashed, then flashed again. Barnaby leapt back just in time.

Cameron snarled and lunged. Her heart in her mouth, Penelope started to call out. At the last instant, Barnaby twisted away; the knife glinted as it slid past his chest.

He reached for Cameron's arm, but Cameron saw the danger and flung himself back. Eyes wild, flicking over the men, the knife waving before him, he backed.

He'd forgotten—or perhaps never noticed—Griselda. Stealing out from behind the screen, she'd lifted a heavy statue from a side table and crept up behind Cameron, keeping close to the wall. Raising the statue, she'd been waiting for her moment; as he backed within reach, she brought it down on his skull.

Penelope scrambled to her feet as Cameron swayed on his. "Not hard enough." She waved at Griselda. "Hit him again."

Before Griselda could, Barnaby stepped forward, brushed aside the knife, and felled Cameron with a jaw-cracking punch.

The force of it lifted Cameron off his feet. His back hit the wall, then his eyes rolled up. His knees buckled; he slid down, ending in a crumpled heap.

Barnaby stood over him, grimacing as he shook out his hand.

Aghast, Penelope flew across the room to him.

Huntingdon clapped him on the shoulder as he passed. "Good work."

Penelope wasn't so sure. She caught Barnaby's hand—his beautiful long-fingered, elegant, and clever hand—stared at the redness already spreading across his scraped knuckles. *What have you done to your hand?"*

To Barnaby's besmusement, the damage he'd done to his hand—minor, it would heal—consumed Penelope's mind. All else was relegated to second place. Nothing would do but for her to hurry him home to Jermyn Street so she could tend his wounds. Salve his scraped knuckles.

That Mostyn had taken the boys under his wing, volunteering to take care of them and deliver them tomorrow afternoon to the Foundling House, set the seal on her impatience to be away.

Something Barnaby decided was in his own best interests; aside from all else, he needed to speak with her—now, soon—before his father said anything to make his life more difficult.

Penelope was relieved when he agreed to leave matters in Lord Huntingdon's and the earl's capable hands. To her mind, there were capable people aplenty to take charge of the fiend Cameron and do all else that needed to be done. The constables would take Smythe and Cameron to Scotland Yard; Stokes would see Griselda home. Penelope's only responsibilities were to see to the welfare of the boys, and Barnaby.

The latter stood highest in her mind. When they reached his house, she dispatched the boys to bed in Mostyn's care and harried Barnaby up to his bedroom. She pushed him to sit on the bed, then bustled into the bathing chamber for a bowl of water.

Returning, setting the candelabra near so she had better light, she examined his hand, and hissed. "Men and their pugilistics." She felt thoroughly shaken; she wasn't sure why. "You didn't need to hit him at all—Griselda could have taken care of it if you'd given her another second."

"I needed to hit him."

She ignored the hard, flat tone of his voice. "I'm very fond of your hand, you know." She immersed the object in question in the cold water. "Both of them. I'm rather fond of lots of other parts of you, too, of course, but that's beside the point. Your hands—" She realized and stopped.

Drew in a huge breath. "I'm babbling." She heard the stunned amazement in her tone, but her tongue just ran on. "See what you've reduced me to? I *never* babble—ask anyone. Penelope Ashford has never babbled in her life, and here I am, babbling like a twit, all because you didn't think—"

He stopped her by the simple expedient of kissing her. Ducking his head, he covered her lips, slowed her racing tongue with his.

His arm slid around her and drew her to him.

Almost instantly, she relaxed against him.

It started off as a gentle kiss—a long, soothing, reassuring exchange for them both. But there was far more between them, more primitive reactions that needed to be assuaged, more powerful needs that rose up and unexpectedly caught them, taking over the kiss, infusing it with passions neither had intended showing, but both desperately needed to appease. To slake. To satisfy.

He angled his head and plundered her mouth, ravaged her senses—and she returned the favor. Shook the water from her hands and plunged them into his hair, spearing through the curling locks to grip his head. So she could hold him steady and kiss him back—claim him as her own just as avidly, as greedily, as hungrily as he claimed her.

As wildly. As unrestrainedly.

When they finally broke the kiss, they were both breathing rapidly, hunger and need—very definitely not just physical—pounding in their blood. The same beat, the same compulsion. She met his eyes, and saw all she felt roiling in the vivid blue—the same tumult of emotions.

The same reason behind it.

The same motive. The same power.

She dragged in a shuddering breath. She'd been meaning to speak; the time was clearly now.

Yet with the moment upon her, one doubt assailed her. He was a confirmed bachelor—everyone in the ton knew that. If she spoke—proposed—and he didn't agree . . . their time together would end. Regardless of her wishes, once he knew she was thinking of marriage, if she couldn't convince him to agree, he would kindly but definitely cut her out of his life . . . and she didn't think she could bear that. If she spoke and he didn't agree, she would lose all they, all she, now had.

If she didn't speak . . . she would lose all they might have.

Yet even if he felt the same emotions she did, that didn't mean he'd see marriage to her as the right path for him.

For the first time in her life, faced with a clear challenge, her courage wavered. Taking this one step . . . she'd never faced such a critical moment in her life. She searched his eyes for some hint, some clue, as to how he might react. And remembered . . . She frowned. "Why did you *need* to hit Cameron?"

He'd made it sound as if the action had held some greater significance beyond simply stopping the fiend.

He held her gaze, then his lips quirked wryly. He lowered his gaze to her lips. "You said I didn't think." His jaw firmed. "You were right—I didn't. It was . . . peculiar. I never 'don't think'—just as you never babble. But from the instant Cameron seized you I . . . stopped thinking. I didn't need to. What I needed to do was perfectly clear without any requirement for thought."

He paused, drew in a long breath. "I had to hit him because he'd seized you. If he'd grabbed Griselda, I wouldn't have felt the same—although perhaps Stokes might have. But Cameron grabbed *you*, and"—his voice deepened—"some time in the past weeks you've become *mine*. Mine to protect. To have and to hold. To keep safe."

He met her eyes, and she saw truth shining in the blue. "That's why I hit him—why I didn't even have to think to know I had to. Needed to." He paused, then went on, "I've heard that's how things can be . . . with a certain woman. I didn't think such a thing would happen to me, but with you . . . it has. If you don't want to be mine . . ." He searched her eyes, then, his voice hardening, said, "It's too late. You already are."

She'd been looking for something to give her heart; it was there, shining in his eyes. "I think we should marry."

Barnaby felt elation surge through him; looking into her dark eyes, he inwardly exulted.

Before he could react, she frowned. "I know it's a startling suggestion, but if you'll listen to my reasoning I believe you'll see it's a sound one, with significant benefits for us both."

This was what he'd planned to achieve. He fought to keep his flaring triumph from his eyes; he wanted to hear all she had to say, all she was so willing to tell him. "You perceive me all ears."

She frowned more definitely, unsure how to read his tone, but then drew breath and went on, "I know—as do you—that there's a long list of logical, rational, socially dictated, and socially approved reasons we should wed." She fixed him with a direct look. "But neither you nor I allow ourselves to be influenced by such considerations—I mention them purely to dismiss them, noting only that a marriage between us would be socially welcomed."

His mother would be over the moon. He nodded and waited.

Her gaze lowered to his lips. "Weeks ago, you pointed out that we deal exceptionally well together. Privately, publicly, socially, and even more remarkably in the matter of our esoteric vocations. We can talk to each other about all subjects that interest us, and more, we enjoy doing so. We talk about things we never talk about with anyone else. We share ideas. We react to situations in the same way. We feel compelled by the same circumstances and to the same end." Raising her eyes, she met his. "As I said at the time, we're complementary. Everything that's happened since has only underscored how correct that assessment was."

She tilted her head, studied his eyes. "You, me—we're not the same, but we—our lives—somehow fit together."

You make me whole. She didn't say the words, but they rang in his mind, conveyed as effectively as if she'd spoken them.

"Together we're more—stronger than we are individually. If nothing else, these weeks have proved that." She paused, then went on, "So I think we should marry, and continue the partnership we've started. For us, marriage won't be a restriction, but instead will enable us to expand our partnership to encompass all the various aspects of our lives."

Her lips firmed; through his hands on her back, he sensed the steely purpose that infused her. "That's why I think we should marry. And that's what I would wish for, if I had my way and you wished for it, too."

Honest, direct, clearheaded, and determined; he looked into her eyes and saw all that and more. All he had to do was smile charmingly, pretend to be much struck by her proposition—her proposal—make some show of considering her arguments, and then gracefully accept.

And then she would be his and he'd have all he desired—without having to admit to, without having to reveal or acknowledge other than in his own mind, what drove him. What power had sunk its claws into his soul and now owned him.

Unfortunately . . . it seemed that power had other ideas.

Honest, direct, clearheaded, and determined . . . wasn't enough. Him simply accepting would never be enough.

"Yes, we should marry." The harshness of his voice made her eyes widen. Before she could start thinking, speculating, he said, "But . . ."

He tried, quite desperately, to censor his words, but with her in his arms, her dark eyes on his, it was suddenly imperative, more important than life, that she knew and understood, completely and utterly. "When we took our first steps into intimacy, if you'd been more experienced you would have realized that a man like me wouldn't have touched you if I wasn't thinking of marriage."

Her eyes widened. She stared at him. A finite moment passed before she managed to enunciate, "From *then*?"

He nodded, jaw setting. "Very definitely from then. You were a gently bred virgin, your brother's sister—no honorable gentleman would have touched you, *except* that I wanted you as my wife and you—at that point—were set against marriage. So I fell in with your wishes, but only because I had every intention of changing your mind."

Her eyes narrowed. "You intended to *make me change my mind*?"

Her tone made him snort. "Not even then, when I knew you less well, did I imagine I'd be able to do that. *I* couldn't make you change your mind, but I hoped, prayed, that you'd come to see that marrying me would be a good idea. That you'd convince yourself to change your stance. As you did."

He'd expected her to follow his comments forward in time, to the present; instead—as he should have known she would—she retreated to the point he'd revealed, but hadn't explained.

"Why did you want to marry me?" She frowned, genuinely puzzled. "Almost from the start of our association, before we grew to know each other well . . . what possessed you to decide you wanted to marry me?"

It took more than an inward squirm—more like an inner wrestle—to force the truth out. "I don't know."

When she stared at him, disbelief in her eyes, he reiterated, "I *don't*." Jaw setting, he went on, "At that time, all I knew was that you were the one. I didn't understand it—but I knew it just the same."

"So definitely you acted on it?" She sounded . . . a touch fascinated.

A dangerous admission, but he forced himself to nod.

Her eyes, dark and luminous, softened. She tilted her head, her eyes on his. "And now?"

The ultimate question.

Looking into her eyes, he forced himself to speak. To confess and have done with it—to tell her all he'd never intended her to know. "I still don't understand why any man in his right mind would tell any woman this, but . . . I love you. Before you walked into my life, I had no clue what love was—I saw it in others, even appreciated it in them, but I'd never been touched by it. So I didn't know how it felt—would feel. Now I know."

He hauled in a huge, not entirely steady breath. "When Cameron grabbed you and he had that knife—I literally saw red. I knew nothing beyond the fact that you—around whom my life now revolves—were in danger. That if anything happened to you, I couldn't live—I might exist, but I wouldn't be truly alive as I have been with you over the last weeks."

He searched her eyes. "You didn't say it before, so I will—*you make my life complete.* I love you, I need you, and I want you as mine—mine for all the world to see and know."

To his surprise, the words had come easily. "I want us to marry. I want us to be man and wife."

She looked into his eyes, then slowly, she smiled. "Good." Reaching up, she drew his head down to hers. "Because that's what I want, too, because I love you, too. It's strange and unexpected, but fascinating and exciting, and I want to keep exploring it . . . with you." Their lips a bare inch apart, she paused. Her ripe, luscious lips curved deliciously. "And you might want to remember that arguing with me is never wise."

He would have laughed, but she kissed him. Kept kissing him when he wrapped her in his arms and kissed her back.

Joined with him—more, urged him on. All barriers fallen, all hurdles overcome, there was no longer any reason not to celebrate to the fullest all they'd found, all they shared—the love, the desire, the passion.

They let all three loose—his and hers combined. Together, as one, they let the tumult rage and devour them.

Let it sweep them into a giddy, desperate, wild engagement driven by their needs. Who took whom, who could more evocatively demonstrate, more effectively convey their devotion—as ever they argued, wordlessly pressed, embraced the question and with abandon gave themselves up to pursuing the answer.

To their mutual delight, to their mutual pleasure and ultimate satisfaction.

To the culminating moment when he had her beneath him, when she arched and took him deep, when her hands clutched desperately as she crested the peak—in that moment, looking down on her face, on the rapture so starkly etched across her features, he couldn't doubt—didn't doubt—that her devotion, her commitment—her love—was the equal of his.

Then the maelstrom took her, shattered her, and glory poured through her—into him. Even as her hands slid limply from his shoulders, the tight clutch of her body drew him with her into the timeless void. Into that moment of exquisitely sharp sensation when nothing mattered but that they were one.

The moment fused them, wrapped them in warm clouds of bliss—in completion, in benediction, in the sureness that this was where fate had wanted them—slumped, helpless in the aftermath of something neither could deny.

Whole. Complete. In each other's arms.

They were married, not as they'd wished within days, but in late January. December arrived and with it came snow—feet and feet of it. Even though their respective ancestral homes weren't that far apart, their mothers jointly declared that too many others would have to brave the drifts to attend their nuptials; consequently, said nuptials had to be delayed until after the thaw.

As Penelope was heard to comment on the drive to the church, she and Barnaby had to count themselves lucky they'd been allowed to wed before April.

The weather did not similarly affect matters in the capital. Cameron was committed to Newgate, and left there to languish pending a full review of the charges to be laid against him; his trial would necessarily have to wait until those from whom he'd stolen so successfully returned to the capital to identify their possessions.

The day after Cameron had been arrested, Stokes and Huntingdon's staff had searched the house. Courtesy of a tweeny who had heard noises in the locked box room adjacent to her tiny room in the attic, they'd uncovered a cache containing the seven items Smythe and the boys had delivered into Cameron's hands.

Riggs had confirmed that Cameron was an acquaintance, one who knew of his house in St. John's Wood Terrace, and that his mistress, Miss Walker, was a slave to laudanum. Riggs had been confounded to learn of Cameron's actions. "He was always such a good fellow, you know. Would never have suspected him of any such thing."

That sentiment was echoed by many; it was Montague who eventually shed light on Cameron's motives.

Cameron hadn't been what he'd purported to be—not since his early schooldays. The son of a mill owner from the north who'd married the local squire's daughter, his gentry-born maternal grandfather had taken some delight in sending him to Harrow.

Unfortunately, courtesy of his schoolmates, his schooldays had given Cameron a glimpse into the world of the haut ton. It became his burning ambition not just to gain entry to that gilded circle, but to belong. So he'd hidden his lowly origins, and had zealously concealed his damning lack of funds.

He'd made ends meet by gambling, which had stood him in good stead, until he'd hit a losing streak. His life had gone downhill rapidly. He'd landed in the clutches of London's most notorious cent-per-cent, a usurer Stokes and his superiors would dearly like to see put out of business, but neither desperate debtors nor dead men tended to talk.

As Cameron's scheme had been all his own invention, he wasn't any help in that regard. Now that said scheme, and the façade he'd constructed, had tumbled down about his ears, Cameron had retreated into himself and largely refused to speak.

Given the seriousness of the thefts he'd planned, and his exploitation of his position as Huntingdon's secretary to that end, knowing as he had that such actions would seriously damage the standing of the still-fledgling police force, and in light of the incitement he'd provided to Smythe and Grimsby to commit murder, kidnap innocent boys and induct them into lives of crime, transportation was the very best Cameron could expect; he would be lucky to escape the gallows.

On a happier note, Inspector Basil Stokes and Miss Griselda Martin were married early in the New Year. Having spent Christmas with their families, first at Calverton Chase, then at Cothelstone Castle, and then having journeyed—commanded by duchessly edict—to join the revels at Somersham Place, there to be subjected to another round of congratulations and teasing, Barnaby and Penelope pounced on the excuse to flee. Braving the roads, they reached the capital the day before the wedding. Just as well, as Barnaby was Stokes's best man, and Penelope stood beside Griselda as her maid of honor.

Penelope regarded the outcome as a triumph. She was quick to extract a promise from the happy couple that they in turn would attend her and Barnaby's nuptials in due course.

Finally, later that month, after she'd succeeded in dancing the wedding waltz at her own wedding—a waltz she'd enjoyed to the very depth of her soul—Penelope stood by the side of the Calverton Chase ballroom, and confessed to her sister Portia, who, with her older sister Anne, had been her matron of honor, "It was so *very* tempting, being in London, to have Barnaby get a special license and simply have done with the matter, but—"

"You couldn't face your mothers' consequent disappointment." Portia grinned. "Neither of you would have ever lived it down."

Looking down the ballroom to where their mother and Barnaby's sat, resplendent on a chaise surrounded by other ladies of similar degree, delightedly receiving the congratulations of their acquaintance, Penelope frowned. "I can't understand it—it's not as if they haven't presided over weddings of their children before. For Mama, this is her *fifth* time, and the countess's *fourth*—surely the gloss should have dimmed by now."

Portia laughed. "You're forgetting one thing. For them, this wedding represents a triple triumph."

"How so?"

"First, you know perfectly well that the entire ton has considered you determinedly unweddable—by your own choice. Your change of mind is a huge triumph for Mama. And similarly for Barnaby—it was greatly feared he would join the ranks of the confirmed bachelors, so of course Lady Cothelstone is in alt. And last but not least, for both Mama and her ladyship, you two are their last. The youngest and last of their offspring." Portia looked down the room to where the two ladies sat. "As of this morning, their work is *done.*"

Penelope blinked; that certainly cast their mothers' happiness in a new light. "But surely," she said, thinking further, "they'll have a similar interest in their grandchildren's lives and marriages."

"Interest, yes, but at one remove—I suspect they'll leave most of the worrying about our offspring to us."

Something in Portia's voice made Penelope look at her more closely. After a moment she asked, "Is that the way the wind blows, then?"

Portia met her eye, and blushed—something she didn't readily do. "Possibly. It's too early to be certain, but . . . it's likely you'll be an aunt again in another seven or so months."

Emily had two children already, and Anne had recently given birth to her first, a son, whose advent had reduced her husband, Reggie Carmarthen, to a state of doting idiocy. "Excellent!" Penelope beamed. "I can't wait to see Simon fussing over someone else."

Portia grinned. "Neither can I."

They both dwelled on the vision, then Penelope substituted Barnaby for Simon . . . and wondered. Children were something she hadn't thought about; they either came or they didn't, but . . . the notion of holding an angelic little Barnaby with golden curls made her feel strange and fluttery inside.

She put the thought away for later examination—she'd barely grown accustomed to being so ridiculously and consumingly in love—as others came up to claim her attention. Everyone in both families, and all their connections, had attended; not only was the Chase full to overflowing, but many of the nearby houses and every inn within reach were crammed with guests.

The oldest was Lady Osbaldestone; despite her age, her black eyes were still sharp. She'd tapped Penelope's cheek and advised her she was a clever girl. Exactly what act had demonstrated her cleverness Penelope hadn't asked.

The afternoon wore on with music, dancing, and general gaiety. The grayness outside made the festive atmosphere inside only more pleasurable.

Eventually, having endured hours of ribbing on his change of heart regarding marriage—to which he had with perfect sincerity pointed out that, as Penelope was recognized as a unique young lady, his earlier dismissal of young ladies in general had never applied to her, which statement had given rise to unrestrained hilarity on Gerrard's, Dillon's, and Charlie's parts—Barnaby found Penelope, deftly excused them both from those with whom she'd been conversing, and whirled her into a waltz.

The dance floor was the one place she let him lead without challenge. Which brought him to his point. "I believe," he said, looking into her dark eyes, "that we should depart. Now."

"Oh?" She raised her brows, but she was smiling. "Where are we departing to? Are we following Stokes and Griselda back to town?"

"Yes, and no." Stokes and Griselda had remained for the first hours of the extended wedding breakfast, but Stokes had had to get back to London; they'd left a few hours ago. "We'll head to London, but by a different route."

He owned a cozy little hunting box not far distant; he'd had it for years, but rarely used it. For tonight, he'd made arrangements to ensure it would provide the perfect venue for their perfect wedding night. He smiled down into her eyes. Before her advent into his life, he'd assumed he was devoid of romantic inclinations. Apparently not so. "I think you'll like where we're going."

Her smile softened, deepened. "I know I will."

She couldn't have guessed; he raised his brows.

"Because all I need will be there—you."

It was his turn to feel the glow that had turned her expression golden. He felt his heart expand, swell.

She saw it in his eyes. "Can I make a suggestion, to improve this plan of yours?"

As he'd expected. "Suggest away."

"See that door over there—past the ornate mirror?" When he nodded, she continued, "If we sweep past after the next turn, we could simply halt, go out, close the door—and escape. If we don't . . . if we try for a formal exit, we'll be hours making our farewells and getting free. We've already thanked everyone for coming. I suggest we leave before we get trapped."

He studied her eyes, then looked ahead as he steered her around the turn. They drew parallel with the door, and he stopped, opened it, whirled her through, closed it behind them—swept her into his arms and kissed her witless.

Then they escaped.

As he'd already learned, regardless of the subject, their two minds were always better than one.

EPILOGUE

Two months later
London

"Incidentally, Stokes sent word this morning—Cameron has departed these shores." Barnaby looked up from the news sheet he was perusing while savoring his morning coffee.

Seated at the other end of the table in the breakfast parlor of their recently acquired town house in Albemarle Street, Penelope glanced up, gaze distant . . . then she nodded and went back to the list she was composing.

Barnaby grinned, lifted his cup, and sipped. It was one of the things he adored about her—she never expected him to regale her with witticisms or anything else over the breakfast cups. In return, she never filled his ears with mindless chatter.

In contented appreciation, he let his gaze rest on her dark head for a moment, then returned to his news sheet.

They'd entertained Stokes and Griselda over an intimate dinner only yesterday. If anyone had told him his wife would be instrumental in drawing his and Stokes's lives closer, facilitating their friendship—that both their wives would—he'd have thought that person demented. But Penelope and Griselda were firm friends and had long ago dispensed with all class-based barriers. He and Penelope dined at the little house in Greenbury Street, around the corner from

Griselda's shop, that Stokes had bought for his bride, every bit as frequently as the other two dined with them.

Penelope had even mastered the art of eating mussels.

Mostyn appeared with more toast. As he set the trivet by Penelope's elbow, she glanced up, pushing her spectacles higher on her nose. "I'll be going to the Foundling House this morning, Mostyn. Please tell Cuthbert I'll need the carriage in half an hour."

"Very good, ma'am. I'll have Sally get your coat and muff."

"Thank you." Penelope returned to her list.

With a correct nod to Barnaby, Mostyn withdrew. Although he didn't smile, there was a spring in his step.

His lips gently curving, Barnaby gazed again at Penelope. When she straightened, considering her list, then laid down her pencil, he asked, "How are Dick and Jemmie coming along?"

She looked up, and smiled. "Very well, I'm pleased to say. They've finally become just another two of the 'lads.' Englehart says they're applying themselves to their lessons. Apparently ever since the idea of training to be constables was mooted, his entire class have been exemplary pupils."

Jemmie had quietly asked Barnaby, on one of his now frequent visits to the Foundling House, if it was possible for boys like him to become constables. After assuring him it was, Barnaby had mentioned the matter to Penelope—who with her customary zeal had taken up the idea and promptly recruited his father to the cause of setting up some sort of apprentice scheme for constables.

Recollections of his father's bemusement when she'd first told him what she wanted him to do floated pleasantly through his mind.

Picking up her pencil, Penelope returned to her list of matters she needed to attend to that day. She was perfectly aware of Barnaby's gaze, of its quality as it rested on her. Perhaps not yet the abiding adoration she'd seen in Lord Paignton's eyes, but it seemed to her an excellent start; she basked in it and quietly held it to her heart.

All in all, marrying Barnaby Adair had been an excellent decision. A wise choice. The only concession she'd had to make was to take him with her whenever she went into dangerous areas, which was no hardship at all, and if he was not available, her coachman and two—not one but two—grooms.

She'd agreed to the latter stipulation without quibble. As in all else, he wasn't seeking to restrict her, but to protect her.

Because she was so important to him.

That, she'd decided, she could accept with perfect equanimity.

"I meant to remind you." She looked up and met his eyes. "Your mother has asked us to dinner tonight. I'm not sure who else will be there, but I'll send Mostyn around to find out. Regardless, we should go."

Looking down, she added the order to Mostyn to her list. "You and your father can talk business—and then I can pester him about our apprentice scheme. With any luck Huntingdon or one of the other commissioners will be there, too, so we can kill two or more birds with one stone, so to speak."

Barnaby smiled, a gesture that only deepened as he imagined his mother's consternation on finding her select dinner party put to such use—and her recently discovered helplessness in the face of Penelope's single-minded drive. "Yes, of course. I'll be home in good time."

He'd avoided his mother's, and indeed the ton's, invitations for years, but with Penelope by his side, he was perfectly happy to attend as she wished.

She was the perfect wife for him; not even his mother doubted it. Which left him in the enviable position of being able to leave all ton-nish females, his mother included, to Penelope to manage. All he had to do was sit back, watch the action, and enjoy her machinations and their outcomes.

Since marrying her he'd learned what true contentment was.

Now he'd given his life, and his love, into her keeping, all was indeed—truly and at last—absolutely well in his world.

Announcement of

THE BASTION CLUB #7,

The Edge of Desire

August, 1816
London

He should make her wait.

Thoughts and conjecture roiling in his head, Christian Michael Allardyce, sixth Marquess of Dearne, slowly descended the stairs of the Bastion Club. He'd been nursing a brandy and his despondency in the library when Gasthorpe, the club's majordomo, had appeared with a note.

A note summoning him to face his past.

That past awaited him in the front parlor, the room he and the club's other six owners, all ex-members of one of the more secret and select arms of His Majesty's services who had established the club as their bolt-hole against the importuning ladies of the ton, had stipulated as the only room in which ladies were to be permitted. In the months since the club's opening, that rule had, incident by incident, fallen by the wayside, but Gasthorpe had rightly shown this particular lady into the formal front parlor.

He really should make her wait.

She'd said she would, twelve years ago, but then another had come along, and while he'd been buried deep in Napoleon's Europe, she'd lightly thrown aside her promise to him and fallen in love with and married a Mr. George Randall.

She was now Lady Letitia Randall.

Instead of the Marchioness of Dearne.

Deep in his heart, where no one and nothing any longer touched, he still felt betrayed.

She'd been Lady Letitia Randall for eight years. Although he'd returned to England ten months ago, and he and she moved in the same, very small circle, they'd exchanged not one word. They hadn't even exchanged nods. Even that was too much to expect of him, given their past. She seemed to understand that; coolly detached, haughtily distant, as if he and she had never been close—never been lovers— she'd studiously kept her distance.

Until now.

Christian—I need your help. There's no one else I can turn to. L.

That was all the words her note had contained, yet between them those bare words spoke volumes.

His feet continued steadily down the treads. He should make her wait, yet he couldn't imagine what had brought her here. Nor could he imagine why his staff at Allardyce House in Grosvenor Square had divulged his whereabouts. His butler, Percival, was a paragon of his calling; nothing short of a force of nature would have induced him to disobey his master's express orders.

Then again, the lady presently occupying the front parlor had qualified as such from her earliest years.

Stepping off the last tread, he studied the parlor door. It was closed. He could turn around and retreat, and let her wait for at least ten minutes. Even fifteen. The desperation in her plea guaranteed she would wait. Not meekly—meek wasn't in her repertoire—but she would grit her teeth and remain until he deigned to see her.

Some part of him wanted to hurt her—as she'd hurt him, as he still hurt. Despite the years, the wound was raw; it still bled.

The faint elusive scent of jasmine drew him to the door.

It was curiosity, he told himself, that had him reaching for the handle. Not the incredible irresistible attraction that had from the first drawn them together—that even after twelve years of neglect and eight years of disillusion, still arced across a crowded ballroom.

And made him ache.

Opening the door, steeling himself, he went in.

The first surprise was her weeds. He paused in the doorway, rapidly assessing.

Seated in one of the armchairs beside the small hearth, the one facing the door, she was clothed in unrelieved funereal black, dull and . . . on any other lady it would have looked somber. On her . . . even fully veiled as she was, the depressing hue did nothing to dim her vitality. It screamed in every line of her svelte form, a humming, thrumming energy, harnessed to some degree but forever in danger of escaping—exploding; she only had to move a gloved hand to instantly attract and fix any man's attention.

Certainly his.

She demonstrated, raising both hands, long slender palms and delicate fingers encased in fine black pigskin; gripping the edge of the black veil she lifted it, setting it back over her piled hair.

So he could see her face.

Finely-drawn features, a pair of ruby lips sculpted by a master, the lower lush and full and tempting. Large, almond-shaped eyes that were an infinitely changeable medley of greens and golds, set above high, chiselled cheekbones. Lush dark lashes, a straight, patrician nose, all set in an oval of perfect porcelain skin.

The epitome of feminine aristocratic beauty not solely because of its composition but also because of her animation. In repose her face was serenely beautiful; awake, her expressions were startlingly vivid.

This afternoon, however, her expression was . . . contained.

He frowned. Stepping further into the room, he closed the door. "Your father?"

He'd assumed the full mourning signified that her father, the Earl of Nunchance, had passed on. But if the head of the house of Vaux had died the ton would have been abuzz with the news. Not only had he heard not a whisper, but Letitia's face, naturally pale, held no hint of sorrow. Despite the years, he could still read her expressions readily; if anything, she seemed to be reining in her temper.

Not her father, then. Regardless of the familial disruptions that were commonplace between the Vaux, she was sincerely fond of her eccentric sire.

Her perfectly arched dark brows drew down in reply, a slight frown that informed him he was being slow-witted.

"No. Not Papa."

The sound of her voice rocked him. He'd forgotten how long it had been since he'd heard it—low toned, with just the faintest natural rasp, it was a voice that evoked visions of sin.

Regardless, today those tones also carried a certain tension. As he watched, she drew in a tight breath, and bluntly stated, "Randall has been murdered."

As if saying the words had released her from some spell, she finally met his eyes. Hers sparked with undisguised temper. "Randall was beaten to death in his study last night. The servants found him this morning—and the idiot runners have fixed on Justin as the murderer."

Christian blinked. "Ah." Moving into the room, slowly to give himself time to dissect her news, he sank into the armchair across the hearth from her. Lord Justin Vaux was Letitia's younger brother. She was presently twenty-eight, nearly twenty-nine, which would make Justin twenty-six. Sister and brother were close, always had been. "And what does Justin say?"

"That's just it—we can't find him to ask. But rather than do so, the authorities have fixed on him as the most convenient scapegoat. They are, no doubt, organizing a hue and cry as we speak."

Letitia bit the words off, her tone acid. Now she'd got over the worst hurdle—getting Christian to speak with her—she felt able to concentrate on the matter at hand.

Which was definitely better than concentrating on him.

Watching him stroll, ineffably graceful, across the room toward her—allowing herself to—had been a mistake. All that harnessed power condensed into one male—a male no one with functioning eyes would rate as anything less than dangerous. His expression was rarely informative, so did little to soften the hard angles of his face, the edged cheekbones, the long planes of his cheeks, the austere set of his features—large eyes set under a broad brow, straight brown brows, surprisingly thick lashes, thin chiselled lips and the strong prow of his nose. His squared chin was a testament to the stubbornness he usually hid beneath a cloak of easy charm.

To him, charm and grace had always come easily. Something she, being a Vaux and therefore attuned to all the nuances of appearance, had always appreciated.

Still did; if anything, the effect he had on her, on her senses, was more pronounced than she recalled. She knew very well just how deeply she still loved him, but she'd forgotten what it felt like, forgotten all the physical manifestations that came with that soul-deep connection.

She hadn't been this close to him for twelve long years. Her decision to keep her distance when he'd reappeared among the ton had clearly been wise; even with a good six feet separating them, she could feel her ribcage tightening, enough to affect her breathing.

Enough to make her feel just a touch giddy. To have her nerves stretching in telltale anticipation.

An anticipation that would never be fulfilled.

Not now.

Not after she'd married Randall.

His gray gaze had shifted from her; now it returned, focused and intent. "Why did the authorities fix on Justin? Was he there?"

"Apparently he called on Randall last night. Randall's stupid butler, who thoroughly disapproves of all Vaux, Justin in particular, was only too happy to point his finger. But you know as well as I do that, all appearances to the contrary, Justin would never kill anyone."

Christian caught her eye, read therein both her temper and her worry. Her anxiety. "You don't believe he would. I might not believe he would. That doesn't mean he didn't."

Baiting a Vaux was a dangerous pastime, but this time, she didn't bite back.

Which told him how deeply worried she was.

And despite the histrionics that were her Vaux heritage—the family wasn't known as "the vile-tempered Vaux" without cause—she wasn't a female who worried unduly.

Which explained why she was there, appealing to him.

To the man she knew him to be.

One who had never been able to refuse her anything. Not even his heart.

She'd held his gaze steadily. Now she simply asked, in her raspy, low—seductive—voice, "Will you help?"

He looked into her eyes, and realized she didn't, in fact, know how he would answer. Didn't know how deeply in thrall to her he still was. Which meant . . .

He arched a brow. "How much is my help worth to you?"

She blinked, then searched his eyes, hers narrowing. After a pregnant moment in which she assessed and considered his true meaning, she replied, "You know perfectly well I'll do anything—*anything*—to clear Justin's name."

Absolute decision, total commitment, rang in her tone.

He inclined his head. "Very well."

He heard himself urbanely agree. He hadn't known he would, hadn't thought what he would ask of her in return, wasn't even sure of his motives in pressing such a bargain on her, but *anything* gave him a clear field.

Revenge of a sort for all the years of hurt might yet be his.

At the thought, he stirred, whether in discomfort or anticipation not even he could tell. "Tell me what happened—the sequence of events leading to Randall's death as you know it."

Letitia hesitated, then gathered the black reticule that had sat throughout in her lap. "Come to the house." Rising, she reached up and flipped down her veil. "It'll be easier to explain there."

She'd thought it would be easier—having places and things to point out to distract him—but having him by her side again kept her nerves in a state of perpetual reactiveness. Ready for anything, to respond to any touch, however slight, to luxuriate in the steady warmth that radiated from his large body, luring her closer.

Gritting mental teeth, she pointed to the spot on the study floor of the house in South Audley Street where she'd been informed her late husband had lain. "You can see the bloodstain."

The spot in question lay between the fireplace and the large desk.

She wasn't particularly squeamish, but the sight of the red-brown stain had her gorge rising. No matter what she'd felt for Randall, no man should die as he had, brutally bashed to death with the poker from his own fireplace.

Christian shifted a fraction closer, looking down at the stain. "Which way was he facing—toward the fire or the desk?"

She frowned. "I don't know. They didn't tell me. And they wouldn't let me in here to see—they said it was too . . . gory."

She'd forgotten how tall he was, how large—forgotten that he was one of the few men in the ton who had always towered over her, who could make her feel . . . protected. That wasn't why she'd turned to him, but at that moment she was grateful for his size, his nearness, for the reminder of life in the presence of stark death. "They've taken away the poker." Forcing in a breath, she turned and waved at a table by one of the armchairs flanking the hearth. "And they've cleared the table—there were two glasses on it, the maid told me. Brandy in both."

"Tell me what you know. When last did you see him?"

The question gave her something to focus on. "Last night. I went to dinner at the Martindales, then on to a soiree at Cumberland House. I returned rather late. Randall had stayed in—he sometimes did when he had business to attend to. He waylaid me in the hall and asked me in here. He wanted to discuss . . ." She paused, then continued, knowing her voice, hardening, would give away her temper, "A family matter."

She and Randall had been married for eight years, but there'd been no children. With any luck, Christian would imagine that had been the subject of their discussion, the subject she'd so delicately refrained from mentioning.

His gaze on her face, Christian knew—just knew—that she was hoping to lead him up some garden path. Declining to follow, he made a mental note to return to the subject of her late night discussion with her husband at some later point. For now . . . "Discussion?" With a Vaux involved, "discussion" could encompass verbal warfare.

"We had a row." Face darkening, Letitia continued, "I don't know how long it took, but I eventually swept out"—a gesture indicated the force of her sweeping, something Christian could imagine with ease—"and left him here."

"So you argued. Loudly."

She nodded.

He let his gaze travel the room. "No broken vases? Ornaments flung about?"

She folded her arms beneath her breasts, lifted her chin, narrowed her eyes at him, and haughtily declared, "It wasn't that sort of argument."

A cold argument, then, one without heat or passion. For her, with her husband, that struck him as odd.

He looked away, again scanning the room. In reality looking away from her, so he wouldn't focus on her breasts. Breasts he knew—or had, at one time, known well. Hauling his mind from salacious images from the past—all the more potent for being memory rather than imagination—took real effort. "So you left Randall here, hale and whole, and then what? What next did you know of this?"

"Nothing at all, until my dresser came rushing in this morning to tell me about the body." She turned away from the bloodstain.

He moved with her, alongside her, as she glided to the window overlooking the street.

"By the time I dressed and got downstairs, the butler—he's an officious little scourge by the name of Mellon—had taken it upon himself to summon the authorities, who assigned an investigator from Bow Street—a weasely, narrow-minded man whose only concern is to close the case as soon as possible regardless of the truth."

She fell silent, but before he could frame his next question, roused enough to say, "One other thing my dresser babbled—she was in a complete tizz—was that this morning the door to the study was locked, with the key on the floor some way inside. Mellon and the footmen tried to force the door and couldn't." Their gazes both swung to the door, a heavy, inches-thick oak panel with a lock that lived up to the door. "Luckily, someone in the household can pick locks. That was how they got in . . . and found him."

Quitting her side, he prowled toward the door. "How far inside— guess from what she babbled."

"A few yards, not more. That's what it sounded like."

He was standing staring at the floor, considering the implications of the key being in that spot, when a girl appeared in the doorway. Looking up, he met her eyes, looked up at her hair, and smiled. "Hermione."

"Lord Dearne." She bobbed a curtsy. "I didn't know if you would remember me."

He let his smile turn charming, as if he hadn't forgotten the scrap who'd been all of four when he'd last seen her. Luckily, her hair was a telling feature; in common with, as far as he'd ever heard, all those born to the house of Vaux, she possessed luxurious dark locks that, despite their darkness, could never be described as anything other than red. When combined with the evidence of her features, a softer, milder version of Letitia's, placing her hadn't been difficult.

Her attention on her older sister, Hermione advanced into the room. Christian noted she didn't look at the bloodstain, but steadily watched Letitia.

He glanced at Letitia; she was looking down, mind elsewhere. She was patently undisturbed by Hermione joining them.

Glancing up, Letitia continued, "That's really all I know of my own knowledge. What I gathered from the investigator—"

"No." Christian held up a hand. "Don't tell me. I want to hear it from him, direct."

She narrowed her eyes at him again. "Without my interpretations?"

Inclining his head, Christian fought down a grin. "Without your appellations."

She humphed, a sound Vaux females had down to an art, then looked at her sister. "Are you all right?"

Hermione blinked. "Of course. I was wondering about you."

Letitia shrugged. "Once Justin turns up, and the fools who call themselves the authorities admit it wasn't him, and start looking for the real murderer, I'll be fine."

Christian inwardly blinked. No sarcasm ran beneath her words— with a Vaux one never needed to guess—yet Letitia had just lost a husband of eight years in shocking circumstances. . . .

He studied her; she was looking at Hermione, but there was nothing in either woman's attitude beyond sisterly comfort. While Hermione was presently a less intense version of Letitia, she'd no doubt grow into her dramatic powers in time. Both sisters seemed very much at ease with each other, the only real difference being in age, and the suggestion of care, of viewing Hermione as a person she needed to protect and watch over, that colored Letitia's eyes.

He stirred. "If you'll summon the butler—Mellon, was it? I'd like to speak with him."

Interrogate him.

Letitia crossed to the bellpull and tugged; the alacrity with which the summons was answered had her smiling cynically—and exchanging a look with Christian. Obviously Randall's staff found Christian's presence noteworthy, enough to hover close.

Despite that, Mellon fixed his gaze on her, ignoring Christian's looming presence. "You rang, ma'am?"

"Indeed, Mellon. Lord Dearne"—she waved at Christian—"has some questions he'd like to ask you. Please answer them as best you can."

Mellon reluctantly turned to Christian, who smiled easily—charming as ever.

She could have warned him; Mellon turned rigidly frosty.

Christian saw, but chose to ignore the man's reaction. "You've been Mr. Randall's butler for . . . how long?"

Mellon drew himself up. "Twelve years, my lord."

Long before Letitia's marriage to Randall. "How did you get on with your late master?"

"It's a . . ." Mellon broke off, blinking, then his chin firmed and he continued, "It's been a pleasure working for Mr. Randall, my lord."

"And the rest of the staff?"

"Feel the same, my lord. None of the staff had any problems with the master." Mellon's eyes cut toward Letitia, but he stopped before he made contact.

Christian paused, sensing the man's antagonism, wondering at its cause. The Letitia he knew was invariably kind to the lower orders; the impulse was bred into her, all but instinctive, not something she could readily change. There had to be some other reason behind Mellon's patent dislike of his mistress.

"Very well." Christian let his voice relax. "If you could tell me what, to your certain knowledge, drawing solely from your own observations, happened last night. Start from the point where Lady Randall returned home."

Mellon's lips primmed like an old woman's, but he was only too ready to oblige. "The mistress came in, and the master asked to speak with her. Here, in the study. They closed the door, so I don't know what was said, but there was a great to-do—we could hear Lady Randall ranting and raving, as she's wont to do."

Ah, Christian thought. *There we have it.* Loyal and devoted to his master, Mellon resented Letitia's treatment of Randall. He made a further mental note to find out more about Randall. He also needed to know more—a lot more—about Randall's and Letitia's marriage. But first . . .

"Did anything occur during the time her ladyship and Mr. Randall were arguing in the study?"

"Indeed, sir." Mellon's eyes all but gleamed with vindictiveness. "Lord Vaux—that's Lord Justin Vaux, the mistress's brother—called to see the master. He said it was the master, not the mistress he wanted. He could hear the carry-on in the study, so he said he'd wait in the library. I led him there. He told me I didn't need to wait on him—it was latish by then. Said he'd show himself in once the mistress had left."

"So you retired?" Christian's tone conveyed his surprise; Percival would never have retired while he was up and about unless he, himself, had ordered him to.

Mellon looked stricken. "Wish I hadn't now, but his lordship's often here—makes himself at home, he does, and the master had mentioned he was expecting him, so, well . . . it was fairly clear he didn't want me about. So I went."

Even without glancing at Letitia, Christian fluently translated Mellon's words. Justin hadn't liked Randall, and had therefore called frequently, "making himself at home," supporting Letitia—very likely keeping an eye on her. That was revealing in itself. Although Justin and Letitia were close, they had never lived in each other's pockets. And there was Hermione, too. Christian glanced at the younger Vaux sister, and wondered if Letitia's protective attitude had some specific cause beyond basic family instinct.

Clearly, Justin had made his dislike of Randall sufficiently obvious, hence Mellon's rabid dislike of Justin.

"So beyond that point, you have no further knowledge of events." He caught Mellon's eye. "You can't say for certain that Lord Justin Vaux left the library and went into the study and met with your master."

Mellon's eyes narrowed. "No, but I can say he didn't leave until more than an hour later. My room's above the front door, and I heard it open and shut. I got up and looked out—just to be sure—and saw Lord Justin making his way down the steps and onto the pavement."

"Which way did he turn?"

"Left. Toward Piccadilly."

Christian looked at Letitia and cocked a brow.

She reluctantly vouchsafed, "Justin's lodgings are in Jermyn Street."

Mellon had given the direction without hesitation; he most probably had seen Justin leave. Christian thought, then asked, "If anyone else had called on your master last night, after Lord Justin had left, or even before, would you have known?"

"Indeed, sir—my lord. If they'd rung the bell, I would have heard—it rings in my room as well as in the kitchen. Even if they'd knocked on the door, I couldn't help but hear, my room being where it is."

There was no point suggesting the man might have been deeply asleep. "Very well." Christian turned toward the bloodstain on the floor. "Let's move onto this morning. What happened once you came downstairs?"

"I was in my pantry, seeing to the cutlery for the breakfast table, when the housekeeper, Mrs. Crocket, came in to tell me that the tweeny as does the study of a morning couldn't open the door. I went straight away, thinking perhaps the master had gone to his study early. Sometimes he does lock the door. But when I knocked, there was no response, not even when I called out. Then one of the footmen thought to look through the keyhole—I was surprised he could as the key should have been in it. Then he turned green, and said as the master was lying on the floor, and there was blood." Mellon paled at the memory.

"What happened then?"

"We tried to force the door, me and the two footmen, but it wouldn't budge. This house is older than it looks—everything's solid and heavy. We were thinking of breaking a window and putting someone through when one of the maids told us the scullery boy who comes in to help could pick locks. We got him up here, and after a time he managed to open the door. As soon as he did, we rushed in . . ." Mellon's eyes were drawn to the bloodstained floor. "And we found the master there, dead. Quite dead."

His voice quavered on the last words. Christian gave him a moment to compose himself before he asked, "I realize this is distressing, but if you could describe how Randall was lying—on his back, or on his face?"

Mellon blanched. "On his back, my lord." His jaw worked. "Wasn't much of his face left to speak of."

Letitia turned away; hand at her throat, she stared out of the window. Hermione, in contrast, paled, but was clearly less distressed.

"So," Christian said, "it would seem Randall was facing the fire, and his attacker. I understand there were two glasses of brandy on the sidetable—had they been drunk?"

The change of subject allowed Mellon to rally. "Both had been sipped, my lord, but neither drained."

"Where, exactly, was the key?"

Mellon looked toward the door, and pointed. "There—by that knot in the wood."

Hermione shifted. Christian glanced at her, and saw that she was watching—and listening—avidly. He glanced at Letitia; she was watching and listening, too, but not with the intensity Hermione was exhibiting. He glanced at the younger girl again. Her eyes were wide; she was definitely tense. Without looking at Mellon, he said, "Put your finger on the spot."

Mellon obeyed, measuring the distance to the door with his eyes. "Best I can recall, it was here."

Hermione's eyes hadn't left Mellon, but as he straightened, she looked at Christian. Expectantly.

Unsure what was going on, he obliged with the obvious question; he looked at Mellon. "How do you imagine the key got there?"

"I can't rightly say, sir—my lord."

"If you had to guess, what would you think?"

"I'd think . . . that Lord Justin locked the door behind him, then slipped the key back under the door."

Christian nodded. Given the position where the key was found relative to the body, that seemed the most likely explanation. Except . . . "Why do you think Lord Justin would do that? If he'd just murdered your master, as I understand it in gruesome fashion, why go to the bother of locking the door and slipping the key back inside?"

Mellon frowned, unable to answer.

"To give himself time to scarper."

The words came from a whippet-thin individual who'd appeared in the hall. One glance at his ferrety features and Christian knew who he was.

The Cynster Family Tree

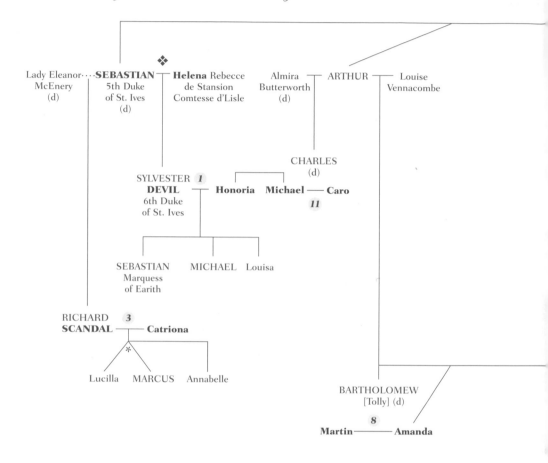

Lady Eleanor····**SEBASTIAN** ─┬─ **Helena** Rebecce   Almira ─┬─ **ARTHUR** ─┬─ Louise
McEnery   5th Duke   de Stansion   Butterworth   Vennacombe
(d)   of St. Ives   Comtesse d'Lisle   (d)
         (d)

CHARLES
(d)

SYLVESTER **1**
DEVIL ─── **Honoria**   **Michael** ─── **Caro**
6th Duke   **11**
of St. Ives

SEBASTIAN   MICHAEL   Louisa
Marquess
of Earith

RICHARD **3**
SCANDAL ─── **Catriona**
         *

Lucilla   MARCUS   Annabelle

BARTHOLOMEW
[Tolly] (d)
8
Martin ─────── **Amanda**

THE CYNSTER NOVELS